DARK RIDER

Robert closed the compartment door and flattened himself against it. The stiffness of desire tightened the crotch of his cut-offs. At the other end of the tiny space, Angelo was already pulling off his T-shirt.

A current of man-scented air brushed Robert's nostrils. He tried to swallow, but the hard lump in his shorts had an echo in his throat. Semi-focused eyes followed the movement of the broad Argentinian's deltoid muscles as Angelo threw the T-shirt on to the upper bunk then began to unzip his shorts.

The sound of metal teeth opening seemed slower than necessary. Was he being mercilessly teased? The thought of Angelo naked and himself still dressed made Robert's groin ache more than ever.

DARK RIDER

Jack Gordon

First published in Great Britain in 1998 by
Idol
an imprint of Virgin Publishing Ltd
332 Ladbroke Grove
London W10 5AH

Copyright © Jack Gordon 1998

The right of Jack Gordon to be identified as the Author of this
Work has been asserted by him in accordance with the Copyright,
Designs and Patents Act 1988.

ISBN 0 352 33243 3

Cover photograph by Colin Clarke Photography

Typeset by SetSystems Ltd, Saffron Walden, Essex
Printed and bound in Great Britain by
Cox & Wyman Ltd, Reading, Berks

SAFER SEX GUIDELINES

These books are sexual fantasies – in real life, everyone needs to think about safe sex.

While there have been major advances in the drug treatments for people with HIV and AIDS, there is still no cure for AIDS or a vaccine against HIV. Safe sex is still the only way of being sure of avoiding HIV sexually.

HIV can only be transmitted through blood, come and vaginal fluids (but no other body fluids) – passing from one person (with HIV) into another person's bloodstream. It cannot get through healthy, undamaged skin. The only real risk of HIV is through anal sex without a condom – this accounts for almost all HIV transmissions between men.

Being Safe:
Even if you don't come inside someone, there is still a risk to both partners from blood (tiny cuts in the arse) and pre-come. Using strong condoms and water-based lubricant greatly reduces the risk of HIV. However, condoms can break or slip off, so:
* Make sure that condoms are stored away from hot or damp places.
* Check the expiry date – condoms have a limited life.
* Gently squeeze the air out of the tip.
* Check the condom is put on the right way up and unroll it down the erect cock.
* Use plenty of water-based lubricant (lube), up the arse and on the condom.
* While fucking, check occasionally to see the condom is still in one piece (you could also add more lube).
* When you withdraw, hold the condom tight to your cock as you pull out.

* Never re-use a condom or use the same condom with more than one person.
* If you're not used to condoms you might practise putting them on.
* Sex toys like dildos and plugs are safe. But if you're sharing them use a new condom each time or wash the toys well.

For the safest sex, make sure you use the strongest condoms, such as Durex Ultra Strong, Mates Super Strong, HT Specials and Rubberstuffers packs. Condoms are free in many STD (Sexually Transmitted Disease) clinics (sometimes called GUM clinics) and from many gay bars. It's also essential to use lots of water-based lube such as KY, Wet Stuff, Slik or Liquid Silk. Never use come as a lubricant.

Oral Sex:
Compared with fucking, sucking someone's cock is far safer. Swallowing come does not necessarily mean that HIV gets absorbed into the bloodstream. While a tiny fraction of cases of HIV infection have been linked to sucking, we know the risk is minimal. But certain factors increase the risk:
* Letting someone come in your mouth
* Throat infections such as gonorrhoea
* If you have cuts, sores or infections in your mouth and throat

So what is safe?
There are so many things you can do which are absolutely safe: wanking each other; rubbing your cocks against one another; kissing, sucking and licking all over the body; rimming – to name but a few.

If you're finding safe sex difficult, call a helpline or speak to someone you feel you can trust for support. The Terrence Higgins Trust Helpline, which is open from noon to 10pm every day, can be reached on 0171 242 1010.

Or, if you're in the United States, you can ring the Center for Disease Control toll free on 1 800 458 5231.

One

Robert pulled up the blinds and stood naked in front of the open window. His skin was sticky, sheened with the sweat of another clammy night in the city. Damp-palmed, he pushed a stray strand of blond hair from his sleepy eyes.

Traffic fumes drifted up from three floors below. A gust of hot air brushed his groin.

He yawned and stretched, hips jutting forward to fuck the morning. There was a heaviness in his balls, part-arousal, part-discomfort. Still half-asleep, his gaze swept the pavement, pausing on the figure of a road sweeper. Eyes narrowed, Robert squinted in the bright light, then focused. The yawn evened out into an expression of longing.

The guy was bare-chested, fluorescent green uniform jacket tied around his waist. Strong shoulders gleamed the pinky brown of a tan obtained through hard work in the open air.

Robert inhaled sharply.

A patch of skin shone in the hollow between the man's hairy pecs, caught by early morning sun. A small metal ring glistened in the right nipple.

Robert's cock twitched. He thought about his mouth around silver coldness, teeth tugging at the decoration. He thought about

1

the road-sweeper's back arching in desire. His fingers tightened around the cord of the blinds.

Below, the road-sweeper's thicker fingers gripped the handle of a brush. The veins on the man's arms stood out, muscles flexing as he bent to sweep another shovelful of litter from the gutter.

Robert cupped his balls, feeling their heaviness. He thought about those thick fingers circling round his length, gripping his prick tightly.

The road-sweeper turned.

Robert's gaze lowered to the back of the man's loose-cut trousers. Just above the tied jacket, a crack of untanned flesh appeared as the road-sweeper emptied his shovel into the cart. Sticky fingers released the blind-cord and brushed his crotch.

Look up.

Eyes pinned to the curve of the road sweeper's arse, Robert ran a finger up the underside of his half-hard prick. The member stretched further under his touch. He thought about that same finger massaging the moist crack, its owner spreadeagled on a bed, arse straining upwards. A shiver of exhaust fumes caressed his balls.

Look up.

The man's entire back was gleaming in eight o'clock sunshine. A fine dusting of blond shoulder hair split in two, travelling down and sideways.

Robert caught a glimpse of thick hair. He wanted to bury his mouth in the deep hollow of the man's armpit.

Someone in a suit appeared from somewhere, obscuring the view.

Robert frowned, running an index finger back down his swelling length.

The suit got into a car. Back in sight, the road-sweeper had removed the jacket and tied it to the handle of his cart. The trousers hung lower than ever.

Robert circled the root of his hard prick with thumb and forefinger, dragging foreskin up towards the head. Lips parted in a sigh.

Look up.

Below, the man turned, plucked a half-smoked cigarette from behind his ear and lit it.

Robert took in the taut outline of well-exercised abdominals. The trousers were equally low-slung front as back. Just above the belt-buckle, a trickle of sweat-slicked hair glinted in the shimmering heat and disappeared beneath rough canvas.

The road-sweeper leant on his brush and dragged on the cigarette, cocking his head and holding the filter between thumb and forefinger.

Robert watched as three girls in short skirts and heels clacked past.

Another pair of narrowed eyes followed the threesome. Smiling lips exhaled smoke in their wake.

Robert stared at the man's face. Mid-twenties. Brown hair honey-bleached by the sun and tied in a loose ponytail. A hint of stubble on upper lip which the razor had missed. He ran a thumb over the head of his cock, moaned and dragged his hand back down to the root. His balls contracted.

Three floors below, another hand rubbed the crotch of heavy work-trousers.

Look up.

'Look up, damn you!' The words hissed through his teeth.

A hand on his shoulder: 'Another hot night?'

Robert spun round.

Angelo's coffee-coloured face smiled at him. A hand waved a fistful of envelopes. 'Post. One for Robert McLeod, Esquire . . .' Huge brown eyes dipped to crotch level.

Robert felt his skin flush up. 'Don't you ever knock?' He grabbed the letters, walked to the bed and pulled on a dressing gown.

'I did. Three times.' A note of awkwardness seeped into the previously happy voice. 'Thought you were sleeping. I was just going to leave the letters and – sorry.'

Robert immediately regretted the edge in his tone. 'No, I'm sorry – this heat is driving me mad! Thanks for the mail.' His fingers shook as he tied the dressing-gown cord, wrist brushing his raging hard-on. 'How are you feeling?' He sat down.

Angelo lounged against the wardrobe. 'I'm OK.'

Robert watched strong features crease and knew it wasn't true. Angelo's girlfriends came and went with the seasons, but Julie had lasted longer than most. He watched his flatmate tug abstractedly at the black curls on the back of his neck.

'Wish I'd cancelled those two weeks' holiday, I miss work – I need something to do, take my mind off . . . things.' He wandered over to the typewriter.

Robert knew the feeling. He opened the first envelope. A circular. He balled the paper, aimed it at the bin. And missed.

'How's the novel coming?' Angelo was peering at sheets of paper.

'OK –' He tore at the second envelope, saw the red printed letters and shoved it into the pocket of his dressing gown. He'd pay the bill later.

'You're not still blocked, then?'

Robert looked into the solemn face, tried to lie then gave up. 'Yeah, still blocked.' He stood up, tossed the third envelope into the air and caught it. 'But at least I've given up worrying about it.'

Angelo perched on the edge of a small chest of drawers. He flicked through a pile of printed paper.

Robert stared at the handsome Argentinian. They'd shared the flat for almost eighteen months now. It had taken six of those months to stop Angelo walking into his room, naked, at all hours of the day and night. Much as he enjoyed the view, his flatmate's exhibitionism was almost too much for a red-blooded man to bear: it took the next six months and the appearance of three of Angelo's very female girlfriends to stop himself returning the compliment. Must be that Latin blood that makes him so unself-conscious about his body –

Robert smiled at a memory of Angelo's muscular thighs. Eyes strolled over the broad shoulders. The smile twitched with frustrated resignation.

– or a complete lack of interest in me. He tossed the remaining letter into the air again.

Angelo looked up from his reading. 'This is good.'

4

Robert sighed. 'Tell that to the publishing industry!'

A wide mouth sloped into one of Angelo's lopsided smiles, the kind that always made Robert's heart miss a beat. 'You need a break – a holiday.'

'You and me both.' He walked to the window, relowered the blinds and angled the slats, half-closing them. As he turned, towelling stretched across the sensitive head of his softening cock and began a reverse procedure. He ripped open the final envelope to distract himself from something he could not do anything about at the moment. Eyes lingered on the letterhead.

'Anything interesting?'

Robert read, blinked and read on. Five minutes later, still mulling over its contents, he passed the letter wordlessly to Angelo.

Large brown eyes scanned, then flicked up. 'Congratulations – or is it commiserations?'

Robert's brow furrowed. 'I've no idea who he is – or was, rather: I didn't even know I had a great-uncle Bethran.'

'Well, he knew about you.' Angelo continued to read the letter. 'A cottage – in Scotland. I've never been to Scotland.'

'It's on an island – off the north-west coast.'

'All mist and rain – that is how I have always thought of Scotland. What is this place called?'

Robert re-read over Angelo's shoulder. 'Kelpie Island. Corrie Cottage on Kelpie Island.' Mist and rain: after three months of near-drought conditions in London, he could do with some mist and rain – and a break. 'The keys are with a lawyer in Fort William. I can pick them up any time. This is great!'

The lopsided smile again, tinged with shyness. 'I'm pleased for you – I said you needed a holiday.' He folded and held out the letter.

Robert laughed, took it. The man was a mixture of lost puppy-dog and Latin god: too appealing for anyone's good. 'Why don't you come too?' The invitation was out before he had time to think about it.

A large eyebrow cocked. 'Do you mean it?'

Robert walked to the window, squinted through lowered slats.

Did he? Below, the road-sweeper had moved off, replaced by an assortment of dustbins awaiting collection. Robert smiled ruefully: the story of his life. 'Of course I mean it.' He could do with the company. Robert turned. 'Go pack your stuff and I'll make reservations.'

The coffee-coloured face beamed at him. 'Scotland! This couldn't have happened at a better time.' He jumped off the edge of the dressing table and bounded forwards. 'We can swim, go hill-walking, hiking, riding –'

'As long as it's cool and wet, I'd be happy just –' He wafted the letter back and forth, trying to create air in the airless room, '– inspecting my inheritance. Always fancied myself as a man of property.'

Angelo aimed a playful punch at Robert's abdomen. 'Land-owner McLeod could do with the exercise.'

'I think they're called lairds, in Scotland – and it's only a cottage.' He couldn't help laughing. 'There might be time for –' he made a face, '– a little hill-walking, I suppose. Now go and pack and let me phone!'

Angelo mock-tugged a glossy forelock and backed towards the door, bowing. 'Sí, Señor McLeod . . .'

Robert continued to laugh, his mood brightening considerably. He lifted an unpaid electricity bill and threw it at the grinning face.

A cottage.

On an island.

Maybe this would be good for his writing.

Angelo caught the crumpled bill, threw it back.

Robert smiled: if the natives were friendly, it might even be good for his sex-life.

Kings Cross station thronged with arrivals and departures. As they waited for the 20.45 Fort William train to appear on the notice-board, Robert lowered his rucksack and glanced at Angelo.

The Argentinian's gaze was fixed on a man and woman, embracing. The woman looked a little like Julie, but Robert knew it was more than the faint resemblance which was taking his flatmate's attention. He continued to stare, watching the way the couple draped themselves over each other.

It was the closeness, the intimacy.

Robert frowned, remembering Archie and their eight months together, before the accountant left for America and pastures new. There had been no one serious since. He gave himself a shake, punched Angelo's shoulder. 'Packed your toothbrush?'

The dark head jerked towards him. Large brown eyes hinted at a mournfulness, then snapped back to life. '*Madre mía*, did I remember it?' Angelo began to rummage in the compartments of his rucksack, then the pockets of tight denim cut-offs.

Robert watched as three packets of condoms clattered onto the station concourse. He grinned, picked them up.

Angelo was holding a toothbrush and looking sheepish.

Robert laughed. 'Expecting to seduce Kelpie Island's entire population of willing maidens?'

'I just got into the habit of carrying them, I suppose.' The coffee-coloured face tinged crimson as Angelo grabbed the condoms.

The blush took him by surprise. Robert often wondered about his flatmate. Part of him put Angelo's easy, laid-back sensuality down to his own fantasies about sexually ambiguous Latin men. Another part was sure he'd caught the swarthy twenty-nine year-old eyeing other men on the few occasions they'd been for a drink together.

He watched Angelo shove the condoms back into his pocket, staring at the two bulges which swelled in the man's tight shorts.

In the background, a distorted voice echoed through the station.

Lust hit him like an unexpected punch in the guts. In his mind's eye he saw Angelo's prick nestling on top of large, weighty balls. He saw himself easing a pink circle of latex over the large head and down the thick shaft.

'Ready?' Inches away, Angelo adjusted the straps of his rucksack.

'What?' Robert's throat was dry. Beneath the thin T-shirt, his nipples rubbed achingly against the light fabric. He was always ready, these days. If Angelo asked him to step behind one of the luggage-carts and take both of those large, heavy balls into his mouth, he'd do it like a shot.

Angelo picked up Robert's rucksack, shoved it at him. 'That's our train. Are you ready to go?'

Relief and disappointment flooded his body. Robert gripped the back-pack. As Angelo marched in front, strong muscular legs covering the station concourse in long, easy strides, heads turned: male and female. A ticket inspector tripped over a small dog, so intense was his study of the striking Argentinian.

Angelo hoisted the rucksack further up his strong back and strode on, oblivious, Robert falling in behind.

Ten hours was a long time to sit up, so they'd booked a sleeping-compartment.

Robert eased himself into the cramped space. He looked around. 'Where's the other –?'

'Here!' Angelo pulled down the upper berth.

Robert sighed. Now there was even less room. He hadn't expected the sleeping-compartment to be quite so small. He could smell Angelo's aftershave, and underneath that, the natural, healthy smell of the man's body.

His flatmate hoisted himself on the upper bunk, feet dangling. 'Very compact, isn't it?'

Robert tried to back away from the splayed thighs, but there wasn't enough space. The legs of Angelo's shorts gaped and he could see a tantalising hint of curly black hair. He moved towards the window end of the compartment.

His flatmate gripped the edge of the bunk, swung gracefully down and grabbed his rucksack.

The small of Robert's back dug into the concealed washbasin.

Angelo was unpacking, bending over the lower berth. 'Top or bottom?'

Robert's eyes were glued to the two firm mounds beneath tight denim. He'd never been quite so close to Angelo before. The crotch of his own shorts was growing increasingly tight. As was his throat. 'Er, bottom. Top. Whatever. You choose.' Under

Angelo's broad frame or straddling those muscular thighs. He didn't care.

'OK, I'll take the top.'

Robert smiled ruefully. It seemed appropriate. He'd often lain awake at night, listening to Angelo and Julie fuck in the next room. She came quietly enough, but his flatmate's grunts and moans carried through the thin wall until Robert had grabbed his cock, caressing himself in sync with the man a few feet away. The memory made him uneasy. He needed to get his mind onto other things. 'Fancy a nightcap?' He tossed his rucksack onto the lower berth, opened it and produced the guide-book he'd purchased that afternoon.

'Yes, why not. Just let me cool down a bit first.'

Robert braced himself against the side of the cramped compartment as ridged, hard abdominal muscle inched past him.

Angelo turned on a tap, filled the sink and immersed his head.

Robert opened the guide-book at random, tried to immerse himself in its contents. Words strobed before him, his eyes constantly glancing left to the tantalising view of a solid rear.

Minutes later, Angelo shook his head like a dog, then buried his face in a towel. 'OK. But just one drink, yes? I don't want your snoring keeping me awake!' He grabbed the key to the compartment and grinned.

Robert followed the tall, broad man out into the corridor. He tried to smile, but the thought of spending a night in such close proximity to this man was no laughing matter.

One drink became two. Then three. The bar emptied as the train chugged north. Together they poured over a map of Scotland.

'Kelpie Island? Are you sure?'

'Twenty-minute boat journey from the mainland.' Robert peered at a selection of tiny dots less than a mile from the country's north-west coast. 'That's what the solicitor's letter said.'

'Well, it's not here.'

'It's got to be.' The tiny dots danced amidst the flat blue of the North Atlantic.

Angelo frowned. 'Must be really small if it is not named.'

Robert nodded in agreement, then pulled the solicitor's letter from the pocket of his denim jacket.

Angelo's head was lowered in concentration. The conversation lulled naturally.

Robert looked from the letter to the top of his flatmate's dark, curly head. Beneath the table, their calves brushed. His leg jumped like someone had just passed thirty thousand volts through his kneecap. He hauled his sun-tanned thighs free and stretched both legs out to the side of the small table.

Angelo didn't stir.

Robert sighed and mentally cursed the meagre dimensions of their sleeping-compartment. Sharing a large flat was one thing: sharing something the size of the double-berthed cabin was something else. He'd been half hard for the past hour. Every time he shifted position, or crossed and uncrossed his legs, his desire for the handsome Argentinian poked through the fly of his boxers and rubbed against the rough fabric of the cut-offs. He tried again to take in the information contained in the letter.

Bethran McLeod – who the hell was Bethran McLeod? His father, when they'd spoken that afternoon, managed to recall a distant branch of the family who had acquired land somewhere in Scotland, late last century. As far as anyone knew, the cottage had been maintained by property agents and seldom used by its subsequent owners.

Robert rubbed abstractedly at the inside of his left thigh. His fingers were greeted by a corresponding twitch. He frowned, tried to will himself soft. The more he thought about his cock, the harder it became. His face felt hot. The single malt whisky had seemed appropriate at the time, and he'd hoped it might help him relax. His body obviously had other ideas. Robert clenched his jaw and re-read the letter.

Corrie Cottage.

No street name or number.

Just Corrie Cottage.

A large property or a very small island? Robert swirled the melting ice in his glass and leant back in his seat.

At the other side of the table, Angelo remained absorbed in map-reading.

Robert glanced at his watch – just after ten-thirty – then scanned the bar, which was now almost empty.

He examined a slumped figure in a hooded jacket a few seats away, who had been nursing what looked like an orange juice since he and Angelo had walked in, two hours ago.

From beneath a baseball cap, alert grey eyes met his, then darted away.

Curious, Robert continued to focus on the man, who was now staring determinedly through the tinted glass window into the night sky.

Late twenties, maybe older. His eyes noted the shadow of blond stubble on a square chin and upper lip.

The train's rhythm changed. A slim hand shot out to steady the almost empty glass of orange juice.

He watched the man's fingers tighten around the stubby tumbler, his own tightening in tandem. The guy had an anxious, almost furtive air about him. Robert's curiosity grew. He shoved the solicitor's letter back into his pocket.

The man removed the baseball-cap, ran a hand over very closely cropped blond hair then slumped back in his seat. It was almost as if he were trying to merge with the upholstery, bury himself in the bar's fittings and fixtures.

The writer in Robert sprang loose. Cropped hair – escaped convict? Criminal on the run from the police? A frisson of intrigue shivered his skin. His craned neck was starting to hurt. Robert knew the man in the cap must be aware of his attention – he was anything but subtle – but still the figure gazed studiously into the dark.

Bank robber?

Robert's eyes dropped to the floor and the large holdall which sat between work-booted feet.

A bank robber who had escaped with the entire proceeds of the robbery?

The train lurched.

Robert gripped the edge of the table to steady himself,

momentarily shifting his gaze. When he glanced back across, he caught the grey eyes for a second. Then the man stood up abruptly, lifting the large holdall and moving swiftly towards the door at the far end of the bar. Robert stared disappointedly into his wake, then finished his drink.

A few minutes later, a large, cheerful guard appeared and checked their tickets.

Robert watched a yawn stretch Angelo's darkly handsome face. 'Want to hit the hay?'

The large brown eyes blinked at the idiom, then smiled. 'OK.'

Robert's stomach lurched with the train. That lopsided smile should come with a government health warning: this man can seriously damage your gonads. He shoved hands into pockets and stood up, praying his erection would have subsided before they reached their sleeping compartment.

Two

_____

I t hadn't.
  Robert closed the door and flattened himself against it. The
stiffness of desire tightened the crotch of his cut-offs. Engine
vibrations shivered up through his feet and made his balls quiver.
The whisky was fuzzing his brain, but he felt anything but sleepy.
The compartment seemed to be shrinking with every passing
second.

At the other end of the tiny space, Angelo was already pulling
off his T-shirt.

A current of man-scented air brushed Robert's nostrils. He tried
to swallow, but the hard lump in his shorts had an echo in his
throat. Semi-focused eyes followed the movement of the broad
Argentinian's deltoid muscles as Angelo threw the T-shirt onto
the upper bunk then began to unzip his shorts.

The sound of metal teeth opening seemed slower than necessary. Was he being royally and mercilessly teased? The thought of
Angelo naked and himself still dressed made his groin ache more
than ever. Robert tore his sweatshirt over his head, fingers
fumbling with belt. Cut-offs went the same way. A combination
of modesty and embarrassment made him keep the boxer shorts
on.

Angelo was humming to himself.

13

Robert only half-heard the rich baritone voice over the rhythmic sound of wheels on track. His eyes had fixed themselves on the nut-brown curve of the man's arse-cheeks and the darker crevice between as Angelo stepped out of shorts, then white cotton briefs.

He tossed both onto the top berth before turning back to the wash-hand basin.

Over the sound of running water, blood pounded in Robert's ears, then fled lower, thickening his already stiff cock. He wanted to spread those lean arse-cheeks and bury his face in the very heart of the man, inhale the musky essence of Angelo's maleness. His gaze never leaving the dark hairy crack, Robert reached up, grabbed the briefs from the top bunk and stuffed them under his own pillow.

Immediately, he felt furtive and underhand. But his body knew no shame. The head of his prick wept a single tear of lust. Robert groaned.

'What?' A brown face turned towards him, half covered by a fluffy white towel.

'Nothing.' The train slowed then lurched. Robert gripped the side of the upper berth to steady himself, but not before the unexpected motion threw him off balance and the back of his head glanced against a badly placed coat-hook. 'Ow!' The pain took his attention from the agony of longing which was tenting the front of his boxers. Fingers flew to the injury.

'You OK?'

Stars twinkled before his eyes. The train lurched a second time, picking up speed again. 'Uh – yes, I –' Fingers located a sensitive area. 'Christ!'

'Let me see.' Concern creased the dark, handsome features. In seconds, Angelo was in front of him, large hands moving over blond hair.

Through blurring vision, Robert stared at the side of Angelo's elegant neck. Two feet below, warm hairy softness brushed his thigh. He tried to move back, and met the coat-hook again.

'Keep still.' One hand gripped his bare shoulder while the other continued to ease his head forward.

The breath was tight in his lungs. The hand on his shoulder was firm and warm. The man in front of him was close. Very close. Too close. A trickle of sweat tracked a course from his right armpit. Robert flinched as strong fingers located the point of impact.

'You will have a bruise the side of an egg in the morning if you don't take some of the heat out of it.'

Robert felt himself steered towards the washbasin. He stood motionless, unable to draw away as a naked Angelo soaked a small hand-towel and pressed it against the back of his head. 'Hold that there for a while.'

The coldness of the water did nothing to cool his hot skin.

'Better?' Angelo folded his arms across a hairless chest.

He managed a nod. One nipple was hidden by a hair-dusted forearm. He focused on the other, which was large for a man: a brown nub in a circlet of darker skin. Robert thought about tracing the outline with his tongue, licking smaller and smaller concentric circles before drawing the hard bud into his mouth, nipping the sensitive flesh between his teeth.

The wet towel was drying in his warm fingers.

Angelo reached up, removed toothbrush and toothpaste from the rucksack on the upper berth.

Robert managed to swallow, watching the play of dim overhead light and shadow on the long muscles of the man's back and shoulders.

He couldn't move.

Couldn't think.

Robert frowned. His balls were swollen and heavy with undischarged spunk. He hadn't had a wank in forty-eight hours and Angelo wasn't making things any easier: any longer and lust would mutate into irritability.

Over at the sink, the curly-haired figure was brushing his teeth and humming again.

With supreme effort, Robert managed to sink to a crouch and crawl into the lower bunk. The taste of whisky and desire soured in his mouth. The smell of his own sweat mixed with the minty tang of toothpaste. His fingers located a small switch behind his head. A pair of thick, hairy calves travelled the length of the small sleeping space as Angelo removed and replaced articles in his ruck-sack. 'Put the overhead light out, eh?' His voice was thick.

'OK!' Angelo was as cheerful as ever. 'Want the window-blind open?'

'No!'

'OK.' The compartment darkened. 'Good night!'

''Night.' He switched on the small reading light on the wall to his right and eased his body between crisp white sheets. The fabric cooled his skin but not his ardour.

Above him, the bunk creaked and dipped as Angelo settled down for the night.

Robert turned onto his side. The head of his cock, which had managed to find the fly of his boxers, made contact with the sheets. He winced. He needed relief. Badly. How quietly could he wank? One hand snaked under the pillow. Robert moved onto his stomach, cock thrusting into the mattress while he buried his face and moaned into Angelo's still-warm briefs.

'Robert?'

He sighed, moving his mouth from the slightly skanky crotch. 'What?'

'I just want to say – thanks.'

Robert propped himself up on one elbow. 'What for?'

'For asking me to come along. I really wasn't looking forward to hanging about London – especially on my own.'

'Forget it.' His cock twitched. He suppressed a groan, beginning to regret the whole thing. 'Good ni –'

'I thought about going home for a while.'

Robert narrowed his eyes. 'To Argentina?' His flatmate rarely talked about his family, let alone the exotic country thousands of miles away where he'd spent the first twenty-seven years of his life.

'Yes.'

Robert knew little of Angelo Caballo's background. The man spoke almost-perfect English, suggesting a good education. He also received an allowance: Robert had seen the long envelopes bearing colourful stamps which arrived each month, containing cheques for an amount in a foreign currency. His flatmate worked for a small firm of joiners in Whitechapel, a job which seemed to satisfy a need other than financial. Was now the time to pry? In the dark, Robert smiled wryly: maybe talking would do them both good. 'Why didn't you – go home, I mean?' He flipped over onto his back, stuffing the briefs back under his pillow and stared up at the bulge in the mattress above.

A sigh drifted down. 'Many reasons.'

Robert detected a hint of melancholy in the rich baritone voice.

'My father is very wealthy. He owns one of the largest beef ranches in the highlands – thousands of hectares of prime pampas, hundreds of thousands of heads of cattle. He is also an educated man, but still my family cling to the old ways.' The melancholy was soured by anger.

Robert was intrigued. 'What do you mean – the old ways?'

'Convention. Tradition.'

'Ah.' Daddy Caballo had a scheme all mapped out for his son and heir – a scheme in which, apparently, the son and heir had no interest. Robert laughed softly. 'It's been happening all over the world, from the beginning of time, Angelo: fathers can never understand why their sons have no interest in –'

'It's not that. If I took over the running of Rancho Caballo I could triple output, increase our profits by two hundred per cent. My father knows this. I think the knowledge hurts him more than my –' he sighed '– disgrace.'

Robert leant out of his bunk, eyes boring up into darkness. He waited for Angelo to continue.

And was disappointed. 'My father pays to keep me here in Britain. I am unsure of what welcome – if any – I would receive back in Valcheta. I have few friends in London, now that Julie has –' The strong, masculine voice cracked with emotion. '– gone.'

Robert felt cheated. He wanted to know more about the misdemeanour serious enough for Daddy Caballo to banish his son to the other side of an ocean. It sounded medieval – prehistoric, even. He tried to brighten the gloomy atmosphere. 'Well, you've still got me!' He knew it was true and wished with every fibre of his being Angelo felt the same.

'You are a good friend and a fine man, Robert. I thank you.'

It wasn't exactly what he wanted to hear, but something in the voice touched him deep inside. Robert fought it and changed the subject as train wheels thundered distantly over points. 'Wonder if we're in Scotland yet?' He swung his legs from the bunk and padded over to the small window. The blind flew up as soon as he touched it.

'Are we? What can you see?'

Robert peered through the glass. Too-large eyes stared back. He flinched, then recognised his own reflection. He wasn't bad-looking, he supposed: six foot, good muscle tone, which was all the more remarkable since he didn't take much exercise these days. A throw-back to his university days, when he'd been on the rowing team, probably: not that Angelo seemed to care, one way or the other. Robert pulled a face and watched his reflection do likewise. Beyond angular cheekbones and short blond hair, dark shapes raced by. Pupils slowly acclimatising, he made out the slow progress of majestic hills in the background, their stately motion a sharp contrast to the telephone poles and solitary trees which flicked past his eyes like accelerated animation. 'Not much.'

'Open the window.'

Robert's fingers gripped the sill, hauling upwards.

Noise rushed in. Then scents.

Damp, night scents – the odour of wet, newly cut grass mixed with a baser undertone of woodlands. And something else, something he couldn't quite identify.

'That's Scotland.'

The voice was very close. Robert moved over as Angelo's naked shoulder pressed into his. 'How can you tell?' He felt rather than heard the sound of his flatmate's laugh as it vibrated across the short distance between them.

'I just can. It's exactly the way I thought it would be.'

A gust of wind buffeted the side of the train, splattering the glass with rain.

Robert jumped back. 'Now I know we've crossed the border: it's raining.'

A fist playfully punched his shoulder. 'You have no soul. A little rain only adds to a country's beauty.'

Catching a stinging, wet faceful of that beauty, Robert closed the window and turned. 'Come on – I need my sleep. Don't want the natives seeing us at anything but our best, do we?'

The glow from the lower berth's reading lamp cast their shadows high on the wall. Robert watched the taller of the two move fluidly past the slighter, then vault up onto the top bunk.

Seconds later he switched off the light and pulled the covers up over his ears. The last thing he heard was the rhythmic wheels of the train lulling him towards sleep.

He dreamt of a faraway country and men with brown European faces who sat astride powerful horses.

He dreamt of a man he had never met, an older, greyer version of Angelo who wore a stern expression and a cowboy hat. One long brown finger pointed past a repentant-looking Angelo towards a tall gate set in the middle of a high fence. Around them, cattle lowed. Angelo was pleading with his father, pleading to stay.

The stern-faced man didn't speak but continued to point.

Angelo turned, dragging his feet towards the tall gate. Crowds of people had gathered – men, women, children – all watching Angelo's slow progress towards the gate from Rancho Caballo.

Fingers fumbled with the gate's catch, then slowly pushed it open.

The crowd was murmuring. An older woman with a black headscarf was crying. Some distance away, a pretty girl with an ornate hair-decoration was calling Angelo's name.

On the other side of the gate, Angelo paused, turned to look back.

The gate was metal, he could see through the slats.

Knocking.

Angelo was knocking on the gate, begging to be allowed to return.

The stern-faced man shook his head once, then gripped the reins of an ebony black stallion and galloped off over the pampas.

Knocking.

Angelo's fist pounded against the smooth metal of the gate. His knuckles began to bleed.

The knocking sounded different. Less loud.

Robert moaned, removed the pillow from his ears and turned over.

More tapping than knocking. And whispering.

Robert blinked awake. Someone was at the door – had they reached Fort William already? He glanced towards the window. No, it was still dark. His ears strained.

Another soft rap.

The ticket inspector! Robert sighed. What was the point of paying for a berth to ensure sleep if the guard had to wake you up to check tickets? Frowning, he grabbed cut-offs, struggled into them and reached for his wallet. His hand was on the door knob when Angelo stirred:

'Wha –? Who –?'

'Go back to sleep.' Robert unlocked the door and dragged two booking slips from a calf-skin wallet. The cut-offs were only half-zipped as he edged the door open a few inches and thrust a hand through.

'Let me in, pal. Please.'

Robert froze, then eased the door outwards another inch or two. From under a baseball cap, alert grey eyes met his.

'Just a few minutes till the guard goes past.' The voice was breathless with fear.

Robert stared at the unkempt man with the holdall from the bar.

Now tinged with panic, the alert grey eyes focused on the far end of the train's corridor, then flicked back to Robert's. 'Please!'

Behind, he could hear Angelo stirring. What the hell – he'd skipped fares often enough himself: everyone did. Robert stepped back, flattening himself against the open door then closed it as the man moved quickly inside.

Angelo's dark outline was now upright on the top berth.

'Shhh! It's OK.' Robert watched the figure in the baseball cap walk to the window end of the sleeping compartment, then turn. Even in the gloom, he could see every nerve in the strong body tensed.

All three remained silent.

Outside, footsteps approached. Then a soft knock.

Robert motioned towards the lower berth.

The man removed his baseball cap and dived onto the bunk.

Robert turned towards the door. 'Yeah?' He hoped he sounded convincingly sleepy.

Voice from the other side: 'Sorry to disturb you, sir. Ticket check.'

His wallet was still in his hand. Waiting a few minutes, Robert opened the door and stared at the bulky guard. He held out their reservations, rubbed sleep from his eyes and yawned. A large hand took the tickets, while narrowed eyes peered past him into the dark space.

A grumpy voice appeared from behind Robert's head: 'It's hard enough to sleep on this damn train!'

Robert mentally thanked Angelo for the back-up.

The guard smiled sheepishly, returning the reservation folders. 'Sorry to disturb you, gentlemen. Have a pleasant night.' He touched the brim of a peaked cap and moved to the next compartment.

Robert's hand was shaking as he closed the door a second time. Adrenalin coursed through his veins like a drug. The excitement and satisfaction of pulling a fast one was immense. He found himself smiling broadly.

'What is going on?' Angelo's deep voice rumbled in the darkness.

'Man-oh-man! This is something I could do without.' The reply was a rushed whisper.

Robert sank to a crouch, switched on the bunk light and stared at the figure on his bed.

The man rubbed his face with relief. 'I need to get to Edinburgh by morning.' Alert eyes appeared from behind palms. 'I can't thank you guys enough.'

Something in the man's accent told Robert he was not British. 'You're Canadian?'

The crew-cut head shook. 'American. Stationed at the Gareloch for eight months. Thought I'd see the London sights, get some R and R in before the unit goes back. Boy, was that a bad idea.' One hand fumbled in the inside pocket of a dirty denim jacket.

Robert shivered. This man could be a criminal, a psychopath – anything! Remnants of adrenalin turned fear into a delicious anticipation.

One freckled hand produced a harmless airline ticket folder. 'Lost track of time, money – and my buddies! The plane leaves Edinburgh at 05.03.'

Robert looked at his wristwatch: just after 4 a.m. An hour or so to kill. 'Probably best if you stay in here – I think the guard patrols the corridors all night.'

'Sure that's OK, now? I don't wanna be –' a sly, knowing expression flickered across the square-jawed face '– interrupting anything.'

Robert frowned. 'You're not.'

The knowing expression softened to faint surprise. 'Ah. Well, I gotta be on that plane, guys – and you two just made that possible.' The man scrambled to his feet. The compartment became more crowded than ever. 'Thanks again.' The square-jawed face creased. The American stuck out a hand. 'Corporal Billy-Bob Monroe at your service and in your debt!'

Robert stared briefly, then seized the hand. Billy-Bob's grip was iron as his arm was pumped up and down. 'Robert McLeod, and this is –'

'Angelo Caballo.' A brawny arm dangled down from the upper and grabbed another hand.

'Good to meet you, Angelo!' The alert grey eyes had levelled just below Robert's waist.

Robert was suddenly aware of his open zip, and the stretching member inside his briefs. He was sweating, and Billy-Bob was very close. 'Move over.' He gripped the edge of the top bunk and hauled himself up beside Angelo.

His flatmate raised one thick black eyebrow, nodding in the direction of the buzz-cut head a few inches away.

Robert shrugged then grinned: two of them, and only one of him. If all this was a con and the American did have nefarious intentions, he would have a fight on his hands.

Below, Billy-Bob had produced a bottle from his holdall and was slugging from it.

Robert wriggled as Angelo eased his legs from behind him. 'Where did you say you were from, Billy-Bob?'

'Stationed in Groton, CT, now – the sub-base – born and raised in Fayetteville, Arkansas. Man, I miss the south, sometimes.' The bottle was held out. Robert shook his head. Angelo grabbed the dark shape, took a slug and coughed.

Billy-Bob laughed. 'Best Arkansas moonshine, buddy. My grandma sends me a jug disguised as her herbal pick-me-up.' He took the bottle back. 'Best tonic I know for getting through your country's damp weather. Mind if I –?' He tugged at the hooded jacket.

'Feel free – it is rather warm in here.'

'Thanks, Robert.'

He watched as the man struggled out of the jacket to reveal a tight khaki vest with deeply cut armholes, which showed off his strong, muscular shoulders. Two dog-tags clanked between two mounds of surprisingly large pectoral masses. The vest itself came next. Robert's eyes glued themselves to the thick hair beneath long sinewy arms as Billy-Bob dragged jersey over his crew-cut head, then wiped his armpits with the garment. 'That's better!' He leant against the wall opposite, staring up and grinning. 'Now you gotta let me show you guys my appreciation.' Grey eyes pinned his.

Robert made a dismissive gesture with his hand. He could feel Angelo's warm, naked thigh beside his.

'I insist. Where I come from, one good turn deserves another.' Billy-Bob had one fist wrapped around the bottle. The fingers of his other hand lingered at the crotch of worn, olive trousers. 'We southerners like to pay our debts.'

The message was loud and clear. Robert's cock understood the sentiment while his brain was still trying to process the words. 'No need, really.' He could take Billy-Bob to the small toilet, let him 'show his appreciation' there. But with no ticket and a suspicious guard, it was much too risky. He swallowed down another frustration. His face prickled with desire and embarrassment: he wanted the American but the compartment was much too small for any mutual 'appreciation' to go unnoticed by the silent man who sat beside him. Robert stared at the shadowy figure inches away and sighed.

Billy-Bob took another drink, then scratched his tufted armpits.

At Robert's side, a whisper of a voice seeped through the darkness. 'What's wrong?'

Robert moved closer to the approximate area of Angelo's ear. 'Nothing.'

Angelo's low laugh drifted back. 'You want him?'

Robert flinched. 'Well, yes – but –'

Angelo's words were half-laugh, half-whisper and for Robert's ears only. 'Let me handle it.' The rich voice grew in volume. 'I hear Arkansas men are better with their mouths than their fists.'

An unfamiliar tone in his flatmate's voice caused Robert's cock to edge another inch up inside his briefs.

'Well, I guess you could say we're flexible.' The American's laugh was low and sexy, loaded with promise.

Robert watched Billy-Bob loosen the webbing belt around the top of his olive army-trousers, then unbutton and drag down the zip.

'How about a little show for my knights in shining armour?' Fingers slipped inside the zip and hooked around a solid rod of flesh.

'With audience participation?' Angelo's tone was even.

Robert shivered. Moisture slicked the head of his now fully erect cock. The small space was thick with the smell of sweat and the fresh, salty odour of lust.

Billy-Bob's angular face flicked between the two of them, grey eyes smouldering. 'Whatever you guys want, I'm up for it!'

Three

Strong legs planted two feet apart, Billy-Bob pushed folds of olive fabric out of the way and wrapped fingers around his shaft. Back arching and shoulders braced against the motion of the train, he caressed the root of his cock. The bottle of moonshine was stuffed in a back pocket. Fingers which had previously held glass were now toying with a large nipple.

Robert leant forward on the top bunk, lips parted. At his side, Angelo was motionless.

Billy-Bob's dog-tags clanked against each other. Hips thrust forward, fucking the air, then circled back and thrust again. 'Like what you see, guys?' The voice was half-taunt, half-plead as the man caressed himself.

Robert was transfixed by the American's cock, which sprouted from out of his fist like a parade-ground sergeant's baton. It was circumcised, the thick, rose-coloured head collared by an uneven circlet of tightening skin. The shaft curved to the left. Pulsing blue veins contrasted sharply with the thin, slightly brownish skin which covered the member. A weapon. A tool. An offering – one he desperately wanted to accept. Words cut through his thoughts.

'About turn, soldier!'

'Yessir!'

Robert blinked. There was a new tone in Angelo's deep voice:

a note of authority which he longed to obey himself. A frisson of uncertainty mixed with the fear of the guard's return and his own mounting need. His flatmate's whispered 'Let me handle it' tossed and turned in his mind.

Corporal Billy-Bob Monroe braced his arms against the wall of the compartment, head thrown back. Under the light cast by the reading-lamp, skin and muscle glowed. Olive pants bagged around hairy thighs. 'Awaiting your orders, sir!' The voice came from a now-lowered head.

Robert glanced left into darkness. His words were a hissed, hoarse whisper. 'What's going on? Do you –?'

A breathy laugh caressed his ears: 'Follow my lead.' The voice resumed an authoritative tone. 'Spread 'em, soldier.'

'Yessir!'

Robert looked back at the American, open-mouthed.

Two large hands dragged trousers to ankles and over boots, then grabbed two small hard mounds, wrenching them apart.

Sex-sweat glued the head of Robert's cock to the fine hair on his stomach. Was Angelo now playing some sort of game with both of them? Arousal blocked any further uncertainty. Robert seized his shaft, tore it free from his briefs. The pressure of the grip made his balls spasm.

Billy-Bob was thrusting backwards now, knees bent and thighs tensed as the hard hemispheres of his arse circled towards them. The dog-tags continued to clink.

Robert could see four finger indentations surrounding a dusky pink, puckered hole. He wanted to fuck that hole. He wanted to grab the back of Corporal Billy-Bob Monroe's shaven neck and fuck his arse then wrench himself out and shower the man's back and buttocks with his lust. Before he knew it, his fist was travelling upwards, then down, pulling foreskin tight then releasing it.

'What is the penalty for possession of illicit alcohol, soldier?'

Robert felt a sharp clenching in his balls. He was building quickly but didn't want to come yet: with Angelo at his side, barking commands in that strange new voice, he didn't know if he wanted to come at all.

'Whatever punishment you wanna issue, sir!'

Robert stared at the bottle-shaped lump in the back pocket of Billy-Bob's olive trousers, which were now crumpled concertina-like under the army boots.

Angelo laughed.

Robert shivered, eyes flicking between the spasming orifice and the man at his side.

'You like moonshine so much let's see just how much you can take, soldier!'

'Yessir!' Billy-Bob whooped enthusiastically. His right hand removed itself from one arse-cheek. Four red indentations glowed as the American fumbled on the floor, producing the green bottle.

Robert stared at the shape, the narrow neck spreading in circumference from one to at least eight inches. His aching cock spasmed against his sweating palm.

'Get it in there, soldier! Get it right in there!' Angelo had to shout over the clatter of train-wheels on tracks.

'Yessir! Right away, sir!' Billy-Bob spat into one palm and rubbed it over the green glass neck.

Robert's heart hammered in his chest. The fear of discovery combined with the shock of Angelo's evident military background turned him on more than ever. He gripped the edge of the bunk and was about to lower himself to get a better look at the man about to fuck himself with a bottle when strong fingers gripped his wrist. He turned his head.

Angelo's face remained a dark, unreadable shadow.

Robert could feel warm breath on his face, smell the tang of fresh sweat. Neither of them said anything. The message was clear: part of the game involved Robert remaining on the top bunk.

From below, a gasp.

His head jerked round.

Fingers of one hand gripping the coat-hook for balance, the other gripping the base of the bottle and holding it steady on the floor, Corporal Billy-Bob Monroe was easing himself down onto a cylinder of green.

Robert watched the man's thickly haired thighs splay out as he bent his knees.

The first inch disappeared.

Arousal dribbled down Robert's spine and into his crack, causing his own hole to tighten then dilate in parallel with the American's rapidly filling anus.

The second inch disappeared.

Billy-Bob was moaning rhythmically now as he continued to bear down on the neck of the bottle, impaling himself on the shining, hollow rod.

Robert had a sudden urge to grind against the mattress beneath him. Inside his boxers, his sphincter was gaping, longing to be clamped around something hard. He stared at the lips of the American's arse which widened to admit more and more of the glass cock.

He had to come.

He had to come soon or when he did he'd blow the roof off the compartment.

'Attention!'

Billy-Bob slowly rose to his feet, staggering slightly. 'Yessir!' The word was a hoarse rasp.

Robert was panting, eyes fixed on the remaining five inches of bottle which protruded from between the American's arse-cheeks. He was surprised the movement upright and the highly charged atmosphere in the compartment hadn't caused muscle to contract and force the object out of the man's body.

'Eyes front.'

'Yessir!' Billy-Bob slowly turned.

Robert stared at the pink, flushed face beneath the blond crew-cut. The veins on the man's neck stood out, taut and pulsing with effort. The clanking dog-tags were silent, adhered to heaving pectorals.

Arms at his sides, Billy-Bob's fists were clenched with concentration. And desire.

Robert's gaze dropped from hard, abdominal ridges to the American's cock. Clear liquid flowed freely from the slit which bisected the engorged head. Billy-Bob's balls had almost disappeared, the delicate skin stretched taut over the tight sack.

'Come here, soldier.'

'Yessir.' The words were hissed through clenched teeth.

Robert's hands were still gripping the edge of the bunk. He knew if they moved anywhere near his cock he'd come in seconds.

Billy-Bob's progress across the short distance was slow and laboured. With each step there was a sloshing sound, as moonshine splashed around in the bottle which tight muscle still held in place.

Robert watched the man's approach, watched the rest of his body disappear from sight until only Billy-Bob's shorn head and broad freckled shoulders were in view.

Alert grey eyes hid themselves beneath long lashes. The American stood between them, head bowed.

Over the thundering of the train and the hammer of his heart, Robert heard Angelo's words:

'Let's see that southern mouth in action, soldier.'

Seconds later Billy-Bob was living up to his name.

Hands gripping a pair of scarlet ears, Robert groaned as lip-sheathed teeth made a firm 'o' over his firmer flesh and Billy-Bob's mouth began to pump up and down on his aching shaft. The motion pulled his balls tight against his body while his slit leaked pre-come freely.

Heat from the man's mouth seeped through tightly stretched cockskin, into his flesh and into the very heart of him. Frowning with desire, Robert pistoned upwards with his hips, thrusting his cock deeper and deeper into Billy-Bob's mouth.

The man began to choke.

Robert gripped the American's skull and forced his head back, opening up his throat and pushing past the gag-reflex. Then hands gripped his waist, pulling him forward. He groaned, feeling the sensitive glans bang off something warm and solid as he fucked the back of the man's throat.

Billy-Bob was making low, animal sounds. The force of the face-fucking made his eyes water, but there was no mistaking the need which painted creases on the pink, freckled features. His Adam's apple bobbed convulsively against Robert's balls, which tightened and relaxed in response.

'Take it all, soldier!'

The reminder of Angelo's presence made his stomach churn.

But he was too far gone to care. Draping his legs over Billy-Bob's shoulders, Robert leant back, lying half-on, half-off the bunk.

As the American pleasured him with his mouth, Robert glimpsed Angelo's slightly mocking face, inches away. The sight tightened muscle deep inside and pushed him over the edge. He thrust one final time. Hips jerked upwards. Hands pressed down, fingers tightening around a bristly skull. Robert threw back his head, body rigid and mind empty as spunk filled Billy-Bob's mouth in short, sharp shots.

The head between his thighs groaned, Billy-Bob's hands working furiously three feet lower to bring himself off. A sudden gasp and the clank of glass on carpet as the bottle of moonshine hit the floor told him the American had managed it.

Robert lay quivering on the top bunk. Stars danced before his eyes. In the receding pleasure of orgasm, his legs were limp over Billy-Bob's shoulders, damp skin stuck to damper skin.

'At ease, soldier!'

Billy-Bob fell back against the compartment wall, then slumped to the floor. 'Man-oh-man! You English guys are something else!'

Angelo's deep laugh filled his ears.

Robert tried to echo the sentiment, but could only croak. Crystallising spunk was making the head of his cock itch. He reached down, readjusting then scratching just beneath his foreskin. To his surprise he was still half-hard. There was movement at his side.

'My jockeys – where are my –?'

'I think they're on the floor.' Robert wondered at the sudden onset of modesty, then suddenly remembered the whereabouts of the white jersey briefs. His mouth dried with the onset of a blush.

'I need to relieve myself – I may meet another passenger.'

Billy-Bob whooped hoarsely. 'Lucky them if ya do!'

Tucking his sticky cock back inside his boxers, Robert sat up and lowered himself from the bunk.

Billy-Boy was still trying to get his breath back as Robert crouched, reached under his pillow and grabbed a handful of soft, Angelo-scented fabric. Retrieving the underwear, he tossed the briefs onto the upper bunk.

'Thanks.'

Robert leant back against the berth, feeling Angelo's hairy calves on each side of his head. An odd mixture of intimacy and detachment coursed through his veins. His mind was visualising the activity above, as white briefs dragged over the groin inches from the back of his skull.

Angelo bounded from the top bunk, grabbed his jacket and unlocked the door.

Robert's eyes flicked from Billy-Bob's sweat-drenched body to the disappearing sight of his flatmate's and back again.

The American wiped his softening cock, then the neck of the moonshine-bottle, with the olive T-shirt and took a slug. 'I needed that!'

'The drink or the face-fuck?' Robert grinned,

Billy-Bob smiled, held up the bottle. 'Both. Three months on-base without any company makes a man thirsty.' A sweaty hand clamped itself to Robert's arse and squeezed.

Robert passed on the moonshine, running his fingers over Billy-Bob's bristling crew-cut. 'I know the feeling.' He glanced up towards the door and thought about Angelo, at present in the tiny toilet at the end of the corridor: his was a thirst only semi-quenched, and a curiosity only partly satisfied.

While choreographing the entire encounter, Angelo hadn't come. Was that what he had excused himself to go and do?

Billy-Bob's hand wandered down the back of Robert's thighs, then slipped between them, knuckles nudging the softness of his loose ball-sac.

Robert half-laughed, half-moaned and grabbed the back of Billy-Bob's neck.

The American kissed his stomach.

The compartment door opened. 'No sign of the ticket inspector now, but you'd better hold on here anyway.'

Angelo's down-to-earth remark broke the tension. Robert eased away as his flatmate vaulted onto the upper bunk. 'So, Billy-Bob-from-Fayetteville-with-a-mouth-like-a-Hoover: what did you think of London?'

Billy-Bob read the signals with a practised eye. He pulled up and fastened olive army trousers one-handed, then sank back to a crouch opposite. 'London's a real cool town. I loved those guys in the red jackets and furry hats, outside your queen's place!'

Robert smiled, one hand coming to rest on the top berth. He could hear Angelo slipping once more out of his briefs. Fingers contacted with soft, damp warmth: he wondered if Angelo had had a sly wank in the toilets.

Words drifted down from above: 'The Beefeaters are even more colourful. Did you get the chance to visit the Tower of London?'

Angelo's voice made the hair on his arms stand on end. As the first rays of dawn streaked in through the uncurtained window, Robert eased the briefs from the top bunk, lowered and held them behind his back.

'Sure did. Got to see St Paul's too.'

Robert listened with half an ear, running the damp fabric between his fingers, feeling Angelo's still-warm piss-splatters against his moist palms.

The train journeyed northwards. Billy-Bob continued to fill them in on the details of his London escapade while he dressed.

Half an hour later, light had seeped into the small compartment. The American was still talking. Robert pulled the plug and let water drain from the sink as he gazed out of the tiny window. The train was slowing. Outside, suburban Edinburgh chugged into view.

A warm, mocha shoulder edged in beside his. 'How's your head?'

Robert turned his face slightly, one hand feeling for the lump where the coat-hook had impacted earlier. It was barely perceptible. 'Fine.' He had avoided catching Angelo's eye since stuffing still-warm briefs into the rucksack beside his own soiled boxers. Now he couldn't avoid it. A coffee-coloured face grinned lopsidedly at him.

'OK?' Large brown eyes refocused on the scene beyond.

'Er, yes.' He stared at the side of Angelo's face, at the dark stubble which etched his flatmate's jaw-line. 'Listen, thanks for –'

'My pleasure!' Angelo laughed. 'You can return the favour sometime.'

Robert was more confused than ever. The Argentinian was no prude or homophobe: Robert knew that already. But tolerating the idea of man-to-man sex was one thing: sitting in the middle of it, issuing orders, was something else.

'Quite a night, yes?'

Robert managed a smile and nodded, wondering if Angelo was aware of exactly how much of a night it had been for a certain blond-haired, blocked writer who still longed to run his fingers through the glossy black locks mere inches away.

'Where are we, guys?'

Robert's head jerked round to look at Billy-Bob, who had consumed an entire bottle of moonshine and seemed none the worse for it. 'Edinburgh. You'd better get ready.' He moved away from the window. 'Let me check for the guard.' Drying his face, he squeezed past the American and cautiously edged open the door.

Outside, three passengers and their luggage were waiting to disembark. Billy-Bob's nemesis was nowhere in sight.

Robert's head flicked back inside the compartment. The train was grinding to a halt and the smell of brake-fluid mixed with the bite of wood alcohol and the stale tang of men's bodies. 'OK.' He beckoned. 'Come on.'

Billy-Bob began to pump Angelo's hand vigorously. 'Thanks for everything, guys –' he winked at Robert '– and I do mean everything!'

Robert smiled. 'The pleasure was ours.'

Angelo grinned. 'Hope you get that plane –' he laughed '– soldier!'

Billy-Bob whooped. 'Yessir!'

Robert's smile stiffened. The whole thing was a game to Angelo, and he wasn't sure how that made him feel.

The train jolted. Their exchange was interrupted by the sound of doors opening and the distant, early morning bustle of Edinburgh's Waverley station.

Angelo levered himself onto the top bunk to allow the

American space to leave. At the door, Robert found himself seized in a bear-hug. Low words brushed his ear: 'You're a lucky fella – that's one hot guy you've got there!'

'Take care.' Robert returned the embrace, frowning at Billy-Bob's assumption, then checked one last time before bundling the man out into the corridor through an open door onto the station platform. As he closed the door and lowered the window, a tall figure with cropped hair was already striding into the distance, army boots thumping on stone, holdall thrown over one shoulder. Billy-Bob paused, turned and saluted.

Robert half-heartedly returned the gesture and watched their unscheduled travelling companion disappear from sight.

An hour later they were in the dining car, eating breakfast. Determined to enter into the spirit of things, Angelo consumed his kippers with relish.

Robert toyed with a piece of toast and gazed out of the window. Last night was a pleasant, erotic memory, but his heart was heavy with a sense of growing confusion. There were so many questions he wanted to ask.

Outside, the lush, green pasture of the Scottish lowlands had given way to a rockier, more mountainous terrain. The sun was shining less brightly from behind a veil of cloud which steadily thickened until it became a shroud.

'These are good!'

Robert looked over at Angelo, who was munching enthusiastically. He decided to broach at least one previously unexplored subject. 'You were in the army?'

Full lips paused, mid mastication. Large eyes narrowed. 'Two years. It was a long time ago.' Angelo swallowed then sawed at the remaining shard of smoked fish.

Robert sighed. So much for that! It was obvious the man didn't want to talk about it.

'More coffee, gentlemen?' The accent was unmistakably Scottish.

Two sets of eyes looked up at the white-aproned steward who held a gleaming silver pot. 'Please.'

Angelo nodded in agreement.

As the man filled both cups, Robert watched the easy grace with which the waiter moved. He frowned: this was becoming an obsession! He dragged his mind onto other things. 'How far is Fort William?'

The steward wiped the lip of the coffee-pot with a spotless napkin and glanced at a hairy wrist. 'An hour and a half or so.' He smiled. 'On holiday?'

Robert nodded. The truth was too complicated.

'Your first time north of the border?'

Angelo replaced his knife and fork on the plate and leant back in his seat. 'Yes. Do you live here?'

The laugh was harsh and guttural. 'I'm Scottish, aye, but from Dumfries – it's very different from the Highlands and islands, or the east coast. Scotland's really about five different countries merged into one.'

Robert gave up with the toast. 'Do you know Kelpie Island? It's very small and we can't find it on the map.' He drew the guide-book from his pocket and spread it out on the table.

The steward moved the coffee-pot out of the way, brow creasing. 'Kelpie Island . . . Kelpie Island. No, never heard o' it – let's have a look at your map.'

Three pairs of eyes stared at the table-top, examining the ragged debris around the north-west coast of Scotland. After about five minutes, the steward sighed. 'You're right – I don't see it anywhere.' He straightened up, lifted the coffee-pot. 'Hold on – the cook's a Tuechter. Maybe he can help. Angus?' he shouted towards the galley.

Robert looked at Angelo and whispered. 'What's a Tuechter?'

Angelo whispered back, 'Don't ask me – my English is barely passable. I have no knowledge of Gaelic. What is a kelpie, for that matter?'

They both stared towards the small, stocky figure dressed in grease-smeared white who stood in the doorway to the kitchen, wiping hands on apron.

'You heard o' somewhere called – Kelpie Island?'

A balding head tilted to one side, then the other.

Robert suppressed a snigger.

'Who's asking about Kelpie Island?' Angus's intonation was strange and lilting, completely different from the steward's. He crossed the lurching train towards their table.

Robert straightened his face and stood up. 'We are. Can you tell us what direction the island is from Fort William?'

Angus stopped in his tracks, staring past him.

Robert followed the stocky man's gaze to Angelo, who was pouring himself more coffee. He sighed: chalk up another one to his flatmate's irresistible charms. 'Kelpie Island? It isn't on the map and –'

'There is no ferry service, but you might be able to find a trawlerman in Mallaig who's willing to take you across. I'm Angus McDougal, of the Tobermory McDougals.'

Robert smiled, stuck out a hand. 'Thanks, Angus. I'm . . .' His words tailed off as he noticed the introduction had been directed at his breakfasting companion, not himself.

'And can I ask your name, my friend?' The balding head inclined towards the curly black one.

The Argentinian looked up, startled. 'Caballo – Angelo Caballo.' He gripped the arms of his chair, made to stand up.

Angus backed away, face a mask.

Robert thought the cook looked as though he was going to cross himself, or make whatever religious sign Tuechters made.

The balding man continued his deferential retreat towards the kitchen, as if in the presence of royalty – or great evil. 'The islanders will know of your arrival. You will be met at Mallaig, Caballo.' The words had a sonorous, loaded quality.

Robert's eyes widened. Was it his imagination, or had the stocky cook just bowed?

Angelo himself now looked confused, hovering between a standing and sitting position. He replied to the swinging galley door. 'Er, thanks, er – McDougal.'

The steward laughed.

'What was all that about?' Robert stared at the space where the cook had been.

'Ignore Angus.' The steward was still laughing. He tapped his forehead. 'Highlanders – they're all daft! But at least you've got directions to this Kelpie Island place.'

Angelo sat down, looking more confused than ever.

Behind them another table required the steward's attention. He smiled at them both. 'Enjoy your holiday.' His expression darkened. 'But watch out for full moons!' Breaking into another gale of mirth, the man walked away, shaking his head.

Robert stared at Angelo.

Angelo stared back.

Their confused faces broadened into grins at the same time.

'Strange man!'

Robert winked. 'Strange country, it would seem.' He glanced left.

Outside, the sky was leaden and rain threw itself at the glass.

Angelo laughed. 'And a wet one.'

'Adds to the atmosphere, don't you think?' Robert smiled.

Angelo's large eyes widened. 'You've changed your tune!'

'I know.' Robert rested elbows on the white linen tablecloth, propping his chin on his hands. His eyes were fixed on the grey sky and the greyer mountains. 'Something tells me a lot of things are going to change, in the course of this holiday.'

Angelo didn't reply.

They sat in comfortable silence, drinking coffee.

An hour later, the train pulled into Fort William.

Four

'Well? How do we get there?'

Robert looked at Angelo, then threw a set of keys into the air and caught them. The main street in Fort William was busy as they walked away from the solicitor's office. 'The cook on the train was right: there's no regular ferry service. We need to go to Mallaig.'

Angelo grinned lopsidedly. 'This is turning out to be quite an adventure, yes?' He shook rain from dark curls.

Robert wiped his wet face. The steady drizzle which had started the moment they left the station was developing into heavier rain; his stomach grumbled from lack of breakfast, and a night's interrupted sleep was catching up on him. The last thing he needed was Angelo's boundless enthusiasm. 'I suppose so.' A hand clapped his back, nearly knocking him off his feet.

'Cheer up! It won't be long now, I am sure.'

An arm draped itself around his shoulder. Robert flinched.

The arm tightened.

So did his groin.

As they walked up the street, two women were walking down.

With their soaking shorts and rucksacks, Robert knew he and Angelo were already conspicuous amongst locals in raincoats and wellington boots. He felt himself redden under the women's curious gaze and began to walk more quickly: Fort William was no urban metropolis – men didn't hold on to each other up here.

The women neared.

Part of him wanted to dig his hand into the back pocket of Angelo's shorts and proudly but untruthfully proclaim: this man is my lover. Another part of him wanted to scream: 'He's from Argentina! They all do this, there!'

The women drew closer.

Angelo slowed his brisk pace.

A prisoner of the strong arm, Robert could only do likewise.

Angelo stopped, parallel with the twosome, who looked like mother and daughter. 'Good morning, ladies.'

Robert cringed at the formality.

In matching cagoules, the women paused.

Angelo executed a small bow. 'We are looking for Mallaig – can you tell us how to get there, please?'

The polite, friendly words rang in his ears. Robert wondered how used Fort William locals were to demonstrative tourists. He looked at Angelo.

The handsome face was beaming.

He looked at the two women.

The younger giggled. The older smiled. 'Mallaig? Bus is your best bet, son.'

Robert watched as directions were given. He tried to take them in, but was distracted by the flirtatious glances which were being exchanged between Angelo and the younger of the two women while he debated various Mallaig-options with the older. Blood returned to his head. Robert's face burned. He moved away from Angelo's arm and found a smile. 'Thanks. I'm sure we'll have no problem now.' He nodded curtly, smile fixed then strode away. The blush became a flush of anger.

Footsteps behind. Then breathless words. 'What's wrong?'

'Nothing!' He walked faster.

'They have a car. They were going to give us a lift to –'

'I don't want a lift! We'll find the bus station.' His stomach churned, jealousy flooding his veins. He scowled. Rain dribbled from his hair onto his face. He wiped it away.

'But I thought with the weather so bad, and you so wet –'

The note of concern in the deep, accented voice made him feel petty. Robert stopped, turned.

Large brown eyes stared into his.

Robert's heart missed a beat. Angelo had been thinking of him and his comfort, when he had been thinking only of himself. He felt stupid: so what if his flatmate was flirting with a woman? Angelo hadn't minded about him and Billy-Bob, last night in the sleeping-compartment. Warmth filled his stomach, mixed with embarrassment at his own irrationality.

The full mouth smiled lopsidedly again. 'Know what you need?'

Robert's skin tingled, anger and embarrassment subsiding into desire. He knew all too well.

Angelo winked. 'You need to get out of those wet clothes and get something warm inside you!'

Robert frowned. Then a chuckle built in his chest, exploding into a hearty laugh at the unintentional come-on.

Angelo was perplexed. 'What is it? What have I said?'

Robert's shoulders shook. He stared into confused liquid eyes. Before he could stop it, his hand snaked out and ruffled wet curls. Angelo's hair was soft between his fingers. 'I'm just grumpy this morning – ignore me. You're right, I just need . . .' The words dissolved into another gale of laughter. He pulled his hand away, and repositioned his rucksack. 'Come on, let's find a bus.' He began to walk purposefully.

'OK.' Angelo was still a little confused. 'But you must promise to tell me if my English is not as it should be in future, yes?'

'I wouldn't have your command of language any other way!' Robert grinned. As a row of covered stands came into view, he could still feel the texture of those thick, dark curls between his fingers.

The bus journey to the coast was brief, most of the scenery hidden by a thick layer of cloud.

Twenty minutes later, they stood on a bustling pier. The smell of salt and seaweed hung in the air. Around them, oilskin-clad figures unloaded their squirming, slippery catches onto the quayside. Others were sorting then packing marine life of all shapes and sizes into various boxes. Robert's nostrils twitched: he'd never been one for fish.

Angelo was spellbound.

Robert strolled on down the pier, avoiding the lobster-creels and their vicious-looking prisoners. Near the end of the long, stone jetty he could see smaller, less obviously commercial-looking craft.

Angelo was walking ahead, now, reading off the names of the boats. '*Highland Lass*. *Amy-Lou*. Mah . . . Magh . . .?'

Robert scanned the Gaelic name. 'I think it's pronounced "*Maree*" . . .'

'Thanks!' Angelo looked grateful. 'Why do boats always have women's names?'

'No idea.' Robert's attention had been taken by a brawny red-haired figure, bare-chested despite the rain. The man wore only a pair of bright, waterproof trousers and heavy rubber boots and sat, cross-legged on top of a pile of discarded fish-boxes, deftly mending a net. Large fingers slipped a needle fluidly between black diamonds of nylon, weaving a neat repair across a ragged hole. There was something soothing, almost hypnotic about the work – and a stark contrast between the size of the man and the nature of the task.

Although seated, he had to be at least six foot five.

Robert stared at blunt fingertips which moved like the pistons of a well-greased machine, slowly and meticulously weaving the darn. His eyes focused on the film of sweat and what might have been fish-oil which shone between the redhead's ginger-tufted pectorals.

'The *Kelpie*!'

Robert tore his gaze away and walked on. 'What?'

Angelo was pointing to the name-plate of a rather delapidated boat which bobbed almost at the end of the pier. 'The *Kelpie*! A good sign, yes?'

Robert peered at the vessel, then noticed a couple who were standing a little away from the *Kelpie*'s gang-plank.

A man and a woman. Both tall, their well-cut clothes incongruous amongst the yellow oil-cloth and tangled nets of the quayside. Other passengers? The straps of the rucksack were digging into his shoulder-muscle. He wrestled his arms free of the backpack, sat it on the wet surface and turned back to Angelo. He nodded in the direction of the tall couple. 'See if they know which boats go across to the island. I'll —'

'You're looking for the *Kelpie*?'

A soft burr stroked his ear.

Robert turned and found himself staring into a very pronounced Adam's apple. He raised his eyes.

The bare-chested giant pushed a straggling lock of heavy ginger hair back into the ponytail which lay over his shoulder like a thick coil of rope. The other hand held a hank of neatly repaired net.

The smell of fish was very strong and mixed with a heavier musk. Robert inhaled and took a step back. 'We're looking for a lift to Kelpie Island, and we were told —'

'If it's passage to the island you're after, you're just in time.' Huge hands gathered up the net expertly, folding it into rectangles. The fisherman turned, heaving the mesh onto the deck.

Robert's eyes took in the veins on sweat-slicked arms. The net had to weigh close to a hundredweight, but the movement was almost effortless.

The redhead lifted a pair of wicker cages and turned back. A smile split the rugged, weather-beaten face. Vivid green eyes moved to Robert's backpack. 'We don't get many tourists, but if you don't mind sharing space with my creels —'

'We don't mind at all.' Robert glanced over at the ramshackle boat. 'The *Kelpie* is yours?' He could listen to this man's accent all day.

A low chuckle. 'Aye — mortgage and all!'

Robert's eyes widened. 'You live on it — her?'

'It's not everyone's idea of home, but I like it.'

The soft burr bored into his ears. Robert watched the redhead glance into the water, then peer at a large watch strapped to a hairy wrist. 'Tide's turning.' Huge fingers grabbed Robert's rucksack, lifted the heavy pack one-handed. 'We'd better get going if we want to catch it.' The man walked towards the gangplank.

Robert stared after him, watching the way strong legs covered the ground between him and the small vessel. A sudden image of bristling ginger arse-hair pushed itself into his mind. Then a voice at his side: 'The *Kelpie* –' Angelo pointed. '– can take us across.'

'I know.' Robert grinned. 'I've just been talking to her skipper. Let's go.'

As they sauntered towards the gangplank, Robert saw the well-dressed couple were already on board.

Angelo bounded across the gangplank, which shook slightly under his weight.

Robert paused, suddenly apprehensive. He'd always considered himself a fair sailor, but there was a big difference between cross-Channel ferries and a vessel which sat this low in the water. He risked a glance downwards into the wide channel between the quayside and the edge of the boat, and immediately regretted doing so. Dark, oily-looking water splashed and slapped against the side of the boat, buffeting the *Kelpie* away from the pier. The small craft looked very unseaworthy.

A laugh from the wheelhouse only increased his queasiness.

Robert looked up.

The broad redhead had pulled on a bright orange waterproof. The jacket hung open, showing the more appealing channel of wind-tanned skin. 'On you come – she's safer than she looks!'

Robert clenched his fists: fine first impression to make! He quickly crossed the gangplank before he lost his nerve completely.

On the deck, Angelo was waiting, holding his rucksack for him. 'I'm going to watch our departure – coming?'

Robert shook his head. He grabbed the backpack, gripping its solidity against his chest. Beneath his feet, the deck was vibrating. He glanced at the back of Angelo's head.

His flatmate was now leaning against the rusty railing which ran in a semicircle around the bow.

Robert took a step forward. The deck rose up to meet his foot before he managed to replace it. The effect was unnerving. He gripped the rucksack more tightly.

Angelo had moved to the stern of the *Kelpie*.

Beyond the curly head, Robert watched Mallaig disappear behind a bank of mist. He shivered, glancing up at the wheelhouse, which seemed to be the only covered area on board. Eyes moved to the rusting metal steps which led there.

Faced with a choice of freezing to death on deck, and passing the crossing in the company of the red-haired giant – even if it did involve risking life and limb up those stairs – Robert knew which he preferred.

With a last glance to Angelo, who was now chatting with the well-dressed couple, Robert released his rucksack and headed for the upper deck.

'The sun will come out soon.'

Robert smiled sceptically, warmer under a heavy, hand-knitted jumper which was three sizes too big for him. He leant against the wheelhouse wall, watching the large hands skilfully perform another task.

'It's true. We have a saying on the island: if you don't like our weather, wait around five minutes!'

Robert laughed.

As if on cue, water-droplets on the window at his side sparkled into rainbow prisms. Robert raised one hand, shading his eyes from the dazzling sun which burst through the glass. 'Where did that come from?'

A laugh erupted from somewhere deep inside the red-headed giant. 'The sun always comes to welcome visitors.'

Robert glanced at the *Kelpie*'s skipper.

One vivid green eye winked. 'It's up to you whether it stays or not.'

Robert grinned, enjoying the feel of the man's sweater against his skin. Beneath his feet, the engine chugged contentedly.

The redhead talked on. 'The Gulf-Stream encircles Kelpie Island – some people think it's responsible for our changeable weather. But I'm more inclined to favour the earthquakes.'

Robert stared. 'Earthquakes?'

The weather-beaten face creased into a broader smile. 'We

44

catch the tail of the San Andreas fault — and St Andrew is Scotland's patron saint.' The skipper brushed a straggle of ginger hair from his now-grinning face. 'The tremors usually only register 2.3 or 4, but its enough to bring on the lambs if it happens in spring.'

Robert's scepticism wavered. 'And is this earthquake season?'

Green eyes fixed his. 'Normally, no.'

The soft burr of the man's consonants sang in his ears.

'Although we had three wee ones last week alone.' The red-haired giant registered Robert's apprehension and smiled. 'But don't you be worrying yourself about any earthquakes. Chances are, you'll not even notice them — city folk rarely do.' He returned his attention to the sea.

Robert did likewise, staring through the rapidly drying window.

The craft was still surrounded by banks of mist. But the sky above was a clear blue and sun sparkled on the sea around the *Kelpie*. The dark waters which had seemed so ominous back at Mallaig were now almost inviting. A smile formed on his lips.

Earthquakes?

His smile broadening, Robert's eyes skirted a fog-obscured horizon then moved lower onto the *Kelpie*'s deck.

Angelo was still in conversation with the handsome blond couple from the pier. Robert saw all three were engrossed in close examination of the guide-book. A low burr joined the deeper hum of the engine: 'Want to steer her?' One hand holding the craft steady, the skipper reached under the control-panel, then turned and beckoned.

Robert hesistated: rowing-boats he could just about contemplate. A vessel this size was something else. But he'd seen how easily the tall redhead had guided the craft from Mallaig harbour — and how much could there be to sailing, anyway? It wasn't as if there was much to bump into, way out here. He smiled. 'Yes, please.' Moving forward, he eased himself between the broad, oilskin clad man and the *Kelpie*'s wheel, placing tentative fingers on the wooden arc. Behind, a deep laugh rumbled.

'Both hands.'

Robert gripped the other side of the wheel. Ahead, the *Kelpie* continued to scythe through choppy waves. He felt the tow of the water tug at the wheel as he struggled to steer a straight course. Then there was another body, very close behind his: 'That's it. Hold her steady.'

The vessel's skipper stood directly behind him. Robert could feel the man's breath on his neck. He could hear the crack of oil-skin as it creased and folded around strong thighs. The man's body shadowed his. Robert glanced down and saw two shiny, yellow legs parallel, each side of his bare legs. Automatically, he leant back, and as he did so, his grip on the wheel loosened.

'Steady! Keep your eyes on the sea ahead.'

Robert inhaled sharply. His fingers tightened around the worn wood of the ship's wheel as he edged forward, away from the warm body behind and closer to the waist-high steering device. One wooden strut pressed into his groin, rubbing against the full-blown erection which was now straining up inside his shorts. Robert groaned.

'That's it – firm but light.'

They stood like that for several minutes. Vibrations from the engine travelled up though the wheel, resounding in his hands and trembling from the lower spar to echo against his tingling balls.

Suddenly, warm fingers were on his waist, slipping up under the hem of the thick jersey. Instinctively, Robert released the wheel and reached up towards a face he couldn't see. One of the skipper's large hands gripped his, replacing it firmly on the wooden arc: 'Both hands – we're coming up to a shallow channel.'

A shiver of panic tingled up his spine. Robert tried to concentrate on what he was doing. He stood very still, staring straight ahead through the *Kelpie*'s rain-splattered window. A large hand squeezed his, then moved back to his waist. Inside his shorts, Robert's cock stretched upwards towards the exploring fingers which were now massaging his stomach. He wanted to say something. He wanted to reach around and slip his own shaking fingers down beyond the waistband of the skipper's heavy water-proof trousers and grasp what he could feel thrusting upwards against the seam of his shorts. But he didn't. If he removed even a little finger from the wheel, he could send the craft hurtling onto rocks. Biting his lip against the growing need in his groin, Robert gripped the wheel until his knuckles turned white.

The *Kelpie* chugged contentedly onwards.

'Dangerous waters, these.'

The skipper's hands were circling upwards now, roughly rubbing themselves over his chest. Robert mumbled a response. Huge palms clasped his pectorals.

'Many ships have met their end here, hulls ripped to splinters on rocks like razors.'

Robert gasped and leant forward, his nipples swollen and sore. The skipper's voice was now filled with a warning which was contradicted by each jut of his oil-skinned hips. Back arching, Robert's cock continued to grind against one of the wheel's lower spars. The sound of the engine faded away in the face of his low moans and the slap of cold, inflexible oilskin against the sides of his legs. The skipper tightened his calves around Robert's, squeezing with iron thighs. The hands on his pecs increased the pressure, then slipped up and over Robert's shoulders, gripping firmly and pulling him back.

'A man needs control, at times like these.'

Robert opened his mouth. His heart was pounding – part fear, part arousal. Sweat trickled from his armpits. Inside the heavy jersey, his skin prickled. Beneath his shorts, his balls were heavy with need. Standing there, leaning back against the skipper, knees buckling and groin thrusting upwards against the steering-device, wild thoughts raced through his brain.

What if he never got to see Corrie Cottage?

What if he accidentally nudged the wheel and sent them all to their doom?

What if he caused a major shipping accident?

What if the other passengers walked in on this? The idea sent further ripples of desire shooting into his balls. He imagined Angelo, standing in the doorway, watching as Robert writhed in the arms of the tall red-haired skipper and rubbed himself against the wheel. The vision made a muscle clench deep in his arse.

Then hands released his shoulders and he was shoved forward. Jammed between the wide spars of the wheel, Robert gasped as rough hands clasped his arse-cheeks, then moved lower. His face was pressed against the vessel's control-panel. Strong fingers probed between his bare thighs then inched up under the leg of his shorts, while another hand gripped the back of his neck and held him still.

'Steady – steady!'

Robert was panting now. The skipper's index finger was caressing the underside of his bollocks. Arms trapped at his sides, hands still gripping the wheel, pressure built deep inside him. He gulped for air, trying to hold back but the vibrations from the engine, the way his cock was crushed against the dashboard and the broad hand which was now trying to ram itself up the wide leg of his shorts was too much for anyone to bear. Lips parted in a grimace, Robert's hips bucked one last time. Then wet, sticky warmth flooded his underwear and he felt his body go limp.

His cock was still pumping the last bursts of thick liquid when sanity returned. Robert levered himself off the wheel and turned. 'The rocks! The rocks!'

A ruggedly handsome face smiled at him. 'Don't worry.'

Knees buckling, he felt a strong arm enfold him, then watched through a haze of fading orgasm as the red-haired skipper deftly reached past him and flicked under the dashboard. The engine changed pitch. Robert focused on the twinkling green eyes, feeling spunk start to dry inside his shorts.

The ginger giant winked. 'Automatic pilot – just in case.' A brawny arm tightened around Robert's waist. Then the skipper moved forward and took over the wheel with both hands.

A frown of annoyance formed on Robert's face. He wondered how many other amateur seamen the huge redhead had taken, in this wheelhouse, hands rooted to the steering-mechanism by the threat of imminent disaster. Then he laughed, his softening cock twitching at the idea. 'Better safe than sorry, eh?' He moved back against the wall, thrusting a hand down inside his shorts to reposition his gummy cock as he stared at his seducer's long red ponytail which hung down over the back of the waterproof jacket.

The response was a warm laugh. 'Indeed!' The man turned.

'I'm Malcolm, by the way.' The giant removed one hand from the wheel and held it out.

'Robert.' He gripped solid, leathery-feeling fingers and felt the pressure returned – and an extra squeeze, just before Malcolm pulled his hand away. Robert gazed up into the weather-beaten face.

On the dashboard, a short-wave radio crackled.

Before he could steer the conversation onto topics more intimate, the red-headed giant did some steering of his own. Robert felt the small craft veer sharply left.

'The mist will clear soon.' A calloused finger pointed straight ahead, then grabbed the radio-handset. 'The best view of the coastline is from the deck.'

'Oh – er, thanks.' A little irked at the summary dismissal, Robert left the wheelhouse and made his way down rusting iron steps. But at least he was warmer and drier, the incipient sea-sickness had been left behind in grey Mallaig and he felt altogether more comfortable – despite the news concerning Kelpie Island's geological instability. As he descended the stairs, the drying spunk inside his shorts was the only indication that what had just happened, had happened at all.

On deck, the couple had moved to beneath the wheelhouse's overhang.

Robert glanced at the pair, then followed their gaze to the prow, where Angelo's swarthy outline was bathed in a halo of sunshine. The man looked like he'd stepped out of some medieval, religious icon. Robert walked towards his flatmate and leant arms on the rail.

Angelo sighed. 'Beautiful, isn't it?'

Although there was nothing to see yet, Robert couldn't help but agree. Sunshine danced on the water. Gripping the rail, he stretched his spine and drank in lungfuls of fresh, tangy air. London's smog-filled streets were part of another world – even last night on the train seemed a lifetime away. He lowered his gaze and stared at Angelo's chiselled profile.

One glossy, black curl hung over the smooth brow, brushing a dense, ebony eyebrow. Long, thick eyelashes flickered in the sunlight, and the coffee-coloured skin seemed to glow. Robert stared at the shadow of facial growth which was just visible above a full, upper lip.

Beneath rapidly drying shorts, a sudden twitch let him know some things remained the same. He turned, glanced up to where the weather-beaten redhead was talking into the handset of a two-way radio.

The twitch increased.

Robert turned, discreetly grabbed his crotch and shifted his re-hardening cock to a less noticeable position.

A slight wind was getting up, blowing his hair back from his face. He closed his eyes, enjoying the heat of the sun and the warm breeze on his skin. Sleepiness crept over him. He stifled a yawn.

'Look!'

Angelo's shout made him flinch. Robert opened his eyes and refocused.

The mist was evaporating and Robert now found himself staring at an unforgivingly rocky coastline. Steep cliffs shot up sheer from froth-speckled waves. An awed voice said in his ear, 'See the white horses!'

Robert watched another wave crash against the fractured coastline. 'Where? How can you see animals at this distance?'

Angelo laughed. '*Caballos blancos* – white horses?'

Robert frowned in confusion.

Angelo's amusement grew. 'The waves! When I was a child, my grandmother called big waves – waves like that – white horses.' He pointed as a particularly large breaker smashed against the foot of a towering cliff. 'Don't you call them that?'

Robert grinned. 'I was brought up in Nottingham – didn't know the sea existed until I was in my teens!'

Angelo stared for a moment. 'Oh – it's a joke, yes?'

Robert laughed. 'No – I am from Nottingham originally, but I really have never heard waves referred to as white horses.'

'Ah.' The curly head nodded, then returned its attention to the approaching land.

As the boat curved around a spiky promontory, a more gentle

geography appeared. Robert watched as rolling hills and grassy plains began to dominate the horizon.

Under his feet, engine-vibrations changed pitch.

He glanced back at the wheelhouse, and caught three pairs of eyes.

The blond couple had joined Malcolm. A triple gaze was focused on himself and Angelo. Robert grinned and waved.

A large hand raised in reply.

Then Angelo's exclamations reclaimed his attention.

Side by side, they stood in the bow of the *Kelpie* as her skipper expertly steered the small craft through a narrow inlet into a calm bay.

Five

The pier was smaller, but every bit as busy as Mallaig's.

On the deck of the *Kelpie,* Robert hoisted his rucksack onto his shoulder and turned to Angelo. 'See any taxis?'

The handsome Argentinian was shading his eyes from the sun and scanning the hills beyond the quayside activity. 'No, but it looks ideal riding terrain.'

Robert laughed. 'All I want at the moment is a shower and some kip. I'll –' The sentence remained unfinished as he spotted their blond, well-dressed travelling companions disappearing into an ancient blue Daimler which was parked at the end of the crowded pier. 'Damn!' He glanced at Angelo. 'Wish they'd hung around – did they mention they were getting picked up when you talked to them?'

'I didn't even get their names.' Angelo shook his head. 'But they were very interested in us for some reason.'

Robert sighed. In Angelo, more like. Still, he couldn't blame them. He stared at the sea of heads on the quayside behind. Some almost flaxen, some a darker gold, others shades of red ranging from Malcolm's bright ginger to deep auburn.

Silhouetted against a lighter canvas, the Argentinian's swarthy handsomeness stood out more than ever.

Out of the corner of his eye, he caught a flash of yellow oilskin.

Malcolm was carrying a series of lobster-creels from the back of the vessel, lining them up alongside the gang plank. Robert remembered he was still wearing the fisherman's pullover. Struggling free of the rucksack's straps, he dragged the brightly patterned garment over his head and moved towards the industrious skipper. 'Thanks.' He held out the jumper.

The pale skin glistened with exertion. Malcolm smiled. 'My pleasure.' He took the pullover and wiped under his arms with it.

Robert caught a whiff of fresh man-sweat. So did his nipples. The buds of flesh stretched against the drying fabric of his T-shirt. He shivered. At the moment, he was too tired to think about anything but sleep, but the red-headed giant was filed away for later. 'Where's the best place to get a taxi?'

A huge hand tossed the pullover onto a hank of net. 'Duncan'll see you right.' One finger pointed.

Robert looked over his shoulder.

'Top of the pier – you can't miss him.'

On the quayside, a group of blond and ginger heads were still focused on the deck of the *Kelpie* and Angelo, who now had his nose stuck in the guide-book. Robert scanned the crowd. There was no antagonism in the stares, only an almost reverential curiosity.

Malcolm's laugh was warm and mildly apologetic. 'We don't see many darker skins around here. Your *friend*'s a bit of a novelty.'

Robert noticed the stress on the word. 'Oh, he's not my friend.' He realised how that sounded, and added: 'He's my flatmate,' a little louder than he'd intended.

Angelo looked up, meeting dozens of stares.

Malcolm chuckled. 'I'd get that taxi, if I was you, before they start asking if they can touch him!'

Robert half-smiled. But there was something in the way the locals were transfixed by Angelo that reminded him of the reaction of the cook, back on the train. A rescue was definitely in order: Angelo was looking more uncomfortable by the minute. 'Maybe we'll bump into each other later.' He picked up the rucksack.

Blue eyes met green twinkles. 'Aye, I'm sure we will.' Malcolm stuck thumbs in the belt loops of oilskin trousers.

Robert grinned, turned and gently steered a confused Angelo across the gangplank and down onto the quay.

Heads turned and pairs of green and blue eyes bored into their backs as they made their way up the pier.

The taxi driver was every bit as eccentric as his vehicle, which had once been a Morris Minor but now looked as though radical surgery had been carried out too late. 'Corrie Cottage?' Gears ground alarmingly.

In the back seat, Robert and Angelo exchanged worried glances.

'Why would you be wanting to go there?' The engine screamed. The car lurched forward, then stalled.

'We're staying there.'

'Is that a fact?' The driver shook the gear-stick, swore and wrenched the choke fully out. The engine screamed again.

'Yes. My great-uncle left it to me –' Robert clutched at the back of the passenger seat as Duncan McBeth of Duncan's Automobiles slammed his foot to the floor. The car took off like a Formula One racer.

'Is that a fact?'

'Yes.' Robert found himself having to shout over a deafening rattle which appeared to come from somewhere beneath their feet. 'Did you know him?'

'Who?' Duncan rolled down the window and waved at a passing cyclist.

Robert leant forward. 'My great-uncle – Bethran McLeod.' His throat was beginning to hurt.

'You southerners have affy soft voices – what was that?'

'Bethran Mc–'

The driver hit the brake.

Robert was thrown back in his seat. 'McLeod!'

'Ah. Would you be the Drumcree McLeods, or the Thurso branch of the family?' Duncan took another bend on two wheels and glanced around, grinning.

Outside, scenery galloped past. Robert kept his eyes on the road ahead: someone had to. 'The – Nottingham McLeods?' He sighed with relief as Duncan returned his attention to the windscreen.

'Hmmm – don't know that branch of the family.' The driver scratched his head, then removed his other hand from the wheel to wind up the window. 'Was your maternal grandmother named Morag, by any chance?'

'I've no idea.' Robert gave up. He glanced at Angelo.

The large dark eyes were closed, the curly head lolling back as his flatmate snored gently.

'Ah.' The car slowed to allow a flock of sheep across the road. 'Well, that's a shame.' The engine idled. Duncan turned, smiled at them. 'Do you mind if I tune in to the Fish Market report?' One hand back on the wheel, the other waved towards a dashboard radio which had seen better days.

Relief flooded Robert's body. 'By all means.' Sheep continued to file past the stationary vehicle. Then a different, equally foreign-sounding accent filled the car, recounting what seemed to be haddock prices.

Robert screened out the sound and took the opportunity to admire the view. Through the window to his right, sunlight danced on tiny waves. To his left, a row of small but immaculate turf-roofed cottages sat amidst lush greenery. He smiled, offered a silent prayer to great-uncle Bethran, whoever he had been.

The air which wafted in through the open window was clean and fresh-smelling, the scenery spectacular. His mind's eye pictured Corrie Cottage: white-washed, rustic but well-equipped, maybe a little garden, a bit of ivy creeping up its two-hundred-year-old walls.

A sigh escaped his lips.

Idyllic.

Grinding gears pulled him back to the present as the taxi lurched forward. 'Not far now!' Duncan yelled over the fishing report. 'What did you say your name was, lad?'

Robert leant forward indulgently, and began the saga once more.

A picturesque cottage on a remote island.

The promise of delights to come, in the form of muscular, sweaty Malcolm.

Nothing – not even eccentric Duncan and his ramshackle vehicle – could take that away from him.

Fifteen minutes later, they stood on a remote, rocky promontory.

Something just had.

While Angelo wiped sleep from his eyes, Robert threw his rucksack onto a patch of scrub-grass and mentally cursed Great-uncle Bethran. 'Look at it!'

Angelo walked slowly forward. 'How many years has it been standing?'

Robert frowned. 'You call that standing?' He stared at a squat, unpainted building with a distinctly saggy roof. Two windows were boarded up. A third winked scornfully at them through cracked and grime-encrusted glass. Robert pulled the bunch of labelled keys from the pocket of his shorts, focusing on the door which swung drunkenly on rusting hinges.

'It looks worse than it is.' Angelo was now walking around the building. 'Structurally, it is probably sound.' He sank to a crouch, slapped a section of brick. 'No sign of dampness or dry rot.'

Robert picked up his rucksack and joined his flatmate. Close up, Corrie Cottage was more dilapidated than ever. 'But it's . . .' The place defied description. He looked up at a huge dip in the middle of the roof, then behind to the fierce, inhospitable peaks which stretched skywards. He couldn't help but feel disappointed.

Angelo stood up, smiling the lopsided smile. 'It is fixable, believe me.' He stepped back, folded broad arms across his broader chest. 'I'm sure we passed an ironmonger's shop in the village. We can –' he searched for the word '– renovate it together.'

'We can?'

'Of course!' Angelo dragged the rucksack from his shoulders and began to rummage through its contents. Minutes later, he was strapping a leather work-belt around his waist, loading two sizes of hammer, a chisel and other implements Robert didn't recognise into worn loops. 'I am a trained joiner, you know. It will make a change to be the boss.'

Robert winced at his flatmate's choice of words: Angelo had been the boss – as far as the twitching member inside his shorts was concerned – for the last twenty-four hours. He dragged his eyes from the strong, muscular chest, his skin flushed with shame.

He had brought Angelo six hundred miles on the promise of a holiday, and here he was lusting after the man who was volunteering to spend that holiday working. 'You don't mind?'

Angelo grinned, brown eyes filled with pleasure. 'Of course not. It will –'

Robert's shaft was uncurling down the left leg of his shorts. 'Be fun?' An opportunity to work, half-naked, beside someone for whom I have long hidden my desire?

'– look excellent on my CV! Especially if you could write a testimonial, saying how pleased you are with my work.' Bottomless eyes smiled at him. 'Would you do that?'

More disappointment coursed through his veins. Why did he torture himself like this? Then Robert remembered tall, red-haired Malcolm, and gave himself a shake: Angelo might be out of bounds, but the *Kelpie*'s skipper held out more definite promise. He laughed and glanced at the shambles of a cottage. 'If we can make this place habitable in two weeks, I'll write you the most glowing testimonial anyone ever had. Deal?' He stuck out a hand.

Angelo spat onto his palm, then gripped the extended fingers. 'Deal!'

Robert shivered as warm saliva coated his hand and strong fingers clenched his. The ache in his groin increased.

Angelo pulled away. 'You check inside while I look over there.' He pointed to a listing pair of outbuildings. 'We need to patch up that broken window before we do anything else.'

Robert winced. The ache which was now fully stretched down the left leg of his shorts needed attention before he could do anything else. 'OK.' He watched Angelo stride away, then walked round to the far side of the cottage. His fingers fumbled with his zip. As he pulled out his cock, he glanced around at the deserted terrain: if nothing else, he had all the privacy he could want.

The rod of flesh pulsed in his grip. Robert closed his eyes, leaning back. Uneven stone dug into his spine. A cool breeze caressed the skin on his stomach and made his balls tighten. He groaned, rubbing Angelo's slowly drying spit along his swollen shaft.

The teeth of the zip bit into delicate ball-skin. Robert turned, one arm braced against the wall of the cottage while the other slid up to the purple crown of his cock. Head lowered, he inhaled the salty smell of his groin mixed with the fresher odour of the sea.

Angelo's firm buttocks danced on his eyelids, shadowed by Malcolm's red-tufted chest. An image of the two men together thrust itself into his mind.

Robert gasped, heart thumping. Fist moved faster.

He pictured himself sandwiched between two very different bodies, face buried in his flatmate's bristling groin while the huge fisherman's thick cock pounded into his arsehole.

'And what might you be up to, laddie?'

The fantasy exploded. Robert gasped, shoving his shaft back inside his shirts and zipping up so fast he ripped a couple of pubic hairs free. He spun round and took two steps forward still trying to zip up.

From under a policeman's hat, a bearded, suspicious face regarded him.

'Er, nothing.' His voice was hoarse. Fingers frozen on the button of his jeans, Robert cleared arousal from his throat. 'I was –' Words failed him.

Suspicion grew in narrowed eyes. 'You were –?'

Robert swallowed again, taking in more of the officer.

Mid-thirties and stockily built, the policeman's chest and stomach were barely restrained by the buttons of his uniform jacket. Solid-looking legs which ended in highly polished leather boots were planted two feet apart. Black-gloved hands held what appeared to be a truncheon.

Sweat drenched his body. Against his zip, a length of throbbing flesh pulsed more ferociously than ever. Robert's mouth opened, then closed again: what little blood was left in his head had just fled southwards.

'I'll tell ye what ye were doing, laddie.' The officer began to circle him.

A flush of heat reddened Robert's face. Uniforms always had this effect on him. Robert stared down at his feet, desperate to hide the effect the man was having on him. His eyes watched the boots.

'Look at me when I'm talking to you!'

Something in the tone demanded obedience. Robert's head shot up.

The square, full-bearded face was inches from his. And glowering.

'You were about to relieve yourself against another man's property!'

Robert took a step back. 'No, I –'

'Don't try to deny it.' The truncheon slapped against a leather-covered palm. 'I know your type!'

Robert retreated further, until roughly hewn stone scraped against his back and even then he didn't stop. 'No, really!' Fingers scrabbled against the wall of the cottage. Words hit his face like blows.

'You day-trippers make me sick!'

Robert cringed. Sweat coursed from his pits, cooling on his shivering skin.

'Over from the mainland, with your city ways – think ye can do what you like, don't you?'

Scarlet-faced, he struggled to avoid accusing eyes. Robert focused down, up, sideways – anywhere rather than that bearded, intimidating face. He had lost the power of speech completely. Whatever the policeman lacked in stature, he certainly made up for in sheer commanding presence.

Something cold and hard pushed itself beneath his chin, raising his head. 'Know what I should do?'

Robert stared down the length of the truncheon into icy blue irises. He tried to shake his head.

Eyes bored into his. 'I should let you urinate.'

Robert froze. From the hardness of his cock, pissing was the last thing his body could handle.

'Then I should make ye clean it up, laddie.'

Chips of ice held him in a vice-like grip.

'I should make ye get down on yer knees and lick yer pish from this man's property!'

Robert's hard-on raged more strongly than ever. He couldn't speak. His stomach churned. It was all he could do to stop himself falling prostrate to the ground and abasing himself beneath the soles of the officer's highly polished boots.

'That's the only treatment mainland types like you understand.'

The tip of the truncheon was forcing his chin higher. Robert felt his eyes start to water. Other liquid was leaking from a slit three feet lower, adhering the head of his cock to the already damp fabric of his shorts.

'Look at me, laddie!'

Robert tried to focus.

Icy pupils bored into his. 'What's wrong with your eyes?'

'Nothing.' Robert blinked back tears. The man was very close. He could smell him. The officer continued to stare into his face. Robert could almost count the man's eyebrow hairs.

'Yer pupils are awful big, laddie – are you using illegal substances?'

'No!' The syllable was more squeak than word. The contemptuous expression on the policeman's face made his heart race and his cock throb.

'You mainlanders are all liars.'

The sneering voice made his guts turn over.

'Hands against the wall!'

Before he could protest further, Robert found himself flipped around and his palms met the surface of the cottage wall. Arms stretched above his head, his heart pounded in his ears as he stared at bare brick. Then a knee was shoved between his thighs, spreading them wider. Robert's balls tightened, and his cock raged harder than ever as rough hands began to pat him down. The disgust-filled voice accompanied the body-search. 'Coming over here, with yer city ways and yer drugs –' The officer's hands moved none-too-gently down Robert's arms and onto his chest, pausing to check his pockets. Skilled fingers worked their way along the seams of his jacket and shirt, then continued down over his arse-cheeks and onto his thighs. 'You think you can get away with anything, don't you?'

The hands paused at the tops of his socks, before starting back up the inside of his legs. Denial formed in his brain, but his vocal-chords refused to function. Eyes wide with fear, Robert began to tremble as the body search continued. The policeman's practised hands were inches away from discovering the full-blown erection which pushed at the zip of Robert's shorts. He had to stop him, had to say something. 'Look, officer –' His voice was a hoarse, lust-filled rasp. '– I –'

A grip like iron clutched his balls, cutting off the end of the sentence.

Robert almost screamed.

The hand tightened. 'Too clever to be carrying them about your person, eh?'

Robert's fingers scrabbled on rough stone. Then his bruising balls were released and a hand grabbed his wrist, twisting it up between his shoulder-blades and turning him round. The four-teen-inch length of hard, black rubber was back beneath his chin: 'Open yer mouth!'

With the truncheon pressing into his Adam's apple, Robert could barely lower his jaw a millimetre, let alone open it. Abruptly, the length of rubber was removed and something hard hit the back of his thighs. Robert's legs gave way. His knees impacted with the stony ground. Before he could as much as gasp, a hand grabbed his chin and leather-covered fingers were forcing their way between his lips. A strangled cry escaped from deep in his lungs. He tried to twist away.

The grip on his jaw tightened painfully. 'Hold still!'

Robert could only obey. Fists clenched, he squeezed his eyes shut. His head was thrown back as the invading digits searched roughly along his teeth, then flicked under his tongue. His saliva-glands went into overdrive. Robert tried to swallow. Couldn't. His mouth was full of the man. Robert felt himself start to choke. His cock battered at the zip of his shorts, desperate for release, while somewhere lower another hole longed to be filled the way the policeman was filling his mouth.

Abruptly, the invading force retreated. The policeman wiped his gloved fingers on Robert's hair. 'On yer feet!' The voice was sour with disappointment.

Robert was amazed at the speed of his journey upright. Relief flooded his body, only to be replaced by a heavier dread at the stocky man's next words. The truncheon tapped the buckle of Robert's belt. 'One hiding-place left, laddie.'

The meaning was clear. Adrenalin raced through Robert's veins, chasing away relief, fear and any thought of argument or escape, leaving only a dog-like compliance. His hands shook as he fumbled with belt and button. In his hurry, the zip jammed half-way down. Robert felt his hot, fleshy rod pulse against his fingers and a new wave of panic swept over his body as the policeman impatiently slapped his truncheon against his palm.

'Come on! Get them off!'

Robert struggled with the teeth of the zip, then gave up and wrenched his shorts down. The waistband stuck somewhere around the top of his thighs. He nearly fell, but a strong hand grabbed the back of his neck and held him steady while another tugged at the garment. Somewhere in the distance, over the sound of his hammering heart, Robert heard the sound of fabric ripping. He knew his hard cock was now exposed for anyone to see. But all he could think about was the cool air which erected the hair on his arse, and the feel of those leather-covered fingers on the back of his neck pushing his head down.

Before he knew what he was doing, Robert gripped his knees and spread his legs as much as the half-off shorts would allow.

Hands grabbed the cheeks of his arse, forcing them apart.

Robert inhaled sharply. Face scarlet, he blinked back tears as one, then two rough fingers forced themselves into his hole. Deprived of blood, his brain had stopped working. He stood there, bent over, naked from the waist down and allowed the policeman access to his body.

The man poked roughly, pausing occasionally to mutter his annoyance.

Robert winced with shame at how easily his sphincter opened to admit the probing digits. More tears welled up behind his eyes.

He let them fall, staring through blurred vision at his own erection which bobbed less than six inches from his drooling mouth. The policeman seemed to be ignoring the engorged member – a fact which made Robert more aroused than ever. Then just when he thought the worse had happened, a new humiliation rose up to torment him.

'Hold yourself open, laddie!'

Unable to refuse, Robert released his knees and reached round. He wrenched the cheeks of his arse more widely apart, and felt his hole gaping for all the world to see. Not for long. Seconds later, something smooth and round and hard was slipping into his arse. The realisation was too much for Robert's straining cock to bear. As the first three inches of the policeman's truncheon forced its way inside him, and the firm hand gripped the back of his neck, Robert's hips jutted forward and he felt the wet warmth of his own lust splatter his scarlet, tear-stained face.

The force of the orgasm made his knees turn to water. He slumped forward, falling against the wall of the cottage while the muscles in his arse convulsed and flexed around the length of the black rubber truncheon. His eyelids shot open and he found himself staring at the well-polished toes of the officer's boots. Abruptly, the hard object inside him was wrenched out, and Robert gasped through the fading ripples of climax as the truncheon impacted across the back of his naked thighs.

'Get up, laddie!'

Almost tripping over the shorts, which hung in folds around his ankles, Robert covered himself. He crammed his softening prick back behind his zip and staggered to his knees. Turning, he forced himself to look up at his tormentor.

The officer wiped the truncheon with a handful of scrub-grass then stuck it back beneath Robert's chin. 'Now I'm going to take you back down to the pier, put you on the first boat back to the mainland and –'

'What's going on here?'

Robert flinched. Deliverance! The truncheon remained beneath his chin as the stone-faced policeman turned to Angelo.

'And who might you –?' The sentence hung unfinished in the air. But the truncheon was removed.

Robert slumped down. His relief was tinged with a disappointment he didn't want to think about.

Above him, his flatmate stuck out a hand. 'Angelo Caballo.'

The rich voice brought Robert to his senses. He scrambled to his feet. 'And I'm Robert McLeod.' He fumbled in the inside pocket of his jacket, removing the solicitor's letter. 'This is my property – I own it. Corrie Cottage was left to me by my great-uncle – Bethran McLeod?' He held out the correspondence.

The gesture was ignored.

Robert stared from the darkly handsome face to the pale bearded one.

The officer regarded Angelo, then stuck the truncheon back in his belt, removed one glove and seized the outstretched hand. 'Hamish Campbell, Mr Caballo.' He touched the brim of his hat respectfully. 'PC Campbell. Welcome to Kelpie Island.'

Robert shoved the letter into a prominent position and met Angelo's eyes.

The officer talked on. 'If you'd let us know you were coming, I would have arranged for you to be met at the pier.'

Robert smiled magnanimously. 'Oh, there was no need – we found a taxi and . . .' He paused.

The half-apology wasn't directed at him: Hamish Campbell was scrutinising Angelo with that same mixture of awe and fear that he'd sensed on the quayside. Robert sighed. What was it with the natives?

Eventually, his presence did register. The policeman turned, removed his hat and smiled. The expression transformed the stern face into a visage brimming with near-benevolence. 'Sorry about the mix-up, Mr –?'

'McLeod.' Robert supplied his name for the fourth time.

'We had a report of strangers hanging about up here. Can't be too careful, you know. Not all incomers are as welcome as Mr Caballo and yourself.' He scratched his beard with a gloved hand, then replaced his hat on his head. 'No hard feelings?'

Robert remembered the sensations he'd experienced at the

mercy of those gloved hands and that truncheon. He smiled and lied.

'Good!' Hamish Campbell positively radiated joy. 'Now, I hope you two gentlemen will be our guests at the ceilidh this evening – by way of a more formal welcome to our little island.'

'Ceilidh?' Angelo looked blank.

Robert smiled. 'A dance, right?' He couldn't help but glance at PC Campbell for confirmation: those feelings just wouldn't go away.

'More of a general get-together, Mr McLeod.' The officer suddenly seemed anxious to leave. 'Seven thirty, in the village hall. You can't miss it. I'll leave you to get settled in.'

Robert watched as the man touched the brim of his hat again, and with one last lingering glance at Angelo turned and marched back to a bicycle which was propped against a boulder.

'Everyone's so friendly.'

'Yes, they are.' At his flatmate's side, Robert continued to stare uncertainly into the wake of the uniformed figure on the bicycle. He frowned, wondering if Hamish Campbell had been teasing him all along: the man's demeanour had changed so abruptly when Angelo had appeared, it was hard to believe there had ever been a threatening, abusive side to the stocky figure who was now waving at them from the seat of his bicycle.

They both returned the wave.

A warm breeze brushed his face as he turned back to Angelo. Sticky sweat was adhering the back of his T-shirt to his shoulders. Robert wiped his face.

Angelo smiled. 'Fancy a swim?'

Robert blinked, then shaded his eyes and gazed down the winding, dirt road to where tiny waves danced, a quarter of a mile below. He yawned. 'Too far.'

Angelo beamed. 'Corrie Cottage has its own ... swimming-pool.'

Robert's eyes narrowed sceptically. 'You're having me on!'

Angelo cocked his head. 'I'm having you on what? I do not understand.'

Robert flinched at the longed-for implication. He sighed and stifled another yawn.

Angelo's full lips widened in parallel.

They both laughed.

'Must be the fresh air.' Robert grabbed his rucksack. Whatever it was, Angelo's swimming-pool could wait. 'I need a couple of hours' kip before I can take in anything else.' He walked purposefully round to the front of the building.

Angelo followed.

Robert paused. For some reason, the cottage didn't look quite so bad now. He took a step back and raised his eyes. The sun was almost overhead, bathing the rocky landscape in a golden glow and glinting off glossy flecks in the boulders. Even the rough masonry of the dilapidated structure was shining.

In the distance, the squawks of the gulls were almost soothing.

Robert felt surprisingly calm, as if they had suddenly been transported into another world. He edged open the door. 'Come on.'

Six

———

The cottage was dark, but dry-smelling. Robert brushed a large spider's web away from his face and peered into the gloom.

'Told you any work would be superficial – the roof is still watertight.'

A sudden beam of illumination above his head told Robert a torch was also part of his flatmate's armoury of joiner's tools.

Angelo leading the way, the soles of their walking boots echoed on bare stone as they investigated the single, large room.

The place was untidy, but the furniture was solid and mainly undamaged. In the centre of the back wall, an ancient fireplace and cooking-range seemed to be in working order. Rummaging in a box, Angelo found an ample supply of candles. Soon the room was bathed in a welcoming, if slightly flickering light.

The smell of wax mixed with a peaty, earthier odour. Robert stared at the single bed which was tucked away in the far corner.

'You take it.'

He laughed as both their voices made the offer.

Angelo was unfastening boots. 'No, it's your cottage –'

Robert smiled. 'And you're my guest.' He scanned, eyes pausing on an overstuffed armchair.

'We could share.' The offer was automatic.

'No, I insist you have the bed!' Robert sighed: he wasn't going through another night like last night. It would take every ounce of willpower he possessed to stop himself permanently lusting after the handsome Argentinian, and he had no desire to spoil a friendship with a clumsy pass which would inevitably result in rejection. 'I want to explore around here a bit more, anyway – don't really feel tired.' He turned away to hide a yawn.

'OK.'

Despite his resolve, Robert tingled with longing. He walked over to a pile of dust-covered trunks which sat against the wall beside the fireplace and heaved the top one over the stone floor.

In flickering candlelight, Angelo's silhouette stripped against fading whitewash.

Robert fiddled with the lock. After a couple of tugs, the battered chest opened with a creak. He sat back on his heels.

On the wall, Angelo's shadow wriggled out of briefs and stretched.

One hand in the trunk, Robert's head remained tilted, eyes lingering on the broad outline of well-muscled arms and arched spine. Licking dry lips, his gaze moved lower, brushing the slight curve of the hard buttocks, then skirted sideways to hover between strong, parted thighs.

'Good night.'

Robert started, then buried his burning face in the chest. 'Good morning, you mean.'

Angelo's low, husky laugh filled the cottage.

Ears straining as the sound was obliterated by the creaks and groans of ancient springs which signalled his flatmate's progression on to the bed, Robert hauled a handful of magazines and newspapers from the trunk and determinedly immersed himself in them.

Yellow light illuminated yellower paper.

Robert stared at the date: Saturday 14 August 1896. *The Times.* Corrie Cottage certainly hadn't been inhabited in a while! He placed the newspaper on the floor and flicked through another: 23 March 1911.

Slowly, the ancient periodicals began to absorb him. He read about the death of a certain playwright, Oscar Wilde, in Paris. He read how Emmaline Pankhurst's protest outside 10 Downing Street resulted in the arrest of herself and five other women. He read about unrest in the Balkans, and thought how little had changed in nearly a century.

As the pile of literature increased on the floor beside him, his eyelids grew heavy. Then fingers brushed a smaller publication, which had been slipped between the pages of the *Country Gentleman*. No title, but the volume was beautifully bound in soft, brown leather.

Robert rubbed his eyes, opening the pamphlet's covers. As he skimmed through, then slowed to a more intense scrutiny of the drawings and photographs which packed the slim volume, his body told him what his brain was still processing.

He'd heard about Edwardian erotica, of course – everyone had. Robert stared at the hand-coloured images which decorated the obviously self-published pages.

Well-dressed, aristocratic gentlemen watched the watery antics of a group of swarthy, half-naked country lads as they washed each other by the side of a stream.

He stared at individual studies of the male nude. Tall men, short men, men on their own.

Robert turned the page.

And men together. He paused, drinking in the more explicitly sexual scene before him.

A handsome, genteel-looking man, on his knees, sucking the generous prick of a sturdy, scowling rustic type.

Robert's hand trembled. The attention to detail was startling in its intensity. The artist had evidently shared a great affinity with both the subjects and objects of his art. He turned a page and found himself staring at a strangely familiar scene.

In the background, mountains very similar to those which towered over Corrie Cottage framed a coloured sketch. The same, aristocratic-looking blond man, now collared and tethered to a stake, writhed with obvious pleasure while another rough bucolic rammed a member of unbelievable proportions between eager arse-cheeks.

Had the artist occupied Corrie Cottage? Had some ancestor of his sat on this very floor and fantasised about some ideal lover, the way he himself had only minutes before? Robert stared at the exquisitely drawn cock, then peered more closely: there was something about the depiction of the tethered man's expression which seemed almost too accurate to be the work of an unknown artist. Perhaps there had been some famous McLeod who had amused himself, on holiday, while exhibiting at the Royal Academy in his professional life.

Still holding the volume, he moved away from the trunk towards a candle. He tilted the illustration to the brighter light, searching for a signature. Then his heart was hammering.

A photograph! Hand-coloured, and outlined in ink to disguise the fact, but definitely an early photographic reproduction!

The implications had his own cock rearing like an untamed beast. Robert dropped the small book and staggered to his rucksack. Hands tore at the fastenings. He rifled through its contents for what seemed like hours before fingers contacted with the object of the search.

One hand pressing Angelo's pungent briefs to his face, the other ripped at the button of his shorts.

Seconds later, nose and mouth were buried in stiff fabric while his fist jerked up and down on his throbbing cock. Eyes closed, Robert was almost too aroused to think about anything as his hand moved faster. The delicate skin on his cock began to burn, only increasing his pleasure. He handled himself roughly, tugging and squeezing with abandon as he visualised his unknown ancestor photographing the scene from life. His body responded to the treatment, balls tightening and tingling towards climax. The room was filled with the dry, agonisingly enjoyable drag of fist on flesh and the sound of laboured breathing.

Robert seized a section of Angelo's briefs between his teeth and sucked the soiled fabric into his mouth. He chewed on his flatmate's underwear, which absorbed his groans as it had absorbed Angelo's piss splatters the previous evening.

He was wanking furiously now. Robert jammed wet fabric into

his mouth, fingers of his free hand plunging lower to pinch the skin of his heavy balls.

Sheer intensity of sensation pushed him over the edge. Mind reeling with Malcolm, Billy-Bob and almost every other man he'd encountered in the past twenty-four hours – but mainly Angelo – Robert's thighs trembled and his legs gave way. Dropping to his knees, he shot into his fist, almost hyperventilating with the force of the release. His head spun. Eyelids sprang open. Robert spat fabric from his mouth and gasped into the candlelight. His shaking fingers filled with warm stickiness as his cock jerked and spasmed.

Falling forward onto the bare floor, his hot face met cold stone. He groped for the saliva-soaked fabric which became wetter still as he wiped the spunk from his slowly relaxing body.

Ten minutes later, the spasms had subsided. Crawling to the bed, he eased a blanket from over the gently snoring Angelo and draped it around himself.

Ten minutes after that, he was asleep.

The scent of coffee woke him. Robert opened his eyes, propped himself up on one elbow and peered at the cooking range.

A large kettle was simmering.

Angelo turned, holding two steaming mugs. 'Sleep well?'

Robert nodded. Nothing like a satisfying wank to send him into deep, soundless slumber. He remembered the small, beautifully bound book. 'I had some interesting bedtime reading.'

Angelo raised an eyebrow.

Robert stretched out an arm and swept the slim volume towards him. 'Take a look at this!' His eyes registered the mugs in his flatmate's hand. 'Have you been to the village?'

The curly head shook. 'Found a box with coffee, milk, bread and lots of other things on the doorstep.' Angelo knelt, held out a mug.

Robert took it. 'That was nice of someone.' He sipped the hot liquid gratefully.

'Yes, wasn't it.' Angelo sat on the floor beside him. He picked up the book casually and opened it at random. 'So what sent you into such a deep –?' His mouth froze.

Robert watched the dark eyes widen. The mug in his flatmate's fist trembled slightly. An uncharacteristic blush spread over the handsome features.

Robert smiled. 'It's really old, don't you think? I was trying to work out what period it's from.'

His flatmate closed the volume. 'I cannot tell.' An expression of discomfort flickered once over the mocha-coloured skin, then disappeared as Angelo grinned. 'But I am amazed you could sleep at all, after looking at this!'

Robert stared at the newly shaven face. The smell of fresh soap and toothpaste wafted into his nostrils. It suddenly occurred to him there was no sign of any plumbing in the cottage. 'You've found water!'

Angelo laughed. 'In abundance. There's a well round the back. Everything else is in an outbuilding.'

Robert felt sticky. The grime of a day's travelling plus the excesses of the past twelve hours clung to his body. Angelo's increasingly soiled underpants were at present stuffed inside his unzipped shorts. 'Shower?' He rubbed a hand over his stubbly chin.

'Of sorts – it's a little temperamental, but it works.'

Robert zipped up, threw back the blanket and jumped to his feet. 'Lead me to it!' He grabbed his shaving stuff and a towel.

'Aren't you going to finish your coffee?'

Robert seized and drained the mug. The liquid burnt the back of his throat. He coughed. 'Happy?'

Angelo laughed, walked to the door, which was still half open.

Outside, the sun had sunk lower in the sky and the tide had ebbed, exposing a narrow band of sand at the foot of the steep cliffs below. Robert rubbed sleep from his eyes. 'What time is it?'

Angelo glanced at a broad, hairy wrist. 'Nearly seven.'

Robert inhaled deeply, filling his lungs with sweet, fragrant air. Oxygen rushed to his brain. Despite the approaching evening, everything seemed clearer, sharper-edged. The colours were brighter, smells more pungent and the distant call of a curlew sharp and tuneful.

They stood there in silence for a while.

Beside him, Angelo sighed. 'There's something, isn't there?'

Robert could only nod.

Angelo talked on. 'It's not the mountains or the beach or the sea or the air – or at least, not just the scenery and the air. There's something else, something –'

A warm breeze caught the words and wafted them out towards the sparkling horizon.

Robert smiled dreamily. It was almost as if Kelpie Island didn't want Angelo to finish the sentence – as if trying to fathom the island's charms would somehow break the spell. He stared happily down at the beach.

'Look at the white horses.' Angelo's voice rumbled against his arm.

Robert laughed. 'The sea's like a millpond! There's not a wave in –'

'No, I mean real horses. Look!' Angelo took a step towards the edge of the sheer drop.

'Where?' Robert peered.

'There!' Angelo was running along the cliff top now, pointing.

Robert jogged, then had to sprint to keep up. 'Where? I can't see anything.'

When he caught up with Angelo, his flatmate had stopped and was scanning the deserted shore. He stuck his hands in the pockets of his shorts.

'They've gone.' Angelo turned, large dark eyes almost mournful. 'There were four or five of them – they were beautiful: white and galloping and –'

'Probably escaped from the local riding school!' Robert gripped his knees, trying to get his breath back. 'Hey, you ride, don't you?'

Angelo nodded. 'It has been a while, but yes – I used to ride a lot, back home.'

Robert looked around, thinking how different the flat, pampas-terrain of the Argentinian highlands must be to this mountainous island. 'Would you teach me – if we can find horses to hire, I mean? Then we could explore on horseback.' He grinned, straightening up and snapping Angelo's hairy thighs with his towel. 'When I give you time off from fixing my cottage, that is!'

The handsome face brightened. 'I would be honoured.' Angelo smiled. 'You'll learn to stay on a horse if I have to tie you there myself!'

The thought made his stomach churn. Robert changed the subject. 'Well, for now you can come and help me work this temperamental shower!' He snapped the towel again.

Angelo aimed a mock-punch at the side of Robert's head.

Robert ducked away, firing little jabs at the rippling abdomen. Then he ran.

Angelo laughed, chased him.

As they jogged back to the outhouses, the magical moment was indeed broken. But it didn't seem to matter any more.

Half an hour later, showered and shaved, Robert was attempting to lock the door of the cottage.

Angelo waited patiently in the background. He was dressed in shorts and a white linen shirt, which showed off his coffee-coloured skin tone to full advantage.

Robert frowned and fumbled. None of the keys seemed to function and the wood around the frame was too swollen and warped to allow the door to even close properly.

'Leave it.'

'But our stuff's in there.' He thrust the key more firmly into the rusting lock and heaved the door with his shoulder.

'The place was wide open when we arrived, and the amount of dust on everything showed no one had been inside for decades.'

Robert paused. 'Think we can risk it?' He was remembering the three double-locks and burglar alarm which held sway over the London flat. Leaving a property with the door not even closed, let alone locked, was something he wasn't used to.

'The fisherman wouldn't take money for the crossing over here; the taxi-driver refused to let us pay for the journey; the policeman invited us to a dance and someone left a box of groceries on the doorstep.' Angelo grinned. 'I think we can trust them with a couple of towels and a few T-shirts!'

Robert smiled. Angelo was right. He was about to shove the keys back in his pocket, when he thought the better of it. Wrenching the door ajar, he tossed the key-ring inside. 'When in Rome, I suppose!'

Angelo looked puzzled. 'What has Rome got to do with –?'

Robert laughed. 'I'll explain while we walk.'

There was only one road: the route the taxi had taken, hours earlier.

They walked side by side. Now adequately versed in another British linguistic peculiarity, Angelo was eager to know about a singularly Scottish custom. 'Cay-lee. Tell me more about cay-lees.'

'A ceilidh's a sort of dance, as far as I'm aware.'

The road curved inland, away from the coast and up a steep incline which had been barely noticeable, despite Duncan the taxi-driver's ancient vehicle. As they walked, Robert was aware of the sound of their voices in the still, evening air.

Angelo laughed. 'I'm not really much of a dancer.'

'Me neither.' Robert could vaguely recall the reception after the wedding of a Scottish friend, and the wild, abandoned spree which almost defied the definition. 'Not this sort of dancing, at least.'

A grumbling sound assaulted his ears. Robert glanced at Angelo, who frowned.

'Will there be anything to eat, do you think?'

Robert felt his own stomach cramp in response. He'd been so caught up in everything else it had slipped his mind that they'd not eaten since breakfast. 'Not sure.' His abiding memory of Scottish ceilidhs was the large quantity of alcohol regularly consumed. 'Tell you what: we'll pop in, to be polite, then go find a restaurant or something. How does that sound?'

Angelo rubbed his stomach. 'That sounds very Roman!'

Robert laughed. 'OK, an Italian restaurant it is.'

They quickened their pace. Although the sun was still a few

hours from setting, the thick trees through which they were now walking did a good job of cutting out what little light there was. Robert noticed no lamp-posts along the darkening, mountain road: when night fell, the wood would hide the road from even the brightest of moons.

'It's so quiet.'

Robert had to agree. No birds sang, the wind had dropped and even the trees no longer rustled. The only noise was their voices and the tramp of the boots on loose gravel.

They walked on, looking around themselves at the ferns and flowering brambles which choked the roadside. Every now and then, thick forest gave way to fields, in which a few sheep and cattle contentedly grazed.

'Listen.' Angelo stopped abruptly in the middle of the road.

Robert stared at him. 'More horses?' He smiled teasingly.

'No, music. Listen.' Angelo cocked his head.

Robert did likewise. Then he heard it.

A distant skirl of pipes drifted over tree tops towards them. The music had a plaintive quality, conjuring up centuries of bloody history, battles fought and feuds settled. Angelo's rich voice joined the lilting sound. 'It sounds so old, so different.'

Robert smiled. Scotland was a different country, and Kelpie Island was different still, a green jewel cast into a blue sea. He gave himself a shake. 'They probably lay it on for the tourists.'

Angelo looked disappointed. 'You think so?'

Robert stared into the trees, listening to the music. Part of him wanted to believe what he'd just said. Another part niggled, wanting to buy into the fantasy. He compromised, winking. 'Perhaps not: perhaps this is special – just for you.'

Angelo smiled lopsidedly. '*Madre mía* – what's so special about me?'

Robert gazed at the handsome, well-chiselled features and knew if he had a lifetime at his disposal, he probably still wouldn't be able to put his finger on it. Malcolm's summation sprang into his mind. 'You're a –' he remembered Angelo's equine background '– a dark horse in a herd of white stallions.'

Angelo raised an eyebrow.

Robert laughed and walked on. 'Everyone here is blond or red-haired – haven't you noticed?'

Angelo shook glossy curls.

'You're a novelty.' Robert punched a muscular arm instead and bit back a tinge of resentment. 'I wouldn't be surprised if every woman in the village throws herself at you!' And a good many of the men, he couldn't help adding mentally.

'You think so?'

Robert managed a wink. 'I know so! Now come on – we don't want to keep the ACAS waiting.' He strode onwards, not wanting Angelo to see the lust in his face.

'The ACA – what?'

Robert glanced over his shoulder. 'The Angelo Caballo Appreciation Society – you'll be knocked down in the rush at this ceilidh!'

His flatmate's laughter drowned out the elegiac sound of the pipes.

Running boot steps pounded behind him. 'And what about you, my friend?'

Robert frowned. Founding member of the ACAS? President?

Angelo drew parallel. 'I saw you and the *Kelpie*'s skipper talking.'

Robert smiled, half-pleased Angelo had even noticed anything he'd been doing on the sail across to the island. His smile broadened at the thought of Malcolm's broad chest. 'Oh, I'll keep myself busy.'

Angelo rubbed his hands together. 'I suddenly don't feel hungry any more.' He grinned. 'At least, not in my stomach.'

Robert laughed, mind well and truly on a more detailed fantasy concerning the contents of red-haired Malcolm's oilskin trousers.

Then another sound shattered the ostinato of pipes.

The sound of a gunshot.

Seven

Robert's head snapped left, in the direction of the sharp crack. 'What on earth was –?'

'Shhh!' Angelo held up a broad palm.

Robert narrowed his eyes, peering into the thickly wooded area.

Angelo took a step forward.

Another crack split the silence.

Robert flinched and only just resisted the impulse to throw himself to the ground.

Angelo took another step towards the edge of the trees.

Robert grabbed his arm. 'Come on – we'll be late for the ceilidh.'

His friend turned, dark eyes filled with interest. 'Aren't you the slightest bit curious? I thought writers were interested in everything.'

Robert frowned. 'There could be hunters; poachers; criminals – wild animals in there!' The frown broke into a wry smile, as he remembered his over-imaginative interpretation of Billy-Bob's identity on the train.

Angelo grinned. 'I knew you were interested really.' He moved forward. 'Let's take a look.'

Robert sighed. 'Just a quick one, then. But if there's any bodies being buried –' he couldn't resist chuckling '– we note the details for my next book then scram and report it to the police, OK?'

Angelo's grin broadened. 'OK.' He zipped up his jacket and winked mischievously. 'You're the writer – you go first.' He pushed Robert forward into the undergrowth.

His feet soon found a path, but branches and bushes stuck out in all directions, above ground level. Robert pushed his way through, smiling at the occasional 'ow!' from behind as a brier whipped back against Angelo.

The wood wasn't as dark as it had looked from the road. Light filtered through sparse, high branches, dappling the earth below. Robert scanned clearing upon clearing. After about ten minutes, he brushed bramble blossoms from his face and turned.

Angelo was picking bits of twig from his hair and fighting the attack of a swarm of tiny but vicious-looking insects.

Robert laughed. 'They've gone obviously – let's follow their example and –'

A loud report obliterated the end of his sentence.

Angelo pointed right. 'Over there. I can see them.' He ducked down.

Robert did likewise, squinting through knee-high bracken. From this angle, he could see an inch or so of pale ankle and a denim-clad calf, but nothing more. Something poked him in the back. Then a hiss: 'Move closer.'

Robert slapped a biting winged creature against his arm and crept forward. He could hear rustlings behind and knew Angelo was following. After a couple of yards, his head poked out in a clearing.

Robert stared up at the back of a pair of boots. He glanced around.

The area was littered with fallen trees and rotting stumps. On the far side, pinned to the trunk of one, was a rectangular sheet of paper, decorated with concentric, squinty-looking circles. A variety of shattered bottles littered the ground.

Robert scanned for more legs.

Just the one pair. Slim, almost girlish.

Robert wriggled back a little for a better look. His foot impacted with something solid.

Angelo grunted.

Robert stuck a hand in his mouth to stop himself chuckling, then moved onto hands and knees and crept down the side of the clearing. Angelo following in his wake, Robert paused behind a tree, side on to the scene. Straightening up slowly, he risked a look around the thick trunk.

A broad-shouldered, narrow-waisted figure in a battered leather jacket stood in the middle of the clearing, feet apart, the stock of an air-rifle wedged in one armpit. A veil of tangled golden hair obliterated the face, which was centred in line with the weapon's sight. One long finger hugged the trigger.

Robert watched every muscle in the slender body tense, then jumped as the sound of shattering glass echoed in the clearing.

A voice hissed in his ear: 'It's just a boy, target-practising. No writing-inspiration here. Let's go.'

This was no mere boy! Robert barely heard the rest of the words. He continued to watch as the youth broke the gun-barrel, hooked it over one leather-clad arm and strode forward. Tangled, unwashed hair bounced with each step. Long limbs covered the ground in a swaggering lope. The gait had the awkwardness of one teetering on the edge of adulthood: aggressively masculine while still retaining the gawkiness of youth – and not quite completely comfortable with either.

Robert smiled, remembering the feeling.

The youth crouched, rummaged in a bag which sat at the foot of a tree-stump, then removed another bottle and placed it carefully on the piece of dead wood.

As he turned, long fingers pushed the veil of hair over one shoulder and Robert caught a glimpse of skin flushed with satisfaction.

The lope of a boy, the body of a man –

Robert inhaled sharply.

– and the face of an angel,

A tug at his sleeve. 'Come on!'

Reluctantly, Robert dragged his eyes from the beautiful face and staggered back through the undergrowth, eyes inches from Angelo's tight rear. He grinned. But the blond youth's extraordinary features lingered in his mind.

As they entered the village, sound led them to the location of the ceilidh. Not the lone piper's lament from earlier, but an exuberant and lively mixture of drums, fiddles and accordions, emanating from a brightly lit building a little to the right of a boarded-up church.

Robert lingered at the bottom of a flight of three stone steps and brushed the remaining few leaves from his hair.

Angelo rubbed his hands together and glanced at Robert. 'Sounds like a real party. Ready?'

Robert grinned. 'Ready!' As they climbed the stairs, he couldn't help but notice that the bright lights and dancing shades which flickered through the windows of the village hall conjured up an image of a fiery inferno. On the last step, double doors burst open.

'Ah, you found us!'

Robert's hand was seized in a vice-like grip. He stared at a vaguely familiar man with neatly clippered red hair, beard and a broad smile.

'Come in, lads. Come in.' The stocky figure clapped a hand on Angelo's shoulder.

Ears ringing, they were pulled into the brightly lit hall. Robert stared at their host. Memory kicked in.

Hamish Campbell was now dressed in kilt, white shirt and black bow tie. Over the shirt, he wore a smart black jacket, three silver buttons decorating front and sleeves. He looked very different from their earlier encounter – both in appearance and demeanour.

Robert glanced over PC Campbell's head and met Angelo's eyes.

His flatmate grinned.

Hamish talked on. 'It's good to have you both here with us tonight.' He led them through the mingled throng of dancers and watchers, all of whom beamed.

In the far corner, leaning on the top of a makeshift bar, Robert caught a twinkling green eye.

Malcolm raised a glass in discreet salute.

Robert smiled in response, eased his hand from Hamish's strong grip, and immediately found the same hand clasped around his shoulder. PC Campbell evidently used his official skills, even when off duty. A low voice whispered over the noise of the band: 'There will be plenty of time for renewing auld acquaintance later, my lad.' The dapper man guided them through the throng and up onto the small dais at the top of the hall, where the band stood. He held up a hand.

The music and dancing stopped.

Disengaging himself from them, Hamish stepped sideways to a small microphone on a stand and tapped it once.

A howl of feedback filled the hall, followed by gales of laughter.

The police officer frowned, stepping back from the microphone. 'Friends!' Hamish Campbell didn't need amplification: his deep, resounding voice reached all corners of the hall unaided. 'It gives me great pleasure to finally introduce our two visitors.' The jovial, bearded face turned. 'I'm sure you'll join with me in welcoming Mr Robert McLeod and Mr Angelo Caballo to our little community.' Hamish smiled broadly, then began to clap.

Other hands joined in.

Robert and Angelo stood, mesmerised and totally surprised, as the entire hall broke into thunderous applause. A few began to cheer and stamp their feet. Then more. Robert's eyes travelled over a mass of smiling, nodding heads, then paused at the back of the hall.

Standing a little apart from the general throng, he noticed the striking couple from earlier, now both dressed in finery which even outdid the dapper Hamish's outfit.

Robert made eye contact with the man, who nodded. As his gaze shifted to the woman, he saw a pair of pale blue eyes already focused on the tall Argentinian at his side.

There was something about her stare which marked it off from the friendly curiosity of the islanders', something more intense and almost predatory. Just for a second, the rest of the hall vanished and it was as if the tall blonde and the darkly striking Angelo were the only two people in the room.

Robert smiled wryly and looked away: the Angelo Caballo Appreciation Society had, no doubt, just found itself a chairperson. His eyes scanned the bar for redheads, where he found plenty, but none were Malcolm's. By the time he refocused, the standing ovation had subsided and the band was playing again.

PC Campbell patted his shoulder. 'Now, Mr McLeod — let's get you a drink. You'll need fortifying. There are many people who want to meet you.'

He felt himself gently but firmly steered from the dais. Robert looked around for Angelo, eventually spotting him a little way off, smiling and nodding with the well-dressed couple from the boat. With a sigh, he turned away, more than a little curious about the relationship between the tall man and his female companion. As his mouth opened to enquire, other words obliterated his:

'Angus McDuff.'

Robert's hand was gripped and pumped vigorously by a wiry man with thinning ginger hair and a face to match.

'Jimmy Dalgleish.'

Another hand seized his. Robert smiled at a stout, bald forty-year-old in a sheepskin waistcoat.

'Hugh McBride.'

Slowly, the faces all merged into one. Someone gave him a glass of something, which at least put an end to the tiring handshakes. As Hamish continued the never-ending series of introductions, Robert nodded and smiled. He drained the glass.

It was replaced.

They made their way up one side of the dance floor, then down the other. After a while, the whisky stopped burning his throat and began to loosen his tongue. Hamish had halted their progress in front of a vast building of a man, almost as broad as he was tall. An arm as thick as most men's thighs was thrust out at him.

'Douglas McVey.' The voice was deep and bassy.

Robert let his fingers be grasped in a surprisingly gentle grip. Hamish cut between them.

'Douglas is the local blacksmith and runs the ironmongers. Any metalwork you need done, he's your man.'

Robert smiled at the hulking figure, and thought of the warped door-frame back at Corrie Cottage. He was about to enquire about Douglas's availability, when Hamish steered him onwards.

'And this is Miss Nicol, our schoolmistress. A valiant and courageous lady!' Hamish beamed admiringly.

Robert focused on a tiny woman with iron-grey hair which was severely pulled back into a tight bun. Perhaps it was only in contrast with the towering blacksmith, but he couldn't help but wonder how someone so small and frail-looking managed to keep order in the classroom. He smiled benignly.

Miss Nicol regarded him coolly. 'You're the writer?' The voice was metallic as her hair colour.

Robert felt himself wither under the cold appraisal. He laughed self-consciously. 'Well, I – er – um, I try.'

Miss Nicol evidently wasn't impressed. 'Then you'll need to try harder in future, won't you?'

Robert felt his face flush up.

Hamish laughed. 'Now, don't tease the boy, Grace.'

The pinched features softened a little. Miss Nicol took his hand, patted it. 'You must come and visit me, Robert. Douglas?' She looked beyond Robert.

In seconds, the hulking blacksmith was at her side. 'Yes, miss?'

The schoolteacher held out her empty glass. 'Another orange-juice, Douglas, if you please.'

An enormous fist carefully took the offering then began to push its way towards the bar.

Robert couldn't help but admire the tiny woman's manner.

The police officer steered him onwards. More introductions were made. Robert was losing track of names and people kept buying him drinks. Unexpectedly, he caught sight of a slender blond figure in a leather jacket, slouching sullenly against the bar. Robert bent his head to Hamish's scarlet ear. 'Who's that?' He nodded in the youth's direction.

PC Campbell sighed. 'That's one who makes Miss Nicol's job all the harder. Young Fingal's off her hands now, but what's good news for the school is bad news for the rest of us.'

Fingal.

Fingal. Robert rolled the exotic name around in his head.

Hamish talked on. 'Out of work and full of mischief.'

Robert watched as Fingal glanced up from scrutiny of the glass in his hand, cast a scornful glance around the boisterous ceilidh, then returned to further moody contemplation of his drink.

His eyes lingered on the heavenly face. The gait of a boy. The body of a man. The face of an angel –

'There's the soul of a devil under that peach-like skin.'

PC Campbell's choice of words took Robert aback. He switched his gaze from Fingal's face and stared at the bearded one.

It was looking as stern as it had done earlier. 'At the moment, it's only minor offences, but unless someone takes that lad firmly in hand, I'm fearful of the consequences for him.'

Robert frowned, remembering himself at that age: sometimes it took a special kind of man to break another man, to force him to submit to his will and toe the line expected of him.

Hamish's face brightened. 'But that's an island problem – we don't want to be bothering you with –'

'It's no bother.' Robert smiled. The words were half whisky-induced, half genuine. 'I'd like to think I could eventually become part of the community here.'

The ruddy face beamed. Hamish slapped him on the back. 'You don't know how much it means to us to hear you say that.' The voice rose in volume, cutting through the sound of the band. 'I'd like to propose a toast. To Robert McLeod, the newest inhabitant of Kelpie Island. May he find only peace and happiness on these shores!'

The responding roar was almost deafening. 'Robert McLeod!' Glasses clinked noisily.

Robert flushed at the enthusiastic salutation. Pride grew in his chest. From the other side of the hall, he caught Angelo's eye as his flatmate joined in the toast. Robert swayed, waving his own glass towards the Argentinian, who was now firmly flanked by the couple from the boat.

Hamish had evidently followed his gaze. 'Young Caballo's made himself some powerful friends there, lad.' Robert turned, one eyebrow raised. The police officer was referring to Angelo in the same, strange way as had the cook on the overnight train to Fort William. PC Campbell's expression was stony, eyes lowered in deference. 'That's Cameron and Rhona Dunbar: Laird and Lady Laird of Kelpie Island, owners of Castle Dunbar and every other inch of this fair isle.'

Robert grinned drunkenly. 'Is it, indeed!' Trust Angelo to get himself in with the local aristocracy. Still, it could come in handy if they required planning permission for any alterations needed to Corrie Cottage.

Hamish's tone grew darker. He shook his head. 'Don't be showing any disrespect now. This island owes a lot to the ministrations of the Laird and Lady Laird. It wouldn't do to displease them.'

Robert hiccuped. 'Sorry, I –'

'No harm done, lad!' The police officer's expression brightened. 'It's bound to take you a while to get used to island ways.'

He sneaked another look at Angelo and his handsome companions. Some people were getting used to 'island ways' like they'd been born to them.

Then Hamish was steering him through the dancing, flailing crowd again. Armed with another glass of the local distillation, Robert smiled and steeled himself for another round of introductions.

An hour later he'd met everyone in the place, band members and all.

Complete strangers had asked him about his parents, his schooling – he'd even had a very interesting conversation with a local historian about writing. People had offered him help with everything from the renovation of Corrie Cottage to free lessons in Gaelic and a cut-price kilt-fitting.

The room was swaying pleasantly.

Dancers shouted good-naturedly around him, beckoning him into their rowdy reels.

Robert grinned and shook his head: it was taking him all his time to remain upright and walking. Right now, a few quiet moments alone with Malcolm was all he really wanted.

He'd caught the fisherman's eye a few times in the course of the evening. But every time he tried to make his way towards the bar, someone handed him a drink or asked how long he was planning to stay. Robert was in the process of trying to shake Hamish free from his side and edge away when a particularly exuberant cry rose up from the dance floor.

Inching through the crowd which had spread off the floor and was now spectating from the sidelines, Robert stared.

To the steady, rhythmic clap of a roomful of hands, Angelo was dancing. With the Lady Laird.

Robert watched, mesmerised, as the couple linked arms and bounded one way, then the other. Rhona Dunbar's long plaid skirt whirled up, revealing elegant ankles, while Angelo's white linen shirt had come loose from his shorts and was swirling free around his taut, bronze stomach.

The stamp of booted feet joined the cacophony.

Then the Lady Laird paused.

Angelo continued to dance around her, his feet moving with an agile grace.

Robert's jaw dropped. Not much of a dancer, his flatmate had said. He stared at the leaping figure.

Angelo's strong arms were now raised above his head, his feet executing some complicated-looking step, half flamenco, half Highland fling. He continued to circle the statuesque Lady Laird.

A sonorous lilt whispered in his ear: 'Your friend's light on his feet.'

Robert turned and found himself staring into twinkling green eyes.

Malcolm's breath was warm and smelled of whisky. The pale cheeks were slightly flushed.

Robert smiled. The brawny fisherman had sought him out. 'Yes, he is.' He turned back to the dance-floor display, enjoying the feel of Malcolm's strong warm body pressed against his.

Angelo was now linking arms with a variety of beaming women, twirling them around this way and that, but always returning to circle the Lady Laird. The dance was spiralling outwards, as each woman took a new partner, who in turn linked arms with someone else.

Eventually, there were more people dancing than clapping.

Robert laughed, shook his head and staggered back as a pink-faced girl tried to grab his hand.

Behind, muscular arms seized his waist, steadying him.

Alcohol made him reckless. Robert reached up, ran his fingers through Malcolm's thick red hair and grinned inanely at the pink-faced girl.

She cocked her head, shrugged good-naturedly then winked before moving on in search of another partner.

Malcolm's breath caressed the side of his neck. Robert pressed back, half undulation, half drunken stagger. Beneath his shorts, alcohol had done nothing to impede an incipient erection. Words brushed his ear.

'Want to get some fresh air?'

Robert extracted the meaning with the skill of an expert. Eyes scanning the crowded room, he saw Angelo was still in the thick of the dance. Another gaze had obviously followed his.

'Your friend's in safe hands. Don't worry about him.'

Before he could say anything else, Robert was firmly propelled towards the open fire exit door.

Eight

Night air bathed his sweating skin, cooling his body and clearing his head. Robert was surprised how much light was still around, although his watch told him it was well after eleven.

He and the tall fisherman walked down the stone steps and leant against a wall.

Robert gazed at Malcolm, taking in what he had been unable to see, back in the crowded hall.

Like PC Campbell, the tall red-haired fisherman was also kilted, but the plaid garment looked completely different on his broad form. A tight black T-shirt covered the deep chest, showing off well-defined pectorals to best advantage and highlighting the pale, freckled skin.

On his feet, Malcolm wore stout boots and thick socks. But it was the kilt itself which took Robert's attention. Unlike Hamish's neat, ceremonial-looking garment, the redhead's plaid was almost haphazardly gathered and draped around his waist. The fabric was held in place by a thick, black leather belt with a large silver-coloured buckle.

Robert watched, dry-mouthed, as Malcolm hoisted himself onto the wall, spreading the knee-length kilt over and around his knees.

Where Hamish looked formal and slightly stuffy in his regalia, Malcolm exuded an untamed, heavily primitive wildness.

Robert could imagine armies of Malcolms, their long red hair flowing in the wind, rough features contorted in battle cries as they raced down the sides of steep glens towards the invading English. A dreamy smile crept over his face.

Malcolm pulled the black T-shirt over his head and tucked it into his belt. 'That's better.' He scratched at the tuft of red hair between his nipples.

Robert's cock twitched, stretching itself against the inside of his shorts. No claymores were necessary to defeat this Englishman! He had been a lost cause ever since the journey across from the mainland.

Malcolm's hair had worked its way loose from the slim leather thong which had held it in the ponytail. Thick red tresses cascaded over pale, well-muscled shoulders.

Robert grinned to himself at the thought of those poor idiots who considered long hair and skirts feminine. He levered himself off the wall and stood directly in front of the fisherman.

Malcolm radiated testosterone from every pore.

Robert moved into the V of splayed thighs. The crotch of his shorts rubbed against the stone wall. Friction made him gasp aloud.

A hand rested on his shoulder, then slid behind his neck, pulling him closer. Green eyes stared into his.

Robert wanted to plunge into those emerald pools and drown himself. His fingers fumbled amidst the vast folds of the kilt, searching for an opening. Warmth seeped up into his hand. He could smell fresh sweat and the slightly seaweedy odour of all things marine, which would for ever remind him of a weather-beaten Scottish skipper.

Their faces were close. Very close.

A jubilant hoot from the dance behind shattered the moment.

Malcolm's generous mouth spread into a grin. He levered himself from the wall, plaid-covered hip-bones jutting out and brushing Robert's groin. Glancing at the incongruously modern watch on his wrist, the fisherman then looked towards the pier. 'Fancy helping with the nets?'

Robert stepped back, trying to re-adjust the very obviously bulge in his shorts. He scrutinised the heavily draped front of Malcolm's kilt for telltale tenting. 'What?' He continued to stare, then sighed with disappointment: you could hide a two-handed sword in there and it wouldn't be noticeable.

'My nets need to be folded for the morning. This time of year the *Kelpie* must be out before the four o'clock tide turns. I could do with another pair of hands.'

Malcolm was sounding more businesslike by the minute. Robert's heart sank. 'OK.' He could only pray 'helping with the nets' was a Gaelic come-on which lost something in translation. Finding a smile, he turned and followed Malcolm down the hill towards the quay.

As he walked, the gentle swing of a tartan-draped arse in front entertained his eyes, while his mind momentorily wondered how Angelo was faring, back inside the village hall.

'Are you sure you have no Scottish blood?'

Angelo wiped his face with the tail of the linen shirt. He was still trying to get his breath back. 'Most sure.' He stared at the handsome woman at his side.

He'd never met anyone quite like Rhona Dunbar. Tall – almost six feet – she carried her height with a surprising grace and elegance, reminding him of the proud, upper-class women who frequented the exclusive cafés and restaurants of Buenos Aires. Although they made his heart beat faster and his cock swell with lust, he knew he was a country boy – albeit from one of the largest beef ranches in Argentina – and would never be good enough to bed any of those haughty creatures.

'You have a natural talent, then.'

Angelo glanced to his other side and smiled at Rhona's fine-featured brother. 'Thank you, Mr Dunbar.'

The aristocratic head nodded once. 'Cameron, please.'

Angelo beamed. 'Cameron it is!'

Rhona's slim hand passed him a glass.

Angelo took it, their fingers meeting for a second.

She smiled. 'He likes Cammie too.' Fingers exerted a light pressure, then removed themselves.

Angelo knocked back the whisky in one gulp. The liquid hit his stomach like an explosion, setting off further detonations of warmth in his head. 'Cammie and Rhona! My friends, you must call me Angelo – Mr Caballo makes me sound like –' his expression darkened '– my father.'

Rhona's voice was low and probing. 'And are you not your father's son, Angelo?'

The warmth in his head increased to a hot, niggling resentment. 'We share a name. Nothing more.' The words came out angrier than he'd intended. Angelo looked from one concerned face to the other and back again. In his haste to change the subject, his eyes paused on the large cameo brooch which nestled at the neck of Rhona's high-collared blouse. He reached up, stroking the delicately carved ivory. 'This is very beautiful.' The relief showed a white stallion, front hooves pawing the air as the animal reared back in wild abandon. One finger traced the intricate detail of the horse's mane.

Then other fingers moved past his.

Angelo watched as Cammie carefully unpinned the decoration and held it out so that Angelo could see the cameo more clearly. He placed the brooch in the palm of his hand. The value of the piece was almost palpable. 'Most beautiful.' His eyes moved from examination of the stallion to the exquisitely featured face inches from his. 'Like its owner.'

Rhona Dunbar took his hand in hers, curling coffee-coloured fingers around the cameo. 'It's yours.'

Angelo stiffened. 'No, I cannot accept such a –'

'Take it.' Long, ringed fingers held his with surprising strength.

They'd tried to buy him before, those haughty, elegant creatures in Buenos Aires. With drinks, with meals, when the allowance from his father had been late in arriving and his guts had tightened with hunger. Then with crisp dollar bills, which they crammed into his shaking fingers.

Angelo wrenched his hand away. 'No!' The ornament slipped

from his fingers and fell to the floor. He watched as light glinted off the carved relief.

Rhona sank to an elegant crouch, her skirts rustling as she retrieved the brooch from under a chair.

Angelo shook the past from his mind, eyes focusing on the Lady Laird's pert, rounded rear as it bobbed before his face. 'Oh! Forgive me!' He watched, shamefacedly.

Rhona straightened up, smiling at him. 'No harm done.' Deft fingers reattached the decoration to the high neck of her white, ruffled blouse. 'It was insensitive of me to offer such a gift when we don't yet know each other well.'

The Laird's voice placatingly rejoined the conversation: 'There was no insult intended.'

Angelo focused on the Laird's well-chiselled features.

Cammie continued. 'Perhaps, by way of making amends, you would do us the honour of accepting our hospitality.'

Angelo tried to extract meaning from the words.

Rhona clarified, red-stained lips very close to his ear. 'Castle Dunbar is close by. Our car is outside.'

In the background, the music was becoming more frenzied, the dancing and general merry-making more rowdy.

'Will you join us for a nightcap in more appropriate surroundings?'

Hunger cramped in his stomach. He suddenly remembered the plans Robert and he had made to leave early and dine at whatever restaurant was still open. His head swivelled, eyes searching the dancing throng. 'Can my friend come too?'

Cameron's laugh was low and hearty. 'Mr McLeod left some time ago, in the company of Malcolm. '

Angelo pressed a hand to his mid-section to deaden the rumbling, which was growing ever louder. 'Is there anywhere around here I can get a sandwich?'

A high, tinkling laugh joined the hearty one. 'I'm sure the castle larder can do a little better than that!' Rhona linked her arm through his. 'Please join us for a late supper, Angelo.' A pink tongue snaked out and licked red lips. 'I'm feeling more than a little hungry myself.' She began to steer him towards the door.

Angelo watched the Laird drape a length of plaid around his sister's shoulders. Rhona's fingers were cool and soothing against his hot skin.

As the threesome left the hall, various villagers nodded and bowed to them.

Angelo bowed and nodded back, looking forward to something to eat. Walking down the steps to the same blue Daimler he'd seen on the quayside earlier, he was slightly irked and more than a little disappointed that Robert had left without telling him.

'Doesn't it ever get dark around here?' Robert stared up into the rosy-tinged night sky.

The nets had been folded, and he and the red-haired giant were now each sitting astride an iron bollard.

Malcolm stretched tired arms and glanced upwards. 'We're approaching midsummer. In June, there's only an hour or two of real darkness.'

The low, lilting voice mixed with the soft slap of water on stone and the muted jangle of anchor-chains as they clanked against the quayside. A balmy breeze ruffled the hair on his arms. Robert smiled. 'How wonderful.'

'Not so wonderful in winter, when the process is reversed – plays havoc with the tides, not to mention the cost of fuel.'

'Ah.' Robert nodded, acknowledging the fisherman's pragmatism.

Malcolm talked on, one broad hand rubbing a large shoulder. 'We have few natural resources.'

Robert was staring up beyond the village, to the majestic peaks which framed the scene.

Malcolm followed his eyes and smiled. 'At least, none which provide electricity, gas or anything else we can use.' He shook his head slowly. 'We have water, of course, but all –' Malcolm corrected himself '– most other necessities of life must be imported from the mainland. Costs go up every year.'

'It's the same everywhere.' He watched tension flick across the rugged features, and noticed the way Malcolm was rotating and flexing his shoulders. Robert got up from the bollard and wandered round to behind the bare-chested fisherman. 'London's getting impossibly expensive.' His hands hesitated only once, before clamping themselves to knotted muscle. The flesh beneath his fingers flinched, then began to relax.

'That feels good.' Malcolm gripped kilted knees, head lolling forward. He groaned.

Robert removed one hand from the task, flicked the mass of tangled red hair on the pale, sweat-slicked shoulder then resumed the back-rub. He dug his thumbs deep into stretched sinew, feeling the sheer power of the fisherman's upper-body beneath his palms. His own arms were a little achy from the net-folding, but he continued the massage, leaning forward and running his hands down over biceps to forearms.

His crotch rubbed against the arc of Malcolm's spine. Robert stifled a groan of his own, as tension seemed to seep from the fisherman's flesh into his. The more thoroughly he kneaded and pummelled at the strained muscle, the more relaxed Malcolm became.

And the harder Robert's cock pushed against the zip of his shorts.

The brawny redhead was sighing and moaning by turns, now. Robert scowled with aching arousal. With every thrust of his hands on the warm skin of Malcolm's back and shoulders, a returning thrust from the base of the man's spine shot arrows of desire into his groin. Robert ground the throbbing neediness of his fully hard shaft against nobbled bone. The massage was pleasuring and torturing him by turns, and even the torture was starting to feel good. In one swift movement his hands were over the broad shoulders, one buried in a tangle of scarlet while the other found and began to fondle a nipple.

Malcolm hissed through clenched teeth.

Robert pulled the fisherman's head back further until tangled hair pressed against his chest. Fingers continued to fondle Malcom's stiffening bud.

Then one of the fisherman's large hands clamped itself to his left arse-cheek. Over Malcolm's shoulder, Robert could see the other fumbling amidst tartan folds. His fingers tightened around a now fully erect nipple. Robert squeezed.

A low moan echoed in the still night air. The fisherman's huge hand paused, then flicked aside a section of kilt.

Robert stared past twitching fingers at the purply-pink head which had poked its way free of the plaid cage. His own cock was now leaking wet desire and staining the inside of his briefs.

Abruptly, Malcolm lurched to his feet and turned.

Robert was breathing heavily. He took a step back, eyes unable to pull themselves away from the fisherman's strong, pale shaft which strained up towards him, flanked by two curtains of tartan. With shaking fingers he unzipped himself, unleashing his own pulsing rod.

In the half light of midnight they stood there, inches apart, then Malcolm reached down, grabbing both cocks and squeezing them in an iron grip.

Robert gasped, gripping Malcolm's shoulder to steady himself as he was pulled closer.

A corresponding hand grasped his waist.

Mesmerised, Robert continued to stare at their two cocks, sprouting from Malcolm's vast fist.

The fist tightened further.

Robert shivered, watching two bisected heads ooze clear liquid, which Malcolm collected in his palm and slathered over the pair of shafts. His balls tightened, knitting together as two cocks bumped and writhed against each other. Panting, he looked up into vivid green pools.

Malcolm's pupils were lust-swollen, expanding ever outwards until his eyes were black, emerald-rimmed circles.

As he stared, three feet below his length throbbed against another length, heavy balls brushing another heaviness.

Then Malcolm's mouth was on his, lips crushing lips.

Robert moaned into hard wetness, tongue desperately probing the inside of Malcolm's mouth as an arm circled more tightly around his waist. His T-shirted nipples met the erect naked tips of the fisherman's buds. Robert panted harder and began to fuck Malcolm's fist.

With every thrust, the skin on his cock dragged against the surface of another cock. A coating of precum cut down the friction but the movement still sent waves of ecstasy through his body – especially when he felt Malcolm's hips rutting back against his.

Robert gnawed fiercely on Malcolm's mouth, shifting a hand to behind the fisherman's neck and forcing the red head closer to his.

Then a hot tongue was in his mouth, twining with his own. Robert's cock jerked as the first ripple of incipient orgasm spasmed in his guts.

Malcolm felt it too, cock pulsing in response.

In the distance, the sound of a car engine.

He tore his mouth from Robert's. 'We need somewhere more private.' Malcolm's voice was hoarse with need.

Cocks jutting in semi-darkness, they pounded across the gangplank onto the deck of the *Kelpie*.

Angelo peered through the Daimler's back window as the car moved smoothly past the top of the pier and up a steep hill.

He thought he'd seen two figures, embracing on the quayside.

A high-powered engine purred beneath him.

'This all must seem very new to you.'

The Lady Laird's low, molten voice dragged his eyes from the window. Angelo refocused on Rhona Dunbar's face.

One plaid-covered arm resting on the back of the passenger seat, the blond, perfectly coiffured head nodded outside to the dramatic scenery.

Cameron shifted gear as the steep incline increased.

Angelo smiled. 'The mountains I am not used to – the pampas are very flat and green. But many things about Kelpie Island make me feel at home.'

Rhona returned the smile. 'I am glad – we both are.'

From behind the wheel, Cameron nodded. 'We hope you may eventually come to enjoy those aspects which, at first, may seem rather foreign to you.'

Angelo's stomach lurched. He'd read about haggis – it was even mentioned in the guide-book as a local delicacy. The very thought of the dish's ingredients sent hunger fleeing from his body. But he knew he was a guest, and remembered his manners. 'I am sure I will.'

The car purred onwards.

Rhona continued to smile. 'So, tell us about Argentina, Angelo. It sounds a fascinating country.'

Angelo beamed. He jumped at the chance. He was also eager to get his mind away from whatever strange and peculiar-sounding food he might be offered when they eventually reached Castle Dunbar. 'My county stretches from –'

As the powerful Daimler smoothly turned corner after corner, under the Laird's expert's guidance, Angelo entertained his hosts to the marvels of a land thousands of miles away.

Robert tore at the buttons of his shirt, ripping the bottom two in his haste to be free of the garment. He looked down.

Malcolm was sprawling on a bed of nets. One hand fumbled with the silver buckle of his belt.

Robert eventually managed to get out of his shirt and started on his shorts. 'Keep it on!' His voice was husky with desire.

Irisless eyes stared up at him. 'What?'

'Keep the kilt on!' Robert scowled, wrenching shorts then underpants down. He kicked the garments over his boots.

Malcolm looked bemused, then complied.

Robert fell to his knees, fingers sinking into nylon net as he crawled up between strong legs. He gripped ginger-dusted calves, drawing his hands up over knees and onto thighs. His cock bounced off his abs as he pushed plaid folds aside and up onto a harder, more muscular stomach.

Malcolm was naked beneath his kilt. A bushy groin lay exposed before him, in all its majesty.

Robert drank in the salty, male smell which joined with the scent of the sea and his own fresh sweat. He gazed at the thick, solid shaft, nestling in a shock of bright red hair. At the root, large bollocks drooped down between splayed thighs.

Robert stared at his catch, at the half-naked Scotsman who writhed amidst fishing-nets.

Malcolm's eyes pleaded up at him. 'Suck me.'

Robert's cock spasmed at the thought of those thick sweating inches. He wanted to bury his face in Malcolm's ginger pubes and feast on his cock and balls. But there was something else he wanted more. He ran a finger down the pale quivering shaft, tracing circles around and over the full balls then travelling on down.

Malcolm groaned, fingers tightening in the nets behind him. He drew up his legs, tensing with pleasure. Booted feet planted a yard apart, he arched his back and lifted his arse off the deck.

Robert's finger continued to travel down. He massaged the wrinkled skin behind Malcolm's balls, his own bollocks knotting and unknotting in desire.

The fisherman's cock jutted upwards into the night sky.

Robert pressed onwards, until the tip of his index finger found the moist, puckered hole. Nostrils filled with the musky heart of the man, Robert nudged one muscular thigh over each shoulder and groaned with anticipation. Malcolm's balls impacted with Robert's forehead as he gripped two hard arse-cheeks and wrenched them apart.

Somewhere above him, someone groaned. A pair of thighs tightened over his shoulders.

Thumbs placed either side of the moist, puckered hole, Robert rubbed his nose along the wrinkled flesh behind Malcolm's bollocks and inhaled sharply.

Bristling arse-hair tickled his skin.

Robert licked.

The body beneath his jerked and writhed.

Robert bit back mounting pleasure and ran a wet tongue from the root of the fisherman's engorged cock up and over the spasming hole.

The body beneath his shuddered.

Robert heaved Malcolm forward until only the man's upper back and shoulders had contact with the deck. Inches from his face, the orifice was tight and quivering. He stared at the wide band of damp hair which bisected the two pale globes of Malcolm's arse, lowered his face an inch and exhaled.

The breath erected each damp hair and caused the hole to shiver and shrink.

Robert pressed with his thumbs, knees digging in just beneath Malcolm's shoulderblades.

The fuckhole popped open, moist and pink and yearning.

Unable to hold back, Robert buried his face between tightly muscled arse-cheeks. Hands gripped the inside of the fisherman's thighs, widening them as he lapped first up then down the hairy crack.

Malcolm's breath was coming in short, sharp pants.

Eyes closed, mind filled with the animal stench of the man, Robert could feel the fuckhole gaping as he circled with his tongue, teasing them both.

Gasps from a little away upped the tension.

Robert smeared his face with the very essence of the fisherman then began to gnaw at the tender pink flesh.

Malcolm howled and drummed his heels against Robert's back.

Robert chewed on. He nipped and bit at Malcolm's arse-lips until the delicate flesh was as swollen as the length of aching shaft trapped between his stomach and the fisherman's broad back. His tongue flicked over and around the hole. Soon the entire area was a rosy wet mass of longing.

Then he plunged in.

Beneath him, Malcolm's body jerked rigid, then seemed to dissolve as Robert probed the inside of the fuckhole. He dived deeper. Spreading the man wide, he thrust with his tongue, breathing in the wetness of sex-sweat and his own saliva. Blood pounded in his ears and was echoed lower as his cock flexed, engorging more with each jab of his tongue. The flesh strained, barely kept in check by the tight foreskin. Malcolm's warm thighs wrapped themselves firmly around his head, deadening the sound until all Robert could hear was the thunder of his heart. Face immersed in the welcoming, spasming orifice, he was drowning in Malcolm.

A sudden movement threw him off-balance. Before he knew

what was happening, Robert found himself flipped backwards. His spine and shoulders impacted with the deck of the *Kelpie*, his fall cushioned by fishing-nets. Blood rushed from his head. Stars spangled before his eyes. Something warm and heavy rested on his ribcage and took his breath away. He gasped. Rough fabric scratched against his neck and shoulders as knees burrowed into his armpits.

Malcolm straddled his chest.

Craning his head, Robert stared at the towering rod of engorged flesh which grazed his bottom lip. He raised his eyes further, gazing at a freckled face which was pink with exertion. Malcolm's long red hair lay in a sweaty tangle over both shoulders.

The fisherman stared down, pupils swollen with desire, hips jutting forward.

Huge fingers linked themselves behind Robert's head, cradling his skull and raising it up.

'Suck me, Robbie. Please.'

His cock nodded its enthusiasm against his damp stomach. Robert pressed his lips to the hairy flesh of the fisherman's bollocks. Then, as Malcolm moved onto his knees and the purple head of his thick cock bobbed urgently against his nose, Robert reached up and around. He gripped the solid cheeks of the fisherman's arse, sheathing his teeth and opening his mouth as he pulled the man into him.

Malcolm was shaking. Vibrations quivered from hard mounds of muscle.

Eyes closed, Robert groaned around the thick shaft as it edged between his lips. The tongue which had previously fucked the hot, skanky centre of the man now flicked across the shiny cockhead, licking droplets of clear salty essence from the tiny slit. The flavour made his guts tighten. He drew the first four inches of cock easily into his mouth, tongue darting in and out of the fisherman's piss-slit.

The fifth was a less smooth movement.

He wanted Malcolm to pound into his mouth, fuck the face off him until that thick rod of desire shot hot sour liquid down his throat.

But he wanted to be conscious when it happened.

Robert gripped the cheeks of Malcolm's arse and slowed the motion, pinkies hooking upwards towards the man's hole as he waited for his gag-reflex to relax.

Re-angling his head as the muscles of his throat slowly untightened, Robert took another inch, running his tongue along and over the great shaft. Lips increased the pressure on the fisherman's length.

A low moan of frustration seeped into his ears.

Robert would have grinned, but there was too much of the man in his mouth to do anything but take more. Releasing his grip on Malcolm's arse-cheeks, he drew another inch between cushioned teeth and slipped a finger between tighter lips.

Malcolm hissed with pleasure as Robert eased a nail's then a knuckle's length into his arse. He drew back, then began to thrust more forcefully.

Ginger pubes ground against his face. The weight of the fisherman's balls smashed off his chin as Malcolm pounded into him. The head of the huge invader was hammering the back of his throat, forcing him to snatch breaths between thrusts.

Inhaling wiry hair, Robert snorted and gasped when he could. With every movement forward, the thick length forced its way more determinedly into his gullet. With every reverse thrust, Robert's finger buried itself more deeply in Malcolm's arse.

The Scotsman was making low, anguished sounds which rumbled from his vast chest. He squirmed and writhed, impaled like some reluctant marine creature caught on an angler's hook.

Robert eased another digit into the tight hole. Muscle clenched around and massaged his fingers. Something trembled in his guts.

The speed of the face-fuck increased. Malcolm's cock battered between his lips with a new urgency.

His neck hurt. The skin on his face was rubbed raw. His mouth was dry, lips starting to bruise around the insistent pummelling. And Robert found himself more aroused than ever.

A sudden wrenching and a wet warmth against his belly told Robert he'd just come. But it didn't seem to matter. No sooner had his balls clenched and shot thick ropes of spunk from his slit than he was hardening all over again. He shoved a third finger into Malcolm and felt the tight tunnel widen to accept the rough invasion.

The fisherman was humping his face furiously now, grunting with lust.

Behind lips, teeth dug into delicate skin, which bruised further under the onslaught. Robert swallowed a cry as the raging cock beat against the back of his throat. His eyes watered, tears streaming down his face. Spunk crystallising on his belly, he thrust hips skywards, fucking the night.

Then Malcolm pulled out, sat back and skewered down on Robert's cramping hand.

A howl tore into the darkness. Another man's passion loud in his ears, Robert blinked as a shower of wet warmth splattered against his hot face.

Nine

Angelo couldn't speak. He stared around himself, awestruck. Long, ringed fingers touched his arm.

'Make yourself at home. I'll just see what cook's left in the fridge, while Cammie puts the car away.' The hand removed itself and the low clack of brisk heels moved over bare stone.

Angelo followed her progress in the direction of an arched doorway. Crossed pikes flanked the lintel. Some feet above, a tiny slit of a window stared down at him. He lowered his eyes and focused on a suit of armour which stood in a far corner of the great hall. He walked towards it, gazing at the ancient, roughly hewn walls which towered up into a high ceiling, vaulted with broad beams. In the centre hung a huge chandelier.

Rhona's footsteps faded away.

Angelo paused, craning his neck upwards and narrowing his eyes in the light. From outside, the squat square building which was Castle Dunbar had looked anything but what he'd expected from a castle. It was much smaller, for a start – deceptively so, as it was turning out.

He slowly crossed the wide expanse of old but polished stone. Angelo looked down at the sparkling surface. As he refocused on the suit of armour, he realised the entire hall was crafted from the same, ebony-freckled stone which littered the boulders around Corrie Cottage.

He stuck out a hand and touched the forged suit. The metal felt cold and rough under his fingers. He flipped up the face-protector and peered inside.

A small spider seemed surprised to see him and scuttled across to the edge of her web.

He grinned, letting the visor fall back in place with a clang that made him jump and echoed up into arching rafters.

When a door slammed behind him, Angelo jumped again. He swivelled round.

Cameron Dunbar smiled. 'You'll not get much sense out of him.' Small strides briskly lessened the floor between them.

Angelo raised an eyebrow.

Cameron made a mournful face. 'Duncan, fourth Laird of Kelpie Island – 589–610.' He laid a hand on the armour's shoulder piece and gave the suit an almost affectionate pat. 'All this metal did little to protect him. He died defending his home and this island.'

Angelo sighed. 'He was so young.'

'He was so unsuccessful.' The present Laird moved away, towards a line of paintings Angelo hadn't noticed. 'Centuries before William Wallace and Robert of Bruce were fighting the English for their independence over on the mainland, my ancestors were waging a different battle – with equal setbacks and failures. Kenneth Dunbar, fifth Laird.' An elegant finger indicated a portrait of a slender blond youth, with bowl-cut hair and a grim expression.

'Who were your ancestors at war with?'

Cameron Dunbar walked slowly on. 'Ewan, sixth Laird of Kelpie Island. Died in this very room.' A fingertip traced Ewan's slim, age-crackled neck. 'Decapitated.'

Angelo shivered, although the night was warm. He tried to remember his geography. 'Were the invaders –' he searched for the correct term '– Viking?'

Cameron didn't answer. He moved to a third, then a fourth portrait. 'Alexander, seventh Laird. Gordon, eighth Laird.'

Angelo stared from ancient chiselled features to the present Laird's face and back again. The man's expression remained sombre. Angelo's curiosity grew. 'Who were they fighting?'

Cameron had paused at a fifth portrait.

Angelo's gaze remained on Gordon Dunbar, a fiery-looking man with a thick blond beard.

'Do you believe in freedom of religion, Angelo?'

The question took him by surprise. Angelo moved his gaze to the last painting, and was surprised even more. 'Um, yes, I think I do.' He took a step back.

The final portrait in the gallery of Dunbar ancestors was of a woman. The style of her hair and the battle clothes she wore were similar to those of her predecessors, the expression equally grim but the features were softer – more full, more sensuous.

'So did Flora, first Lady Laird of Kelpie Island. 960–1044.'

Angelo blinked: whereas her male antecedents had all been killed in their early years, Flora Dunbar had apparently lived to what was considered a ripe old age, even now: in the eleventh century, her long life must have been very rare.

'Flora was thirty-eight when her brother Gordon and a hundred islanders were massacred by Christian zealots from across the sea.'

Angelo was transfixed by the woman's delicate features, her piercing blue eyes and the long sweep of her neck.

'Kelpie Island's green fields and rolling hills ran with the blood of our people. Gordon Dunbar's young wife fled in panic. No male heir was available to take a stand against our persecutors. For three hundred years we had fought, and now the fight seemed over, the end inevitable. So Flora took up the claymore and vanquished those who wished to colonise and bend us to their will, force the islanders to accept their ways.'

Angelo listened, entranced.

'This year is the thousandth anniversary of her victory.'

He shook his head in admiration tinged with disbelief. 'How did she do it? What did –?'

'Is Cammie boring you with our bloody history?'

The soft voice made the hair on the back of his neck stand on end. Angelo turned from his study of vividly painted blue eyes and gazed into other, larger-than-life pupils which glinted warmly at him.

The resemblance was striking. He stared, even though he knew it was bad manners to do so.

Rhona smiled over his shoulder at the portrait of Flora Dunbar. 'People say I look like her. I don't see it myself.'

Angelo gave himself a shake. The uncanny resemblance refused to leave his mind.

Rhona had changed out of her evening finery and now wore a tight, plaid skirt and cream blouse. A hand-knitted cardigan was draped casually over her shoulders. She held a tray, from which tempting odours drifted up and twitched his nostrils.

'Let me help you.' Angelo reached out and gripped the edges of the shining salver.

She smiled and let him, then turned reprimandingly to her brother. 'It was rude of you to keep our guest hanging around out here, Cammie.'

The Laird frowned. 'I was merely –'

Rhona interrupted. 'There's time enough for all that later.'

Angelo watched as a look passed between brother and sister. He glanced away. From the wall in front of him, a row of other blond, similar faces seemed to gaze at him in curiosity.

Then a particularly appetising smell wafted out from the tray in his hands. Angelo's stomach grumbled.

Rhona's tinkling laugh filled the hall, joined seconds later by Cameron's.

She turned her elegant face once more to Angelo's. 'Now that you have food, let's see if we can find you somewhere comfortable to eat it.'

Accompanied by audible hunger pangs, Angelo followed the Laird and Lady Laird towards a wide door in the centre of the far wall.

Robert's heartbeat was returning to normal.

A wet tongue licked a smear of spunk from above his left eyebrow.

Robert grinned, pulled the red head down and searched for Malcolm's mouth with his own.

The kiss was warm, affectionate. The salty tang of the fisherman's fluids sent a ripple of arousal rolling through his body. His own orgasm had crept up on him so unexpectedly he had barely been conscious of it. But the solidifying spunk which adhered his foreskin to the hair on his stomach was undeniable. He moaned into Malcolm's mouth, draping a thigh over the sweaty body which lay between his legs.

Slowly, the fisherman pulled away.

Robert gazed up at his rugged-faced lover.

Malcolm eased himself up, lowered a shaggy head and playfully bit one nipple.

Robert arched his back and closed his eyes. The fabric of Malcolm's kilt brushed over his skin. He felt sleepily satisfied, and wanted nothing more than to curl up amongst the nets which had provided such a comfortable bed.

But his red-haired Adonis had other things on his mind. Robert was jolted from soft nylon onto rough wood as Malcolm unceremoniously tugged the nets from under him. 'Hey!' His eyelids shot open.

Green eyes twinkled down at him. 'You might be on holiday, but some of us have to work.'

Robert scrambled to his feet. 'Spoilsport!'

A low, hearty laugh rumbled in his ears. 'There will be other nights, other opportunities.' Malcolm reached over and ruffled his hair with a huge hand. 'I have a living to make.' He removed his hand and gripped the edge of the nets.

A cool night breeze wafted over his skin. Robert shivered, then found himself grinning. 'OK – but next time, we use a bed like ordinary people!'

Malcolm laughed again. 'There's nothing ordinary about you, Robbie McLeod!'

He smiled at the nickname. This red-haired god who stood before him was also extraordinary: as extraordinary as the sex they'd just had together. He winked. 'OK, nets it is.' He rubbed the skin of his back where the nylon mesh had left diamond-shaped indentations. 'And tomorrow night I get to go on top, agreed?'

'Agreed!' Malcolm began to fold.

Still grinning, Robert quickly pulled his briefs over a half-hard cock, then grabbed the rest of his clothes and struggled into them. In minutes he was dressed and helping with the net-arranging process, already looking forward to their next encounter.

Fifteen minutes later, he stood on the quayside, watching and waving as the *Kelpie* chugged out from the bay into the North Atlantic. Robert's arms ached from the exertion of the net-folding. His mouth was sore from the force of the face-fucking.

The boat's hooter tooted twice in response, then disappeared from view.

Robert turned and strolled down the deserted pier. It was at least an hour's walk back to the cottage. Muscles battered and stretched, he set off at a jaunty pace.

At the top of the pier, just outside Duncan's Automobiles, the ground began to tremble.

The movement was slight, but unsettling.

Angelo sprang up from the large, comfortable couch, eyes flicking between each of his hosts.

Cameron smiled. 'Don't worry – it will pass. We've been having these tremors all week.'

Above the enormous fireplace, an imposing, primitive etching of a horse slipped one of its mountings and shifted askew.

The Laird moved swiftly to right the work of art.

Angelo watched a tray of cut-crystal glasses dance on their shiny silver surface. The sound tinkled in his ears. Then a single glass leapt off the table and bounced on thick carpet.

Angelo bit back the beginnings of panic. Breath stopped in his chest. The sensation of instability beneath his feet brought back memories of the sudden earth tremors which from time to time would shake the vast magnificence of the pampas. He remembered the way the old women would quickly cross themselves, heads bowed as they murmured silent prayers.

And he recalled the effect such tremors had on the cattle and horses, giving rise to mass stampedes.

The Laird and Lady Laird were both staring at the primitive etching of the stallion which hung over the fireplace.

Static electricity prickled the atmosphere in the room. The air seemed to ripple, as though the shudders in the earth were producing parallel rifts in the very ether around them.

Angelo clenched his fists, feeling his fingers brush damp palms.

The tinkling of crystal faded to an almost inaudible shimmer, then died to a long, high note before disappearing completely.

Rhona knelt, picked up and replaced the fallen glass with the others.

Breath flooded from his lungs.

Cameron seized a decanter of whisky and strode over. 'That was more violent than usual – I think we need another drink.'

Angelo shook his head, waiting for the last dregs of panic to drain from his body. His brain needed to be clear, not fogged by more whisky. 'Thank you for the food.' He placed his empty glass on the broad mantel. 'I must be getting back. Robert will be worried.' The last sentence was on his lips before he could stop it.

Two disappointed expressions turned to amused curiosity. Then Rhona was at his side. 'Of course you must go to him. We didn't realise you and your friend were –' piercing blue eyes twinkled teasingly '– more than friends.'

Angelo laughed, still perplexed by the words which had come out of his mouth, minutes earlier. 'We're not! That is, of course Robert's more than just a friend. He's a –' Angelo ran a hand through thick curls and scratched his head.

Two pairs of gently mocking blue eyes waited for an answer.

'Robert's a city boy. He is unused to country places and –' He smiled lopsidedly and shrugged. 'I worry about him!'

Rhona's laugh was soft and genuine.

He saw the Lady Laird exchange a fleeting glance with her brother, then return her beautiful face to him.

'You feel protective – it is only natural you are concerned for your friend.'

Cameron had produced car keys and was jiggling the bunch in

his hand. 'Of course you must go – we're only sorry we kept you so long. Let me give you a lift.'

There was no trace of resentment in the words, but Angelo was embarrassed nonetheless: he didn't want to appear rude or ungrateful for the Dunbars' hospitality. But he did want to leave, and quickly: the earthquake had been very unsettling. Searching for a pleasant note on which to end the rather strange evening, he eventually found one. Angelo picked up his jacket, eyes focused on the primitive etching. 'Does someone on the island keep horses?'

Rhona raised an immaculately plucked eyebrow.

Angelo struggled with his jacket. 'I promised Robert I'd get him into the saddle and –'

'You ride?' Cameron's voice was surprised.

Angelo nodded. 'It has been a while, but the terrain around here is ideal for riding and it seemed like a good way to see more of the island.'

Rhona unfolded the collar of his jacket, easing the sleeves over his shoulders.

Angelo shivered under her touch. Then heard her words in his ear: 'I keep a small stable here at Castle Dunbar. It would be a pleasure to provide you with a suitable mount.'

Angelo moved away. His cock was stiffening.

Rhona talked on. 'Tomorrow afternoon? About two?'

Angelo looked from brother to sister. Rhona Dunbar was having an undeniable effect on his body, but now was neither the time nor the place: it was not right to make advances to a man's sister without first obtaining permission from the man himself. He switched his attention to the Laird, and was surprised to see a faint smile of curiosity mixed with desire play across the generous lips.

'Tomorrow?' Rhona repeated her offer.

'Yes! *Mañana* – I will return then. With Robert.' He bowed swiftly, then backed out of the room and walked briskly towards the main door. Angelo was half way down the driveway before he remembered Cameron had offered him a lift back to the cottage.

He quickened his pace and hoped he had not insulted anyone.

Ten

———

In the strange half-light, half-dark, Robert tramped along the coast road, whistling. Malcolm had been right: the shivers had felt more like the passing of a large juggernaut than an earthquake. But it had still been unnerving to feel the tremors beneath his feet with not so much as a bicycle in sight.

As he walked, the sound of the sea gently lapping against the shoreline to his right became almost hypnotic. He stopped whistling, listening to the soft whoosh of the waves and the determined crunch of his boots on the gravel surface. His body glowing with post-climactic energy, Robert felt he could walk for ever. Sleep was the last thing on a mind still filled with the tastes, smells and sensations of the broad red-haired fisherman. He broke into a jog.

On the left, jagged peaks crept into view, silhouetted against a grey-blue sky.

Robert found himself smiling.

In no time at all, the road curved up steeply and the sound of the waves faded.

Robert jogged on, slowing slightly as the incline increased. Ahead, he could see the sagging roof of Corrie Cottage.

Was Angelo home yet?

He laughed aloud. 'Home': less than twenty-four hours on

Kelpie Island, and he was almost unable to imagine ever living anywhere else.

Halfway up the hill he paused and looked back. Below, the sea was a distant, glassy millpond. Robert narrowed his eyes, searching the horizon for fishing boats.

The faint, pink line was empty. No engine sounds spoilt the vision of complete and utter stillness.

He turned and continued his way up the hill. His thoughts turned to his flatmate. For all his bravado and easy relaxed manner, Angelo was rather unworldly in so many ways. A faint feeling of guilt swept over him: he'd brought someone who was basically a green, country boy and a foreigner in a foreign land to an even more foreign land – and then abandoned him to the tender mercies of complete strangers! Robert began to run towards the building, feet pounding and sliding on loose grit.

What if Angelo had become lost on the way back from the ceilidh?

What if he'd fallen into a ditch, or – worse – over a cliff?

What if some drunken locals had mugged him?

Robert's heart pounded louder than his feet as he remembered the youth with the airgun.

What if –?

Reaching the cottage, he wrenched the door open and stared frantically inside.

Empty!

He dashed back outside and ran to the edge of the tall cliff, eyes darting along the road below. The ceilidh must have finished hours ago. There was only one road up to the cottage, and Robert hadn't passed another living creature, let alone Angelo.

He rubbed his face. Thoughts of police launches and hill searches burst into his mind. He saw himself, pale and drawn, waiting with mounting trepidation as an army of local stalwarts, Malcolm at their head, unloaded their fishing nets to reveal the drowned, beautiful body of –

A noise crept into his ears over the thump of his worried heart. Robert slowly turned his head towards the sound.

Humming, which grew in volume as Robert moved towards the outhouses.

Then the humming burst into a jaunty song.

Spanish words broke over him in a wave of relief. Robert gripped the handle of the outhouse door and hauled it open.

The sound of running water and singing swelled out. From under the shower-head, a coffee-coloured face grinned at him. 'I wondered where you'd got to!'

Anger distorted feelings of relief. 'Where I'd got to? You were the one who ran off!'

Angelo laughed. 'Me? The last thing I saw was you and that big fisherman dragging each other out of the cay-lee.'

Robert watched as Angelo nonchalantly continued to wash his handsome body. The shower-stall had no door, and every soapy inch of Argentinian manhood was clearly outlined by the beams from a torch jammed behind the shower-head. He scowled. 'I'm surprised you noticed anything, you were so wrapped up in that couple.' He moved closer, anger mutating into an equally hot emotion.

Shoulders braced against the back of the outhouse, Angelo parted well-muscled thighs and lathered his cock and balls. 'You mean Cameron and Rhona?'

'Oh, it's Cameron and Rhona now, is it?' Robert's snort was tinged with desire as his eyes fixed themselves on the thick length of Angelo's shaft. 'To everyone else it's the Laird and Lady Laird, but to you they're Cameron and Rhona!' He knew he was being irrational. He knew, at the ceilidh, he had only had eyes for Malcolm's brawny body.

'Actually, he likes to be called Cammie.'

Robert watched the way his flatmate handled the heavy ball-sac, parting wet, shiny thighs to wash underneath. His own cock, still sticky from his time with Malcolm, was pressing urgently against the zip of his shorts. 'Cammie, indeed!'

Angelo rinsed his groin, then grabbed the bar of soap and reached around. 'Yes, Cammie. They are very nice people, Robert – very friendly and hospitable.'

Robert's jaw dropped and his nipples tingled as Angelo half-turned and began to soap between his arse-cheeks. 'You and I were supposed to be going for a meal. I was hungry. Cammie and Rhona gave me something to eat.'

Robert's mouth snapped shut. At that precise moment in time, he hated Rhona and Cameron Dunbar more than any other two people on earth.

And he wanted Angelo's thick cock inside him more than he'd ever wanted anything else in his life.

Knees bent, one arm braced against the side of the outhouse, Angelo continued to wash.

Embarrassment joined the lust. Robert's face flushed up: he felt annoyed and aroused and awkward and foolish all at the same time.

Low humming competed with the sound of water on stone and flesh. The wet, glossy head was lowered.

Robert watched the way his flatmate's hands soaped the deep, dark crevice. Then: 'Have you eaten?' Angelo began to rinse, placing the soap back in its holder.

The small bar slipped onto the floor. Mutely, Robert sank to a crouch. One hand snaked between two broad feet. He gripped the soap, staring at the four ebony hairs which adhered to its soft surface.

'Have you?'

'What?' Robert's eyes darted upwards.

Angelo was towering over him, wet and glistening.

Robert swallowed hard, eyes level with his flatmate's large bollocks.

Angelo reached down, plucked the soap from Robert's slippery fingers and laughed. 'You've been fishing!' He winked, grabbed a towel from a hook on the wall and brushed past.

Robert stood up, sniffed himself. Then laughed. His flatmate had a talent for defusing tension – tension he himself was usually responsible for causing. 'It's that obvious?'

The Argentinian dried himself briskly. 'You smell like a tuna-canning factory!' He nodded to where the shower was still running. 'The water's quite warm now – must be a thermal spring.'

Robert began to undress, imagining those liquid brown eyes on his naked body as he washed the last traces of Malcolm and his fishing-nets from his skin.

The curly head was buried in soft folds of towelling.

Robert kicked off boots and socks, eyes fixed on Angelo's heavy cock which swayed languidly from side to side as the man dried his hair.

Hot water. A soothing wash. Angelo watching.

The coffee-coloured face appeared from the towel, grinning. Angelo grabbed the soap, thrust it at him. 'Go on – before the warm water runs away.'

Robert's hot skin tingled. Was it his imagination or was there something new in the words? His flatmate was lingering in the outhouse, almost looking for an excuse to hang around and watch him wash. He smiled, hooked thumbs into the waistband of briefs and revealing the half-hardness within. Eyes never leaving Angelo's smiling face, Robert stepped under pounding jets – and roared as gallons of icy water flooded down over his head and shoulders.

Angelo's chuckles cut through gasps and shivers.

Robert tried to leap from under the shower-head.

Strong hands gripped his shoulders, holding him there.

Robert spat near-zero water from his mouth. 'You bastard!'

Angelo was shaking with laughter. 'It will feel warmer soon. Really.' He grinned good-humouredly. 'Now get clean, and I'll make you a sandwich.' With a mock-punch to the side of his dripping head, Angelo turned and strolled naked from the outhouse.

Robert stood there, seething. But he could never stay angry with Angelo for long. Slowly, his lips relaxed into a half-smile. The water did seem to be getting warmer. He stared down at his now-shrivelled cock, laughed and began to wash.

Half an hour later he was munching his fourth sandwich. Hunger had been the last thing on his mind, but the first bite had brought his appetite back with a vengeance.

They both sat cross-legged on the cottage's stone floor, dressed only in T-shirts and underwear.

Angelo smiled across at him from over the brim of a coffee-cup. 'Is he nice?'

Robert took another bite, chewed. 'Who?'

'Your fisherman.'

Robert swallowed, wiping his mouth on the back of his hand. His shoulders twitched into a shrug. 'He's OK.' Curiosity pricked at the back of his mind. 'Is she . . . nice?' He still couldn't bring himself to say the woman's name, but at least he could now introduce her into the conversation without scowling.

'Who?' Angelo sipped his coffee, bathed in candle-glow.

Robert laughed. 'Mrs Laird, or whatever her name is!'

Angelo grinned lopsidedly. 'Rhona is Cameron's sister.'

'Ah.' He felt the now-familiar green-tinged emotion tug at his guts. Robert pushed it firmly away and fixed a friendly, disinterested smile to his lips. 'So did you get to use your condoms?'

Angelo looked appalled. Suddenly he was on his feet. 'Rhona is a very noble lady! I would never presume to –'

'Hey, calm down!' Robert slapped a hairy, muscular calf. 'I didn't mean to imply anything!'

The coffee-coloured face stared down at him.

Robert stared up, saw confusion and anguish in the deep brown eyes. The tall Lady Laird was evidently something of a prickly issue. He sighed: the last thing he needed was a love-lorn Argentinian moping around for the rest of their stay. Time for a subject change. Robert stuffed the last of his sandwich into his mouth and jumped to his feet. 'So you don't think there's much work needing done?'

Angelo regarded him curiously.

'Here, I mean!' Robert patted one of the large struts which held the roof in place.

'Ah.' Angelo joined him at the east wall of the cottage. He began to tap, working his way up and along the stone surface.

Robert followed.

When he'd tapped and listened around the entire four walls, Angelo dragged a table into the centre of the room and climbed onto it.

Robert passed him a candle, staring up past the flame into dark rafters. 'Well?'

His flatmate peered up, then jumped down. 'No, I don't think so – it's a little damp, but nothing serious. Yet.'

Robert heard the foreboding in the word.

Angelo perched on the edge of the table, sinewy legs braced. 'Don't worry. The sagging you can see from outside may just be age. We'll probably only need to replace the guttering, and perhaps a new roan pipe.'

Robert perked up.

'I'll get a better idea of the state of things when we remove the slates tomorrow.'

Robert felt his heart sink again. 'That sounds like a big job.'

Angelo shook his head. 'Might not be – if you can go to the village and get supplies, I'll make an early start.' He smiled, lying a hand on Robert's shoulder.

Robert felt uncomfortable. Angelo was going to so much trouble, and all he could do was harbour lustful ideas and get jealous every time his flatmate looked at a woman! He moved away from the reassuring hand before it started to have its usual effect on him. 'Make a list of what you need.' He mock-bowed. 'I'm now officially a builder's mate.'

Angelo laughed, pulling his T-shirt over his head. 'Builders need lots of sleep.'

Robert glimpsed large, brown nipples just before his flatmate blew out the candle and turned to extinguish the others.

'I insist you take the bed tonight.'

Robert could only nod: it had been on the tip of his tongue to suggest they double-up, but he couldn't guarantee that same tip wouldn't be more interested in exploring other possibilities.

Slowly, the large room returned to semi-darkness.

His sense returned with the night. In the gloom, Robert watched as Angelo's shape grabbed a blanket from the bed and wrapped it around himself.

'An early start, remember – goodnight, my friend.' Angelo sounded relaxed and at ease.

Robert managed a laugh. 'Night – but I bet I'm up first.' As he walked slowly towards the bed, the drag of his lengthening cock against his thigh shot a renewed shiver of lust through his body.

The sun was already high in the sky by the time he staggered from the bed and outside into fresh morning air.

Angelo had dragged the table and two chairs from the cottage and was sitting on one, head bent.

Robert yawned.

Angelo turned. 'I win the bet – you make dinner tonight.' He nodded to a polythene-covered box in the shade beneath one boarded-up window.

Robert rubbed his eyes, crouched and flicked back the covering.

Angelo talked on. 'Another present – from your friend with the boat, I think.'

Robert stared at three neatly gutted and filleted fish. Another yawn settled into a smile as he remembered Malcolm and last night's activities on the deck of the *Kelpie*. He recovered the box and walked to join Angelo.

A large hand pushed a pot of coffee towards him. 'Sleep well?'

Robert stretched, eyes following his arms upwards into a cloudless, blue sky. 'Very well.' It was true. Lulled into unconsciousness by a combination of Angelo's body smells and memories of Malcolm, his sleep had been deep and soundless. 'What happened to all that rain Scotland's suppose to get?'

Angelo tapped a pencil on the table-top. 'The weather knows we're here, perhaps, and doesn't want to spoil our holiday.'

Robert guffawed. 'Even you're starting to sound like an islander!'

Angelo looked perplexed.

Robert poured coffee into a mug then leant back in his chair. He swept an expansive arm around the imposing vista. 'All this is rubbing off on me already. I can barely remember London.'

Understanding broke onto the handsome face. 'Mmmm – I know what you mean. It's like –' he searched for the phrase '– coming home, yes?'

In the distance, seagulls called. A soft breeze drifted in from the North Atlantic. Robert closed his eyes contentedly. Angelo's voice was low. 'I feel more part of this community than I ever felt in London – or the country where I was born, for that matter.'

Something in the words made Robert open his eyes. Recalling several veiled references on the journey to Fort William, he stared at the suddenly wistful face. 'Want to talk about it?'

The question broke the spell, and Robert could have kicked himself.

Angelo lowered his head and continued to scribble on the notepad in front of him. 'No, but I do want you to go into the village and get me these.' He tore off then slid the sheet of paper across the table-top.

Robert took it, eyes scanning the neat handwriting. When he looked up, his flatmate had moved and was now standing, staring out over the horizon. Robert frowned. What was the big mystery? Had Angelo got some local girl pregnant, been exiled in shame? What was the enigmatic 'disgrace' to which he had referred on the train? He pushed his curiosity to the back of his mind.

None of his business, anyway. 'OK – any idea how much this lot is liable to come to?'

Angelo didn't reply.

Robert shrugged, finished his coffee. As he grabbed his jacket and began to walk into the village, he hoped the local ironmonger accepted credit cards.

He strode along the coast road, following the same route they had taken last night. Out at sea, a few fishing boats were making their way back towards the pier, which curved out into the vast blue millpond, a mile or so ahead. Robert wondered if the *Kelpie* was amongst the little flotilla, then remembered the box of fish and knew the tall redhead must have returned home hours ago.

In the fields which lined the right-hand side of the road, potato-pickers took a rest from their work to give him a wave.

Robert returned the salute.

The islanders were more visible this morning – and friendlier than ever. A group of women, drying fish on the rocky beach above high water mark, shouted 'good mornings', then returned to their task.

Robert answered, his mind turning to his own profession. He'd packed paper and pencils, but there hadn't been time yet to sit down and see whether the island could work the same magic on his writer's block which it was conjuring around his frame of mind.

So the cottage was ramshackle.

So – despite Angelo's tactfulness – it would take a small fortune he didn't have to repair it.

For some reason, it didn't matter. Robert grinned into sweet island air and had his grin returned by a group of passing villagers on bicycles.

All that mattered was that he and Angelo enjoy their stay here.

Robert followed the road as it turned up into the hills.

And if their first night was anything to go by, enjoyment was Kelpie Island's middle name.

The highlands were even more striking in full daylight than they had been the previous evening. Robert stared up at purplish-brown crags and peaks, their heather coating set off by the blue, cloudless sky behind.

Although bright, the sun had none of its London fierceness and gently warmed his neck and bare arms as he climbed further up. But the incline was steeper than it looked.

After fifteen minutes or so, he paused, resting against the moss-covered rocks of a dry-stone wall. As he waited for his breath to return to normal, Robert inhaled the sweet smell of honeysuckle.

Far above the industry of the coast, the hilly road was as silent as ever, except for the low hum of bees in the blossoms by his side.

He hauled himself onto the wall and stared between the trees of the wood opposite. At times like this, it was hard to believe there was anyone else on the island.

Then something flashed in the undergrowth. Robert blinked, narrowing his eyes. The sun behind his head was glinting off some object fifteen or twenty yards into the wood.

Robert levered himself from the wall and crossed the road. He recalled the blond youth with the airgun from last night, and frowned. Although there were no shots this time, as he watched sun reflect from deep in the forest, he remembered what Hamish Campbell had told him and knew young Fingal was up to no good. Feeling almost resentful at the youth's malevolent intrusion on such a heavenly day, Robert pushed his way into the bushes.

Eleven

Robert strode purposefully into the woods, ears pricked for the telltale sounds of shattering glass or the ping of a target missed. He was now virtually a resident of Kelpie Island, after all, and anything which was causing a problem for the locals was his problem too.

The sulky, sneering face from the ceilidh emblazoned itself on his mind. Despite the delinquent Fingal's beautiful features, he was coming round to the opinion that PC Campbell was right. The angelic-looking youth needed a good talking-to.

Ahead, the sun continued to reflect off something shiny and golden.

His resolve grew. He marched through thick bushes and swept bramble briers away from his path. Robert stopped a few feet from the same clearing where he and Angelo had watched last night's target practice. The sun had moved, and the golden flashes were no longer obscuring his vision. He blinked.

A heap of clothes lay on top of a tree-stump.

Robert's eyes swivelled left.

Leaning against the same uprooted trunk on which an array of bottles had been balanced the previous evening, was a pale vision, topped by a straggling crown of blond hair which glinted in the sunshine.

A pale naked vision.

Robert took in the sight.

Fingal was taller without his leather jacket and slouching demeanour. He also looked older and younger at the same time. The angelic face was tilted up towards the sky, bathing itself in the sun's warmth. Light-blue veins stood out on the long neck, merging into long, subtly developed muscle over broad shoulders. The light shone on trails of sweat which tracked Fingal's skin, drenching his body in a golden glow. Arms braced against the tree-trunk, bare feet planted amidst the leaves and moss of the forest floor, the youth arched his back in obvious pleasure.

Robert's eyes moved over the smooth, hairless chest, pausing at two tiny, almost flat, pink nipples which thrust themselves heavenwards. His own hard buds were suddenly straining inside his work-shirt. He sank to a crouch.

Surrounded by greenery and the background of trees, Fingal resembled an ethereal wood-sprite, languidly sunning himself. Caught up in his own thoughts, the youth hadn't heard Robert's noisy journey from the road. This was another Fingal – a fantasy twin, who only emerged within the safety and privacy of his very own dream-like glade.

Robert stared, entranced by the other-worldly tableau. He held his breath, not wanting to exhale in case he blew the airy vision away. Then his eyes settled on something all-too solid.

Lying in the hollow beside Fingal's right hip-bone, sprouting up from the bushy blondness between his splayed thighs, a heavy, flaccid cock was also enjoying the sunshine.

Robert stifled a groan, one hand moving to between his thighs and the tightening he could feel there.

The naked vision remained perfectly still, like a detail in a painting. Around him, birds chirped and called to each other. The flutter of wings in the canopy of branches above was the only movement.

Abruptly, Fingal roused himself. He moved slowly at first, swaying with his arms outstretched as he strolled to touch the branches of bushes and shrubs. Then he began to dance.

Robert watched the rhythmic steps, admiring the half-man, half-boy's grace.

Long limbs loped elegantly and unselfconsciously. Fingal threw his arms wider, as if he were trying to embrace everything around him. Large feet moved with an easy dignity from this tree to that. Tangled blond curls fell over the man-boy's shoulders. The angelic face remained focused on something up beyond the trees. A thick tube of flesh slapped resoundingly against one thigh, then the other, with each sway and twist of his body.

Robert's eyes were fixed on the mercurial performance.

The boy moved from an open-armed position to its mirror image. Fingal hugged himself, running hands up and down over his ribs and began to rotate. His head was lowered now, a curtain of gold falling to obscure the perfect face. The youth pirouetted three times, sinking lower and lower with each corkscrew move- ment until he was crouched in the clearing, a compact bundle of pale skin and golden hair. Then, as if in response to the climax of some music only he could hear, Fingal threw out his arms and leapt into the air. Legs splayed as he jumped, his cock swinging between parted thighs.

Robert stared at the flailing vision. His guts churned with lust. He wanted to tear off his clothes and join in.

Unexpectedly, whatever unheard music was guiding the dance changed emphasis.

The youth quickened his steps, weaving between thorny bracken. He swooped from this bush to that, seizing handfuls of leaves. Long fingers tossed flakes of greenery into the air. Whoops of joy filled the clearing as bramble and blaeberry leaves rained down onto the dappled ground.

The man-boy was moving faster now, darting in and out between trees as if he was chasing something.

Or something was chasing him.

Fingal dipped to the ground and seized a long, pliable-looking branch, which he swung above his head with a wild cry. A wiry arm brandished the ash switch, slashing at passing briers and bushes.

The pace of the performance increased until Robert's head sang with the sound of feet on leaves, the swish of the branch through the air and the slap of engorging cock-flesh on stomach-flesh.

Fingal's strange tribute to nature was becoming increasingly frenzied.

The breath caught in Robert's throat as a new sound joined the others. He almost felt the sting as the man-boy suddenly brought the pliable bough down hard across his pale, hairless chest.

The youth was galloping freely now, swatting his upper body until the flawless skin on his chest and shoulders was a zebra's coat of thin, red welts. With each flick of the woody switch, Fingal's verve and abandon increased.

As Robert watched, balls sweating, the focus of the thrashing changed and the switch was criss-crossing lower, lashing pale thighs and legs.

The whack of wood on skin shimmered in the air.

One lightly muscled arm held high above his head, Fingal drew the limb back further then brought the branch down hard across the length of his semi-erect cock.

Robert wanted to close his eyes, but couldn't.

The man-boy thrashed his groin again.

Robert winced with each sharp swat, while his own hard length throbbed inside his shorts with an unexpected desire. Transfixed by the crotch-whipping, he saw that with every whack the rod of flesh between Fingal's slim thighs grew a little harder until it jutted out and up from the bush of wiry blond hair.

The youth danced on, covering the ground in leaps and jumps. He threw himself into the air, bringing the birch down hard across his lengthening prick each time he landed.

Robert could hear the sound of his own heavy breathing over the sound of wood on flesh and Fingal's increasingly aroused whoops and cries.

When the man-boy finally hurled the branch into a bramble bush, the flesh protruding from the blond bush was thicker and more turgid than ever.

The dance increased in speed and intensity. Every now and then as the youth raced out from behind a tree, Robert caught a glimpse of the striking face.

Fingal's golden hair plastered itself to his sweating skin. His blue eyes were wide and staring, pupils huge. Nostrils flared with exertion. The youth's full lips were parted in something which was neither smile nor frown but beyond both.

The figure had become a dervish, swirling and stamping then swaying and gliding by turns. Quicksilver fingers grabbed at a nearby elder bush. Fingal's other hand snatched a second trophy from a brier of blaeberries.

Robert's heart leapt as he saw redness seep from between one, then two clenched fists.

Fingal was dancing faster than ever, hurling himself into the air as he smeared his welted skin with the fruits of the forest.

The man-boy slapped palms against his chest, drawing his hands down over his stomach and into the golden V between his thighs. Scarlet and purple slashes streaked the long, lithe limbs.

The hair on the back of Robert's neck stood on end. He couldn't drag his eyes from the whirling athletics taking place mere yards away.

No longer part of some rustic idyll, Fingal was grunting now, moving with uneven strides. The previous elegance had been replaced by an animal-like gait. Two stained palms rubbed themselves over the perfect features and on into his hair. The swollen purplish-red head of the youth's thick cock was picked up by every berry stain which now painted most of his body. In seconds, the transformation was complete: the swaying blond angel gave way to a loping red devil.

A bare foot impacted with a dead branch and kicked it into the air.

Then as suddenly as the manic dance had started, it stopped. Fingal threw himself against the trunk of a tree, scarlet-stained hands gripping the angry rod of flesh which sprouted from the pink-tinged pubes. The man-boy began to fondle his cock ferociously. His blond head lolled forward, hair obliterating his face but Robert could still hear the growls and gasps of a man on the verge of ecstasy.

The red-streaked chest rose and fell violently. Long muscles on the boyish arms stood out as Fingal dragged frantically on the length of pulsing man-flesh between his thighs. He threw his head back, face tilted upwards. The man-boy stood there, features creased in concentration. He stared intensely towards Robert.

Robert flinched as their eyes met momentarily. But the man-boy's gaze was unfocused, and Robert realised Fingal was too absorbed in his own need to register another presence in the glade with him.

Abruptly, his fist pausing at the engorged head of his swollen cock, the youth flipped around and began to thrust against the trunk of the tree.

Robert watched heaving arse-cheeks clench then unclench. Breath caught in his throat.

Fingal's arms were wrapped around the broad trunk, fingers scraping on bark as he rubbed himself against the solid surface. Twin red-streaked hemispheres rose and fell with each thrust.

Robert's calf spasmed with cramp. Biting back a yelp, he staggered to his feet. Despite the pain, he remained transfixed by the rutting figure, rooted by the hot arrows of desire which pierced his own groin.

Fingal fucked the tree desperately with a need as other-worldly as Robert's first view of him had been, thrusting his groin urgently against the mossy bark.

Rubbing his right leg, Robert stifled a moan.

The man-boy drove his way towards climax.

Robert stared at the berry-stained back, eyes moving down to the clenched arse-cheeks and quivering thighs.

Fingal's knees were bent. Two hard mounds thrust forward then up in a scooping movement, as if the youth was trying to gouge a hole in the tall tree.

Robert staggered left until he was standing side-on to the boy-tree coupling.

Seconds later, the beating of wings filled the clearing as a flock of birds suddenly took flight from upper branches. Fingal's howl of release reverberated in Robert's own cock. On the verge himself, he watched open-mouthed as the man-boy pressed his face to rough bark and shot against the trunk in short, jerky movements.

Still entwined with the towering tree, Fingal slid slowly down. He slumped backwards, sprawling amongst fallen leaves. Arms once more stretched outwards, the spent, red-stained body faced the sky and offered itself.

Robert stared at a darker section of the tree, where Fingal's spunk now smeared the bark. Then he turned and made his way back to the road on rubber legs, unsure of what he had just witnessed but unable to deny the effect it had had on him.

The remainder of his journey passed quickly. Robert shook his tousled blond head several times, partly in disbelief at what he had just witnessed, partly to dislodge the unsettlingly erotic thoughts which still teased his mind.

He tugged Angelo's list from his pocket and scanned it.

Two pounds of three-and-a-half-inch tile nails.

One pound of masonry nails – four inch.

Three pounds of headless timber tacks.

Tarpaulin – nine square yards.

Two gross slate roofing tiles.

As he descended the hill into the village, a large figure on the other side of the road raised a massive hand in salute.

Robert returned the gesture, taking in the blacksmith's enormous bulk.

Last night, in the confines of the village hall, Douglas McVey had seemed a larger than life character. To see the giant of a man in broad daylight and the open air was to appreciate the sheer bulk of the man.

Robert stared after the blacksmith, who was carrying a huge holdall. Tattooed biceps and forearms bulged in the morning sunshine. Various implements hung from a broad belt which was slung low around surprisingly narrow hips. Robert blinked, thinking of Vulcan himself as Douglas McVey ambled up the steep incline. As the blacksmith approached the brow of the hill it dawned on Robert this was probably the best man to help him.

He shouted.

Douglas ambled on, oblivious.

Robert shouted again, hands cupped around his mouth to help carry the request.

The blacksmith disappeared from sight.

Robert sighed, then turned back to the village and began to search for an ironmonger's.

Fifteen minutes later, thanks to helpful directions from almost everyone he'd asked, Robert stood in front of a small shop. The legend above a closed and locked door read 'D. McVey'. He peered more closely, looking for an Opening Times sign. But as with the other few establishments which made up the main street, Douglas McVey's ironmongers seemed to open and close when the owner felt like it.

Robert shoved his hands in to his pockets and sat down on a nearby wall. He was thirsty from the walk. His feet ached a little, but he didn't want to return to Angelo empty-handed. He frowned, kicking his heels against the wall and staring disconsolately at the ground: his first day as a builder's mate wasn't getting off to much of a start.

'Stop that immediately!'

Robert flinched at the words. His feet hovered inches from the dry-stone surface. He looked up and found himself pinned by a pair of iron-grey eyes.

Miss Nicol's stern expression softened. 'Ah, Mr McLeod – I didn't recognise you there.' The schoolteacher was wearing a smart tweed two-piece. Her grey eyes were still shot with steel.

Robert leapt off the wall. 'Sorry, I –'

'Over three hundred years old, this wall.' A neat hand patted the ancient stone. 'And it will stand for another three hundred, if the tremors –' She regarded him solemnly '– and the vandals leave it alone.'

'Oh – sorry, I – er –' Robert's tongue was tying itself in knots.

Miss Nicol smiled, waving away his halting apology. 'You weren't to know, Mr McLeod.'

'Robert, please.' He stared dry-mouthed at the petite figure and wondered what it was about the woman's tone which made him feel fourteen again. 'And I'm truly sorry.' He kicked a few loose scraps of crumbling stone into the side of the wall and hoped she didn't notice.

'That's all right, Robert.' If she did, Miss Nicol made no comment – nor did she make any attempt to provide him with her first name. Her tone became more soothing, something which Robert found even more intimidating than her previously harsh words. 'What brings you to the village? I would have thought you and your handsome friend would be busy, this beautiful morning.'

He flinched again. Was that a wink, or did Miss Nicol have a speck of dust in one of those steely eyes? Before he knew what he was doing, Robert found himself retelling the whole roof saga.

The schoolteacher listened sympathetically, nodding from time to time.

'And so I have this –' Robert fumbled in his pocket, then held out Angelo's now much-crumpled piece of paper '– and nowhere to buy anything.'

Miss Nicol took the list, pewter eyes quickly absorbing the details.

Robert shuffled uncomfortably from one foot to the other. Why did he feel like he'd just been caught smoking behind the bicycle-shed – or worse?

'Not to worry, Robert – I might be able to help you.'

He looked up, surprised.

The schoolteacher's laugh was even more disconcerting than her offer of assistance. The sound tinkled in his ears and increased his discomfort.

Miss Nicol clarified. 'We had some work done to the school roof, recently – the builders left behind sacks of surplus supplies and several boxes of tiles. I'm sure there will be at least something amongst them to make your journey this morning worthwhile.' She turned and began to walk briskly away from Douglas McVey's ironmongery shop.

The words 'Yes, miss' sprang involuntarily to his lips. Robert fell in behind.

The village school was a small, Victorian building with a pristine roof of shining, new-looking slate tiles.

Miss Nicol removed a large bundle of keys from the pocket of her tweed jacket and opened a large door.

The smell hit him immediately: floor polish, school dinners and the rubbery/canvas scent of old plimsolls.

Ahead, Miss Nicol's sensible square-toed brogues slapped soundly on ancient linoleum. Her curt, no-nonsense tones sliced through his thoughts as they walked past several oak doors with frosted glass panels. 'Wait in here, Robert.' She unlocked a second door, held it open.

He shuffled into the room, heart thumping as the door closed behind him. He stared around, taking in the orderly rows of desks and chairs. The walls of the schoolroom were decorated with maps of the world and ordinance survey charts of what looked like Kelpie Island itself. From the ceiling above, two antiquated striplights hung suspended. He turned and found himself facing the blackboard and the large desk which stood in front. Legs turning to water, he stumbled towards it.

The smells were stronger in here. Robert closed his eyes and inhaled the floury odour of chalk dust and the dry smell of cloth-bound exercise books. But it was the undertone of ancient, well-worn leather which hit home most powerfully. In a matter of minutes Robert was back in Form Three of Nottingham Second-ary School – specifically, the room of Mr MacTavish, the geography teacher.

His cock twitched at the memory. He could remember little of Mr MacTavish himself, apart from a strong Scottish accent and the stench of of pipe-tobacco. But the sensations he'd experienced waiting outside Mr MacTavish's room returned to arouse him a decade and a half later.

Robert groaned. A tingle spread over the cheeks of his arse, travelling up to his face. One hand darted to the tenting crotch of his shorts and the half-hard member stretching itself there. His breath was coming in huge gulps, blotting out everything except the sound of his struggling lungs.

'What are you up to?'

His eyelids shot open. Robert spun round.

Miss Nicol was carrying a large box, eyes fixed accusingly on his.

Embarrassment burned his skin. 'Nothing! I –'

'You have the look of a boy who is hiding something.' She placed the box on the floor and closed the door.

Guilt scorched itself on his face. Robert tried to turn away. A surprisingly strong hand gripped his chin.

'Tell me what you were thinking about, or it will be all the worse for you, Robert.'

Skin on fire, he could only obey. Robert struggled for words. A trickle of sweat ran from his left armpit, evaporating somewhere around the waistband of his shorts. Every inch of his skin prickled with embarrassment as he stared at the floor, rubbing at a spot on the worn linoleum with the toe of his boot. 'I – er –'

'Speak up!'

He gulped. 'There was someone – when I was at school –' His throat tightened. Robert coughed, trying to clear it.

'And?'

His heart hammered in his chest. Robert's slick fingers twisted at fabric.

'Hands out of pockets, boy!'

Robert flinched and obeyed, wiping damp palms on the thighs of his shorts.

'That's better. Now tell me about this "someone".' Miss Nicol's voice was briskly authoritative.

He took a deep breath, trying to give himself time. But the action only succeeded in filling his head with more smells and unleashing more memories. His balls were sweating now. Robert exhaled more than just air. 'Johnny Fisher. He was three years above me.' Just saying a name he'd not thought let alone spoken for almost two decades made his heart thump harder than ever. It also cracked the dam he'd built around those years. Words flooded out. 'Johnny was captain of the rugby first eleven, president of the debating society, head boy.' Something fizzed in his ears. He talked on, through the noise.

'Johnny was tall and not particularly handsome. His nose had been broken during a match against a rival school, but he was the most beautiful man I had ever seen. He was nice, too – Johnny hated bullying, and if he found any of that sort of thing, he came down hard on the culprits.'

His voice cracked. The years swept away and he was fourteen again, trembling with shame. But Robert couldn't stop talking.

'I tried out for the second eleven, joined the debating society – did everything I could just to be near him. But Johnny didn't know I existed. I knew I couldn't have him – someone like him wouldn't notice someone like me.' Sweat gathered on his forehead, plastering his hair to his face and dripping into one eye. Robert wiped it away. His guts churned. 'So I had to make do with what was Johnny's.' He looked up, skin burning. 'Please can I go now?'

Miss Nicol regarded him with faintly amused curiosity. 'Not yet, boy. I want to hear it all.'

Robert blinked rapidly, then looked back down at his feet. Rooted to the spot, sweating with embarrassment, he continued.

'I took his pen. No one noticed. It was much like any other pen. But it was special to me because it was his.'

He remembered fondling the biro, caressing then rubbing the implement between hot palms in his room at night and thinking that Johnny's fingers had gripped the pen the way Robert longed to have Johnny grip him.

'I took a bar of soap he'd used.' Heat from his face travelled down over shoulders and chest. Robert was amazed something which had happened so long ago could still affect him. He'd hidden the rough bar of red soap under his bed, sleeping with it crushed in one fist, until his mother had found it amidst rumpled bed-sheets and thrown it away. To this day, the harsh scent of carbolic made his nipples ache.

'Then I took his –' He broke off, wanting to run from the room. The half-hardness inside his boxers refused to let him.

'Spit it out, boy!' Miss Nicol's words bristled with impatience.

Robert's response was whispered. 'I stole Johnny Fisher's jock-strap.'

'Don't mumble!'

Robert's head shot up with such force that jangled nerves

tingled at the back of his neck. He shouted the words. 'I stole it! I stole Johnny Fisher's jockstrap!' Defiance mixed with shame and cooked a heady brew. Beyond the geography classroom in this school on Kelpie Island, Robert was reliving the sequence of events all over again.

Disgust painting his moustached face, Mr MacTavish strode to the door and opened it.

Robert wanted to find the deepest mine-shaft in Nottinghamshire and throw himself down it.

Johnny Fisher walked into the room.

Robert couldn't look at the face which permeated his dreams and haunted every waking hour. He couldn't look at Mr Mac-Tavish. So he looked at the floor. A solemn voice soared past his lowered head: 'Is this yours, Fisher?'

In his mind's eyes, Robert saw the item dangling from Mr MacTavish's fingers. He saw the elasticised sports-support, off-white straps connecting an adjustable waistband and a jersey pouch still warm from where Johnny's cock and bollocks had nestled during that morning's rugby practice.

The same jockstrap he had carried in the inside pocket of his school blazer until a search for late homework had tugged the beloved object from its hiding place for all to see.

His already crimson face flushed a more excruciating red. Johnny's mildly surprised voice sliced into his torment and doubled his humiliation.

'Don't think so – mine's in with the rest of my sports kit.'

'Take a closer look, Fisher.'

Praying for the floor to open up and swallow him, Robert heard Johnny's footsteps on worn linoleum. Then more surprise filled the rich voice: 'Oh yes – this is mine. There's the stitching I ripped when I was in too much of a hurry undressing last week.'

Robert groaned, remembering the way he had run his fingers over the join between crotch-piece and arse-straps.

'I was sure I packed it away with my rugby kit.' Surprise gave way to confusion. 'How did it get here?'

Robert's abasement was almost complete. Mortified, he tried to close his ears as Mr MacTavish retold the details of how Robert

McLeod had reached furtively into Johnny Fisher's sports bag and extracted the soiled garment from between the folds of a First Eleven jersey. Then the stern voice took on a more directly chastening tone.

'You have stolen from another, McLeod. It is only fitting that the wronged party be present when you receive your punishment.'

Robert's knees began to shake. He was going to be sick. Blood fizzled in his ears. Standing there, cringing and ashamed before the boy he desired most in the world was greater punishment than any disciplinary action Mr MacTavish could choose to take.

'You are a disgusting creature.' Miss Nicol's voice brought him back to the present. Robert could only nod in agreement. The sound of a drawer opening made him raise his head.

On the other side of the desk, the small woman with the iron-grey hair and the steely eyes was now holding an eighteen-inch length of thick brown leather.

Blood fled from Robert's face. His cock hardened further. He stared at the tawse, remembering its rigidity and stiffness.

Other teachers preferred the writing of lines, or detaining the guilty after school as means of punishment. But Mr MacTavish favoured the corporal variety – specifically, the traditional Scottish tawse. It was rumoured that he soaked his in a bowl of salt water, once a week, to keep it hard and inflexible.

Robert's Adam's apple bobbled convulsively. The leather strap in Miss Nicol's hand was new and unwieldy-looking. Its length poked up into the air, fanning out slightly so that he could see the two distinct fingers of tanned hide.

'You know what to do, Robert.'

He knew only too well what was expected of him. Fingers fumbling with the zip, Robert wrenched his shorts down over his thighs. He tugged at his boxers, but his hard, aching cock was caught in the fly and he had to lift the waistband up and over its stiff length.

Robert stared down at his erect cock, remembering his shame, fourteen years earlier, when Mr MacTavish had commanded him to take down his shorts and prepare to receive his punishment like a man.

'Bend over!'

Robert leant forward, slippery palms gripping just above his kneecaps. The bare cheeks of his arse quivered. Trapped between stomach and thigh, the head of his cock pushed at the tight foreskin.

'This is for your insolence.'

The first stroke of the tawse made him gasp and retreat from the crack of leather on flesh as it resounded in the still air of the classroom. He could imagine how he looked: a grown man, arse exposed and vulnerable under the scornful onslaught from this tiny woman. The thought made his hole spasm. Robert heard the sound of an arm drawn back. He braced himself.

The second stung more sharply, slapping heavily across both cheeks. Robert whimpered, fingers digging into the skin around his kneecaps. Head hanging between his legs, he stared at the floor as stars spangled before his eyes.

The third made him flinch. Robert inhaled sharply, biting his lip to stop himself crying out.

As the fourth stroke of chastisement impacted on his reddening arse a sob escaped from his mouth.

He felt the fifth and six somewhere deep inside his brain, in a place where he knew no pride, no shame – nothing, except the sensations which churned in his guts and threatened to send him coming all over Miss Nicol's well-polished floor. Stiff warm leather touched the back of his neck.

'Cover yourself, boy.'

Robert staggered slightly, then hauled up his shorts, flinching as the fabric dragged over his tender rear-end. He turned.

Miss Nicol was smiling at him. 'Let that be a warning, Robert. There is a time and place for arousal – and my classroom is neither.' She nodded towards the large box beside the door. 'I trust you will find something there to help with your roof.'

'Yes, miss! Thank you, miss!' Robert scurried backwards in the direction of the exit. He wasn't quite sure if he was expressing gratitude for the building supplies or the six of the best the faintly amused looking schoolteacher had meted out to him.

Miss Nicol nodded briefly, giving nothing more away.

Robert groped behind himself for the door handle, then seized the box and rushed from the building. As he ran up the village's main street, legs pumping and a box of building supplies clutched to his chest, his cock was still hard.

Twelve

_____

Overhead, the sun was making its way towards midday.

Angelo positioned the ladder against the front wall of Corrie Cottage, then leant on it to ensure it was steady. He checked his belt for the tools he would need, then tentatively mounted the first rung.

It gave a little under his weight, but held.

Angelo continued to climb. Drawing level with the edge of the roof, he paused to clear moss and the remnants of birds' nests from the ancient, cast-iron guttering. The downpipe was completely choked: there was more work involved here than he'd reckoned. Grabbing another soggy handful of leaves and twigs, he hurled them groundwards then rested an arm against the top rung of the ladder.

Even clearing the guttering was a going to be a two-man job.

Angelo stared over the sagging roof at the craggy mountains behind. He could just see the black/blue edge of the small loch behind the cottage.

He smiled ruefully. The water looked very inviting. Maybe later he and Robert could take a swim, before they went up to Castle Dunbar for an afternoon's riding. Angelo dragged his eyes from the tempting vista and returned to the task in hand.

He worked slowly but steadily. After half an hour or so, he had repositioned the ladder three times and cleared the entire front section of guttering.

'Need any help?'

Angelo looked down.

A vast mountain of a man stared up at him. 'Douglas McVey – Lady Rhona said you might be in need of some assistance.'

Angelo smiled, negotiating his progress back down the ladder. 'Thanks.' He held out a hand, then noticed it was caked with grime and made to wipe his palm on the back of his shorts.

Douglas was too quick for him. The blacksmith gripped Angelo's fist firmly. 'Nothing wrong with a bit of dirt, lad. The sign of good honest labour.'

Work-hardened skin rasped against his. Angelo smiled. 'If it's good honest labour you like, there's plenty to be done around here! I'm not sure we can pay you much, but –'

Douglas McVey's soft, bassy laugh drowned out the end of this sentence. 'Call it a welcome present.' He gave Angelo's fingers a final squeeze, then shrugged the large holdall from a large shoulder.

The bag clattered to the ground, spilling its contents.

Douglas crouched and spread the sides wide.

Angelo stared at the blacksmith's thick neck as the man lifted the tools of his trade and placed them in a neat row on the rocky ground. 'You are employed by Lady Rhona?'

The vast head and shoulders tilted upwards. Douglas nodded reverentially. 'That is my honour. Generations of McVeys have been ironmonger and blacksmith to the Dunbars of Kelpie Island.' He moved forward onto leather-covered knees and regarded Angelo with equal deference. 'I would be proud to serve you too, Caballo.'

'Well, I can't deny it would be good to have some help.' Angelo took a step back, wiping his hands on the tail of his shirt. 'If we can clear the guttering then maybe we can see exactly how much work needs to be done on the roof.' Angelo rubbed his palms together.

Douglas McVey straightened up. 'Sounds like a good idea.'

Angelo found himself dwarfed by the man's shadow. He stared from the giant of a blacksmith to the flimsy, half-rotted rungs of the ladder then up onto the sagging roof. Maybe this wasn't such a good idea after all. He hoped the Dunbars had Employee Liability insurance.

He needn't have worried.

A testament to the underlying sturdiness of the roof of Corrie Cottage and the large man's skill at distributing his weight, Douglas McVey was soon lying prostrate on the roof and hauling handfuls of debris from the guttering. Angelo used the ladder.

The two men worked well together. When the rusting pipe around the edge of the roof was free of obstacles, they started on the slates themselves. Perched on a plank of wood he had discovered in one of the outhouses, Douglas levered each slate loose with the ripper then tossed it down to Angelo, who divided the roofing material in two piles: one damaged, one undamaged.

The sun climbed higher in the sky as they worked on in comfortable silence. The wind dropped, and the only sound was the faint lap of waves on sand from the beach far below. After an hour, the top section of the roof was cleared. Now minus his shirt, and with a red bandana wrapped around his forehead to keep his sweaty hair out of his eyes, Angelo straddled the plank of wood beside Douglas and gazed through bevelled struts to the joists below. A deep voice rumbled at his side: 'Looks not too bad.'

'But how does it sound?' Angelo seized a hammer from his belt, leant down to tap a length of wood. He couldn't reach. 'Hold me steady.' Easing himself further down into the darkness of the cottage, he felt strong hands around his legs. One hand gripping a bevelled strut, he balanced his weight then delivered two sharp blows to a thick section of timber.

The responding thuds confirmed Douglas's opinion.

Angelo wriggled lower, feeling thick fingers edge down the inside of his thighs. He tapped a second joist.

Equally sound.

He grinned in the darkness. Replacing a few struts was a two-day job, at most. With a bit of luck, the roof could be repaired completely before their holiday was over. One arm braced against a concave strut, Angelo pushed himself back into daylight.

When he resurfaced, Douglas's leather waistcoat was draped over the chimney head and the man's solid, hairless chest gleamed with sweat. Angelo noticed the man's upper body was a mass of faded tattoos. Two twinkling rings glinted in fat, bullet-like nipples.

Overhead, the sun was a harder task-master than either had anticipated. 'Come on – we've earnt a break.'

Douglas nodded his large head, then began to make his way back to the ladder.

Relaxing against the cottage wall, Angelo refilled his own and Douglas's glass with more of the clear, ice-cold water he had drawn from the stone well. He stared at the blacksmith's broad, ink-decorated chest and vast hairy belly.

His attention was noted. Douglas smiled. 'Fifteen years in the merchant navy.' A huge finger indicated a blue anchor and chain which rippled on his right bicep. 'Served my time as a stoker, on the East Indies run.' The finger moved to the palm tree which glistened on his other forearm.

Angelo examined the outline of a horse which reared up from the waistband of heavy trousers, then grinned at the two naked women who stretched out a hand to each other across the blacksmith's sweat-slicked pectorals. 'Every picture tells a story, yes?'

Douglas laughed. 'The story of a man who spent half his time deep in the boiler rooms of cargo freighters and the other half in the tattoo-parlours of Jakarta!'

'I don't believe you.' Angelo winked. 'I've heard about those Sumatran girls.'

The blacksmith traced the red tongues of flame which licked around the horse's hooves. 'And what you've heard is true, Caballo. They are very accommodating.' He sighed. 'But my size was a problem, even for them.'

Angelo blinked, taking in the sheer vastness of the man at his side. Douglas had hands like coal-shovels, and Angelo knew what that meant. His eyes zeroed in on the root of those tattooed flames.

The blacksmith took another drink of water. 'I turned to men on my third year below deck, Caballo.' Douglas moved round, displaying his back.

Angelo examined the tapestry of interlinked designs which covered the man's shoulders.

Douglas flexed his deltoid muscles and a pair of scarlet imps wriggled. 'I got the twins in honour of two brothers from a brothel in Padang.' The sinewy ripple continued down. To the left of the man's spine, a beautifully coloured parrot seemed to spread its wings. 'He reminds me of Nico, a longshoreman in Georgetown.'

Angelo goggled at the blacksmith's muscle-control.

To the right of the man's spinal column, an intricately worked pair of scales sat, finely balanced between 'guilty' and 'innocent'. Douglas gripped his wrists. Muscle tensed and the balance shifted, first one way, then the other.

'Don't tell me – a lawyer?'

Douglas chuckled. 'A judge!' The vast body swivelled back round to face him. 'A man takes his pleasures where he can, Caballo.'

Angelo nodded. He felt comfortable with Douglas – more comfortable, if truth be told, than he did around Robert these days. Thinking about his flatmate's boyishly handsome face, and the way his blue eyes crinkled when he laughed, Angelo flexed aching shoulders, turned his head and grinned conspiratorially. 'So what does a man do for relief around here?'

Douglas raised a pink sweating face and stared at him. 'Relief?'

Angelo's grin broadened. He winked again. 'When a man has worked up a sweat, and more.'

Understanding broke over the huge face. 'Ah. I have a small vegetable garden. My onions won first prize at –'

'No, no!' Angelo frowned: he'd chosen the wrong word again. Using the international language, he grabbed his crotch and rubbed it.

The blacksmith's face creased knowingly. Then Douglas laughed. 'Most of our young people are already married, or betrothed.'

A slow disappointment seeped over Angelo.

'We live by ancient rules, here on Kelpie Island. Part of that code involves chastity for the young and fidelity for the older – something outsiders do not usually understand.' The amicable face took on a more sober expression.

Angelo sighed. An island consisting of either virginal or faithful women. Just his luck!

Sensing his frustration, Douglas placed a hand on Angelo's sweating shoulder. 'You have a young man's lust, Caballo – a healthy, vibrant lust. Let me tell you what I learnt to do during long months at sea – what generations of Kelpie Islanders have done.'

Hand lingering at the crotch of his shorts, Angelo felt that lust start to grow as Douglas turned his head and stared up at the mountains.

'The need comes upon me as often as it does upon any other man. I am only human.' The blacksmith levered himself from the wall of the cottage and stood in front of Angelo, blocking out the sun with his enormous form. The bassy voice was lowered in volume. 'I pleasure myself, but do not spill my seed.'

Angelo raised an eyebrow, trying to visualise exactly what this involved.

Douglas elaborated. 'It has been the way of men on Kelpie Island for many centuries, passed down from grandfather, to father and on to son.'

They stood there, inches apart. Angelo could feel the heat from the blacksmith's powerfully masculine body radiating against his. He looked up into Douglas McVey's solemn face. 'Don't just tell me – show me!' With a flick of his wrist, Angelo unzipped himself and felt the flaccid length slap across his palm.

The sonorous voice rumbled. 'It would be a pleasure, Caballo.' Douglas McVey unfastened the heavy metal buttons of his fly and slipped a huge hand inside.

Angelo felt his shaft begin to thicken.

The weighty rod of flesh which the blacksmith was pulling free from beneath the creases of his heavy leather trousers was every bit as awesome as the rest of the man. Not so much long as thick, a vast, wrinkled foreskin covered the organ, obscuring the head in a mass of loose, brownish folds. Drooping downwards, the cock was pulled towards the earth with a gravity all of its own. The magnitude of Douglas Mcvey's thick manhood surpassed anything Angelo had ever seen.

'Power, Caballo.' Douglas flipped out one then two massive balls, nestling in a sack of puckered, hairy skin. 'The power which is manufactured deep in a man's arse and is collected here.' He hefted the solidness in the palm of his hand. 'We owe our existence to these, Caballo.'

Angelo couldn't take his eyes off the colossal pouch of flesh which covered the blacksmith's calloused palm and hung over as far as the second joint of his thumb. A small gold ring glinted in each.

'The energy which resides here is the very essence of the male animal, and must be treated with respect.'

Angelo was surprised at this eloquent speech from a man who had not spoken more than ten words in the past two hours. Abstractedly, his fingers began to caress his shaft. He couldn't help wondering what Douglas's cock would look like erect.

As if on cue, the plump, corrugated member twitched.

The blacksmith's voice was low. 'The very spirit of a man is held captive here. It is a wild spirit, a powerful spirit which can be harnessed and put to good use.'

A pulsing within his fist told Angelo arousal was taking over from mere curiosity. He looked up from his hand.

Douglas was staring at him. A faint smile played across the hearty face. Three feet below, fingers were moving. 'Good honest toil can take a man's mind off his hunger. But he is ultimately an animal, with animal needs and urges. When the urges are strong, a man longs to plunge himself into whatever tight hole he can find. He longs to feel constriction around him as he ploughs between soft thighs, hairy arse-cheeks or the bristling hindquarters of another animal.'

Angelo's fingers began to move more quickly. Before he knew it, he was thrusting into his hand. His eyes dropped to Douglas's fist.

The wrinkled rod was steadily stretching, swelling to fill the loose foreskin. Heavy blue veins thickened on the shaft, carrying blood to the engorging organ until the creases rolled back completely to reveal a fat, purple head.

And a ring. The circlet pierced the velvety flesh of Douglas's wide slit.

The blacksmith's voice was becoming hypnotic.

'That first push, as a man thrusts against a hole. The moment of resistance, at which he is balanced on the edge of a precipice. For those few seconds, a man is alone in the world with his cock. He is his cock, and his cock is all he is and ever wants to be.'

Angelo's fingers tightened around his shaft as the pace increased. Feet planted firmly apart, he arched his back and began to fuck his fist more determinedly.

Douglas sighed. 'No, Caballo – not like that.'

Angelo froze. His cock spasmed, leaking a tiny pearl of anticipation as Douglas gently but firmly unwrapped his fist and replaced Angelo's fingers with his own.

'Like this.'

Angelo stared down at his shaft, which sprouted like a young sapling from within the blacksmith's giant hand. Douglas held him loosely, fingers barely exerting any pressure at all. A finger caressed the middle of his ball-sac.

'Understand?'

Angelo understood that he wanted to pump into this warm, alien fist, wanted to push his balls up against the teasing finger. He tried to sound casual. 'OK. What happens now?' His eyes were fixed on the man's turgid shaft.

'Now you let me pace things.'

Angelo exhaled as a rough thumb moved over his slit, smearing the clear liquid which was still oozing from the tiny gash.

Then a thumb and forefinger tightened around the swollen head.

Angelo's slit winked open, the delicate flesh within pink and moist.

'You have a handsome cock, Caballo – a powerful cock.' The digit-ring increased the pressure.

The slit yawned wider than ever.

Then the finger began to rub the middle of his sack. Angelo groaned. His balls jumped, then fled, each into its own discreet pouch.

His slit was gaping now. He writhed against the cottage wall, hands grabbing at rough stone as a thick index finger abruptly plugged his piss-hole.

'It takes two hands to tame the cock of a Caballo.'

Angelo wanted to take the blacksmith's huge member between his own palms and feel the blood pumping through those thick veins. But he could only gasp. He looked down.

While Douglas himself seemed calm, the man's cock stretched out from his solid belly with a firm jut which belied the soft words.

Then three fingers and a thumb began to squeeze.

Angelo inhaled sharply, fingertips clawing at the rough stone behind.

'Feel the potency, Caballo.' The grip grew tighter.

Blinking back discomfort, he stared down at his groin. Douglas's thick, calloused fingers were digging into Angelo's shaft. The large, purplish head was swelling further, barely kept in check by the taut foreskin.

The tip of Douglas's index finger rotated slightly inside Angelo's slit.

The motion sent a wave of pain-pleasure coursing up his spine. Angelo's head lolled back against the cottage wall, then dropped forward. At the other end of his shaft, a finger probed. 'You are heavy with essence, Caballo.'

Angelo's balls mashed and twisted together against the rough length of the blacksmith's little finger, which was as thick as most men's thumbs.

'Male essence.' Douglas's smallest finger curled itself up and under his balls, nipping and constricting the hairy flesh.

A clenching deep inside made Angelo groan again. 'I'm going to come.' His voice was breathy and hoarse. He could feel heat from the blacksmith's meaty body. Open-mouthed and panting, he sucked in the smell of healthy toil, the stench of his own lust, and the musky scent of another man's body. Douglas moved closer. Then Angelo became aware of low words, which seemed to come from inside his head: 'You will feel pleasure, but no essence will be lost.'

The muscles in Angelo's thighs were tensed and trembling. Against the wall of Corrie Cottage, his arse-cheeks were almost scraped raw as he ground himself up and down the rough surface.

Douglas McVey's fist held him in a vice. Angelo's cock was sealed at both ends now – a finger jammed into his slit, while a smaller digit had ringed the bottom of his shaft, just above the balls.

Ripples of desire grew into a fierce current of need. 'No, no, no –'

'Aye, Caballo!'

The blacksmith increased the pressure until Angelo thought the man's fingers would rip his cock in two.

The current overflowed into a crashing wave. As strange, unfamiliar sensations shot up his shaft, Angelo bucked and reared, held prisoner in Douglas's iron grip. His legs gave way and he slumped to the ground.

Eyes open, wide with passion, Angelo heard the hammer of hooves as the final wave broke over him. Every muscle in his body shuddered. He was staring at the earth, Douglas's vast fist still clamped around his cock.

Then the earth swallowed him up.

When he came round, a now-dressed Douglas was gathering up his tools and replacing them in the holdall.

Angelo moaned. 'What happened?'

The blacksmith turned, heaving the bag over a broad shoulder. 'Too much sun, my friend.'

Angelo raised his head up from where it was cushioned by his shirt and blinked.

Douglas sank to a crouch. 'Stay there until you feel better.' His vast hand pushed a damp, black curl back beneath Angelo's bandana.

'I feel –' Stretching tingling limbs, Angelo pulled himself

upright. A satisfying warmth was spreading through his body. 'I feel wonderful!' He leapt to his feet. 'We can finish that roof easily now. Let's –'

'Calm down, Caballo.' Douglas's laugh was low. 'There will be plenty of time for that later.'

But Angelo was already striding towards the ladder, tool-belt clanking around his hips. At the bottom rung he paused, remembering his manners. 'Thanks for all your help.' He smiled at the blacksmith.

Douglas bowed. 'The pleasure was mine.'

Angelo grinned. Energy was coursing through his veins – he'd never felt so alive, and couldn't wait to get back up on the roof. 'I'll buy you a drink later – two drinks.'

The huge face beamed. 'Your satisfaction is my reward, Caballo.' He bowed again.

Angelo stared, then gave up trying to work out what the man was on about. 'OK, but if you are passing please visit us again. I know Robert will want to thank you himself.'

Douglas nodded. 'I'm sure we will meet again.' And with that curt, enigmatic farewell, the vast man turned and made his way along the cliff-top back to the road.

Angelo watched him go, wisps of fog starting to clear from his brain. Last thing he remembered before waking up was staring at the blacksmith's heavily veined cock, and a strange sensation in his head. Angelo pushed the section of lost memory to the back of his mind and climbed jauntily up the ladder.

Robert would be pleased when he saw how much work they'd done in a mere morning.

Thirteen

The first thing he heard was the sound of hammering. The first thing he saw as he rounded the last bend in the road was a head of bandanaed curls poking up from the roof of the cottage.

Robert heaved the box of supplies onto his other shoulder and quickened his pace. The journey from the village to Corrie Cottage seemed to become shorter each time he made it – even with his load of nails and tarpaulin. And although he was hot, tired and more than a little dusty, it felt like only a moment ago that his arse had been bare and trembling under Miss Nicol's heavy tawse.

His cock pressed itself against the teeth of his zip with each step.

Reaching the cottage, he dumped the box beside a pile of slates then stared up at the roof.

Angelo was completely absorbed in his work. Strong muscular thighs straddling an open section of roof, he was bent over and punching nails with short, sharp blows.

Robert stepped back, eyes focusing on the flaring legs of his flatmate's shorts and an area of shining, sweat-slicked skin just beneath. He dragged his eyes away, refusing to allow his cock to be teased any further. A yard away, he noted the bevelled sections of timber which his flatmate was in the process of replacing with sturdy, straight lengths. He looked back up at the industrious figure. 'Hey!'

The Argentinian paused, hammer held high over his shoulder. Spotting Robert, he grinned and waved, then slid his legs over a section of new timber to the edge of the roof.

Robert laughed as Angelo almost fell down the ladder and landed at his feet in a cloud of dust.

Angelo removed the bandana and wiped his glowing face. 'What took you so long?' Large brown eyes fell on the box. He sank to a crouch and began to rummage.

Robert hesitated, then provided an abridged version of his morning while his flatmate sorted through the box of building supplies.

'This is excellent – and she gave them free of charge?'

Robert winced, the cheeks of his arse still stinging where Miss Nicol had extracted a price of sorts. 'Yes – everyone's so helpful.'

His flatmate laughed. 'I too had a little help.'

Robert recalled the large figure he had passed on his way to the village. 'Don't tell me – the blacksmith?'

Angelo glanced up. 'How did you know?'

Robert winked. He leant against the ladder, surprised at the blush which was creeping across his flatmate's handsome, grime-smeared face. 'Oh, I have my sources!'

The blush creased into panic.

Robert laughed. 'I passed him on my way into the village.' His teasing was increased by curiosity. 'He looked very able.'

The Argentinian's face was now a portrait in awkwardness.

Robert couldn't resist it. 'Give you a helping hand, did he?'

Angelo goggled.

Robert chuckled, nodding upwards. 'With the roof, I mean.' His features were a mask of innocence. 'What else could I have been talking about?'

His flatmate's expression froze for a second, then Angelo guffawed. 'You have a dirty mind.'

Robert's chuckle increased. 'And you have a dirty face!' He flicked a smear of grime from Angelo's cheek.

151

The Argentinian rubbed his face with a sweaty forearm, then raised one arm and sniffed. 'And I smell like a dog.' He frowned.

Robert wanted to bury his face in each of those armpits and lick Angelo clean.

Then his flatmate was stripping off the filthy T-shirt. 'Let's have a swim!'

'What, now?'

Angelo threw his T-shirt at Robert's head. 'Yes, now! You've not seen the swimming pool, have you? Or the stones.'

Robert pulled a faceful of Angelo-scented fabric from his head. 'Stones? What stones?'

Angelo was kicking off his boots now. 'Come on – I'll race you.' He disappeared round the side of the cottage in a cloud of dust.

Gripping the warm, sweaty T-shirt in his fist, Robert followed.

The swimming pool turned out to be a blue-green loch almost completely surrounded by waist-high reeds. A red-beaked moorhen was escorting her brood across the still surface.

Poised on the end of a natural jetty, a naked Angelo turned and beckoned, before diving into the blue-green depths with barely a ripple.

Robert kicked off his own boots and socks. He walked towards the edge, enjoying the soft grass beneath his bare feet.

On the far side of the loch, Angelo surfaced, gasping and rubbing his face.

The moorhen shrieked and ran across the top of the water, chicks scattering in her wake.

Robert laughed. 'Cold?' He pulled off his T-shirt, then sat down and dangled his feet in the watery depths.

Angelo shook his wet head and cupped hands around his mouth. 'Yes, but it's wonderful! Come on in.'

'In a minute.' Arms braced behind him on the smooth, shiny rock, Robert threw back his head and enjoyed the early afternoon sunshine on his face. A breeze from the hills rolled down and cooled the air around him, making the conditions ideal for sunbathing. He hugged his knees, feeling the sun on the back of his neck. Robert closed his eyes and listened to the sound of his flatmate's naked brown body scything through the water. His mind's eye provided every detail – from the curve of long muscles stretched on coffee-coloured arms to the mocha skin on the Argentinian's hard arse as he fought the resistance of the water.

Robert waited for his hard-on to subside. His thoughts were turning to the whereabouts of his sun-block when something grabbed his foot. His eyelids shot open. He looked down.

A water-spout erupted around Angelo's bobbing head and shoulders. The handsome face grinned up, water dripping from thick eyebrows. 'Come on in – it's no fun on your own.' The full mouth slumped into a mock pout.

A hand tugged at his ankle. Robert stared to where crystal clear water was lapping around two large brown nubs. Erected by the cold, Angelo's nipples thrust themselves out into the loch. Robert looked across the silvery blue surface, searching for something to focus on. 'What's that?' His eyes alighted on what seemed to be a large table within a rough circle of rocks, on the far side of the loch.

Angelo continued to bob in front of him, treading water. 'That's the stones.'

Robert raised one hand to his forehead, shading his eyes from the sun. He peered through shards of glinting light, which reflected off the shiny surface.

'Want a closer look?'

Robert nodded. Framed by the majesty of the towering mountains behind, the strange stones were definitely intriguing. It was hard to believe some earth tremor had disgorged them in exactly that position. On the other hand, they looked so old and so ancient it was even harder to visualise some primitive people hauling the great slabs up to this rocky promontory.

He got to his feet and prepared to take the long way round. 'Meet you over there.'

Angelo had other ideas. He grinned mischievously.

Then Robert felt a sharp tug on his ankle. Next thing he knew, water was engulfing him.

The loch was deep and weed-filled. And icy. Robert's hard-on shrivelled. Water gurgled in his mouth and his nose, fizzing in his ears as he sank like a stone, arms flailing. He kicked his legs, feeling his soaking shorts drag as he pushed himself through blackness towards light. Lungs bursting, he broke the surface and gasped.

Angelo was a yard away, laughing. 'It is much quicker this way. Really.'

Robert spat water from his mouth. His shorts were heavy with the stuff and flapped uncomfortably around his thighs. He frowned at the sleek, dark head. Angelo's curly hair was plastered to his skull, and looked like some exotic water-creature.

'Come on.' His flatmate turned and began to swim towards the far side where the stones glistened in the sunshine.

'Oh no you don't!' In one quick movement, Robert unfastened then kicked his legs free of the shorts and underwear. Then he lunged across the sparkling surface. Hands gripping two broad shoulders, he reared out of the water and pushed.

Angelo's shout of surprise was cut short as his head disappeared.

Robert grinned, then gasped as a hand grabbed his right leg and pulled him under.

The water didn't feel as cold this time. Blinking in the clear depths, he tried to wrench himself free of his flatmate's strong grip. And failed. Robert fumbled for a grasp of his own. His hands found and held onto Angelo's biceps. He stared at the face, inches from his.

The bandana had floated away. Angelo's thick, black hair fanned around his head like an inverse halo.

Then his flatmate pushed himself backwards.

Robert found himself pulled forwards, then upside down. He lost his grip, and made a grab for Angelo's waist. Hands slipped, grasping warm thighs instead. His flatmate's fingers were tight around his ankles now, Angelo's thighs spread and icy beneath his palms.

The two men writhed, each trying to best the other. Air bubbled around them. The water churned. Then, mid-twist, something solid impacted with Robert's skull. He raised his head, and found himself staring at Angelo's hard cock. The organ bobbed against his nose. Large balls slapped languidly against his upper lip. Hands tightening on his flatmate's calves, Robert opened his mouth. Then began to choke as water flooded into his lungs. Next thing he knew Angelo's hands were under his arms and they were both shooting towards the surface.

As strong, Argentinian arms dragged him towards a bank of reeds then began to pump his back, all Robert could think about was Angelo's thick cock swinging through icy, ball-shrinking water.

He lay half-on, half-off the lochside, slumped and groaning. The man was super-human!

Angelo's large hands pressed down, pushing up towards Robert's skull.

Robert turned his head and coughed a mouthful of water onto muddy grass.

'Are you all right?'

The hands paused, then moved.

Robert disgorged another mouthful of loch, then wiped his lips on the back of his hand and eased himself up. 'I think so.' He turned.

Angelo was crouching, his coffee-coloured face pale with concern.

Robert managed a weak laugh. 'Trying to drown me now, eh?'

'No, no! I –'

'It was a joke.'

'Ah.' Angelo's face returned to its sombre examination of Robert. 'But you are all right?'

'I'll live.' Robert looked away from the concerned expression. He stared at the length of unnaturally engorged flesh which hung between his flatmate's splayed thighs. Not an erection exactly. Angelo's prick was somewhere between half-hard and hard – a difficult state to maintain, especially around sub-zero water.

He lay there recovering as his lungs ejected the last of the loch.

Angelo turned away. He picked up a pebble, rolled it between his fingers then hurled the tiny rock into the middle of the glassy water.

Robert stared from rippling concentric circles back to Angelo's now-contemplative face.

The man was suddenly miles away, oblivious of everything.

After a while, Robert pushed a hank of wet hair from his eyes. 'What are you thinking about?'

'Nothing.' Angelo picked up another pebble and threw it into the loch. 'And everything.'

'You're not enjoying yourself?'

'Yes, I am. But –' The sentence hung unfinished. Angelo grabbed a handful of gravel and peppered the blue-green surface with tiny missiles.

Robert's smile tilted into a frown. Maybe he was taking Angelo for granted. He rested his hand on a sun-warmed shoulder. 'I'm really grateful for your help with the cottage.' Robert squeezed the solid flesh.

'I enjoy working with my hands.' Angelo seized another handful of grit and let it trickle through his long fingers. 'That's not the problem. Something strange happened when you were away.'

Robert blinked. A sudden breeze blew down from the vast mountains. He shivered. 'Want to talk about it?'

Angelo turned towards him. The handsome face shone in the sun's rays.

Robert removed his hand, smiling encouragingly.

Angelo began his tale.

Fifteen minutes later, Robert's mind was racing. 'And you don't remember anything else?'

The curly head shook slowly. 'One minute he was squeezing my cock, the next I woke up on the ground.'

Robert stared at the swollen length which was now resting against his flatmate's left thigh, and envied Douglas McVey the privilege. 'Did you – er, come?'

'No – I don't think so.' Angelo flicked his cock from its resting place. The heavy organ slapped on the smooth surface of the rock.

'Did it hurt?' The idea of his gorgeous flatmate with the huge blacksmith was doing things to his mind.

'No.' Angelo's chuckle was low and almost normal-sounding. 'It was just – strange. And I've felt a little odd ever since.'

Robert smiled. One confidence deserved another. Dangling his feet in the cool water, he told Angelo about his morning's adventures. 'And that did hurt!' Squirming slightly at the memory of Miss Nicol's heavy tawse, he raised one arse-cheek from cool stone and rubbed still-smarting skin.

Angelo was grinning now. 'Six of the best? I bet it did!'

Robert laughed. 'It was as if she knew the effect it would have on me, right from the start.'

Angelo winked. 'Don't underestimate women, my friend. They can be very surprising.'

Robert's eyes widened. He found himself wondering what sort of games Angelo got up to with Julie. He pushed the image away with a grin. 'This whole place is very surprising.'

Angelo nodded in agreement. 'I usually like surprises.' Brown fingers curled around the seven semi-flaccid inches. 'But what am I going to do about this?'

Robert bit back several suggestions. 'Cold showers?'

Angelo laughed. 'That swim didn't help a bit!'

Robert smiled, enjoying the intimacy. He was getting to know Angelo in a way he hadn't anticipated. It had been a long time since he'd felt as close to a man he hadn't slept with. 'Want to know what works for me?' Or used to, he couldn't helping thinking as his own slowly drying cock twitched against the inside of his thigh.

Angelo groaned. 'Exercise is no good – I worked like a madman on your roof and it only made things worse.'

Robert scrambled to his feet. 'It's all in the mind, anyway.' He glanced at the all-too physical length which swung between Angelo's legs as his flatmate dragged himself upright. 'So you need your mind distracted. Let's go and look at these stones – last one there's a jessie!' Robert whooped, tearing off towards the large, black-flecked rocks, Angelo racing behind him.

With a head start, and the added advantage of a cold-shrivelled cock, Robert beat his flatmate easily.

Out of breath and panting, they both leant against one of the smaller rocks.

Robert stared. He could now see the stones were positioned in a definite circle. Counting ten in number, they surrounded a large, flat slab structure in the middle. 'It looks very old.' Robert levered himself off the tall, upright stone and began to walk around the others. 'What do you suppose it's for?'

'For?'

Robert turned, and saw his flatmate was sprawling on the circle's centre-piece.

'Why does it have to be for anything?' Angelo ran his hands over the smooth surface.

Robert continued to walk. 'Most standing-stones had some significance at one time.' He touched one of the rocks, running a finger down the side of the weather-beaten edifice.

'What's a – standing-stone?'

Robert smiled. He continued his inspection, giving Angelo a brief lesson in the reputed uses of Stonehenge and other pagan monuments. When he'd finished, Angelo leapt off the middle slab as if it was on fire.

'You mean these might be special?'

Robert laughed. 'Long ago, yes.' He slapped one of the stones. 'But now they're just curiosities.' A sudden prickle spread over his palm. He yelped.

Angelo was at his side. 'What is it?'

Robert stared from the black-flecked stone to his still-tingling fingers and back again. 'Static, I think.'

Angelo was standing in the background, now, peering over Robert's shoulder. Above their heads, light glanced off one shining surface and refracted onto another, less smooth stone. His voice was low, uncertain. 'Maybe we should go.'

Robert watched the light-show with fascination. 'No –' He turned, mesmerised by the darting, flashing pinpricks which glinted and bounced off the black-flecked stone. The area where Angelo was standing was a sparking arch of dancing light. A smile broke over his face. 'It seems to like you!'

'What seems to like me?'

'Whatever's doing that.' Robert stared, entranced by the broad, naked figure surrounded by a near-rainbow of prismed rays. Angelo looked like a detail from a Blake etching. The air was crackling around them, and he could smell ozone. Eyes shifting to the left, he noticed Angelo and the fireworks display had taken someone else's attention. Robert lowered his voice. 'Don't look now, but we're not alone.'

Angelo flinched. 'Who? Where?'

Robert moved closer, wondering if the blond boy from the woods was enjoying his bird's eye view of Angelo's arse, and how long he'd been watching their naked antics. He lowered his voice. 'Fingal – the kid with the gun.' Robert squinted at the far bank of the loch. 'He's hiding in those reeds.'

Angelo ran a hand through his dark curls. 'Do you think he's a peeping Tim?'

Robert guffawed. 'It's Tom – and if what I saw in the woods this morning is anything to go by, Fingal's more likely to be part of the show than a member of the audience.'

Angelo looked puzzled. 'What?'

Robert dragged his eyes from the handsome face back to the other side of the loch. Blond Fingal was gone.

'What do you mean?'

Robert laughed. 'Let's go put some clothes on and I'll tell you.'

As they walked back to Corrie Cottage, taking the land route this time, Robert was only half-gratified to see Angelo's erection had eventually subsided.

Fourteen

W ashed and dressed, Robert cooked the fish Malcolm had thoughtfully left that morning, while Angelo secured the section of tarpaulin across the de-tiled roof.

They dined alfresco, the early-afternoon sun shining overhead while Robert retold what he'd encountered on his way to the village.

Angelo ate heartily, grinning through mouthfuls of freshly caught haddock. 'He didn't see you?'

Robert shook his head. 'Don't think he would have noticed an army if it had tramped past him!' He swallowed the last piece of fish and pushed his plate away.

His flatmate laughed. 'So the performance wasn't for your benefit?'

Robert took a drink of water. 'No, I'm sure it –'

Angelo was still munching, but the large brown eyes were now focused over Robert's shoulder.

'What?'

Angelo continued to grin. 'He's still there –' he nodded '– on a boulder. I think perhaps he followed you back here.'

Robert spluttered into his glass.

Then Angelo was on his feet, beckoning. 'Please join us.' He gestured with his fork.

Robert turned round, craning his neck.

The blond man-boy was indeed sitting about fifty yards away, just behind the cottage. The leather jacket lay over another rock, and Fingal's bare arms were crossed in front of his slender chest.

Angelo shouted again. 'Hey, you!'

The man-boy's attention was focused somewhere out to sea and he either didn't, or chose not to, hear Angelo's invitation.

'Leave him.' Robert watched the way Fingal's blond hair sparkled in the light. The man-boy looked as much part of the rocky landscape as he had seemed at home in the leafy glade. 'Perhaps he's used to coming here to get some peace and quiet – after all, the cottage hasn't been occupied in a while.'

'This is your property now.' A note of unease entered his flatmate's voice. 'And your land. He is trespassing.'

Robert's head swivelled back to Angelo. The darkly handsome face was shrouded in suspicion.

'I don't trust him.'

Robert almost laughed. 'We don't know him! Every other islander has been friendlier than we could have hoped.' He knew the answer to the question before he posed it. 'Why should Fingal be any different?'

'He has a gun.'

Robert took the point, then countered it. 'If he had any intention of doing damage, he could have easily taken pot-shots at us, by the loch.'

Angelo remained sceptical. 'I still don't trust him.' He pushed his plate away.

Robert sighed. 'I'll have a word.' He stood up.

'Too late – he's gone.'

Robert returned his attention to the rock which Fingal had been occupying, and saw it was empty. The leather jacket was gone too. 'Oh well – I'll have a word with him later.' He sat back down, perching on the edge of the table. His eyes swept over the roof of the cottage and on up to the mountains behind. A cooling breeze swept down. 'Fancy a hike?'

Angelo's face tilted upwards. 'Where?'

Robert pointed to a faint path which tracked the south face of one of the smaller peaks. 'Up there – I bet the view's stunning.'

His flatmate's expression brightened. He turned his head to examine the trail.

Robert talked on. 'We can take a picnic, spend the rest of day exploring. With the short nights the island gets at this time of year, we don't need to be back until –'

'Oh!' Angelo leapt to his feet. 'What time is it?'

Robert glanced at his wrist. 'Half past one. Why?'

'Rhona has invited us to go riding at two o'clock – I almost forgot.'

Robert frowned. The thought of an afternoon with the Lady Laird had generated more enthusiasm than any suggestion of hiking had. He struggled for a smile. 'That sounds fun! She knows about a riding school?'

'Rhona keeps a small stable herself.' Angelo was scooping up plates and condiments from the table and heading in the direction of the cottage.

Robert followed, listening.

'I'm sure she is an excellent horsewoman.' Angelo dumped the dishes into a bucket of water. 'The very person to give a beginner instruction.'

Robert felt his hackles rise. It was one thing to have Angelo teach him to ride and laugh at his mistakes. To be the brunt of joint hilarity was something else. 'Er – no thanks. I think I'll stay here and do some writing.'

Angelo was rummaging in his rucksack. Eventually he located his shaving-gear. 'Oh. OK.' He grabbed a towel and headed off towards the outhouse.

Robert scowled in the darkness. Two shaves in the space of four hours. The Lady Laird was honoured! He kicked the leg of the bed, then sat down, seething. A quiet afternoon, tramping the hills was what he'd had in mind. Now – thanks to Lady Bountiful's boundless hospitality – an even quieter afternoon hanging about here was the only thing on offer. Robert drummed his heels against the stone floor, and wondered what Malcolm got up to during the day. He sighed, knowing the red-haired fisherman had to sleep sometime. Getting to his feet, he wandered aimlessly over to a dust-covered mirror and wiped a section free of grime.

A slightly sun-tanned face stared back at him. Robert peered critically at his reflection.

His nose was too small, his eyes were too big. Robert ran a hand over his chin. Blond stubble ground against his palm. He could do with a shave and his hair needed cutting. Pushing his thick blond fringe out of those too-big eyes, Robert scowled. No wonder Angelo wasn't interested in him: he looked like a bit of scruff!

Drifting in from outside, the sound of running water and Angelo's out-of-tune singing made his stomach clench. Robert swallowed down resentment. His eyes moved from the mirror to his rucksack, and the notebook and pencils every writer carried with them. Maybe this would be a good opportunity to get some thoughts down on paper – his imagination was certainly finding plenty of stimulation around here. Dredging his mind for ideas, he moved his gaze to the pile of trunks, and the slim, leather-bound volume they contained.

Robert smiled wryly. He grabbed his rucksack and hauled it outside.

By the time he'd spread his writing equipment out on the table, the fresh sea air was mixed with the scent of aftershave. Angelo had changed his clothes three times, finally settling on another of those almost transparent linen shirts and a pair of well-fitting denim jeans. 'You are sure you won't come too?'

'Quite sure.' Robert gripped his pencil more tightly and underlined the same word a second time. 'You worked all morning – now it's my turn.' He tried to keep his tone light. 'Enjoy yourself!' He risked a glance at his flatmate.

Silhouetted against the horizon, Angelo was more handsome than ever. He grinned lopsidedly, a large hand ruffling Robert's hair. 'Wish me luck!'

'You don't need luck.' Robert found a weak grin. 'She'll not be able to resist you – neither will the horses!'

Angelo guffawed. 'See you later.' He winked, striding off along the top of the cliff.

Robert watched him go, then pushed the hurt aside and concentrated on the blank sheet of paper before him.

Angelo tramped through heather beside green fields. He followed the same, snaking stone wall as he had done the previous night.

After fifteen minutes, Castle Dunbar's turreted tower appeared ahead.

Angelo walked faster. Robert drifted into his mind. Angelo frowned. He was a little disappointed Robert had turned down Rhona's kind invitation. A smile twitched at his mouth. He was sure the blond Englishman and the aristocratic Laird would have a lot in common – and a fourth member of the hacking party would have given Angelo time to get to know the Lady Laird a little better.

Pausing at a stile, he crossed it and marched more determinedly. But Robert had work to do. Angelo knew how important the man's writing was to him, and understood Robert's desire to have some time to himself. His smile spread into a grin: either he'd have to make sure Rhona's brother approved of his intentions, or hope Cameron Dunbar had other plans for that afternoon.

The coast receded below him, the incline steepened and the wind grew stronger. Angelo paused in front of a large tree to get his breath back. Leaning against the broad trunk, he gazed down.

Corrie Cottage was a tiny speck in the distance.

Behind him, the rugged peaks were larger than ever. He stared at the winding path which twisted around the closest. Robert had been right: from any point on that trail, the view over the island would be marvellous. He smiled, hoping it was a bridle path. Then something caught his eye, near the summit of a larger peak to his right.

Angelo screwed up his eyes in the sunshine.

The wind which had been whistling through his clothes died abruptly, and his ears filled with the thunder of hooves.

Angelo watched, transfixed by the white steed which was

galloping down the side of the mountain. The rhythmic pound of hooves echoed in his ears.

He smiled. Proud and haughty, the animal reminded him of the Lady Laird. Angelo glanced away for a second. Castle Dunbar was about quarter of a mile to his left. As owners of the island, Rhona and Cameron evidently allowed their beasts to roam free over the vast hilly countryside. He approved: wildness was something to be treasured, not broken to the will of man. His thoughts lingered on the Lady Laird as he turned back to watch the horse.

Wind whipped his hair back from his face.

The terrain ahead was motionless. The steed had vanished.

Angelo shrugged, and resumed his journey towards the castle.

Cameron Dunbar opened the strutted, wooden door almost as soon as Angelo's fist impacted on the studded surface. He smiled. 'Again, welcome.' The Laird moved back, drawing the door back further. 'Rhona has asked me to entertain you while she gets ready.'

Angelo nodded respectfully.

'Please come in.'

As he entered the great entrance hall Angelo couldn't help but notice how different the vast room looked in daylight. Even Cameron Dunbar had an earthier air to him. Angelo regarded his host, who was dressed today in torn jeans and a heavy, leather-looking apron which covered the top half of his body and hung down as far as his knees. His hands were hidden by huge gloves and a pair of perspex goggles perched on top of the blond head.

Cameron bowed apologetically, closing the door behind him. 'You must excuse my attire.' The low burr of his voice lowered further. 'I must start the final process.'

Angelo cocked an eyebrow.

The Laird smiled. 'A little hobby of mine – would you like to see?'

Despite his impatience to be with Rhona again, Angelo remember Robert's phrase from the day before: he was in a man's house, paying suit to his sister, and he wanted to make a good impression. 'When in Rome!'

Cameron Dunbar laughed, eyeing Angelo's pristine white shirt. 'Better take that off – it's a wee bit dirty, downstairs.'

Angelo did as requested, draping his shirt over a high-backed chair. An icy draft blasted across him, erecting his nipples. When he turned around, Cameron was gripping a large ring in the middle of one of the flagstones, hauling at the square. Damp air seeped out from underneath. With a final grunt, he lifted the stone.

Angelo walked across the floor and stared at the roughly hewn steps which led down into a glowing area. A strange hum was emanating up from the trapdoor.

Cameron moved forward, then disappeared down the steps into the pulsing orange light.

Angelo hesitated, eyes flicking up another set of larger stone stairs, to where he knew Rhona would be dressing for the ride.

A voice from below rose up. 'Watch where you're putting your feet – these stairs are rather treacherous.'

One foot on the top step, Angelo almost changed his mind. Then he remembered his manners and the importance of Cameron Dunbar's approval. Steeling himself, he moved carefully into the deep hole.

Castle Dunbar was like an iceberg. As Angelo followed his host through a serious of twisting, candlelit corridors, he saw there was as much, if not more, of the building below ground as above. He stared up at vaulted stone ceilings as he walked past various iron-barred rooms which looked like cells but were probably ancient storerooms.

The initial chill was fading. Angelo noticed the air was actually getting warmer, as if they were nearing the centre of the earth itself. The hum was getting louder too. It sounded like some sort of machinery. Rounding a sudden bend, Angelo almost bumped into Cameron Dunbar.

'Here we are!' The Laird patted Angelo's naked shoulder with a gloved hand, then walked to a long table and a large copper vessel which dominated the space.

Odours filled his nostrils. Angelo inhaled the scents of herbs and spices – some familiar, some not. The hum was augmented by a bubbling sound, which was coming from the huge copper pot. A vague smell of yeast underpinned the more obscure fragrances.

Angelo grinned. 'A still!'

Cameron Dunbar raised a goggled head from his inspection of a small control panel and laughed. 'No, not quite. Though a potent brew, this contains no alcohol.' He clapped a gloved hand to the copper vessel.

Curious, Angelo moved closer. 'What is it then – some sort of medicine?' Back home, he knew some of the older women on his father's ranch swore by the healing properties of certain herbs.

The Laird was fiddling with a dial on the control panel. The hum dropped in pitch to a low rumble. 'Medicine?' He turned, wiping sweat from his aristocratic brow. 'Yes, I suppose you could call it that.' He moved to the middle of the bench and beckoned.

Angelo followed, and found himself staring at the open pages of a very ancient-looking book. The paper – if it was paper – was yellow with age, the script tiny and densely packed.

Removing one glove, the Laird ran a neatly manicured finger along one line, then another. 'This belonged to Lady Flora. It is her own recipe for what you would probably call a tonic.'

Angelo tried to read the minuscule writing, which blurred before his eyes. 'Is it English?' Behind, the still hummed on.

'An arcane form of Old Scots, I believe.'

Angelo inhaled the sweetly scented air. 'What does it contain?'

Cameron laughed. 'Ah – that I cannot tell you.'

Angelo looked at the aristocratic face.

Cameron tapped the side of his elegant nose. 'Family secret. There's even a legend the brew will lose its power if anyone outside these walls learns of the ingredients.'

Angelo nodded sagely. 'The healers who live on the pampas have similar rules. I understand.'

The Laird's face took on a new expression. Cameron regarded him admiringly. 'It is rare to find someone so in tune with our ways, my friend. You are a very unusual man.'

Angelo felt himself flush up. He turned away, glancing around the small laboratory, and changed the subject. 'You have a power-source down here?' His eyes came to rest on the corridor which had led them down here. Suddenly he wanted to be back up on ground level.

'Yes –' Redonning his glove, the Laird embarked on a brief tour of the distillation area, explaining what each piece of equipment did and its part in the overall process.

Hands clasped behind his back, Angelo nodded patiently. The Laird certainly managed to communicate his own enthusiasm for his hobby, and Angelo found himself quite engrossed in the semi-lecture.

They had almost reached the final stage. Angelo stared at a corkscrew length of tubing which led from the main fermentation cask to just above another vessel. He was getting impatient – was Rhona still getting ready? Had she forgotten about him? He attempted to bring the impromptu lesson to an end. 'Is your – elixir for sale?' A single, amber drop condensed on the end of the copper piping and fell into the collection vessel below.

The Laird was adjusting a tap behind the second fermentation tank. 'For sale?'

Angelo nodded. 'Yes. Where can I buy some? I would like to –'

Cameron Dunbar's voice was low and vaguely amused. 'Oh, I don't sell it.' He plucked a small beaker from the work-bench and moved past Angelo. 'As I said, it's just a little hobby of mine.' One gloved hand angled the glass beneath the curled tubing while the other increased the flow. 'But I would be honoured if you would give me your opinion of this season's brew.'

Angelo took a step back, watching as the beaker began to fill. Refusal formed on his lips. Then he remembered his manners. He smiled. 'The honour is mine.'

The Laird held out the vessel.

Angelo stared at the golden liquid, then gripped the glass. He inhaled its fragrance. Chateau Dunbar smelled of mountain streams and heathery plains, with an acrid undernote which was vaguely familiar. Angelo closed his eyes and let the aroma fill his head. Then he took a sip.

Somewhere in the background, Cameron was still talking.

Angelo didn't hear the words as the first trickles of the aromatic liquid slipped over his lips. A slightly bitter taste, then a burning sensation tingled over his tongue. Then his mouth was filled with a sweet warmth which soon radiated throughout his body. The drink possessed both the sharp bite of alcohol and a honey smoothness. Angelo could almost feel the brew seeping through muscle and sinew until it emerged through his skin, where it glistened like a second distillation.

'Good?'

Angelo's eyes opened. He was glowing from the inside out. 'Very good!' He stared at the empty beaker, which Cameron immediately refilled. 'I bet this helps keep you warm in the winter.'

The Laird smiled. 'Oh, it has many uses.'

Angelo knocked back a second glass. The effect this time was less dramatic but equally pleasant. His brain was completely unaffected, while his body pulsed and hummed like the generator which powered the still.

Cameron repositioned the collection vessel under the copper spout. 'Some have reported it helps rheumatism. Others say it gets rid of warts. I've even heard the elixir has amazing results in the −' He winked. '− bedroom department!'

Angelo licked the last few drops from his lips and grinned. The liquid had reached his groin, where a faint twitching told him the Laird's testimony was no idle boast. 'I've never tasted anything quite like this.' He stared at the beaker. 'I think 1998 will be − a very good year!'

Cameron laughed, patting his shoulder.

Angelo grinned. They were both chuckling when the slap of boots on stone made him turn.

In the doorway, bathed in the orange glow from the wall torches, the Lady Laird was a vision in cream jodhpurs and black hacking jacket. She carried a hat and a small riding crop.

Angelo's cock took another leap.

Rhona Cameron smiled. 'I see Cammie has been plying you with his devilish brew.'

Angelo was aware of a tingling in his nipples.

The Laird moved to beside his sister. 'Just a taste – the first of the season.'

Side by side, the resemblance between the Dunbars was more striking than ever. Suddenly, amidst the backdrop of laboratory equipment, Angelo felt like a specimen under their joint scrutiny. A jolt of sensation shot through both nipples. His eyes moved from Cameron to Rhona and back again.

The Laird was a striking man. The undeniably noble set of his features, the patrician sweep of his neck and the broadness of the shoulders made him look every inch a gentleman.

An aftertaste lingered in his mouth, not unpleasant but tainted and more acerbic than the brew itself.

Unexpectedly, Angelo found himself visualising a naked Cameron Dunbar. And a naked Rhona. He pictured himself kneeling between the Laird and Lady Laird, servicing one, then the other with a mouth still prickling from the taste of the amber liquid.

Then another golden liquid was pouring over his face, running through his hair and stinging his eyes. Gasping, Angelo opened his mouth and accepted two sour, acidic torrents. Beneath his shorts, a hard length was pushing up towards his waistband. He bathed in the steaming fluid, an arm encircling each of two sets of thighs and pulling his benefactors more closely over him.

A concerned voice rang in his ears: 'Are you all right?'

Angelo blinked.

Rhona Dunbar stood on one side of him, her brother on the other. Two brows were creased with worry.

Angelo blinked again, chasing the disturbing image from his mind. 'Yes, I'm fine.' He rubbed his damp face with damper palms.

'What were you thinking of, bringing our guest down here?' Rhona's voice was mildly reprimanding as she chastised her brother. 'And without a shirt!'

'It's OK – honestly.' Angelo felt slightly foolish. He grinned sheepishly, nodding to the copper fermentation cask. 'That stuff's more powerful than it looks.' He shoved his hands deep into his pockets. His fingers made contact with the engorged length of his cock, and he pulled them out again.

At his side, Cameron was apologising.

Angelo's legs tingled. 'I just need some fresh air.'

Rhona shot her brother an irritated look, then smiled at Angelo. 'You need a good, refreshing ride through the mountains.' She placed a hand on his arm. 'Let's get you a mount.'

Cameron's expressions of regret followed them along twisting corridors.

As he emerged back into the great hall, Angelo suddenly found himself wishing his English friend had agreed to come too.

Fifteen

Robert frowned at the three lines he had written in the past hour, then set down his pencil. Why hadn't he gone with Angelo?

He leant back in his chair, then stood up and began to pace.

Above his head, seagulls squawked, mocking his attempts at writing.

Robert scowled up at them. Irritation at himself became anger. 'Piss off!' He batted at the birds with his arms.

One swooped down, dive-bombing him.

Robert waved his arms more vigorously.

Another gull joined the raid.

In seconds, Robert was engulfed in a flapping, shrieking flock of white wings and vicious orange beaks.

Then a gunshot rang out.

Robert threw himself to the ground, arms over his head. His face contacted with something wet and fishy-smelling. Heart pounding, he recognised a scrap of haddock which had evidently fallen from either his or Angelo's plate at lunchtime. He raised a tentative face from the rocky ground.

A few yards away, a slouching figure holding an airgun.

Robert staggered to his feet. He marched towards Fingal, grabbed the weapon and wrenched it from the youth's hands.

'What the hell do you think you're playing at? You could have killed me!'

Behind, the sound of beating wings and cries told him the gulls were retrieving the morsel they had been after all along.

Fingal kicked sulkily at a rock. 'I know what I'm doing. I fired into the air to scare the birds.' The toe of a heavy boot impacted with the rock a second time. Eddies of dust puffed up around the youth's foot. 'I'm a good shot – if I wanted to kill you, you'd be dead.'

Robert's initial panic was subsiding, but he still didn't like the idea of strange, armed youths skulking around without his knowledge. 'What are you doing here, anyway?'

Beneath heavy leather, slender shoulders shrugged. 'It's a free country.'

The man-boy's studied indifference was really starting to annoy Robert. He grabbed one arm and shook it. 'This is my property. You can't just –'

'It's not your property.' Fingal jerked his arm free of the grip.

'Of course it's mine!'

Hands shoved in his pockets, the youth sauntered away. 'The Dunbars own everything around here, so if this is anyone's property, it's theirs.'

Robert walked after him and grabbed a shoulder. He felt slim muscle flinch under his hand. 'Stand still when I'm talking to you!'

Fingal twisted away again. 'Why should I?'

Robert sighed. The angrier he got, the more obstreperous Fingal became. He tried a different tack, remembering the other side of the man-boy to which he had been witness earlier in the day. 'Listen, I don't mind if you come here.' Robert placed the airgun on the table and modulated his voice. 'Just let us know you're around, OK?' He smiled. 'So we can wear our bulletproof vests.'

Fingal was standing with his back to the cottage, staring out over the cliffs. Tangled golden hair gleamed on the shoulders of his leather jacket. Abruptly, he sank to a crouch, then picked up a rock.

Robert waited for an answer.

Fingal stood up and hurled the stone towards the horizon.

Robert remembered PC Campbell's complaint about Fingal's lack of productive employment. His eyes moved to the various scattered rocks and other detritus littering the area around the cottage. 'Are you looking for some casual work?' Maybe it would keep the boy out of mischief. Robert quickly totalled the money he'd brought with him.

Fingal spun round. 'I've seen you!' The beautiful face was a twisted mass of resentment.

Robert flinched. Angelo was right – the youth had been aware of his presence in the woods that morning.

Fingal sneered accusingly. 'I saw you last night with Malcolm and I saw you today in the loch with Caballo. You're fucking him, aren't you?'

Robert's mouth remained open, then closed abruptly. He stared at Fingal's furious face, trying to read beneath the expression. 'Not that it's any of your business, but no, I'm not –'

'Don't deny it – I've seen you!'

Robert scowled and gripped the edge of the table. 'And I've seen you!'

The boy stiffened.

Robert stared at the shocked face. He felt a moment of sympathy which was soon overwhelmed by resentment at the man-boy's previously judgemental tone. 'People who cavort naked in the woods aren't in a position to cast aspersions!'

Colour drained from the angelic face.

Robert immediately regretted his own sneering tone.

Before he could soften his words, Fingal pushed roughly past him and ran back towards the road.

'Wait! Don't go!'

Fingal ignored him.

Robert scowled ard grabbed the gun. 'Hold on – you've forgotten this!' The wind blew the words back into his face. Before he knew what he was doing, Robert was tearing after the boy.

Fingal ran like the wind, legs pumping. His blond hair fanned out like a golden cloud behind him.

Robert's heart was beating fast as he pursued the leather-clad figure down the hill towards the road. Skidding and slipping on loose gravel, he slowed then increased the sprint to close the gap between them.

At the bottom of the rough road, the youth unexpectedly swerved left up the side of another hilly incline.

Robert frowned and continued pursuit.

The man-boy leapt from rock to rock like a mountain goat, deftly finding his footing on the rocky terrain.

Robert's breath was laboured now, lungs bursting. His legs felt like lead and his heart hammered painfully against his ribcage. One boot slipped into a mossy pool. Water seeped into his sock, soaking his foot and weighing it down. He wrenched himself free and pushed onwards.

Ahead, Fingal was increasing the distance between them.

Wind tore at Robert's face, slowing him down further. The rocks were giving way to a heathery glen. The springy shrub cushioned his pistoning feet but made running more difficult. Clenching his fists, he put all his last reserves of energy into one final spurt.

Fingal was less than three yards in front.

Robert could hear the youth's breath coming in short, rasping gulps. With supreme effort, he launched himself into the air and seized a booted foot.

The rugby tackle brought them both to the ground with a thud. Breath rushed from Robert's body. He tightened his grip on the youth's ankle, managing to avoid kicks from the other leg.

Fingal might be faster, but Robert was stronger and heavier. He dropped the air-pistol and he flipped the youth over. Knees securing Fingal's legs to the ground, he gripped bony wrists and pulled the man-boy's arms flat above his blond head. He pinned him against the heather and held him there with his weight.

A wild pink face stared up at him. Fingal arched his back, cursing like a trooper in his struggles to get free.

Robert was still gasping for breath. He tightened his grip on the bony wrists and held on, lowering his body onto the writhing form beneath. His arms shadowed the length of leathered arms, his bare legs holding denim-covered ones at bay. Then his returning breath caught in his throat.

Jutting through the man-boy's jeans, an unmistakable outline pressed into his groin.

Robert eased himself up and looked at the scowling face. Then two sets of eyes were directed downwards to the growing bulge in the youth's jeans. 'Are you going to tell me what this is all about?'

'Will you get *off* me?' Fingal's voice was hoarse, the huskiness only partly from exertion.

'Will you run away again?'

The golden head shook slowly.

'I'm going to trust you.' Aware of a response in the crotch of his shorts, Robert rolled from the pink-faced boy and propped himself up on one elbow.

Fingal stared at the sky. 'I'm nearly twenty-one and everyone treats me like a child!' There was no sulkiness in the voice. The youth sounded surprisingly matter-of-fact.

'Maybe you sometimes act like one.'

'You're going to tell them, aren't you?'

Robert raised an eyebrow. 'Tell who what?' A damp strand of tangled hair had adhered itself to one high, pale cheekbone. He reached over and pulled it free.

The youth flinched. A blush spread over the ashen face.

Robert watched Fingal's white teeth gnaw at his bottom lip.

'You're going – to tell – that I –' Panic, fear, shame and confusion fluttered across the striking features.

A warm sensation in his stomach joined with the lust between his legs. Robert smiled. For a second, the man-boy was again transformed from delinquent devil to an angel who had fallen to earth.

Fingal turned his head away, unable to articulate any further.

Robert couldn't help himself. Stretching out a hand he leant over and tilted the other-worldly face towards his. 'It's OK – I won't tell.' The pressure of his mouth on Fingal's was light, affectionate. Then leather-covered arms were around his neck and soft lips opened under his.

The man-boy's kiss was passionate and filled with urgency.

Robert groaned, slipping his hands under the youth's narrow waist and raising Fingal up against him. Before he knew what was happening they were gnawing at each other. Robert sucked the man-boy's tongue into his mouth, feeding on him while Fingal wrapped slender thighs around Robert's hips.

His hands slid up under the youth's T-shirt and felt the warm, lightly muscled flesh of his back and shoulders.

Fingal's mouth was wet and tasted sweet. His skin was fragrant, and Robert wondered vaguely through a haze of arousal if that was what elderberries smelled like.

The body beneath his shuddered as Robert ran his hands down the smooth skin of Fingal's sides then paused at the waistband of his jeans.

The youth inhaled sharply, hands moving from around Robert's neck to grip his arse-cheeks.

Their two cocks lay side by side, separated by layers of fabric.

Fingal bucked his hips, grinding his groin against Robert's, which responded with equal urgency.

He had already seen every inch of that boyish body, but now he needed to touch it, taste it and feel it respond under his. If Fingal wanted to be treated like a man, that's how Robert would treat him. Wrenching his mouth away, he licked Fingal's saliva from his lips and wriggled out of his T-shirt.

Fingal was struggling free of the leather jacket then pulling an off-white jersey over his head.

Eyes focusing on those two tiny nipples, Robert lowered his head and took one bud between his teeth, feeling the delicate flesh stiffen under his attentions. The fingers of one hand tangled in golden hair, Robert cupped the man-boy's pec, squeezing gently as he continued to alternately suck then nibble the responsive tissue.

Fingal arched his back and grabbed Robert's head, trying to stuff more of himself between eager lips.

Robert's slit was leaking pre-come as it rubbed against the youth's stout shaft. He moved to Fingal's other nipple, circling the bud teasingly with his tongue as his hands moved lower, to the fly of the man-boy's jeans.

Then other hands were helping him.

Together they wrenched denim then black briefs down over pale thighs. The air around them rippled with the sound of their breathing.

Fingal kicked off boots then jeans while Robert tore at his own shorts.

Seconds later, he was staring down at a naked vision spread-eagled on a bed of purple heather. Robert lowered his face to kiss the bulbous head of the cock he'd admired hours earlier.

Fingal's foreskin was pulled tightly back.

Robert ran his tongue over the velvety flesh.

The youth's fists tightened around clumps of heather, wrenching the plant free from the ground as he moaned with desire.

Robert curled his fingers around the thick shaft, rubbing the underside with his thumb as he continued to tongue the glans.

Fingal's cock was damp and sour-tasting.

Robert ran his tongue around the ridge just below the purple head then darted back to the slit, sucking droplets of lust from the tiny hole. He nibbled the fragile skin around the opening, before moving back down the length to nip and tease more.

'Oh, please – please – please . . .'

Robert's own cock was engorged with need, his balls pulled up tight and heavy. The ambiguity in the words made him pause. Then Fingal's hands were clawing at his back, hips bucking the swollen shaft against Robert's face.

'Fuck me – fuck me – fuck me . . .'

Moving between the quivering legs, Robert released the youth's cock and spread Fingal's thighs wider. He licked one finger then shoved his hands under the man-boy's arse-cheeks, which were pistoning up from the heather.

The tight pink hole was already moist with desire. Robert pressed the pad of his wet index finger to the spasming orifice and pushed.

Fingal's yelp of pleasure made Robert's cock throb more urgently. A knuckle's length sank past the tight sphincter and into the man-boy's writhing body. Wet warmth gripped his finger. Robert felt the circle of muscle relax, then reclench around the finger-joint. He continued to push, curling the digit and hooking upwards towards the youth's balls. Robert began to rub.

A howl echoed around the glen. Then Fingal was bearing down on Robert's hand, eager to take more and more.

The sounds of pleasure grew in urgency. The man-boy was panting now, his words coming in breathy gasps. 'Your prick – shove your prick inside me . . .'

Balls tingling, Robert wrenched his finger from the tight hole and groped towards his discarded shorts. His stash of condoms tumbled free. In seconds, his swollen length was encased in a sleek latex membrane. He spat into his palm, slathering saliva over his shaft, then spat a second time, using his spit to lube the youth's spasming arsehole. As he looked up, he saw Fingal's blond head and shoulders levering themselves upwards from the bed of heather.

The man-boy's eyes were wide with lust.

Robert met the gaze. From the tightness of the youth's hole, he knew Fingal was a virgin. Taking a finger was one thing: taking the girth of a man's cock was something else. For a second, he hesitated.

Fingal registered the delay. He arched his back. 'Put it inside me – please! Now! I don't care if it hurts – I want it to hurt!'

Robert grabbed the discarded leather jacket, pounded it into a rough pillow and shoved it under two heather-scratched buttocks. Then, long hairless legs around his waist, Robert gripped his shaft and positioned the head of his cock against the pink pucker. He leant over the naked, writhing youth, linking the fingers of his hand with Fingal's and watching the passion-filled face. Then he lowered himself, using his weight to penetrate the youth.

Fingal's virgin hole resisted the invasion.

The sensation of dragging against his sensitive glans made Robert's eyes water. Holding his iron shaft steady, he leant forward again.

The circlet of muscle trembled, straining under the assault. A shudder passed along the youth's rigid legs and shivered into Robert's waist.

He clenched Fingal's hand in his, pushing with all his might.

The sphincter shivered, but refused to relax.

Robert released his aching shaft. Tension was mounting in his balls, and he didn't have time to get Fingal as relaxed as he would have liked. He looked around, scowling with lust and frustration.

His eyes fell on the clumps of heather the youth had torn from the ground in a spasm of longing. A flash from that morning tore through his mind.

Grabbing the bushy stems, Robert reared back, clasped his shaft again, holding the ring of latex firmly at the root and pushed one last time. As he did so, he brought the rough sprigs of heather down sharply across Fingal's chest.

The man-boy gasped. Three feet below, another hole spasmed and the head of Robert's cock slid into a slick tunnel.

Strong muscle parted to admit him, then reclamped itself around each inch of his aching length. Robert clenched his teeth. He pushed on in, trying to ignore Fingal's arousing squeals, until the taut hairiness of his balls met the smooth cheeks of the man-boy's arse. The branch of heather slipped from his fingers, landing on the youth's stomach.

Immersed to the hilt, Robert paused and stared down, heart thudding beneath his ribs.

Fingal was writhing and thrashing under him.

Robert gripped the flailing wrists and pinned them to the ground. Then he began to withdraw.

The undulating sinew of Fingal's arse walls rippled along his shaft. Delicate cockskin dragged deliciously, making Robert groan all over again. He pulled out to the last of his seven inches, until the head of his cock was the only thing holding him and Fingal together. Hovering there, feeling the need of the youth beneath him join with his own desire, Robert luxuriated in the tight grip of virgin hole. He stared down at the man-boy's broad shoulders. The slim chest was slick with sweat. A trio of reddening lines across Fingal's left nipple bore testament to the heather-swat, minutes earlier.

Robert's balls spasmed. A man's body, with a man's needs. Virgin or not, Fingal deserved to be fucked like a man. Holding nothing back, Robert thrust forward again into the moist opening.

The youth's cries lowered in pitch as Robert pumped slowly and thoroughly, ploughing the narrow tunnel until Fingal grunted in sync with his thrusts.

Robert increased the pace, speeding up the fuck.

Fingal's ankles locked behind him, pressure from his heels pushing against Robert's waist and matching him, thrust for thrust.

Robert blinked sweat from his eyes. Heather dug into his knees, scraping the skin raw. He changed position, altering the angle of the assault so that the head of his cock bumped against the rounded gland halfway up Fingal's fuck-tunnel.

The youth gasped and arched his back in pleasure. The head of the man-boy's swollen prick brushed Robert's tensed stomach, jamming itself and the heather between their sweating bodies with every jutting movement of Robert's hips.

He was close to coming: the feel of the youth's arse tight around his shaft, the wetness of Fingal's wrists held slick in his fingers, the way the man-boy's cock shuddered on his flat stomach with every jolt of Robert's body were all helping to push him over the edge. But he didn't want to come yet. A man's first fuck should be special. Robert tried to think of something else as he hammered into the body below his.

He raised his head and stared up at the mountains which framed the coupling. His mind broke free and he thought about the privately published volume of erotica he'd found in the cottage. He thought about whoever had occupied Corrie Cottage, wondering if they too had found the natives more than willing to indulge their every whim. Malcolm's flowing red hair joined the vision, which was soon augmented by PC Campbell's disapproving face and Douglas the blacksmith's sweat-sheened, tattooed biceps.

Fingal's balls were pressing into his stomach. A sudden tensing in the body beneath his told Robert the man-boy was about to come. He tore his eyes from the hills beyond. His bruised and battered cock renewed the assault, pistoning into the youth's now well-fucked arse with short, jabbing strokes.

Seconds later, a howl of release startled a flock of nearby gulls into flight as Fingal thrust upwards, impaling himself on Robert's cock and shooting between their stomachs.

Riding on through the youth's climax, Robert only heard a thundering in his ears as he collapsed on top of Fingal.

Sixteen

Angelo looked at the hard hat which the Lady Laird held out and shook his curly head. 'I have never used one.'

Rhona smiled an amused smile. 'You've never fallen off a horse?'

They continued to walk towards the stable.

'Many times.' He tapped his skull. 'But I have a hard head – all we cattlemen do.'

The Lady Laird's laugh was low and husky. 'Ah, you gauchos! Born in the saddle, I bet.' She moved left to hang the protective headgear over a hook on a door.

'Not quite.' Angelo stared at the slim figure in front of him. Rhona Dunbar walked with an easy, confident stride. The slap of her knee-length boots on the cobblestones echoed in his head and made his cock twitch. His legs glowed with the after-effects of Cameron's home-brew. 'But I could ride before I could walk. It is the way of the pampas.'

A long, low-roofed building appeared ahead, built from the same shiny black-flecked stone as Castle Dunbar. Angelo inhaled a familiar equine odour. He could hear snuffling and the clatter of iron shoes on stone. It had been a while since he'd been on a horse – London had many stables, but a sedate trot through Hyde Park wasn't his idea of a satisfying ride. His mind flashed back to the milk-white steeds he'd seen on the side of the mountain.

Rhona opened the stable door, stood back to let him go first.

Angelo hesitated, deferring to the lady.

She laughed. 'You are our guest, Angelo.' She nodded him ahead.

Angelo smiled and entered. The smell was stronger here. He wrenched a handful of hay from a nearby bale and walked over to the first stall.

Rhona was already there, stroking the mane of a gentle-looking piebald mare. 'Maxie was my first mount – father bought her for me when I was five. She's more than earnt her keep, but she's getting too old for much more than a gentle hack.' The Lady Laird turned her head towards him as the ancient animal nuzzled her neck. 'And I've got a feeling we will be requiring something a little more strenuous today.'

Angelo held out the handful of hay and felt Maxie's large, blunt teeth snatch it expertly from his fingers.

Rhona patted the black and white neck, then moved on.

The next stall contained a bigger, reddish-brown horse which neighed appreciatively as its mistress approached. 'Ginger is Cameron's favourite mount.' The Lady Laird ruffled the bay's thick mane, then scratched Ginger's withers. 'A spirited gelding –' she laughed '– and wasted on my brother.'

Angelo cocked an eyebrow. 'The Laird does not like spirit?'

Rhona laughed the same, slightly mocking laugh, now tinged with a more serious note. 'Cammie has a lot on his mind these days. He has little time for the horses.'

'Ah.' Angelo still didn't understand, but moved on anyway. The sound of hooves kicking against wood made him jump back.

'Now, Caliban! Be nice.'

Unlike the mare or the gelding, this animal had not come forward to greet them. Angelo stared at the stallion's inky coat. He could almost feel the sheer male vitality of the animal which stared back at him from the far corner of the stall. Beside him, Rhona sighed. 'Beautiful, isn't he?'

Angelo took in the powerful animal, noting the toss of its proud head and the breath which streamed from the flaring nostrils. Densely muscled hindquarters gleamed in the darkness.

'I bought Caliban for stud six months ago – more took him off the trainer's hands than bought, actually.'

Locking eyes with the horse, Angelo moved closer, then leapt back as Caliban reared up, pawing the air with his front hooves. He recognised the dark spirit within, and would have liked to spend more time with the animal. But, as far as a mount was concerned, he wanted the shining palomino he had seen on the mountain side.

Rhona was already leading two chestnut horses from adjoining stalls. 'Meet Thunder and Lightning. Irish thoroughbreds – brother and sister. I thought they . . . Her words tailed off as she noticed Angelo's expression. 'What's wrong?'

He glanced around. 'Where is the white horse?'

Rhona narrowed her eyes.

Angelo tried to hide his disappointment. 'I presumed the palomino was part of Castle Dunbar's stables. I am mistaken.' He tried to generate enthusiasm for the handsome chestnut gelding before him, raising a hand to stroke its nose.

The Lady Laird regarded him curiously. 'Where have you seen the white horse?'

Angelo smiled, remembering the thunder of hooves and the bright flash of milky mane. 'On the beach below the cottage – and on the mountain, on my way here. Is he wild, or does he belong to someone else?'

Rhona's striking features took on a darker set. 'You have seen the Kelpie, Angelo. He belongs to no man.'

A sudden violent snorting and the sound of splintering wood made Angelo turn.

Caliban's hooves impacted with the stable door a second time.

The Lady Laird passed Thunder and Lightning's reins to Angelo and tucked a wisp of blond hair back under her hat. 'Excuse me a moment. I must lead him around the paddock, settle him down a bit.'

Angelo was quicker. He moved in front of her. 'Has he ever been ridden?'

'Caliban? No – according to the trainer, he's unmountable. Wonderful lineage, though – just the beast for stud.'

Angelo grabbed a blanket and saddle from over an empty stable half-door. 'May I?' He strode towards the door of the third stall.

The Lady Laird gave him a sidelong glance. 'Think you can?'

Angelo smiled. Having been done out of the vibrant palomino, the evil-looking Caliban was the next best thing. He nodded, then stared into the stallion's ebony eyes. 'Do I have your permission?' The question was directed at both horse and owner.

The latter laughed. 'Be my guest, but I'm going to insist on protective headgear.' Rhona led Thunder back into his stall before walking her own mount out into the yard.

Angelo was waiting for a response from the dark shape in front of him. Caliban's answer was a sudden snort. But at least the kicking had stopped.

Saddle slung over his shoulder, he unfastened the stall door and stood back.

The seventeen-hand stallion regarded him warily, then walked slowly out into the yard.

Sweat cooled on Robert's spine. He held the condom tight around the root as his softening cock slid out of the gasping man beneath him, curling limp and sore in the crevice of Fingal's arse. Raising his head from the crook of his young lover's neck, he stared down at the beautiful face.

Fingal gazed up at him, features creased with worry. 'You won't tell them, will you?'

Robert kissed a blond eyebrow. 'I won't tell anyone, not if you don't want me to.' His dry mouth moved up over the damp forehead, lips brushing each of the worry-lines which had appeared there. 'But who are "they", exactly?' He propped himself up on one elbow and surveyed the spent, naked figure.

Fingal's legs slipped from around Robert's waist. 'Hamish, Douglas, Miss Nicol – all of them!' The full mouth curved downwards into a frown.

Robert sighed. 'OK, but why the big secret?' He eased the

condom off, allowing his naked cock to loll against the boy's thigh.

'No big secret.' One pale arm reached down. Fingal stuck a finger into a drying globule of spunk, then began to rub the viscous liquid into the hot skin of his chest. 'Just don't tell them, eh?'

Robert laughed. 'Fine by me.' He gripped two slender biceps and leant back, pulling Fingal on top of him. He rather liked the idea of having just taken this youth's virginity, but he could be discreet if discretion was called for. 'Angelo's OK, though? He knows when to keep his mouth shut.'

Straddling Robert's waist, Fingal looked confused. 'Who?'

'My flatmate – you saw us swimming earlier? Tall, dark hair and –'

'Caballo?' Fingal's hair cascaded around his shoulders in blond tangles.

Robert grinned. The youth's balls pressed against his stomach. Somewhere behind Fingal, his sore cock twitched. 'Yes, Caballo, if you like.' He stretched up a hand to caress a now slightly more prominent nipple. Must be the air, or something. Robert found himself ready to fuck again, almost immediately.

The blond head flicked right then left. 'Where is Caballo?'

Robert's fingers found their target. He gripped the pink nub, rolling it between his fingers.

'Where is Caballo?' The voice was more urgent now, the caresses ignored.

Robert tugged at the bud of flesh and grinned more broadly. 'Angelo's out riding – he won't be back for a while.' He released the youth's nipple. Something occurred to him: Fingal was obviously up for sex in a big way – Angelo had seemed to get something out of their encounter with Billy-Bob, on the train. Perhaps –

'He's with them, isn't he?' Fingal's words cut through his thoughts.

Robert looked up at the panic-streaked face. 'No, actually – he's with Rhona Dunbar.'

The youth jumped off Robert and began searching the heather

for his clothes. 'Then you can't tell him.' Fingal dragged black briefs over scratched thighs then grabbed his T-shirt.

Disappointment froze in Robert's stiffening cock. 'What's the hurry?'

The question only made Fingal dress faster. 'You won't tell him, will you – about any of this?'

Robert stared as the youth struggled into jeans, then boots. He was starting to become irritated. 'Look, Angelo and I are friends – we tell each other things.' Despite the afternoon's earlier exchange of confidences, Robert suddenly wondered if he would be privy to what happened between his flatmate and the haughty-looking Lady Laird.

Fingal shrugged on his leather jacket, then grabbed the air-pistol. 'Swear you won't tell anyone – Caballo in particular. He will tell them, I know he will!'

It was on the tip of his tongue to admit Angelo already knew about the target-practice and youth's excesses with the switch and the elderberries. Robert got to his feet, brushing sprigs of heather from his arse and thighs. 'I'm not swearing to –'

'Swear!' Fingal cocked the gun, levelling the barrel at Robert's head.

'Fuck off!' Robert laughed, getting into the game.

But the angelic face was deadly serious. One long finger hovered millimetres from the trigger.

A sheen of cold sweat trembled over his body. His irritation grew to annoyance. Robert brought one hand up underneath the gun, knocking the barrel skywards. His other hand grabbed a smooth throat. 'Don't you ever point that thing at me again!' Beneath his palm, an Adam's apple bobbed convulsively.

Then Fingal wrenched himself free, turned and bounded back down the hill.

Heart pounding in his chest, Robert watched him go. As the vision in the leather jacket, blond hair streaming disappeared from sight, he frowned.

PC Campbell had been right: the youth was bad news.

Bad news, but a good fuck.

Trying to ignore the sour taste the incident had left in his mouth, Robert grabbed his own clothes and began to dress.

Caliban accepted a bit and bridle, but baulked at any attempt to saddle him.

Angelo sank to a crouch, picking up the heavy leather seat and blanket for the third time.

Caliban swished his tail and threw back his head in satisfaction.

A few feet away, mounted on Lightning, the Lady Laird was watching. 'I told you – he's unridable. Lead him around the yard a couple of times and leave it at that.'

Crouching in front of the huge stallion, Angelo knew when he was being goaded. He also knew sheer brute force would never succeed with this steed. He rose slowly to his feet, kicking the saddle over to a far corner of the yard. The hard hat was perched uncomfortably on top of his head. Unfastening the chin-strap, he tore the protective covering free and tossed it aside the way Caliban had rejected the saddle.

Man and beast eyed each other.

Two streams of confrontational steam poured from the animal's nostrils.

Angelo wiped his sweating face with a sweatier forearm. He tried to clear his mind of all distractions.

'You're too alike, you two.'

Lightning snorted impatiently, hooves clacking on cobblestones as she echoed Lady Rhona's sentiment.

Caliban remained suspiciously silent.

Standing directly in front of the huge horse, Angelo took a step closer. He began to talk. 'There's a saying on the pampas: it takes a man to break a mare or a gelding, but more than mere man to ride a stallion.' He stared into the horse's dark eyes.

Caliban returned the stare.

Angelo talked on. His voice was low and relaxed, almost casual. 'Stallions are never broken – any true horseman knows this. To break such an animal as this is to make him less than his nature. Then he ceases to be, and any man who tries becomes less than a man.' He moved closer, feeling hot breath on his face. 'We are alike. Neither of us needs to become less, in this. Together, we can become more.' Angelo tilted his head upwards, closing the distance between himself and the steed.

Caliban's reins hung loose around his proud head.

Angelo's breath brushed the glossy nose. Slowly, he reached up and gently gathered the leather straps into his hand. 'You will let me do this, because I am no threat to any part of you.'

A low snort escaped Caliban's foam-flecked nostrils.

Still talking, Angelo moved smoothly round to the animal's right flank. 'We will ride together, and the weight on your back will be a small price to pay for the pleasure I will give you.' His other hand stroked the warm neck.

Caliban turned his large head slowly, following the movement and the words.

Inside, Angelo was a bundle of doubts. He had seen this done once – by one of Rancho Caballo's more elderly horsemen, a man whose body and bearing had been ground down by decades of life herding cattle. His voice was very low now, barely audible. 'Come, my friend.' His fingers tightened in the thick mane. 'You have nothing to lose and everything to gain.' The heavy muscle relaxed for a second, and Angelo saw his opportunity. Marshalling every ounce of strength, he lashed the reins around one wrist and vaulted onto Caliban's back.

The gasp from behind was obliterated by Caliban's snort of surprise. The steed tossed his head in annoyance, then lowered his neck.

Gripping the thick mane, Angelo knew Caliban was about to throw him. He leant forward, flattening himself against the warm back and whispering in an erect ear. 'I am no threat. You are the boss. You always will be.' Closing his eyes, Angelo allowed his body to go limp across the animal's flanks. He pressed his face into the rough mane and waited.

After an interminable pause, Caliban raised his ebony head and snuffled his assent.

Relief flooded through Angelo's body. He sat up, tightened his thighs around the animal's flanks and seized the reins with both hands. Glancing across at Lightning and her mount, he saw Lady

Rhona was awestruck. It was the first time he'd seen anything except haughty self-confidence on those aristocratic features. Angelo winked, gathering the reins towards his body. 'Well? Are we going for this ride or not?' Turning Caliban's head towards an open gate at the far end of the yard, he applied a little pressure with his thighs, then felt himself thrown back with sheer force as the horse took off at speed.

As they galloped past the stables, the sound of hooves and the huskiness of the Lady Laird's laugh followed Angelo and Caliban out onto rocky moorland.

Man and horse were a single unit of tensed, sweating muscle.

Whether it was the friction which came from riding bareback or the rhythmic pounding of the hooves beneath, Angelo was surprised to find his cock stiffening inside his jeans. He had been forced to shorten the reins and raise his knees to grip Caliban's flanks more tightly in order to keep his seat. The position threw him forward, bringing his crotch into contact with the animal's withers.

The stallion made no further attempt to throw him – he didn't need to. The very speed at which the horse was racing across the ground was enough to unseat the most experienced of riders.

Countryside flashed by.

Ears flattened against his head, Caliban galloped like an animal enjoying its first taste of freedom.

Angelo smiled. The wind tore at his face and hair. The rhythmic tattoo of hooves on earth filled his head. He'd forgotten how exhilarating a good ride could be. Shut up in a stable was no life for a beast such as this. The confines of city life were a distant memory as horse and rider covered the ground with long, graceful strides.

Every sinew of his body was alive and tingling, and Angelo knew Caliban felt the same. If the animal stumbled at this speed, it would be certain death for both of them. The knowledge only increased the pleasure.

But there were other dangers. Angelo didn't want Caliban to

become overheated or dehydrated on his first ride. Much as he was loath to rein the horse in, he knew he had to sooner or later.

Peering around the side of the animal's sweating neck, Angelo's eyes spotted something which made his heart pound harder than ever.

A drystone wall loomed ahead, running from as far as he could see in the north, and joining with another along the bottom of a field. There was no gate.

He shortened the reins, digging his calves more firmly into Caliban's back.

The horse seemed to increase rather than decrease the pace of the gallop.

Somewhere behind, Lady Rhona's shout of warning rang in his ears, then was carried away on the wind.

The wall was mere yards away now.

Angelo tugged at Caliban's mouth, trying to force the animal to change direction, if not slow down.

The stallion's hooves pounded determinedly onwards.

Angelo was about to start praying when he suddenly found himself soaring into the air as Caliban leapt the wall, clearing the top stone by at least six inches.

The impact on landing made his teeth rattle. He fought to control the horse, which was slowing down anyway. Still not quite believing the jump, Angelo tightened the reins further and brought Caliban to a shuddering, shaking halt. To his right, he noticed a small pool. He led the trembling animal across to the water, trying to calm himself as well.

Gratefully, Caliban lowered his head.

One eye on his drinking horse, Angelo turned his head and watched Lightning carry her mount to the other side of the wall.

Seventeen

Robert was staring at the notepad in front of him, still confused by his encounter with Fingal, when a crunch of boots on gravel made him flinch.

He leapt to his feet, ready to snatch the gun from the youth if he was back for a rematch. Green twinkling eyes regarded his clenched fists.

'Did I startle you?'

Robert looked at Malcolm, then laughed. 'You did, but it was a pleasant startle.' The smell from the tall figure before him was stronger than ever.

The kilt was gone. Dressed in a white, scale-stained T-shirt tucked into yellow oilskin work-trousers, the fisherman was carrying a box, which he placed in a shaded area near the door to Corrie Cottage. 'Thought you could do with more supplies – don't let me interrupt your work.' The redhead nodded to the notepad and pencils.

Robert sighed. 'You're not interrupting.' He sat down, pushed out a chair and indicated for Malcolm to do likewise. 'Thanks – you must let me pay you, this time.'

The tall fisherman accepted the chair and thanks, but shook his ponytailed locks at the offer of money. 'No need.' He stretched out his legs, gazing around him, then focusing on the man across the table. 'This is payment enough.'

Robert's cock tugged inside his shorts. He hadn't had the opportunity to shower yet. He smiled at the rugged fisherman. 'Well, if you won't accept money . . .' He let the end of the sentence dangle tantalisingly, surprised at his own arousal. Less than thirty minutes ago he'd been locked in passion with the delinquent, if angel-faced youth. Now his balls were starting to fill all over again.

A hint of a blush shadowed the stubbly, weather-beaten face. Malcolm pulled his eyes from Robert's face and directed them towards the table-top. 'I have a favour to ask.'

Robert's smile broadened. 'Name it.' He glanced at his watch: nearly four. Angelo had been away almost three hours already. But, if he'd been gone this long, he probably wouldn't be back for a while yet.

Malcolm looked sheepish. 'The washing facilities on board the *Kelpie* have packed in. Can I use your shower?'

Robert grinned at the brawny man's sudden coyness. 'Of course – I was about to have a wash myself.' He nodded to the notebook. 'Not working works up quite a sweat.'

Malcolm laughed. 'Thank you.' He began to pull off his heavy rubber boots and thick socks, then hauled the creaking oilskins down over familiar ginger-dusted thighs.

He was naked beneath.

Robert watched appreciatively, enjoying a better view of the man's equipment than he'd been able to the night before in the half-darkness and hurry of their time on the *Kelpie*.

The fisherman's heavy bollocks had rubbed a hairless area on the inside of his thick thighs.

Robert couldn't take his eyes off the pendulous sack which swung like a net weight between pale legs.

Then Malcolm turned to pick up his clothes and Robert's previous vista was replaced by a view of two rounded half-moons of milky flesh. He focused on the ginger tufted crack between the fisherman's arse-cheeks and remembered the feel of that bristling hair against his face as he'd thrust between those two hard mounds with his tongue. Robert winced as his cock trapped several pubes in its rush towards erection. He stood up, pulled his T-shirt over his head and locked eyes with the ruggedly handsome man.

Green twinkled back at him. Malcolm sank to a crouch, stretched out a hand and began to unfasten the buckle of Robert's belt.

Hands resting lightly on the well-muscled shoulders, Robert felt strong fingers unzip him. He heard the fisherman's sharp intake of breath as his cock leapt free from its prison of fabric. Robert stared down at the top of Malcolm's lowered head, then gasped as a stubbly, unshaven chin rubbed itself against the delicate, stretching skin.

Odours drifted up: the smell of sweat, fish and another rich saltiness which had nothing to do with the sea. Remembering his encounter, only half an hour earlier, Robert tried to pull away, conscious of his unwashed state.

Malcolm's hands slipped around and clasped Robert's arse-cheeks, holding him there. The pale face looked up at him. The fisherman licked a patch of crystallised spunk from the back of Robert's shaft. 'Whose body am I tasting?'

Shivers – half embarrassment, half arousal – coursed over his skin. He remembered the way his cock had curled in the crack of the man-boy's arse.

Eyes still on Robert's face, Malcolm's tongue darted up to the head of his stiffening cock and flicked a globule of congealed spunk from under the stretching foreskin. 'This is yours, I know.'

Robert moaned, unable to form words. He knew his groin must smell worse than a cheese-factory in a heat wave, but Malcolm was nibbling and chewing at the wrinkled skin as if it were the tastiest of cordon-bleu delicacies.

'Hamish?'

Robert's 'no' was more moan than syllable.

'Douglas?'

The word vibrated over his glans. 'No – ah!' Robert's denial stretched itself into a groan.

Malcolm's teeth were running around the rim between the

head of Robert's cock and the rest of his shaft. More vibrations set off parallel detonations in his balls as the fisherman laughed.

'Fingal!'

'No – oh, yes!' Robert remembered his half-promise of secrecy. His brain swam with slurping sounds and the feel of the fisherman's tongue on and under his foreskin. 'Does it matter?' He looked down, watching the man clean his prick.

Malcolm looked up. 'No – I like the thought of your cock in other men. I like tasting their bodies on you.'

Something spasmed in his bollocks. Robert kicked off shorts and briefs, grabbing the back of Malcolm's red head and pushing the fisherman's face hard into his groin.

A large hand was gripping his shaft now. Malcolm's fist slid down Robert's cock, pulling the foreskin back further still until the swollen, purplish bulb was exposed in all its glory. Hips bucking, Robert bent his knees. He wanted to ram his length into the fisherman's face the way he had shoved himself into Fingal's tight arse.

A low laugh drifted up through the slurping sounds. Malcolm tightened his grip, and raised his red head. The skin around his lips was wet and pinkish. The large man stood up, wiping his mouth on the back of his hand. 'Now I want to wash the rest of you.'

Robert recalled the icy water which poured from Corrie Cottage's ancient shower, and frowned: no level of arousal – even his – could survive those temperatures. 'Let's stay here. I want to –'

'Come on.'

The fisherman's fist was still clamped around his cock. Grinning broadly, his freckled shoulders and chest gleaming in the afternoon sun, Malcolm hauled Robert towards the outhouse.

As he wrenched open the slatted door, he thought he saw two horses – one black, one red – outlined against a distant mountain.

Then Malcolm slapped his arse and pulled him into the shower.

Rhona Dunbar led Lightning further up the steep incline and through a narrow opening in the drystone wall.

Minutes later, the two horses stood side by side on a naturally formed plateau.

The wind had died down, leaving only a cooling breeze to caress Angelo's sweat-soaked hair. Every nerve in his body was alive and tingling. His fully hard cock rubbed between Caliban's withers as the animal grazed contentedly at a patch of grass. Basking in post-exertion glow, he savoured a satisfaction which was almost sexual.

'You were made for each other.' The Lady Laird's voice was low.

He bowed his head, accepting then deflecting the compliment. 'Caliban is a fine animal. He did all the work, but I wouldn't recommend riding him every day.'

'Your modesty does you credit, Caballo.'

Angelo smiled, then remembered the bitter golden brew which he could still taste on his lips. 'Cameron's tonic also played its part, I think.' He switched his attention back to the marvellous view. 'All this is yours?' He gazed down over a patchwork of fields towards the rocky coastline and beyond. Any further reference to what had happened between him and the wild, black stallion would spoil the moment.

'All this, and more.'

Angelo turned his head, noting an ambiguity in the words.

Skin flushed from the ride, Rhona Dunbar pushed her riding-cap further back on her head. 'Land taxes, feu duty, government levies, utility charges.' She sighed. 'There are many burdens on a laird, these days.' The aristocratic face attempted a smile. 'But don't let me bore you with my problems. Tell me you will accept Caliban as a gift.' She laughed. 'As stud material, he falls a little short of my requirements.'

Angelo cocked his head.

Lady Rhona explained. 'He shows as much interest in mounting my geldings as my mares.'

Angelo leant over and patted the side of the animal's neck. 'So you too like snails and oysters, my fine friend!'

'What do you mean?'

Angelo raised his head. 'On the pampas, we have a saying: some men like snails. Some prefer oysters. Others allow themselves the pleasure of both.'

The Lady Laird's pretty face creased with further confusion.

Angelo blushed. 'Sophisticated people call it –' he searched for an appropriate translation '– "anything that moves"!'

Rhona Dunbar's laugh was hoarse and earthy. 'Now I know why you and Caliban hit it off so well!' She smiled slyly.

Angelo shifted in his seat. He had not intended to be quite so honest with this beautiful rider: some women were uneasy with such things. Julie had been one of those women.

The Lady Laird noticed his discomfort. She reached over, resting a well-manicured hand on his shoulder. 'You and the blond Englishman are lovers?'

Angelo flinched. 'No! We're . . . just friends!'

Sky blue eyes gazed into his. 'But you want there to be more, don't you?'

Angelo looked away. 'How did you . . .?'

Rhona squeezed his shoulder. 'Call it a woman's intuition.'

Angelo sighed. As far as Robert was concerned, he was just some rough, bumbling foreigner who got his English phrases mixed up and was guaranteed to say the wrong thing at the wrong time in the wrong way. Robert wasn't interested in the likes of him.

Rhona let her hand rest where it was. 'Tell me about it.'

Angelo frowned. 'Ten years ago, I . . . slept with a man. One of our ranch hands. Juan.' Angelo remembered the passion: the hardness, the feeling of lying beside the handsome Brazilian cattleman.

Rhona's hand squeezed reassuringly.

Sweet memory soured into bitter resentment. 'My father caught us – beat and sacked Juan on the spot, then told me I was no son of his and exiled me to –' He paused, recalling the Brazilian's soft blond hair – like Robert's hair. His eyes returned to the Lady Laird. 'It was just horseplay – nothing really happened.' Angelo recalled Juan's body: slender but well-muscled and hairless – like Robert's. The good-looking Brazilian had the same almost boyish air about him: long, powerful legs, an arse that looked its best in tight jeans and an easy, relaxed manner. But whereas Juan's eyes had been brown and smouldering, Robert's clear blue pupils signalled an Englishness which made Angelo's pulse race and his balls tighten. 'But –'

'You wanted it to?'

Angelo found himself aroused both by her presence and the thought of Robert's naked body. He tore his mind away from both. 'We'd better get back.'

'There's no rush, is there?'

Angelo gathered Caliban's reins up in his hands. 'No, but I think we've covered more ground than either of us intended to.'

Rhona smiled wryly at the unintended double meaning. 'Yes, we have. It will take a while to get back to the castle.' She gently tugged Lightning's chestnut head towards the gap in the wall. 'You can tell me about Robert as we hack, if you like.'

Angelo shook his head: his mind was already dwelling too much on something which wasn't to be. 'No, you can tell me more about your island.' Applying a little pressure to Caliban's inky flanks, he followed Lightning's swaying rump.

The Lady Laird was a well-informed and interesting guide. As their mounts passed burns and pasture, she pointed out and named wildflowers and birds. 'Kelpie Island is volcanic. This land spent millennia below sea level before a great earthquake spat it upwards. But unlike many other igneous areas, our soil is too sulphurous to grow much more than grass and heather –' she laughed '– despite what Douglas may tell you about his onions!'

Angelo chuckled. He pointed to three large boulders, a little distance away. 'What type of rock is that? Everything here seems to be built from it.'

'Ah. That's low-grade granite. An ancestor of ours believed it was going to be a way to make his fortune, but transportation to the mainland proved too costly and Kelpie Island's particular form of the stone isn't as hard as the Aberdeen variety.' Her voice took on a more serious tone. 'Especially these days.'

Angelo watched as the Lady Laird dismounted elegantly and picked up a small handful of chips. She shuffled them between slim fingers, then cast them to the ground and held her hand up for his inspection.

The pale palm was smudged with blackness.

'What is it?'

Rhona wiped her hand with a lace-edged handkerchief, then remounted Lightning. 'A peaty deposit, I think. Weakens the rock.'

They rode on, and the nature lesson continued. Angelo learnt that the island's main revenue came from fishing these days, but restrictions on quotas, from European regulators, were hampering even that.

'One thousand years ago, Flora Dunbar saw off invaders who wanted to take our island. But when the bank on the mainland calls in the outstanding mortgages, I doubt we will be able to fight any more. Kelpie Island will fall into the hands of strangers, and our customs and way of life will disappear for ever.'

As Castle Dunbar's turrets appeared in the distance, Angelo looked across at his attractive companion. 'Can't you reason with them?'

Rhona shook her head. 'We have tried. Where debts are concerned, these people have no respect.'

Over the hills came the elegiac sound of music.

Rhona sighed sadly. 'He who pays the piper calls the tune. And Cameron and I have no money left.'

Angelo felt himself affected by the mournful music. 'There must be something you can do.'

She reined in Lightning and stared up towards where Angelo had seen the white horse earlier that day. 'Only the Kelpie can save us now.'

Angelo cocked an eyebrow. 'What is a Kelpie anyway, and how can it save the island?'

'Later, Caballo. I will explain later.' The Lady Laird gripped Lightning's flanks more tightly, and tugged his head left. 'Caliban looks like he's had enough of a rest. Race you back to the castle!' Digging her boots in against the animal's chestnut coat, Rhona and Lightning were off, her horse living up to its name.

★　★　★

Corrie Cottage's shower had been built for one – and one small man, at that.

Having efficiently washed his own, brawny body under the icy water, Malcolm eased back and out of the shower cubicle.

Robert released his breath. His cock, which had been pinned upright between his own and the fisherman's stomach, remained there at an almost ninety-degree angle.

Malcolm grinned. 'Turn round.' He lathered the bar of soap between huge hands.

Robert lowered his eyes to where the redhead's shaft curved up towards him, then did as he was instructed. Arms braced against the wall, he planted his feet a yard apart and arched his back.

The icy water was getting warmer by the minute. Robert let the stream break over his head and cascade down his neck and shoulders. His arse-hole was hungry for the man, eager for Malcolm to thrust into him and fill the empty hole between his buttocks. Droplets shimmered down his spine. Robert shivered with anticipation as rivulets ran into his crack and made his sphincter clench and unclench. Seconds passed. Then minutes. His head dropped between his arms. Robert stared at his cock, watching the stiff shaft flex and jump with expectation. He was just about to glance over his shoulder to see what was taking so long, when something firm and slippery wrapped itself around his right ankle.

Malcolm's soapy fist travelled up Robert's calf, then back down again.

Robert shivered as the process was repeated on his left leg. His foot was removed from the floor of the shower, each toe soaped and rinsed individually. Malcolm did the same with the other foot. Robert balanced himself against the shower wall while unexpectedly careful fingers washed between his toes. He wriggled and almost giggled when the fisherman hit a ticklish spot.

There was a low chuckle from behind, then a wet hand patted his arse and his foot was returned to the floor. 'Stand still.'

Then both ankles were gripped. Malcolm ran two soapy palms up and over Robert's legs, carrying on up his thighs and moving from inside to out and back again.

Robert felt his knees start to buckle. He'd never been washed before. To his surprise, the thought of this giant of a redhead painstaking soaping the rest of his body was almost as much of a turn-on as the cock-cleaning. He allowed his legs to bend, palms dragging down the wall of the shower as he thrust his arse out to meet the advance of the lathering hands.

Malcolm soaped efficiently, thoroughly coating Robert's tight bollocks and up into his crack.

Robert's teeth sank into his bottom lip. His ball-sack clenched. He bit back the first surge of climax.

As he washed, Malcolm began to talk. 'So, you're enjoying your stay?'

Robert winced as hands cupped his buttocks. 'Yes!' The word came out more forcefully than he'd intended. The tenor of the fisherman's question wasn't quite what he'd expected.

'That's good.' The hands moved up to his waist, curving around to soap Robert's stomach. 'The weather's been great – and only one tremor so far, too.' Malcolm's palms swept up, rubbing Robert's pecs and making his nipples stand to attention. 'How are you finding the cottage?'

Robert moaned. His head dangled loosely between his shoulders.

Malcolm burrowed into Robert's armpits with businesslike fingers, coating the thick hair with soap then working it into a lather. 'I said, how are you finding the cottage?'

Robert scowled. The fisherman really did expect an answer. Half-annoyed, half-amused that the conversation was more like one a man might have with his barber than an exchange between two naked, hard bathers, he cleared his throat. 'Apart from not having a roof at the moment, the cottage is fine.'

'Good – that's good.' Malcolm's fingers left the now-drenched hair of Robert's armpits and travelled up to his shoulders and down over biceps.

Robert could feel the fisherman standing between his splayed thighs. He could feel the head of Malcolm's swollen cock chafing against his arse-cheek as the man rubbed and lathered his upper and forearms. He was acutely aware of a pressure in his groin which told him he wasn't going to be able to hold on much longer. The redhead evidently liked lots of foreplay. Robert dug his fingers into the back of the shower cubicle as Malcolm continued to soap the side of his arms. If you can't beat them –

'Er –' He gritted his teeth in concentration. 'Tell me, exactly what do I own, around here?'

Malcolm laughed. 'Own?' He continued to run his hands down Robert's arms, soaping his wrists.

'Yes, own. I mean, I know the cottage is mine, but do I own the land around it, or what?' Robert gasped. Water ran into his mouth as the fisherman caressed his wrists. Malcolm's shaft was thrusting between his thighs, rubbing against the underside of his bollocks.

'The Laird and Lady Laird own every inch of Kelpie Island, and the waters as far as a mile out from its shores. You own the stone from which Corrie Cottage is built, nothing more.'

Robert frowned. Some inheritance – literally, a pile of bricks.

Malcolm talked on, his strong hands moving to Robert's neck and shoulders. 'But ownership is mostly a double-edged sword.'

Robert groaned. He could feel the fisherman's nipples grinding against his shoulder-blades. He pushed back against another wet, slippery body, cursing the philosophical direction the unwanted conversation was taking.

'As the tremors remind us, we are all in the lap of greater owners, my friend.'

Robert shivered as wet lips brushed his ear. He pressed his hot face against the cold metal of the shower wall, hooking hands around the body behind him. He knew whose lap he wanted to be in, at this precise moment. An image of himself, straddling the fisherman's hairy thighs and impaled on the man's hot rod burst into his mind. Robert gripped Malcolm's hard arse-cheeks, pulling the man closer until his bollocks were resting on top of the fisherman's throbbing shaft. Despite the small-talk, his message was read loud and clear.

Pushing Robert gently forward, Malcolm eased himself away and patted his bathing partner's rump. 'Too close, my friend – it was risky, even last night.'

Robert spun round, wiping water from his eyes. One hand flapped left, then found the rope which controlled the flow. He yanked the shower off. 'What do you mean?'

The fisherman's rugged face was a solemn mask. 'Tomorrow is midsummer's eve. A very special day for all islanders.'

Robert stared.

Malcolm corrected himself. 'All male islanders, that is. From midnight yesterday until midnight tomorrow, we must deny our appetites.'

Robert struggle to understand. 'You mean, like a sort of contracted Lent?'

The solemn mask cracked into a mischievous grin. 'We acknowledge a more ancient religion, and our practices involve more than giving up chocolate for a few weeks.'

Robert laughed, then looked down wryly at the thick length of manhood which still sprouted from between the fisherman's wet thighs. 'Seems such a waste.' His eyes moved to his own cock, the head of which reached out towards the fisherman's.

Malcolm flicked the shower back on and playfully tapped Robert's bucking shaft. 'But there's nothing to stop you.' He winked, his fist tightening around the stiff cock.

Robert sighed. It wouldn't be the same, knowing Malcolm couldn't come. An arm draped itself over his shoulder:

'I'm sorry – I shouldn't have mentioned it. But I thought it was better you knew. I don't want you to think I don't find you attractive.'

Robert encircled the broad waist and suddenly found himself thinking about Angelo. He already knew one man who didn't want to fuck him. Now he had a second, who did, but because of some strange island tradition, couldn't, at the moment. Douglas, Hamish – all out of bounds, due to the same rules. His mind wandered to the unpredictable Fingal, who apparently didn't abide by island law. Was this what the boy had been so desperate to keep secret? Before he had a chance to ponder any longer, Malcolm's mouth was on his and the fisherman's strong fist was sliding up Robert's shaft.

Robert groaned into the man's mouth, feeling his tight bollocks impact with Malcolm's fingers each time he thrust into the broad, soap-slidy hand. Water coursed over them, adding to the salty wetness which was leaking from Robert's slit. Malcolm was pushing him back, manhandling his shaft until Robert felt the wall of the shower against his shoulders and the familiar tingle deep in his arse.

He opened his mouth wider, wanting to return the kiss but only capable of moaning as the fisherman's tongue explored the inside of his lips and the man's fist tightened around his aching cock.

Robert thrust upwards, pounding into the finger-vice. Water soaked his blond hair, running into his nose then scattering around their joined mouths. He fucked Malcolm's meaty fist fiercely, hands gripping two wet shoulders until a grunt tore itself from his lungs and he shot ropes of warm milky whiteness over ginger-dusted knuckles.

Malcolm's arm was round his shoulders, holding him firmly against the shower wall as he coaxed the last few drops of spunk from Robert's quivering prick. Then he broke the kiss, leaving Robert to gasp as he released his cock and, raising his hand, began to lick Robert's come from in between his giant fingers.

Later, as they walked, dripping, into the sunshine, another implication of Malcolm's words about 'island ways' sank in – for Robert's handsome flatmate.

All male islanders were practitioners.

Every female on the island would be at a loose end.

Robert thought about Angelo, at present out riding with the striking Rhona Dunbar, and tried to be happy.

At least there would be one smiling face on Kelpie Island over the next twenty-four hours.

Eighteen

A ngelo felt a strange sense of anticlimax.

The horses had been rubbed down and watered, and were now back in their respective stalls.

His body wasn't as sore as he would have expected after such a long absence from the saddle. On the contrary, he felt very much invigorated.

Unable to settle, he had been pacing around the drawing room at Castle Dunbar where Lady Rhona had left him, ten minutes earlier, while she went to change. Angelo stared up at the large etching of the white horse which hung over the vast fireplace.

Back on the pampas, after such an exhilarating experience, the men often got drunk on the local brew or fucked their way through whatever assortment of men or women was available.

Angelo turned his head from the primitive painting and stared at the door. Then he looked towards the decanter of whisky and the tray of glasses which sat on the sideboard, and remembered he was a guest, and guests didn't help themselves to drinks – regardless of how badly they might need one.

He began to pace again, taking in the furniture which he had, on his previous visit, thought looked antique but now, in the light of the Lady Laird's confession as to their financial straits, he saw was merely old. Faded wall-hangings and ancient furnishings gave the room an air of bygone days and earlier splendours.

Angelo smiled, fingering heavy velvet curtains. He decided he liked this room, despite its shabbiness. It was how castles should look. He found himself wondering about the other rooms. Turning his attention again to the door, he saw it was not quite closed. Although he knew it was considered bad manners to wander uninvited around someone else's property, Angelo couldn't help himself. Curiosity getting the better of him, he strode across the flagstone floor, seized the handle and walked out into the hallway.

A quick investigation of the three other doors leading off the great hall revealed two dusty storerooms and a vast, well-equipped kitchen.

Back in the hall, Angelo raised his eyes and took in the sweeping staircase. The banister was fashioned from a heavy, dark wood and decorated with intricate carvings. Angelo traced one of the designs with a finger, noticing the relief was in the shape of a rearing horse. He smiled. The Dunbars admired the equine form almost as much as he did. Angelo moved his hand along the stair-rail, examining each of the details.

The carving told some sort of story, which seemed to involve a horse, and an army who fought on foot.

Halfway up, he paused, turned.

Below, from the family gallery, the eyes of countless generations of Dunbars regarded him with the same amused indulgence as both Rhona and Cameron had.

Above his head, an ornate chandelier dangled majestically from the vaulted ceiling.

Angelo continued his climb.

What Castle Dunbar lacked in furniture it made up for in sheer breathtaking architecture. Carved wooden panelling on the stair-well around him took up the story from the engraved banister. The rearing horse had been replaced by a woman with short, masculine-looking hair who was now leading a band of men against a much larger army.

As he absorbed the detail and tried to work out what was happening in the relief, voices drifted down from upstairs.

Angelo paused, head cocked as he listened to the low husky tones of Rhona Cameron. Even at this distance, he could hear the excitement in her voice. He climbed the last few steps and stood motionless, listening to the words.

'It is he! I knew it the moment I laid eyes on him, on board the *Kelpie*. Now we have definite proof. Look, Cammie! It's coming true.'

Ears straining, Angelo struggled to catch the Laird's reply.

But Cameron's words were inaudible.

Swivelling his head left then right, he traced the conversation to a door straight ahead, at the end of a long corridor. Aware of every soft fall of his walking-boots, he made his way down the narrow corridor as silently as he could, eager to find out more.

The door was ajar.

Angelo moved closer.

Then a sound like a gunshot split the low words from inside.

Angelo cursed under his breath and hastily removed his foot from the creaky floorboard.

Too late. The door was wrenched open and he was staring into the Lady Laird's surprised face.

Rhona's blond hair hung free. The smart equestrian outfit was gone. In its place, a white, floor-length gown skimmed the curves of the Lady Laird's slim body like a passing cloud. Pinned to the garment's high neck was the same cameo brooch he had admired last night.

The vision in white took his breath away. 'Er – I was – you were . . .' Angelo struggled to explain his presence. 'I wondered where you had got to!'

'Sorry, Angelo.' Rhona smiled, stood back and beckoned him in. 'I apologise for keeping you waiting. Please join us.'

Transfixed, he found himself moving through the doorway.

Angelo stared from one large free-standing candelabrum to another. Like the basement which housed Cameron's distillation equipment, there seemed to be no electricity in this part of the castle either. At the far end of the spacious room, an enormous postered bed was hung with heavy curtains. Just behind him, at the other end, another set of curtains told him there was a window here. The walls were panelled with the same dark wood as the stairwell, and even at this distance Angelo could see the saga which had broken off at the stairs was continued in here.

Smells drifted into his nostrils: a sweet herbiness, the scent of his own body and the lingering equine odour of Caliban's tangled mane. Angelo soaked up the atmosphere. He wondered vaguely whose bedroom this was, though in truth, the room bore more resemblance to a private chapel than anyone's sleeping-quarters.

'I gather you have achieved the unachievable.' Cameron stood up to greet him.

Angelo shook his head. 'Caliban was a fluke. I –'

'Oh, I don't mean our bad-tempered stallion.' The Laird had also discarded his previous outfit and was now clad in a plaid dressing gown. He smiled, nodded over Angelo's shoulder to where Lady Rhona was closing the door and lowered his voice. 'You seemed to have charmed my sister – no mean feat, let me tell you.'

Angelo blinked, uncertain how to reply.

Cameron Dunbar seemed to enjoy his discomfort. The Laird sat back down on the sofa on which he had been lounging and patted a space beside him. 'Rhona is very choosy about who she likes – someone in her position has to be.'

Angelo nodded soberly, then took the seat offered. On the other side of the room, he could see the white-clad figure moving elegantly from the door to a chair opposite.

Rhona sat down, tucking neat ankles behind shapely calves.

Angelo notice her feet were bare. It suddenly dawned on him what was going on here: he was being sounded out as a potential suitor. He relaxed a little, and waited to be asked about his prospects.

Five minutes later Cameron Dunbar's hand was resting on his shoulder and Angelo was still waiting. The Laird did most of the talking but his words were more statements than questions.

Angelo listened to the low, Scottish voice, enjoying the soft burrs and warm vowels. He found himself entranced by the expressive face, almost unaware of the Laird's hand as it began to rub his shoulder.

Cameron Dunbar was a handsome man.

Angelo glanced across to where the Lady Laird sat, watching their one-sided conversation.

Rhona Dunbar was a handsome woman.

The Laird talked on, and Angelo returned his attention to his host. Gradually, he became so wrapped up in the sound of Cameron Dunbar's voice that the words ceased to have any meaning. Tones caressed his body, flowing over his neck and chest, then resounding in his stomach. The process reminded him of the technique he'd used with Caliban; it was as if the very pitch of the voice was striking at something deep inside him. His cock, hard and pulsing from the ride, was soon pushing at the waist of his jeans. And when the Laird began to stroke the side of his neck, Angelo stretched out a hand and returned the gesture.

Cameron's skin was warm and smooth. Angelo felt the pulse of blood throb beneath his fingers. His other hand settled in the crotch of his jeans, half to cover, half to fondle the stiffness there.

Then another hand was covering his.

Angelo glanced down.

Lady Rhona was kneeling in front of him. Delicate but remarkably strong fingers nudged his aside, then tightened over the bulge in his jeans.

Angelo felt his cock jerk beneath her hand. He groaned, swivelling his head between two aristocratic profiles. His hips bucked upwards and he stretched out his legs around the kneeling vision in white. Leaning back on the couch, he traced the strong jut of Cameron's jaw-line and moved down to slip behind the Laird's neck while Cameron's fingers wandered down towards the buttons of Angelo's shirt.

Two hands were working in the crotch of his jeans now. Heels resting on polished wood, he raised his arse-cheeks from the sofa, feeling denim slide down over his thighs. Freed from the confines of fabric, his shaft shivered in the cool air. Angelo rubbed the back of Cameron Dunbar's neck. His head lolled over the back of the sofa.

Then his mouth was opening in parallel to the mouth around his left nipple as another mouth lowered itself over the head of his straining cock.

Angelo moaned, fingers scrabbling to grip the padded edges of the couch. His back arched as Cameron flicked a wet tongue across his tensing bud. Then the heels of his boots were bracing themselves against the wooden floor as Rhona's tongue mirrored the movement over his glans. He stared upwards into darkness, eyes unfocused with arousal.

Cameron flicked his tongue again, then nipped with his teeth.

Angelo's balls spasmed. He bit back a cry which turned into a sigh of pleasure as Rhona's sheathed teeth made their way down his shaft.

Cameron sucked the bud, drawing the erect nub further into his mouth. Then fingers gripped Angelo's other nipple, twisting the tender flesh between thumb and forefinger.

Angelo's gasp was cut short as the head of his cock impacted off the hard cartilage at the back of the Lady Laird's throat. He thrust upwards with his hips, slamming his aching rod deeper and deeper while the pain in his right nipple faded to a warm glow.

Rhona slid her lips back up the length of his prick, lingering at the ridge just beneath the head.

Cameron twisted a second time, just as his sister moved to take one of Angelo's balls into her mouth.

This time Angelo almost howled. The torment being inflicted on his nipples was joining with the intense sensations produced by Rhona's wet mouth around his ball. Everything seemed heightened, more sensitive than ever. He could feel the diaphanous fabric of her gown against the skin on his thighs, while Cameron's rough robe chafed against his chest.

His nipples grew hard and red, bitten almost raw by the Laird's sharp teeth.

Rhona turned her attention to his other ball, giving it the same treatment, then drawing his whole sack between her lips and rolling the dimpled flesh around her mouth.

Cameron was nipping the skin around Angelo's buds now,

nibbling and gnawing until the entire area was swollen and tingling.

His sister spread Angelo's thighs wider and began to nuzzle the delicate skin of his perineum while his aching balls rested on the bridge of her aristocratic nose.

Angelo thrashed and writhed. Sweat poured from his armpits and between his shoulders, dribbling down to gather in the hairy crack of his arse.

The Dunbars worked in tandem, like a well-disciplined team. One each end of Angelo, they tortured and pleasured his aching body until he didn't know what felt good and what didn't. He hovered on the edge of orgasm again and again under Rhona's ministrations, only to be brought back from the precipice by a particularly vicious nip of the Laird's teeth.

Abruptly, strong arms gripped beneath his and Angelo found himself being half-carried, half-dragged towards the large bed. He caught a glimpse of white, floating fabric as his head hit the pillow. Then Rhona was kneeling at one side of him, Cameron at the other. Angelo watched through a haze, cock sticking to his stomach, while the Laird tugged at the belt of his plaid robe.

The garment fell open to reveal a deep, well-muscled chest. Shrugging his arms from the heavy sleeves, Cameron smiled the same slightly mocking smile Angelo had seen on Rhona's face.

Then Angelo's attention was taken by something three feet below.

Dangling between tensed thighs, Cameron's thick, half-hard cock was kept at bay by a leather and metal cage. Black straps circled the member's length, a heavy single thong bisecting the large head. Drawn up tight at the root of his cock, the Laird's balls were encased in a series of shining chrome rings.

Before he had the opportunity to comment, Angelo felt his legs gently nudged apart. He stared down at Rhona Dunbar, waiting for her to undress also.

She remained between his legs, thumbs caressing the skin on the inside of his thighs. And she remained fully dressed. Lowering her head, a veil of silver hair descended, obscuring his view of her actions. But the sensations were all too clear: the process was starting all over again.

Before he could do anything, Rhona was straddling his chest and the onslaught reversed itself. Angelo felt a bound cock poke against his lower leg as a rougher, stubbled mouth descended onto him.

The folds of Rhona's gown spread out over his stomach as she gazed down at him.

Angelo's hands gripped her waist, wanting to thrust up into her slender body as the Laird's unshaven chin rasped against his shaft.

She smiled, and when she spoke her voice was hoarse with passion. 'We need you, Caballo.'

Angelo ground his throbbing length against the firm cheeks of her arse. 'Anything!' Then he flinched as a breathy laugh between his splayed thighs made the air on his stomach shiver. Cameron's voice took over.

'Anything? That is indeed a generous offer.' Then the Laird was kneeling at Angelo's shoulder, sitting back on his heels and licking Angelo's arousal from around his mouth. The tethered length of his cock probed the air inches from Angelo's nose. 'Rhona has told you about our problem.'

Something twisted in his guts. Although he would indeed have given either this man or woman anything he had at that precise moment, Angelo clarified his words. 'I don't have much money, but what I have is –'

'We don't want your money, Caballo. We want you.'

Angelo's cock pulsed beneath Rhona's silk-covered thighs. 'You have me, beautiful lady –' he glanced right to where the Laird sat, also smiling '– as do you, my lord.'

Cameron's well-manicured hand pushed damp curls back from Angelo's forehead. 'The honour is ours, Caballo. The legend said you would come, when our need was great. And you have.'

Angelo's brow creased.

Rhona took over the explanation, staring deep into Angelo's eyes. 'Tomorrow, at midnight – one thousand years to the day when my ancestor, Flora Dunbar, saved the island from disaster –

the Kelpie will join with the Dark Rider, and the earth's ancient secrets will be revealed.'

Angelo blinked.

Rhona outlined Angelo's mouth with a delicate forefinger.

'Will you be our special guest at the ceremony, Caballo?' Cameron's voice was low and mesmeric.

Angelo tried to kiss the finger. It moved away, then eased itself between his lips.

The Laird continued. 'Tomorrow night we will fulfil what legend has foretold.'

She was fucking his mouth with one, then two fingers, forcing them between his lips then drawing them back out slick with his spit. Angelo fed on the invading digits, trying to suck them further into himself. Then the creature astride his chest paused, three fingers rammed into his mouth.

'I am high priestess of Kelpie Island, Caballo. Will you join us?'

Unable to think, almost unable to breathe, need swamped his body. At that precise moment, Angelo would have sold his soul in order to feel release. He nodded mutely.

Rhona's aristocratic face smiled down at him. 'Good.' She drew her fingers slowly from his mouth and sucked at them. 'We will begin your instruction.'

The pressure in his balls was unbearable. With a grin of lust, he reached up towards the shimmering white figure.

Half an hour later he was limping back across the fields in the direction of Corrie Cottage.

'Instruction' had involved several more glasses of Cameron Dunbar's bitter-tasting home brew and an invitation to return to the castle at midnight tonight, to begin ritual preparation.

Angelo sighed, pulling leaves from a passing hedgerow. He paused, looking back over his shoulder to the fading turrets of Castle Dunbar. He wished his command of English was better – there was so much he didn't understand. Throughout the ensuing conversation with the Lady Laird, Angelo had made a mental note of words and phrases. Maybe Robert could explain them to him.

Other things were fading: the strange atmosphere in the large, wood-panelled bedroom; the beguiling voice of the Laird and the sensual, easy grace of his sister.

One thing was as strong as ever: the need for release.

He walked on, re-adjusting the heaviness inside his jeans. A fabric-covered outline twitched at his touch. Angelo doubted it was possible to be this aroused and not come spontaneously. Slowing his pace, he stuck a hand down the front of his jeans and gasped at the hardness he felt there. He'd not been this stiff since his teenage years.

A frown momentarily creased Angelo's forehead. He remembered the size of his hard-ons at fifteen – and their frequency. He only needed to pass a handsome man or beautiful woman and his cock was up and around like a hungry beast, eager to thrust into whatever was available.

Unexpectedly, he found himself thinking about Robert. Having spoken the words he'd only previously thought, to Rhona Dunbar, a sudden surge of lust sped through his body and caused his swollen balls to clench painfully.

Angelo groaned. His prick throbbed against his fingers. Withdrawing his hand, he broke into a run. Wild images tossed around his hormone-addled brain.

Robert in the shower, damp and tousled.

Robert asleep on the floor of Corrie Cottage, his boyish face relaxed and dreamy.

Robert swimming in the loch, soaking shorts clinging to his slim hips.

Robert lying beneath him, face creased with desire and –

Legs pumping, Angelo pounded across fields, leaping hedges and walls with a Caliban-like abandon.

Robert dried the lunch dishes and replaced them on the side of the cooking-range. Wiping his hands on the towel, Robert gazed around the cottage and sighed.

Malcolm had left an hour earlier. They had made a date for the day after tomorrow when, the fisherman had assured Robert, he would be free from whatever form of self-restraint the entire male population – with the exception of the wayward Fingal – had suddenly decided to practise.

Robert balled up the dish-towel and hurled it across the gloomy room. After an encouraging start, the holiday was turning into frustrating drudgery.

Where was Angelo?

What had happened to the walks and hikes they'd planned?

What had become of their great intentions for the roof of the cottage?

Robert shoved his hands into the pockets of his shorts and stared up at the sky through a rip in the tarpaulin. OK, happy-ever-after and roses round the door had been unrealistic, but neither had he expected to be abandoned and left to do the housework while Angelo was off seducing an abundant supply of sex-starved maidens.

It was true what they said: one only ever really got to know someone when one holidayed with them.

His flatmate had several irritating habits, the least of which, at the moment, was going wherever his cock led him.

He left the cap off the toothpaste.

He never made the bed.

He used whatever towel happened to be around, whether it was his or not.

He didn't seem to realise that dishes had to be washed after they had been used.

Tearing his eyes from the exposed beams and timbers in the roof, Robert surveyed the trail of Angelo's discarded clothing which littered the stone floor, and began to seethe.

He'd invited Angelo along because he'd felt sorry for him – out of the goodness of his heart, he'd saddled himself with a companion who had, first of all, proceeded to tease and torment Robert with his body, only to go to the other extreme and disappear completely at the first whiff of nookie, without even offering to do the dishes!

Robert stomped over to his rucksack and began to sort through his laundry. Angelo hadn't said when he'd be back. Telephones were apparently unknown, on the island, and there was no way for Robert to contact his flatmate at the Dunbars' other than to go to the castle itself – and no way was he going to do that.

How dare Angelo go riding with the Lady Laird when he'd offered to teach Robert to ride first! How dare he prefer to spend the afternoon galloping around the countryside with some fat-arsed minor gentry than hike up the mountains with him – the person who had made this holiday possible!

Robert tore his clothes from the backpack, and threw them into the air in fury. Then, crumpled up inside a T-shirt, he found a pair white briefs which he knew weren't his. The fabric was stiff and encrusted. He froze. The anger faded, to be replaced by a sudden sadness. Robert pressed the soiled briefs to his face, inhaling the fragrant odours of the man.

He was lonely. And jealous. And unhappy.

Then a whirlwind burst through into cottage, grabbed his waist and threw him onto the bed.

Nineteen

'What the –!'

The breath was knocked out of Robert's body. Powerful hands gripped his shoulders, holding him tightly. A well-muscled thigh thrust itself between his legs, pressing into his groin and pinning him against the narrow bed.

Adrenalin spurted through his veins. Robert tried to fight back but his attacker was stronger and had the advantage of surprise.

Huge brown eyes stared inches from his face, pupils swollen with desire. Then Angelo's mouth was open on his mouth, kissing him hard. Full lips covered his, and Robert was responding, palms running over his flatmate's back as Angelo moved his hands to cradle Robert's head.

The kiss was wet and out of control. Their tongues flicked and thrust against each other. Teeth glanced off teeth. Head spinning, cock throbbing, Robert opened his mouth wider, wincing as Angelo gnawed at his lips. His hands found the waistband of the Argentinian's shorts. He wrenched Angelo's shirt free, pushing up under white linen and feeling his flatmate's warm, solid flesh beneath his sweating palms.

He had to check.

He had to know this was real and not some trick of his mind.

Robert cupped the sinewy mounds of Angelo's shoulders, then

218

ran his fingers down the sides of the man's broad back. Muscle and skin quivered. He gripped the sides of Angelo's body, and felt a very real hardness flex against his hip as he ground his own desire against the knee which pinned him to the bed.

Angelo moaned into his mouth, sucking on Robert's tongue. Then he pulled away, gasping.

Hoarse words seeped into Robert's ears as parted lips tracked a wet line of kisses over his face. 'I've wanted you for months, years! I've wanted you —'

'Shut up!' Robert raised his head, grabbed a handful of damp glossy curls and pulled his flatmate's face back down to his. His back arched up into the kiss, feeling the full weight of his flatmate's chest pressing down onto him. He thrust with his tongue, nose bumping against a stubbled check.

Then Angelo was grinding back, mouth and groin gouging into him.

Robert's lips were bruised and sore. The skin around his mouth stung. His whole body ached, wanting to make this moment last but desperate for more. He wanted Angelo naked, on top of him.

He wanted Angelo's prick inside him.

The thought was shared. Still joined at the mouth, they were tearing at each other's clothes. Angelo eased away, hands moving from Robert's head to fumble with the buttons of his shorts.

Robert tried to stop his fingers shaking. He gave up, hauling at Angelo's white linen shirt with a clenched fist and ripping buttons in his haste. Somewhere below, he felt his shorts being roughly lowered. He gasped as metal zip-teeth bit into his thighs, then he kicked the garment free.

Then two sets of hands were tugging at Angelo's jeans. Robert felt the pulse of the man's hard cock beneath his fingertips. Inside his boxers, his own throbbed in response.

Angelo wrenched his arms free of the torn shirt. He threw himself onto his back, arse-cheeks clenched and rising off the narrow bed in the struggle to get out of his jeans.

Robert's stiff length poked up through the fly of his boxers. Unable to take his eyes from the display, he eased the waistband up over his shaft, then paused, transfixed.

His flatmate's cock was a solid seven-inch tube of flesh. Robert watched veins fill further, as Angelo's rapid heartbeat pulsed along the thick length, pumping more blood towards the swollen, velvety head.

The prick shone like a rod of dull steel, arcing up from dense black pubes. Thin cockskin stretched impossibly tight, encasing the flesh beneath in a glossy, lustrous wrapping. The glistening member twitched and bounced with each jut of his flatmate's hips as he tried to get his jeans off.

Anticipation throbbed in his groin. Robert scrambled down the bed. Hauling off Angelo's boots and socks, he gripped dusty denim turn-ups and dragged hair-covered legs free.

Then Angelo lunged forward, knocking Robert off his heels and kissing him again.

Robert pulled away. There would be enough time for kissing later. His balls tingled. His arsehole was spasming open, gaping for the man.

Angelo crouched over him, panting. The shining, sweat-slicked cock thrust outwards from his groin, his bollocks large and heavy beneath. A yard above, the handsome face scowled with desire as Angelo tore open a condom and encased his prick.

Robert moaned. He leant back, grabbed his knees and pulled them towards his chest. His head made contact with the wall but the pain barely registered as he bore down, relaxing his sphincter and staring at the man above him.

Angelo was breathing heavily. Dark eyes were focused between Robert's splayed thighs.

The attention made Robert's prick throb. The dusky pink hole contracted, then gaped again.

Then Angelo's chest was resting on Robert's calves, and the velvety cockhead was jabbing around the entrance to his body.

Robert moaned with frustration at several near misses. He released one knee and reached down, wrapping his fist around the base of Angelo's thick, latexed length and guiding the missile towards its destination.

His flatmate's arms were braced at Robert's shoulders. Angelo's cock flexed against Robert's palm as he allowed the more experienced player to ease his prick forward.

Robert closed his eyes in sheer pleasure, rubbing the head of Angelo's length around his spasming hole, teasing them both. Warm pre-come oozed from his flatmate's piss-slit and gathered in the condom's tip, which felt warm and sticky around the crinkled orifice. His own prick was leaking freely now, a single luminous thread joining the head of his cock to the light dust of fuzz on his belly. The fingers of one hand tangled in the Argentinian's damp, glossy hair, Robert swung quivering legs over Angelo's shoulders and leant the fat head against his own hole. The sheer size of the bulb made his sphincter tense. Robert tried to relax, wanting Angelo inside him in a way he had never wanted anything before.

Above, Angelo's hips began to buck, stabbing at the tight orifice.

Robert winced. Holding Angelo firm in his fist, he eased himself forward onto the vast cockhead.

The skin around his hole dragged.

Angelo groaned, stopped stabbing and began to push.

Robert gripped glossy hair more tightly. The muscles in his thighs stiffened. He felt the beginning of cramp in his right calf but ignored it, trying to focus tension everywhere but the one area which needed to be relaxed.

Then Angelo was teasing his mouth with a dry tongue.

Robert's guts flipped over. His lips opened and he drew Angelo's tongue into his mouth as other lips parted, and the engorged head of the Argentinian's meat edged into his body.

Robert bit down hard, feeling the circle of muscle widen to admit the hugeness. The cockhead was stretching his arse-lips until he was sure he would tear. His eyes watered, then Angelo was kissing them and easing forward, filling Robert's wet tunnel inch by inch.

The fingers of his right hand met the cheeks of his own arse. Robert released his grip on the invader, moving his hand to rest on the hairy flesh of Angelo's arse as the cock sank into him.

The member seemed to swell as it entered his body, pushing at

the lining of his arse. Robert's head began to swim. He bit back
the beginnings of panic. It had been a while since he had taken
anything this large.

Angelo was holding him tightly, raising his upper body up off
the bed.

His head lolled back. Blood rushed to Robert's brain. His legs
slipped from his flatmate's shoulders, yawning wide to admit the
last three inches of the invasion. Lungs stopped working – he was
scared to take another breath. His heart hammered in his chest,
and he could feel another heart hammering back.

Then the solid hairiness of Angelo's bollocks brushed the cheeks
of his arse and Robert knew he had taken it all. His legs slipped
further, ankles locking behind Angelo's back, one heel resting at
the top of his flatmate's crack. Breath rushed from his lungs and
he gasped for air.

His arse bulged with Angelo, stuffed full of the thick cock.
Robert felt himself lowered back onto the bed. Despite the
discomfort, he felt complete – whole.

They were both breathing heavily.

Robert lay there, getting used to the feeling of unbelievable
largeness in his body. His own cock was glued to his stomach, and
when he moved, tiny hairs pulled and snagged with drying pre-
come.

Angelo's face was buried in his neck, lips moving soundlessly.

Robert opened his eyes and looked down between them.
Angelo seemed to be growing out of the V between his legs. He
couldn't see where his body stopped and his flatmate's began. It
was as if the cock in his arse had become part of him, in the same
way as his own cock, sandwiched between their two bodies, was
part of Angelo.

A curly head raised itself from his neck. A single bead of sweat
dropped from the end of Angelo's nose and landed on Robert's
cheek. Robert reached up, stroking the side of the man's neck.
Angelo turned his head, kissing the heel of Robert's hand and
bracing his arms against the mattress.

Then the vastness inside him began to retreat. Robert flinched.
He tightened muscles, trying to keep Angelo's cock there.

Groaning, Angelo continued the withdrawal.

The walls of Robert's arse rippled with sensation as the huge head made its way back down the fuck-tunnel.

Angelo was growling. Robert could feel the man's whole body trembling. He slumped back onto the mattress as Angelo's cock-head again stretched his arse-lips into almost nothing.

Then Angelo pushed back in and Robert screamed with pleasure.

The fuck was slow at first. Angelo ploughed his arse with firm, measured strokes, flexing coffee-coloured hips when he drove in and dipping down so that his tensed abdominals came into contact with Robert's aching cock each time he withdrew.

Arching his back up off the bed, Robert met each thrust head on, and heard the creak of ancient springs beneath him in parallel to the slap of their stomachs.

The pace increased. The sound of flesh-on-flesh speeded up. Robert's foreskin rolled back further as Angelo pounded into his arse. The sensitive glans was rubbing between his lightly fuzzed stomach and the matted hair on Angelo's belly. Robert grunted each time the man's cock slid into him, gasping each time Angelo pulled out.

Soon they were both bathed in a swamp of sticky sweat. Robert tensed his arse-muscles around the throbbing shaft, holding it tightly and feeling the sharp needles of pain-pleasure recede in the face of a hotter, more intense sensation. He pressed his heels against Angelo's buttocks, upping the tempo until they were moving in sync. Creaks, grunts and growls become one low noise, merging with the liquid sound of fucking to blot out everything else.

Robert stared up at Angelo's straining face. He opened his mouth to catch droplets of exertion as they rained from his flatmate's skin and hair. Angelo's swollen balls slapped off the cheeks of his arse. Every muscle in Robert's body was alive and sizzling.

Angelo fucked enthusiastically, wordlessly, like some wild animal caught by its own base instincts.

Robert felt a familiar feeling building in his balls. The heavy sack throbbed mercilessly. He wanted to come, but he wanted to feel Angelo spurt into his arse before he did so.

Then strong hands slipped beneath his shoulders, pulling him upright.

Robert blinked in surprise as Angelo leant back. Eyes unfocused, he hovered, impaled on Angelo's cock. The throbbing shaft sank more deeply inside his body.

Then Angelo was leaning back still more and Robert was falling forward. He yanked his feet out of the way as the Argentinian's body fell back against the mattress and Robert found himself on top, staring down at his sweat-streaked lover. He braced his arms against Angelo's chest. Two slime-streaked inches of exposed cock glistened between them.

Robert's own prick stuck up at an almost ninety-degree angle in front of him. Angelo's hands were on his waist, his feet flat on the bed. Robert could feel his flatmate's knees either side of his spine.

Then Angelo moved his legs. Robert squatted over the Argentinian's fat cock, lowering himself slowly back onto the full length. As Angelo arched his back in pleasure, Robert lost his balance. Hands slipping from his flatmate's chest, he sat down hard.

The head of Angelo's cock slammed up inside him, ploughing fiercely and hitting the bump of flesh halfway up his fuck-tunnel.

Robert roared. A shudder shook his frame. He felt a strong desire to piss, but the sheer stiffness of his erection made this impossible. Angelo was groaning again, digging his fingers into Robert's waist. Waiting until the waves of discomfort had eased to a more bearable ripple, Robert leant back and began to pull himself up and down seven inches of solid meat. His thigh muscles clenched tightly. His sweating balls ached against the root of his shaft. Muscle strained with effort. Robert threw back his head and stared blindly up through the hole in the ceiling at the blue sky beyond.

His arse was on fire, tiny flickers of pain ignited by friction burst into flames of intense sensation as he hauled himself up, then slammed back down.

Angelo's hips were bucking upwards from the bed as he jabbed his cock into Robert. Each time the head of that member glanced off the rounded gland, Robert's balls spasmed. He was close – so close. The Argentinian's prick had become an ossified staff which never grew soft and only existed for Robert to fuck himself on. His mouth hung open, his arsehole throbbed and rippled around Angelo's prick as Robert was tossed about. Now bouncing on the rod of iron, he rode its length like a bareback horseman, gripping tightly and slamming it up into himself.

Then Angelo was lunging up from the mattress, hands on Robert's shoulders as he held him there and twisted his prick upwards in short, corkscrew-like movements.

Something tightened deep inside him. Arms around Angelo's head, his flatmate's face buried in his chest, Robert felt tension explode out of him as he came in the Argentinian's lap. Torrents of milky liquid shot from his slit, spurting onto the man's chin and dribbling down Robert's stomach.

He shot a second slitful, his sphincter tightening and relaxing around Angelo's relentless cock which fucked him on through the climax. Robert's head was spinning with the force of the orgasm. A third rope of spunk leapt from his cock, and he felt rather than heard Angelo mumble against his chest. He was held more tightly than ever, the spunk and the breath squeezed from his body.

Robert slumped over Angelo, gasping. His limbs had turned to rubber, but the cock in his arse was as stiff as ever.

Through a daze, he felt himself lowered back onto the bed. Strong arms wrapped themselves around him. His last conscious thought was of Angelo's persistent hardness throbbing inside his exhausted body.

He woke up still locked in an iron embrace. Breath caressed the back of his neck.

For a fleeting second Robert didn't know where he was or who was holding him. Then the body which enfolded his murmured something in Spanish, and he remembered. Robert turned his head and opened his eyes.

Huge brown pools gazed down at him. 'You looked so peaceful. I didn't want to move until you woke up.' Angelo rubbed at the smear of crystallising spunk on his brown forehead, and grinned lopsidedly.

Robert's stomach lurched. Angelo's cock remained inside him, remained hard. Handsome features closed the gap between their faces. Robert felt the tip of his nose being kissed.

'I must use the bathroom.'

Every fibre of Robert's being resisted the idea of Angelo going anywhere – even if anyone could piss with a hard-on like that, which he doubted.

Angelo's full lips moved to his neck, hands bracing themselves on his waist as he drew out.

Robert groaned at the emptiness. He watched Angelo carefully unroll the condom from his still-hard cock and place it on the beside table.

'Coffee?' Angelo eased himself from the narrow bed and stood on the flagstone floor.

'Mmm.' He watched appreciatively.

Angelo paused on his way to the door, stretching his arms above his head. The play of muscles along the broad shoulders and down over the lean back was caught in a sudden shard of sunshine.

As the man's naked, muscular outline disappeared through the doorway, Robert glanced at the condom and saw it was empty. He rolled over into the Angelo-scented space, inhaling the smell of his Argentinian lover's body and searching for the tell-tale dampness which would tell him Angelo had wanked afterwards, then shoved his freshly condomed cock back into Robert while he was sleeping. The idea made his stomach lurch a second time.

Angelo's side of the tiny bed was damp with sweat only.

Robert smiled dreamily and settled back down. What a man! Edging onto his back, he winced slightly as the swollen lips of his arse came into contact with rough blanket. He wasn't up to another Angelo-style fuck at the moment, but he could always manage to suck him off.

The thought of taking the size of load Angelo must be ready to blow by this time made his sticky cock twitch between his thighs. He found himself grinning idiotically. So much for Miss Hoity-

Toity Dunbar! Angelo had come tearing into the cottage as if the devil himself was in pursuit.

Robert pulled the covers over his head and bathed himself in the odours of what had just happened. Part of him still couldn't believe it, but another part knew better than to think about these things too much. He lay there, luxuriating in afterglow and looking forward to the rest of their stay.

In the distance, he heard the sound of footsteps on flagstone, and the clatter of cups. Minutes later, the smell of coffee drifted into the bed, followed by a dipping in the mattress.

He pulled back the covers and accepted the mug which Angelo was extending.

His flatmate looked a little sheepish as he cupped his mug in large hands and raised it to his mouth. 'Sorry if I – you know – gave you a fright. I . . .'

Robert grinned. The man's shyness was more endearing than ever, now that he knew what a beast the Argentinian was in bed. 'I know. Don't be sorry.' He threw back the covers further and scratched his balls. 'I'm not.' He laughed. 'Surprised, maybe. I thought you were straight.'

Angelo cocked his head. 'I thought you weren't interested in me – that way.'

Robert gulped down the rest of his coffee and sat the empty mug on the floor. He ran a hand through tousled, glossy locks and pushed Angelo's curly hair out of the dark brown eyes. 'I'm interested in you in every way.' Robert felt his guts flip over. He hadn't meant to get heavy, but the words were out before he could stop them. Heart hammering, he wanted to kick himself.

Angelo merely smiled, gently taking Robert's hand and kissing the inside of his wrist.

Robert's stomach melted at the blush which was spreading over his flatmate's lowered face. But he didn't want to push things – not now. He and Angelo had all the time in the world. Tucking his ankles underneath himself, he eased his hand away. 'How did your afternoon go?'

Angelo raised his face. 'Very enjoyable! Cameron distils his own medicinal tonic.' He smiled. 'And Rhona is a most able horsewoman.'

Robert actually managed to smile back. 'I'm sure she is. Tell me more about the Laird's home-brew – is it whisky?' He snuggled back down, his face resting on Angelo's thigh.

Draining his mug, the Argentinian bounded from the bed. 'Oh! I almost forgot. You must help me. What is a –' Angelo's brow creased with concentration '– rune?' He smiled proudly, remembering another word. 'And what's an atavar?'

Robert's face hit the mattress. 'A what?'

'Rhona has invited me to a ceremony! The words are written in runes.' The handsome face grinned. 'She is an atavar! What is that, exactly?'

Robert frowned and sat up. 'I'm not sure – runes are a very old form of written language, but –'

Angelo continued. 'The runes say I am special. Rhona and I are going to save the island!'

The frown slipped into a scowl. What a line! 'Oh yes? And what exactly does fucking her have to do with saving anything?' He heard the sneer in his words.

As did Angelo. The coffee-coloured face peered at him. 'What's wrong? What have I said?'

Robert shook his head. 'Nothing.' He clenched his fists beneath the covers and swore he wasn't going to let petty jealousies spoil anything.

Angelo continued to peer for a few seconds, then resumed. 'There are rituals to undergo. I am to be present at her ceremony – the guest of honour, I think. Cameron mentioned a dark rider –'

Robert guffawed.

Now Angelo was scowling. 'Don't mock me – you are always mocking me!'

The solemnity of his flatmate's words made Robert laugh even louder. His voice dripped scorn. 'Oh, come on – rituals? Ceremonies? Dark riders? I had a feeling that pair were into something kinky, but I didn't think they'd go this far just to get into your knickers.'

Angelo's eyes darkened. 'My knickers have already been got into, as you put it!'

Robert flinched. Straight from fucking the Lady Laird to fucking him. He was a poor second! His face reddened with a mixture of hurt and fury. 'Don't you dare get mixed up in whatever nonsense is going on up at that castle.' He leapt from the bed. 'Rituals, my foot!' He spat the words and began to dress.

'What's wrong? Why are you upset?'

Fingers furiously dragging on his clothes, Robert turned away to hide his scarlet face. He knew he was being irrational, but Angelo's confusion merely added to his irritation. 'I'm not upset!' He stuffed feet into boots and hurriedly tied his laces. A hand placed itself on his shoulder.

'Tell me. I don't understand. What is an atavar?'

Robert shrugged the gesture away. Gathering what little dignity he could muster, he grabbed Angelo's dirty laundry and hurled it at the bed. 'I don't want you going near that pair again – and, if you do, you'll be on the first train back to London!' Before his lover had a chance to reply, Robert stalked towards the door and out into evening sunshine.

Twenty

A ngelo pulled a sweaty T-shirt from his face and stared into the doorway. His head was a little fuzzy from both the exhilarating sex and the lingering after-effects of Cameron Dunbar's powerful brew. He wanted to go after Robert, tell him that it had been talking to Rhona which had finally given him the nerve to act upon his feelings, but everything else he had said in the past fifteen minutes only seemed to make his lover angrier, and there was no guarantee further words would be any different.

He frowned, leaning back against the stone wall. One hand settled between his splayed legs, absently fondling the half-hard cock which lounged against his thigh. Angelo dandled his swollen cock between thumb and forefinger, then slipped a hand beneath his balls and hefted the sack in his palm. Why wasn't he going soft? Ever since the encounter with the tattooed blacksmith that afternoon, his cock had felt strange. The Laird's acrid-tasting tonic seemed to increased the effect.

He closed his eyes, remembering what it felt like to be inside Robert's body. The thought made his nipples tingle. He'd come, seconds after his boyish blond lover had ejaculated against his face. But it had been the strangest orgasm he'd ever experienced. Instead of shooting from his cock, his seed had seemed to return to somewhere just beneath his balls and add to the vast heaviness there. He could still piss; his cock didn't hurt. It just felt . . . strange. As did his whole body.

Angelo sighed, then swung his long legs over the side of the bed and stood up. He stared around the cottage, which seemed very empty without Robert.

A shiver ran across his mocha skin, erecting the fine hair on his chest and stomach. He stood there, naked, staring at the rumpled bed where he and Robert had fucked together only hours earlier.

Why hadn't the Englishman let him explain? Why was he so against Rhona's ceremony? The Lady Laird and her brother had both warned him Robert might not be in agreement. Angelo had assured them the blond Englishman was broad-minded, and would not object.

Angelo sighed. He'd been wrong – again! Resentment coursed through his veins.

How dare Robert forbid him to go!

Confusion mixed with the resentment. Angelo rubbed his face. People were always trying to tell him what to do: his father, Julie, his superior officer back in his army days. He'd spent his life trying to please them, do what they wanted him to do – and where had it got him? His handsome features creasing into a scowl, Angelo quickly dressed and began to gather up his possessions.

He was his own man.

A man who made his own decisions.

If Robert didn't like it, he could – Angelo scowled – do as they did in Rome!

Mind racing, Robert walked for miles. His feet took him along the coast road in the opposite direction from the village. He passed the occasional sheep, grazing on the grass at the side of the rocky shore, but encountered no other signs of life.

Just as well. He clenched his fists: if he were to meet one of the natives he couldn't guarantee they'd get an appropriate response.

His legs were wobbly from the fuck. His arse tingled with the memory of Angelo's cock. His face burned with hurt and anger.

He walked faster, and the images in his head speeded up to match his pace.

Angelo and Rhona Dunbar.

Angelo and himself.

Angelo and Rhona Dunbar, watched by Cameron Dunbar.

The thoughts twisted at his guts. He tried to push them from his mind but the images refused to go.

The crunch of boots on gravel and the occasional mocking shriek from the gulls overhead were the only sounds to break the silence. Even the sea was still, glinting like an orange-pink mill-pond under the low sun.

The serenity annoyed him. Robert broke into a run, feet pounding along the rough country road. He had no idea where he was going, he only hoped if he ran fast enough and long enough the feelings inside would subside.

Eventually, they did. Gasping for breath, his entire body trembling, Robert paused against a huge rock and stared out at the sea. His chest heaved. Eyes closed, he braced his arms against his knees and lowered his head, filling his aching lungs. As air rushed into his chest, his brain began to clear. He suddenly felt very stupid. His fists unclenched themselves and his body slowly relaxed.

He'd acted like a spoilt little boy.

He wasn't usually the jealous type. Robert smiled wryly, remembering the afternoon session with Fingal and Malcolm. He was hardly in a position to get possessive: indeed, the thought of Angelo with other people – men and women – had always turned him on.

A wisp of resentment returned as he pictured the striking Lady Laird. Robert straightened up and opened his eyes.

He was an idiot!

From a nearby boulder, an orange-beaked herring gull squawked in agreement.

Robert sighed. Angelo was so attractive, other people were bound to be interested in him. The adult way to tackle the problem was to acknowledge it – regardless of how vulnerable admitting his jealousy made Robert feel. He turned his head to look back along the winding road.

On the furthest away of four rocky promontories, he could see the steep hill which led up to Corrie Cottage. As he stared, Robert became aware of a deepening in the silence. The gulls were mute, and even the soft breeze had died away.

Then the solid rock beneath him quivered.

He leapt up, eyes fixed on the fourth promontory. The very air seemed to shimmer as the tremor swept the ground under the soles of his boots.

The steep bank of cliff rippled; solid rock momentarily turned to liquid.

For almost a minute, everything hovered on the verge of impermanence. Then the vibrations subsided as suddenly as they had begun.

Robert realised he'd been holding his breath when air gushed from his lungs. Behind, a flock of sandpipers soared into the sky, twittering and swooping around him. He stood there, birds darting and circling in front of his face. The minor earthquake was more awe-inspiring than fear-inducing, a reminder there were greater forces at play.

As he walked back towards the cottage, a tiny trickle of rocks made its way down the cliff.

Robert smiled. Nothing like a potential landslide to help put things in perspective. He and Angelo needed to talk. Talking could work out almost anything.

The soles of his boots slapping rhythmically on gravel, Robert began to whistle.

The cottage was empty, but tidier.

Robert sighed ruefully. Angelo too had felt the need to think things through. He noticed the Argentinian had cleared away the dirty laundry and stashed it somewhere, along with his rucksack. Taking off his jacket, he lit two candles, then sauntered around the back of the cottage.

The small loch was smooth as glass.

Angelo had obviously gone further afield to cool off.

Robert rubbed his sweating face. He needed to make amends.

Inside the other outhouse, he rummaged through the boxes of supplies which Malcolm had brought, extracting two already gutted fillets and a still reasonably fresh loaf of bread.

Soon the table in front of the cottage was adorned by another two candles and a small glass filled with yellow flowers Robert picked from the reeds around the loch. The warm evening air was filled with the mouth-watering smell of sautéing fish.

Robert showered and changed, then set two places either side of the table and smiled. When Angelo returned, they'd eat then talk. His stomach rumbled with hunger as he walked to the edge of the cliff and gazed back at the purple-tinged mountains behind the cottage. He visualised Angelo, stalking amongst clumps of heather, walking off justifiable irritation at his flatmate's fit of pique. Robert smiled.

Not merely flatmates any more.

Lovers.

A yawn of contentment stretched his lips. It had been an eventful day, all in all. Turning, he walked back to the cottage, checked the cooking fish then pulled out a chair and sat down at the table.

The sky above the horizon was a tapestry of orange and pink, its threads picked up and sewn into the mirrored surface of the sea below. Golden hues shimmered around the cottage, bathing its dirty stone in a yellow glow.

Robert rested his chin on his hands. The perfect setting for an intimate dinner à deux. He yawned again, stretching his legs out under the table and clasping his hands behind his head. Drowsiness tugged at his eyelids. In the distance, a curlew's call echoed in the twilight. Leaning back in his chair, Robert felt the day's excesses take their toll on him. His head lolled slowly left, eyes closing.

As a writer, he'd always prided himself in the ability to snatch sleep when and where he needed it. And he did want to be alert and refreshed when Angelo returned.

He woke up with a start, shivering.

The candles had gone out, but something else was burning.

Robert leapt to his feet and dashed into the cottage.

The large room was filled with a thick pall of smoke and the stink of wax and charred fish.

He grabbed the plate, rushed outside and jettisoned two blackened fillets over the cliff.

A flock of hungry seagulls followed the burnt remains downwards.

Robert stared. The sky had changed. He looked around, shaking sleep from his brain, then glanced at his wrist.

Seven a.m.

He quickly checked inside the cottage again, but the room was as empty as it had been the previous night. Robert rubbed the stiff muscles in his chilled shoulders.

Where the hell was –?

A gentle tap on the open door made him jump. Robert jerked round and found himself staring at a penitent, angelic face.

Fingal held a box, which he extended. 'I didn't know if you'd be awake.' The youth looked embarrassed. 'I wanted to bring you this and – er – say sorry about yesterday.' Delicately formed nostrils twitched. 'Is something burning?'

'Forget about that.' Robert sighed. 'Have you seen Angelo?'

Fingal sank to a crouch, placing the box of groceries just inside the cottage. 'Caballo?'

'Yes, Caballo!'

The beautiful face looked at him. Something flickered across the heavenly features, then Fingal stood up. 'He has gone.' It was statement, not a question.

'Well, yes – he's not here, at the moment.'

'Caballo has left.'

Robert raised an eyebrow, then began to rummage around the cottage.

Fingal remained in the doorway, watching.

After a quick search, Robert was forced to agree: all Angelo's possessions, including his jacket and rucksack, were nowhere to be found.

Robert sat down on the bed and stared at the floor. What had he done?

'You and Caballo had an argument?'

Robert looked up. 'Yes – but Angelo wouldn't just leave.'

Fingal pushed a straggling blond lock from his face. 'People sometimes have to leave when they are angry, or confused.' A blush tinged the pale skin. 'I was angry and confused yesterday – that's what I came to tell you. I –'

'Later!' He didn't need this – not now. Robert pushed past the startled youth and surveyed the area around the cottage. 'Where the hell is he?' His eyes refocused on Fingal, who was now slouching sullenly against the wall.

Leather-covered shoulders shrugged. 'I told you, he's gone.' Fingal kicked at a rock with the toe of his boot.

Realisation crashed around Robert. His last words to Angelo slammed back into his mind. 'And I know where!'

Leaving the sulky youth leaning against the wall of the cottage, he stomped down the narrow path.

Cameron Dunbar opened the door when Robert began to kick the heavily bossed surface.

'I want to speak to Angelo!'

The Laird tightened the belt of a tartan dressing gown around his slim waist and blinked sleepily. 'I beg your pardon?'

Robert wiped his hot face with his forearm and repeated the request.

Cameron's aristocratic brow creased with concern. 'What makes you think he's here?'

'Oh, he's here all right!' Robert pushed past the startled Laird and strode inside. 'Angelo! We need to talk!' His voice echoed up in the high-ceilinged hall. Robert was too angry to take in much else as he walked to the foot of an immense staircase and stared up. 'Angelo!' he shouted more loudly. 'Come on, I –' A hand grasped his shoulder.

'Calm down, Mr McLeod.'

Robert shook his arm free of the grip, and walked from the staircase towards the first of three doors. He pushed it open.

Nothing.

The same was true of the other two.

The Laird remained at his side. 'What do you –?'

Robert spun round, grabbed the lapels of the heavy plaid dressing gown and almost lifted Cameron Dunbar off his feet. 'Where is he? What have you done with –?'

'Release my brother!'

The authority in the voice sent a shiver of fear through Robert. His grip loosened.

The Laird took a step back, smoothing the rumpled fabric of his robe.

Robert stared up at the figure which stood at the top of the dramatic staircase.

Rhona Dunbar's silver hair hung loose over her slender shoulders. The rest of her body was draped in a white, gauzy nightgown.

Then Cameron Dunbar's arm was around Robert's shoulder, patting placatingly. 'You are upset. Come and sit down.'

Dragging his gaze from the icy eyes of the Lady Laird, Robert allowed himself to be steered towards one of the open doors.

Inside, the Laird led him to a vast, overstuffed sofa and lowered him onto it.

Cameron Dunbar patted his shoulder. 'Now, what's this all about?' The Laird took a chair opposite, long hairless legs stretching out from under the dressing gown.

Robert sighed. Behind, a door closed softly. He was feeling a little calmer, but that only made his outburst more difficult to explain. 'Have you seen Angelo?'

The Laird pressed immaculately manicured fingers together. His aristocratic brow furrowed. 'As I told you, I saw him yesterday afternoon, when he and Rhona returned from the ride.'

Robert frowned. 'He didn't come here, last night?'

The Laird pursed his lips. 'My sister and I were out for a large part of the evening. We did not return until late. If Caballo did come to see us, he would have found the castle empty and left.'

'What's wrong?'

The husky voice at his shoulder caused Robert to flinch: he hadn't realised Rhona Dunbar was in the room. His head swivelled round.

'Mr McLeod has come for Caballo.' The Laird's voice rumbled from behind.

Glacial blue eyes pinned him. 'Why would Caballo be here?'

Robert suddenly felt very foolish. No way was he going to admit his worst fears to this handsome woman. He had been mad to come here at all. Levering himself up from the sofa, he faced the Dunbars. 'I apologise for bursting in like that. I overreacted.'

Rhona moved to beside her brother, leaning against the side of the armchair in which the noble-faced man sat. 'That's all right – you are obviously worried. Please tell us why.'

Robert gazed from one Dunbar to the other. The family resemblance was so striking, and there was such a palpable closeness between brother and sister it was hard to tell where one stopped and the other began. Cameron's voice joined his sister's entreaties.

'We want to help, Mr McLeod. You and Caballo are our guests – important guests. Tell us what has happened.'

Robert sighed, his own fears rushing back through fading anger. Before he knew what what happening, he was telling his hosts the whole story – minus certain embarrassing details, of course. He fiddled with a button on his jacket. 'So I stormed out, he stormed out, and I've not seen him since.'

The Laird and his sister exchanged fleeting looks. When Rhona spoke, her voice was low and soothing.

'Caballo is a complex man. What happened between the two of you last night may have more implications for him than you realise.'

Robert blinked. He'd never thought of it like that. It hadn't occurred to him that he was perhaps Angelo's first male lover, and that fact alone may have given the handsome Argentinian problems he couldn't talk about – with Robert, in particular.

The Laird smiled reassuringly. 'Go home. Go back to the cottage and wait. Give Caballo the time he needs. He will return to you in due course, I am sure.'

'But where is he? Where has he been all night?'

Rhona moved from behind her brother's chair and crouched in

front of Robert. 'Probably just walking and thinking. Haven't you done that – when things were difficult for you to grasp?'

He found himself nodding.

The Lady Laird took his hand in hers and patted it.

Robert felt surprising strength in those long, delicate fingers.

'Go back to the cottage. Caballo will return to you when he is ready.' She glanced around at her brother, giving Robert's hand one last squeeze. 'Don't worry – things will work out. Cameron will give you a lift home.'

Robert sat in the passenger seat of the ancient blue Daimler, scanning the countryside for tall dark men with curly hair.

The car drove smoothly down a steep hill and on through the village.

Robert sighed. Angelo could be anywhere! He returned his attention to the man at his side.

In the driver's seat, Cameron Dunbar was dapper in a green waxed Barber jacket and matching cap. He looked every inch the rural aristocrat.

Robert narrowed his eyes, peering at the patrician profile. Suddenly he knew where he had seen those noble features before.

Cameron slowed to allow a flock of sheep to cross the road.

Robert seized his opportunity. 'Do you paint?'

The Laird smiled. 'Walls and outhouses only, I'm afraid. But I believe a relative of yours was a rather accomplished water-colourist and photographer. Great-uncle Fergus and his groom spent many hours up at Corrie Cottage, fascinated by what was then fairly new technology. But I've never seen any of his work.'

He had. Robert stared. The exquisite, privately published volume of erotica swam before his mind.

Sheep continued to swarm around the car, despite the best efforts of a gnarled shepherd. The Laird switched off the engine and turned his head towards Robert. Cameron chuckled. 'Great-uncle Fergus caused a scandal in the family when he ran off with one of the stable-lads on his wedding night.'

A hand slapped the Daimler's bonnet.

Robert swivelled his head and saw the woolly herd had

eventually been manoeuvred into an adjoining field. The shepherd touched the brim of his hat and waved the car on.

Cameron raised a hand in reply, then restarted the engine. 'Yes, I suppose there are more black sheep in our dynasty than the white variety, if you think about it.'

The powerful engine purred beneath Robert's thighs.

The Laird's voice was low as the Daimler continued its smooth journey. 'And dark horses, for that matter.'

There was something almost ominous in the words, as if they were a reference to something beyond Robert's ken. He shook the feeling away.

An ancestor of his had photographed then hand-coloured some of the most intimate and erotic watercolours Robert had ever seen – featuring an ancestor of Cameron Dunbar's and his groom. 'Could you hang on a minute, when we get to the cottage?' Robert gripped his seat-belt as the large car swung steeply upwards over the rocky ground. 'I think I have something which belongs to you.'

Ten minutes later, he wrenched the lid of the dusty trunk open, knocking aside a small slip of paper in his hurry. Having retrieved the book, he slipped the volume through the open window and into the Laird's hand.

Cameron looked at him, bemused, then turned the first few pages of the book. When his face returned to Robert's, blue eyes glowed with pleasure. 'Thank you, but this is yours. I cannot accept anything of this obvious value.'

Robert stepped back, hands clasped behind him. 'Please. You've been so kind, bothering with my worries.' He didn't want to think about the fact that the cottage was still empty.

The Laird sighed. 'I would like to look at it in more detail, I must admit.' He slipped the slim volume into the glove compartment. 'Tell you what: I'll keep it safe for you, until you get the chance to have it valued. How's that?'

Robert tried to smile. 'OK.' He looked over the roof of the car to where a small fishing boat was making its way back from the mainland.

Cameron reversed behind the cottage, then paused on his way back down. 'Caballo will return. Try not to worry.'

Robert nodded and waved as the sleek vehicle made its way back down the dusty track.

Only when he was back inside, closing the trunk, did he find Angelo's note.

Twenty-One

Sorry I didn't say goodbye. Please don't try to find me.
Angelo

Robert stared at the sprawling, almost childish script: it bore little resemblence to the Argentinian's normally neat hand. His stomach churned. Angelo must have been very angry when he'd written it. Robert reread the two brief lines over and over again until the words blurred before his eyes. His legs wobbled. He sat down hard on the cold flagstone floor, still holding the letter. Then his brain began to work.

'Goodbye.'

Angelo was leaving. Leaving the island. When?

Robert swore under his breath, cursing himself for not having seen the note before Cameron Dunbar and the car had left. Maybe there was still time to cadge a lift into the village. He bounded up from the floor and rushed outside.

At the edge of the cliff he shaded his eyes against the overhead sun and stared down at the coast road.

The large, blue Daimler was nowhere in sight.

Heart pounding, Angelo's gut-wrenching rejection gripped between his fingers, Robert ran down the steep incline and on to the road.

★ ★ ★

He asked a group of women, picking potatoes in a field.

They all remembered Angelo from the ceilidh, two nights ago, but no one had seen him since.

Robert ran on.

Half a mile along the road, a bicycle bell sounded behind him.

Robert paused, lungs aching.

Hamish Campbell regarded him curiously. 'What's all the rush, my lad?' He dismounted, leaning the cycle against a wall.

Robert eyed the vehicle, then pushed the bearded policeman aside, grabbed the handlebars and jumped on. As he sped off along the coast road, PC Campbell's outraged shouts followed him. Robert pedalled furiously, wondering what the penalty was, in these parts, for taking and driving away a bicycle.

Cycling up hills was hard work. As he pedalled with leaden thighs, he rehearsed his words to Angelo: 'It doesn't matter. Whatever happened, it doesn't matter. We can forget the whole thing. Just don't go.'

He stood up on the pedals, pushing hard against them and feeling the ancient frame rebel under his urgency.

Just outside the village, he passed a surly-looking Fingal, nearly falling from the bike in his haste.

'Hey! Where are you going?'

Robert was too breathless to reply. He swerved around a group of locals who were standing outside 'Duncan's Automobiles', barely avoiding a woman with a pram as he raced on down to the pier.

Robert glanced at his watch, but he couldn't make out the time. He knew Malcolm made the same trip over to the mainland each day, and prayed that was his only trip.

Fishermen scattered ahead of him.

Robert ignored their scramble, waving others out of the way as the wheels of the bike spun along the quayside. He scanned the array of berthed craft. A sense of elation prickled over his skin as he registered the *Kelpie*'s distinctive bow at the end of the pier.

Behind, he was aware of shouts and cries, and the sound of running feet.

Robert put on a final spurt. He could now see Malcolm, sitting astride a bollard, diligently mending his nets.

The *Kelpie* was still in dock. Angelo could be on board, waiting for Malcolm to set sail with his cargo.

Then something squished beneath his front wheel and the bike went into a skid. Robert stared at the trail of fish innards which adhered themselves to his front tyre. He struggled to maintain a straight path, but the cycle was swerving out of control towards the edge of the quay. In desperation, he slammed on the brakes, then gasped as he was thrown forward into the air.

He landed in a tangle of fishing nets, the hard ground impacting against his spinning head. In the background, he heard a vague splash as he looked up into startled green eyes. His mouth opened and closed soundlessly, like a fish gulping for air.

Strong fingers seized his collar, wrenching him to his feet. An angry voice bellowed in his ear, 'What do you think you're playing at, my lad?'

Still trying to answer, Robert was frog-marched through a gathering crowd. A red-faced Hamish Campbell glowered at him, tightening his grip when Robert tried to break free.

'Assaulting a police officer. Theft of the property of Grampian Police. Malicious destruction of said property.'

Robert was still too out of breath to form words. Minutes later he was hauled into a tiny cottage, which evidently doubled as the village police station.

PC Campbell pushed him into a chair, then stared at him, arms folded. 'Now, are you going to tell me what this is all about, my lad?'

Taking a deep breath, Robert began.

The bearded face stared sceptically from the other side of the table. 'So where is Caballo now?' He held a pencil and had been writing down every word of their exchange in a small, black notebook.

Robert sighed. 'I don't know – that's what I've been trying to tell you.'

PC Campbell loosened his tie and loomed over Robert. 'Why were you in such a hurry to leave the island?'

Robert peered up into threatening eyes. 'I wasn't trying to leave! I was trying to find Cab – Angelo.'

'And why would Caballo be wanting to leave?'

Robert reddened. 'I – er – we had an argument.'

The policeman seized on his words and twisted them. 'An argument, eh?' He rubbed his shoulder. 'You pack a powerful punch, my lad. Did this argument involve violence?'

Robert shot to his feet. 'No! Not unless throwing dirty socks at someone counts as violence.'

'Sit down, please.' The voice was icy.

Robert remained on his feet, glowering at the man opposite. 'I'm sorry I took your bike – there wasn't time to explain. And I'm sorry it ended up at the bottom of the harbour. I'll pay for the bloody thing.' He looked towards the door and tried to calm down. 'Now, will you –?'

'Sit down!'

The man's tone demanded obedience. Robert sat, legs shaking.

'What was this argument about?'

Robert lowered his head. 'Something and nothing. I was – er – upset. We both were.'

'Ah. Emotions were running high, eh, lad?'

'I suppose so.' Robert looked up and saw the expression on his interrogator's face. 'But not in that way!' He frowned. 'You should be out looking for Angelo, not wasting your time with me.'

PC Campbell regarded him coldly. 'Volunteer constables are doing exactly that as we speak, my lad. But something tells me you know more about the whereabouts of Caballo than you're letting on.'

Robert gripped the edge of the table. 'I haven't seen him since last night. We –'

A knocking sound made him pause.

PC Campbell glanced round at the door with irritation. 'Later!' He turned back to Robert. 'Go on.'

'We had a row. I walked out.' He suddenly remembered the

note and began to search his pockets. 'Angelo wasn't there when I got back to the cottage, and I found this –' he drew out the crumpled scrap of paper '– about an hour ago.'

The knocking increased.

PC Campbell ignored the sound. He snatched Angelo's note, eyes scanning the words. When the bearded face raised itself from the paper, Robert saw the policeman was looking at him strangely. 'You found this where?'

Robert sighed with relief. At last he was starting to be believed. 'In the cottage, on top of a trunk. I –'

One final knock made the door shudder. Then it opened, and Robert was staring at Malcolm's flushed face. Their eyes met for a second, then the fisherman looked away, focusing on PC Campbell.

'Caballo is safe –'

Robert's heart soared, then plummeted as Malcolm finished his sentence.

'– I took him across to the mainland on the morning tide.'

Hamish Campbell's deep laugh filled the room. 'Good! I'm glad that's sorted out.' He turned to Robert. 'I'm sorry I gave you a hard time, lad, but we can't be too careful.'

Robert was staring at Malcolm. 'Did Angelo say anything? How did he seem?'

The tall fisherman avoided his eyes and left the room as abruptly as he had entered, silently closing the door behind him.

Officer Campbell talked on. 'I don't think we need bother with a report.' He closed the notebook, replacing it in the breast pocket of his white shirt. 'Gives me an excuse to put in a request for a new bicycle!' A smile twitched the corners of the bearded mouth and the policeman winked. 'I've had a yearning for one of those new mountain-bike contraptions – thirty gears they have.' He walked towards the door and opened it.

Robert remained seated. Angelo was gone. He didn't know what to do.

Hamish stood in the doorway, rubbing his hands together. 'Now, what about a wee dram to show there's no hard feelings?

Duncan round the corner usually keeps a bottle in his office for occasions like this.'

Robert got to his feet slowly. 'Er – no thanks.' His head was still a little fuzzy from the fall.

'Och well, as ye like, lad.'

Still unable to take in the events of the past twelve hours, Robert walked stiffly from the room. PC Campbell's now-genial voice continued in his ears: 'What are your plans now, can I ask?'

Robert moved from the dim stuffiness of the office out into bright sunshine. 'I'm not sure.' He squinted in the glaring light.

At the head of the pier, villagers were going about their business. Robert watched Malcolm's broad-shouldered outline move down the quay, then noticed another, slimmer form lounging against a nearby wall.

The stocky policeman at his side focused on the slouching Fingal. 'Excuse me, lad. I need to have a word with that waste-of-space.' Large feet quickly crossed the ground to the wall.

Then a slap echoed in mid-morning sunshine.

The sound pulled Robert from his daze. He moved swiftly towards where the compact policeman was now gripping Fingal's leather-covered shoulder.

The youth rubbed his face, where the man's hand had struck. His voice showed no sign of his usual sneer. 'I wasn't doing nothing! I –'

'Haven't you caused enough problems?' Hamish drew his arm back a second time.

Fingal cringed.

'I should –'

'He was waiting for me, weren't you?' Robert moved swiftly in between them: the boy looked so vulnerable, despite the previous air of delinquent bravado.

The blond head jerked left. Blue eyes stared gratefully at Robert, then nodded. 'That's right.' He stared at Hamish, pink lips tilted downwards into a sullen pout. The insolent tone was back. Fingal poked one finger into the middle of PC Campbell's uniformed chest. 'And there's nothing you can do about it!'

Robert watched the policeman's bearded face grow scarlet with rage. Then the man seemed to swallow down his fury. He gave Robert a sidelong look. The words were low and controlled: 'Watch that one, lad. He can't be trusted.'

Robert stared back. 'Don't worry, I'll keep an eye on him.' Fingal certainly did seem to incur the islanders' disapproval, whatever he did.

A flicker of scepticism crossed the still-seething features. Then Hamish sighed and walked away.

Robert turned to Fingal, who was looking triumphant. He punched a leathered shoulder half-heartedly. 'Don't know about you, but I could do with some breakfast.' The youth was one way of keeping his mind off this disaster of a holiday, until Robert had a chance to pack and follow Angelo back to the mainland.

A draught of cold air wafted across his hot skin.

Angelo awoke with a start. A sheen of sweat cooled on his numbed body. There was something on his face. He opened his eyes and stared into blackness.

Fabric-blackness.

He tried to raise one hand, remove the blindfold. Something tightened around his wrist. His arm wouldn't move. Angelo tried his other hand.

It too remained bound.

He turned his head left then right, staring blindly for the tethers which restrained both arms above his head. Adrenalin spurted through his veins. Angelo strained at the bindings and arched his back, but managed to raise his upper body less than an inch from the hard surface to which it was secured.

The effort made more sweat seep from his burning skin. He slumped back down, heart pounding. As he did so, something solid pushed up into him.

Angelo gasped, trying to take his weight on his heels. It was useless. Sensation slowly returned to his hips and legs, and a new wave of panic broke over him.

His ankles were also tied, forcing his thighs apart and holding them there. Other bindings criss-crossed his body. He could feel straps around his thighs, holding something in place.

Something hard.

Inside him.

The realisation made his skin prickle and his stomach churn. He could feel the object now, poking up into him. The base of whatever it was stretched itself around his arsehole and penetrated for at least six tapering inches inside.

Angelo groaned. He had barely been aware of the intrusion when he'd first woken up, but now the object seemed to extend further up into him with every writhe of his hips.

A tightness increased in his groin. Something rigid clasped the base of his balls, a stiff circle of inflexible material set between the full, hairy sack and the rest of his quivering body. Each heavy ball was divided off from the other by a thin thong of something more pliable, which was biting deep into delicate flesh.

Adrenalin now pumping around his blood-starved brain, his mind trying to recall what had happened.

The blackness before his eyes was echoed by the emptiness of his mind. It was as if he had always been here, tied down and spread wide. He felt like a piece of meat, trussed up for some aristocrat's table.

As he strained at his invisible bindings, a soft hand brushed the inside of his leg.

His bound cock spasmed within its ringed confines.

The hand made its way down the inside of his thigh, pausing at his foot.

Angelo felt a tightening as the tether was adjusted.

Then fingers soft as silk moved to his other ankle and checked the restraint before moving on up over calf, knee, halting to linger again at the sensitive skin on the inside of his thigh.

Every hair on his body stood on end. Angelo groaned. The muscles in his arse hugged the thick object in gut-wrenching contractions, and would have forced it out of his body if it wasn't for the series of straps and buckles around his hips and waist which held it firmly in position.

The hand continued. One long finger traced the outline of his bound cock, moving up over his trembling stomach.

His abdominals were iron hard with tension. Angelo opened

his mouth in a silent cry as something tight gripped his right, then left nipple in a hot, searing embrace.

Then soft lips kissed his forehead and consciousness dissolved.

Fingal turned out to be a surprisingly accomplished cook.

Robert sat at the table outside the cottage, staring dolefully towards the horizon while appetising odours drifted up from the plate in front of him. He looked up at the eager-to-please face, and pushed the breakfast away.

Now minus his leather jacket, Fingal stood there in jeans and a washed-out denim vest. He chewed on a strand of corn-coloured hair. 'I'm sorry.'

Robert shook his head. 'It's not your fault – I'm just not as hungry as I thought.'

The youth sank to a crouch before Robert's chair and gazed earnestly up at him. 'I mean I'm really sorry.' He tucked long legs under himself and leant his face against Robert's thigh. 'For all the trouble I've caused.'

Robert rested a hand on the golden head. Fingal's skin was warm and soft. He raised his eyes from the beautiful creature at his feet and returned his gaze to the sparkling blue sea.

Would Angelo be on the train home by now? Or would he be wandering around Mallaig, trying to find a bus?

Fingal nestled more closely between his legs. 'Hamish is right. I'm bad news.'

Robert laughed, running his fingers through tangled hair and pushing it back from the angelic face. 'Tell me something I don't know!' Fingal was a handful, certainly, but nothing Robert couldn't handle.

The youth rubbed his head, cat-like, against Robert's palm.

He enjoyed the gesture and found his thoughts straying from Angelo's whereabouts. 'By the way, what is a Kelpie? Where does the island get its name?'

Fingal's arms hung loose around Robert's waist. 'Why do you want to know?'

Robert felt the beginnings of an erection. He stroked the soft stubble on the youth's face. 'Just curious. Is it a Gaelic word?'

'It's just stories.'

'What sort of stories?'

Fingal's hands moved along the waistband of his jeans.

Robert could feel the youth's warm breath through the fabric of his shorts.

'Fairy stories. Myths.'

'So tell me about them. Tell me about the Kelpie.'

Fingal rubbed the root of Robert's cock with his chin. 'The Kelpie's a water-spirit. A horse, which can assume human form.'

Robert stretched out his legs, one hand cupping the back of the youth's neck. He was intrigued. 'A spirit? Good or bad?' He felt his cock inch up beneath the boy's face.

Fingal's words were muffled as he gently gnawed the outline of Robert's stiffening shaft. 'It's a trickster. The Kelpie beguils men and leads them to their doom.' The boy's low laugh vibrated over Robert's swelling length. 'A thousand years ago, Flora Dunbar made a pact with a Kelpie. The water-spirit gave her the strength to defeat King Flannon and his Irish army. In return, Flora promised to pay tribute to the Kelpie every year.'

'Indeed!'

Fingal raised his head from between Robert's splayed thighs, fingers lingering on his zip. 'Told you it was all rubbish!' He grinned, blue eyes alight with desire. 'People believe it foretells the future, too.'

'That's interesting. What did the Kelpie predict?' Robert luxuriated in the youth's attentions as Fingal unfastened Robert's shorts and licked a wet line from navel to groin:

'There will come a time when the fish would leave the waters, the ground will tremble and King Flannon's descendants will again try to conquer the island.' The beautiful face looked up mischievously. Fingal's pupils were enlarged with lust. 'Serves the Dunbars right for taking out their mortgage with the Bank of Ireland!'

Robert had stopped caring about the Kelpie. He raised his hips, allowing the boy to ease his shorts down. He gasped, kicking his feet free as the corn-coloured head reburied itself in his groin.

Fingal's tongue was everywhere, laving around the head of Robert's cock then flicking back down to lap at his balls.

Robert groaned. He leant back in the chair, hooking his legs up and over the boy's leather-jacketed back and pulling the angelic face more firmly against him. A sudden sharpness made him cry out.

The blond head flew up. 'Sorry, I'm not very good at this – I've never sucked a man before.'

Robert smiled at the admission. 'You're doing fine – just keep those teeth behind those lips. But there's more to pleasuring a man than just sucking.' He grabbed a handful of tangled hair and gently but firmly pushed the boy's head back down between his thighs. Stretching back, he raised himself up until he could feel Fingal's breath on his pucker.

The boy rebelled.

Robert gripped the sides of Fingal's face. 'Lick me!' He tightened his legs around the leather-jacketed torso and held him captive. Then he groaned with pleasure as a tentative tongue snaked against the sensitive flesh. 'Yes . . .' Robert could feel the boy's reluctance and looked forward to instructing him further when he had more time. Fingers twined in thick blond hair, hauling the wet mouth away from his hot hole, and pushed it against his aching shaft.

More at home, Fingal's lips parted to encase Robert's length. Then began to move.

Shimmers of sensation darted into Robert's balls. The boy sucked like a novice, awkward but eager to please. The thought that his was the first cock in either of Fingal's sweet holes heightened Robert's pleasure as he dragged the wet mouth up and down his hard prick.

After a while, they built up a rhythm and Robert ploughed deeper, allowing the boy's gag time to relax and get used to the thickness in his mouth.

Fingal's low moaning sounds were punctuated by the occasional rasping grunt as Robert's pubes cut off his breath. The boy's mouth was a warm wet glove, snugly cradling his cock. Robert lowered his hands, feeling the muscles in Fingal's neck strain against his fingers as he struggled to take more and more of the man-meat. Soon, the boy's tongue was flicking along and over Robert's length like he'd been born to the task.

Robert felt himself start to lose control. He thrust into Fingal's face-hole more fiercely, feeling his balls slam off the bum-fluffed chin.

The boy's moans were deeper now, a combination of anguish, tiredness and a constant desire to take more and more.

Robert scowled with the approaching climax. The boy's mouth was as good as his arse had been: firm and tight and made for a man's prick. Balls clenching, fingers tightening in thick blond hair, Robert's opened his mouth and thrust one last time into the sweet hole.

Fingal gasped, then his fingers tightened around Robert's thighs as he tried to stop himself choking.

Through the shudders of his orgasm, Robert visualised his spunk flooding the boy's mouth and trickling down his throat. The image made him spurt a second time. And a third. Hauling the boy's head from between his splayed thighs, Robert stared at unfocused eyes and watched a milky globule drop from Fingal's bruised bottom lip.

The man-boy looked more beautiful than ever: face smeared and reddened by the friction of the face-fuck, eyes wild with lust, lips red and wet and swollen.

Robert grinned, holding the boy's hot face between sweating palms. He waited until his breathing had returned to normal.

Fingal 's eyes seemed to glow. 'We are good together, no?'

Behind the lust, Robert could sense something else – something he didn't want to have to think about right now. He racked his brain for something to talk about, and remembered their previous line of conversation. 'So the Kelpie tells fortunes too?'

The beautiful features took on a more serious cast. 'It also said that, after all this had happened, the Dark Rider will come to the island and join with the Kelpie. When this happens, the earth will give up her secrets.'

Robert couldn't help laughing: it was the same spiel the Dunbars had fed Angelo.

Fingal pouted. 'I told you it was daft.'

Robert ran a finger around the sulky, spunk-splattered lips. 'It's not daft. A certain amount has come true.'

Fingal sneered. 'Oh yeah – there have been tremors, the fisherman are finding less and less to catch, and Caballo has come, but I –'

'Caballo?'

'It's all nonsense!' Fingal reburied his face in Robert's groin, nudging the softening shaft with his small nose.

Robert pulled the boy's face upwards. 'The Dark Rider is Caballo?'

Fingal frowned. 'Caballo means horse in Spanish – didn't you know?' The blue eyes glittered momentarily with panic, then a frown transformed itself into a beguiling smile. 'You're better off without him.' Eyes fixed on Robert's, the youth spread his fingers around Robert's sticky cock. 'I can make you happier than he ever could.' Still maintaining the gaze, Fingal flicked his tongue across the sensitive glans.

Robert shivered.

'But I'm sorry about the note – it was the only way I could think of to get you to myself.' The youth's eyes were all pupil.

Robert gripped slender shoulders and slowly stood up. 'You wrote that note?'

Blue eyes widened. 'I thought you knew! When you rescued me from Hamish –'

Robert stared at the scared face and felt a strong desire to slap the boy himself. Instead, he pushed Fingal into a chair and loomed over him. 'Hamish knows that note isn't from Angelo?'

Fingal nodded.

Sweat cooled on Robert's skin. 'If Angelo hasn't left the island, where is he?'

Fingal frowned. 'Caballo is where he should be, according to legend. With Rhona and Cameron!'

Twenty-Two

Robert's blood turned to ice-water. 'Rhona and Cameron told me they hadn't seen Angelo.' Fingal's fingers gripped his thighs.

'He's not Angelo any more – he's Caballo now. Tonight is Midsummer's Eve. He will be used in the ceremony.'

Robert stared sceptically at the beautiful face.

Fingal talked on. 'There's nothing you can do. They have him, and they will keep him.' He pressed his face into Robert's groin.

Robert grabbed a handful of golden locks, forcing the youth's head back and focusing on the large blue eyes. He didn't know whether to believe the boy or not. Everything which came out of that beguiling mouth was a mixture of half-truth and lie.

Fingal's bottom lip trembled.

Robert increased his grip on the boy, hauling Fingal to his feet. They stood there, eye to eye, as Robert remembered the sudden change in the policeman's attitude when he had shown him the purported message from Angelo. He released the corn-coloured hair, grasped both bare shoulders and shook Fingal hard. 'If this is more of your fanciful ideas –'

'No! No!' The boy danced like a marionette. 'It's the truth.'

Robert snorted, then released the trembling shoulders.

Fingal collapsed in a heap and began to babble. 'You're the only one who ever took me seriously. I wouldn't lie to you – I love you!'

'You don't know the meaning of the word!' Robert folded his arms across his chest, furious. He had to do something – the Dunbars couldn't keep Angelo against his will, regardless of what they thought he was. 'Come on – if you love me, you'll help me.' Seizing an arm, he roughly pushed Fingal towards the cliff road.

Castle Dunbar was small but intimidating, a fact he hadn't noticed on his visit earlier.

Fingal sniffed as Robert pounded on the door. 'They won't let you in – not now the rituals have started.'

Robert frowned at the ancient but solid timber, then grabbed Fingal and walked around the squat structure. There were no other doors, and the windows were narrow slits set high into the walls. He cupped his hands around his mouth. 'Angelo!'

A nearby flock of sparrows rose into the air and flew away, as the name echoed around him.

Robert shouted again.

This time, silence was the only response.

Fingal sniffed. 'You're wasting your time.'

Robert stared at the youth, who was now looking very sorry for himself. A tingle of pity sliced through his anger. He shook it away. 'Maybe the Dunbars own this island, but kidnapping is still kidnapping.' He turned and began to march down the steep hill which led to the village.

Fingal slouched along behind him.

Douglas McVey's huge arm paused above the anvil, enormous fingers gripping the shaft of a heavy blacksmith's hammer. 'Leave well alone.' The deep bass voice vibrated up from within the densely tattooed chest.

In the schoolroom, Miss Nicol regarded him cooly. 'Stop interfering. You don't understand island ways.'

Duncan leant against the bonnet of his mongrel vehicle, removed his hat and scratched his greying head. 'There are some higher laws than man's, Mr Robert McLeod.'

Robert clenched his fists to stop himself hitting someone, and marched down to the pier.

Groups of locals watched his progress suspiciously, but made no attempt to stop him.

Malcolm was again sitting astride a bollard, painstakingly weaving a large needle in and out between the weft of his net.

Robert stopped in front of him. 'Why did you say Angelo had left? Why did you lie?'

Malcolm paused, mid-darn. Green eyes gazed up at him, then shot Fingal a disappointed look. 'I had to. You would have interfered. Caballo has been sent to save us, Robbie. It has been foretold in legend.' The emerald eyes glinted. 'It must be this way.' Malcolm resumed his work.

Robert sighed. He was getting desperate. He stormed back up the quayside and into the cottage which doubled as a police station.

In the middle of the floor, PC Hamish Campbell was crouching, examining the chain of a seaweed-covered bicycle which lay on top of a large sheet of plastic. He looked up as they entered.

Robert frowned with determination. Unofficial methods had failed. 'I want to report an abduction.'

The policeman wiped his hands on a small towel and got to his feet. 'You do, do you, lad?' The ruddy face was mildly amused, the tone indulgent. 'Just let me get my notebook and I'll take the details.'

An hour later, Robert emerged from the police station. His complaint had been registered.

PC Campbell had promised to get every available man onto the search for Angelo. He had vowed to interview the Dunbars at the first opportunity. He had written down everything Robert had said very carefully, and had even tried to take a statement from Fingal, who had admitted writing the note but would say nothing else.

As early-afternoon sun sparkled down from overhead, Robert had a feeling the pages were being torn from PC Campbell's notebook at this very moment. He looked at Fingal.

The youth stared back adoringly. 'Please let me help – let me make you feel better.'

Robert sighed, stretched out a hand and ruffled the golden hair. 'I'm not the one who needs help.'

The blindfold had been removed.

Angelo blinked into the darkness. There was a smell: a faint, herbal odour which reminded him of Cameron Dunbar's home-brew. Then he flinched. Oily warmth was being rubbed into his skin by strong, purposeful hands. He moaned, bracing himself against the tethers as fingers circled his clamped nipples, then down over his stomach to his groin.

Other hands held his trussed cock out of the way while the oil was rubbed into his pubes. He arched his back as the fingers continued on down to his sore, swollen balls.

His guts spasmed and two rings of muscle tightened around the plug in his arse. 'No . . .' The word became a moan, betrayed by the tingling in his nipples and the throbbing in his cock.

The hands were multiplying. Two? Four? Five? Angelo tried to count them, pairing each touch with an unseen face and two invisible eyes which were obviously focused on his naked, exposed body.

The thought sent a ripple of fear up the length of his shaft, a ripple which broke across his glans in a wave of longing.

Then his legs were moving.

Angelo tried to swallow but his throat was too dry. He fought the movement, but his ankles continued upwards, raising his splayed legs into the air.

The hands were spreading oil into his arse-crack, under and around the end of the plug then up to the base of his spine. Beneath the slick, scented film his skin glowed with a heat which seemed to radiate out through every pore in his body.

Then a wet finger was outlining his mouth, circling inwards over his lips.

Angelo raised his head.

Another hand supported his neck as he drank thirstily. He could taste the same acrid, bitter liquid as earlier, but it was wet and soothing on his burning throat.

His body slipped and slid in its rough tethers. He lunged forward, wanting more.

A soft finger pressed itself to his lips and the vessel moved away.

The unseen hands were moving down his legs now.

Angelo shivered with each touch, shuddering as his thick hairy thighs became moist and lubricated by the fragrant oil. The massage continued over his knees, then up over his elevated calves.

His arse was in the air, his weight supported by his shoulders and back. Angelo felt warm hands massage his buttocks, kneading the hard flesh and thoroughly soaking the short hair.

He bucked his hips, fingers twisting to grip the coarse rope which bound his wrists. His entire body was drenched in a mixture of oil and musky sweat.

A finger lightly touched one of the tight clamps which bit into his nipples.

Then his back was arching more than ever, his mouth open in a silent plea as his nearly numb flesh was released. His chest was on fire. Blood pounded back into the tender buds and a new pressure inflamed the stiff tissue.

Angelo threw back his head, twisting left then right. Veins stood out on his neck, pulsing as his blood raced. His cock thrashed within its leather cage, straining at its bindings while the cold metal circlet behind his balls tightened unbearably and threatened to spring open.

His nipples were alight, burning upwards into the darkness. With the sensation, memory returned to his fuzzy, lust-addled brain.

Long blond hair. A husky voice. Talking to him, telling him things when all he could think about was the body beneath the filmy gauze gown. 'Rhona?' The name was a whisper.

And drew a whispering response. 'Yes, Caballo. I am here.' Soft lips touched his right nipple, shooting twenty thousand volts of longing through his tormented body.

There was movement between his legs.

Angelo ignored it. He leant upwards towards the voice, then

flinched as a growing heat in his arse began to eclipse the burning in his nipples.

A hand brushed his thigh.

Other hands gripped his legs, holding him steady as warmth continued to seep into his body.

Adrenalin spurted through his veins. Angelo clenched muscle, trying to halt this more intimate invasion.

His defences were useless. Buried in his arsehole, the thick plug continued to leak liquid into him. The sensation made his hot skin flush scarlet. Helplessness drenched his body.

Something flared in the darkness. One, then two candles sparked into life.

Angelo stared up at the pale face above his. Rhona Cameron stood behind him, gazing down. Her eyelids were half-closed. A small, secret smile played around her lips.

'This is your destiny – our destiny.'

Rhona's lips were not moving.

Angelo squirmed as the pressure inside him grew. Neck straining, he looked away from Rhona Cameron to the masked figure between his splayed thighs and the voice of Cameron Dunbar.

One hand held the end of a thin tube. The other poured the contents of an ancient-looking stone ewer into the funnel.

Angelo turned his head, gazing at the flickering shadows which decorated the walls of what he now recognised as one of the dungeons in Castle Dunbar's cellar. Five shadows? Six?

As Angelo's insides swelled with the liquid, a low monotone hum began to fill his ears. Rhona's warm fingers were stroking his face, running their tips over his forehead and up into his sweat-soaked hair.

'Caballo. Caballo.'

Eyes wide, Angelo stared at the figure in front of him. The ewer was at an almost one hundred and eighty degree angle to the funnel now. His stomach churned with the accumulated pressure of the warm liquid. The sensation was beyond discomfort. A second layer of sweat broke out on his sheened skin and his eyes began to water.

Raised above him, his cock buffeted his slick stomach.

Around the walls, the monotone hum became recognisable syllables.

'Caballo . . . Caballo . . . Caballo . . . Caballo . . .'

Then the masked figure was replaced by Rhona's shimmering form. Blond hair was tinged orange by amber candlelight. She was still stroking his forehead, while her other hand was busy between his legs.

Angelo groaned, then gasped with relief as the pressure inside him was eased abruptly. He felt the liquid leave his body the same way it had entered, heard it splatter into a container beneath him. He writhed in his bonds, sharp spikes of shame and helplessness wracking his tethered body and making his sore nipples swell more than ever.

'You have been cleansed on the inside.' Rhona loomed over him. 'Now you must be made clean on the outside.'

The last droplets of the ritual process dripped from the centre of the plug. Angelo was still bathing in temporary relief as silver twinkled in the smoky candlelight, and the sharp blade of a razor began its descent over his slippery chest.

Breath caught in his lungs. Blood froze in his veins. He heard rather than felt the scrape of finely honed metal as it crept over the rounded flesh of his right pec.

After each drag of the blade, more oil was applied.

Angelo watched pale, blurry hands flash in the gloom – hands attached to wrists which disappeared into the folds of heavy black sleeves.

Only Rhona was discernible amongst the dark mass of robed figures moving around him. Her voice ebbed and flowed over the low chant, her finely boned face appearing then disappearing in front of him.

His chest was shaved, the razor descending down over the thick ridge of hair which tufted his abs until it reached his dense public thatch.

Slim fingers curled around his strapped cock.

Angelo inhaled sharply, staring at a ring which adorned the

middle finger. On a broad silver shank, the cameoed relief of a rearing white horse glinted in the half-light.

Other fingers poked and probed his groin, stretching the skin flat while the sharp blade continued its progress.

A shiver racked his body as the razor curved effortlessly over each taut, swollen testicle. Angelo winced as his balls writhed upwards in their delicate sack, trying to escape the threat of sharpened steel. The attempt was foiled by other metal: a cold, broad circle held his manhood still.

As his denuded body quivered, the oil massage followed in the wake of the unflinching blade. The liquid soothed where the scraping reddened and removed. He felt the cheeks of his arse wrenched wide.

Then the blade was moving over his perineum.

Coarse ropes bit into the skin around Angelo's wrists and ankles as he twisted and writhed, inflamed with a desire now tinged with apprehension.

Suddenly Rhona was at his side, tracing the raw circlet on his left wrist with a soft fingertip. She kissed the tender flesh. 'So much strength. So much power.' The words were a murmur against his bruised skin.

His body went limp in its bonds. The sharp blade moved on.

Rhona was holding his lolling head now, crooning words he couldn't understand.

The chant was taken up by the others, filling Angelo's head with alien vowels and consonants.

His smooth, hairless balls quivered between his splayed thighs. The cheeks of his arse stung. Angelo felt as though an unseen layer had been stripped away.

The Lady Laird's hands caressed his hair.

A thousand tiny insects trekked their way over his scalp.

Rhona's voice rose over the incantation. 'You are almost ready, Caballo.'

'Yes.' The word fell from his lips.

'You came to us, Caballo.'

'Yes.' The razor was working its way down his muscular legs

now, rasping through the ebony coating of hair and abrading his skin. He barely felt the friction.

'The Kelpie will join us, Caballo. The spirit of the great horse will come into my body.'

'Oh yes.' He was mesmerised by her husky voice, more aroused than ever by the thought of feeling her slim white body beneath his. He wanted her to crawl on top of him, then and there, and impale herself on his bound, helpless cock.

'We will move mountains, Caballo. The ancient treasures of Kelpie Island will be revealed for all to see.'

'Yes . . . yes . . . yes . . .' His grazed skin was bathed in a sweat of oil and longing. Angelo gripped both robes and bucked with his hips, fucking the air. As he did so, the plug moved inside him. His sphincter spasmed, sending arrows of pleasure along the walls of his arse. With every jut of his hips, the fat plug skewered itself more firmly into him.

Then his mind seemed to break free and he was looking down on a writhing naked man, his coffee-coloured skin hairless and glistening in yellow candlelight. Spreadeagled on a long bench, the man's nipples shot upwards like pink bullets and his cock sprouted from a bald crotch.

The sight made his bound shaft twitch uncontrollably. Dangerously close to sensory overload, Angelo's mind rejoined his body and sank into blackness.

Fingal standing dejectedly on the quayside, Robert approached the third boat.

And received the same third answer. A stocky, gnarled-looking man shook a grey head.

Robert emptied the contents of his wallet onto the deck of the *Highland Lass*, then took off his watch and added it to the bundle. 'Please. I need to reach the mainland.' Maybe the police in Mallaig would do something.

The fisherman sank to a crouch, gathered up the money and the watch and held them out. 'Tomorrow, laddie. But not today. Nothing sails from Kelpie Island today.'

Robert glanced over his shoulder at the red-eyed youth. Biting back a curse, he snatched the notes and watch and walked back to his blond companion. He gripped Fingal's arm and pulled him towards a secluded corner of the busy quay. 'This ceremony –'

The youth wrenched his arm away. 'I can't tell you.'

'Yes, you can!' Robert pinned the distraught youth to the sea wall. 'You want to help, don't you?'

The blond head nodded tentatively.

'I know when the ceremony takes place, but not where.'

Fingal turned his head, a veil of tangled locks obscuring the angelic face. 'I can't! In a thousand years, no outsider has ever learnt the location of –'

'I'm not an outsider!' Robert gripped a lightly stubbled chin, forcing the boy to look at him. 'I live here, yes? I own the cottage, so technically I am an islander.'

Fingal's blue eyes darted left and right, pleading with those in the background.

Robert grinned maliciously. 'They won't help you – I'm the only friend you've got – you said that yourself!' He stared at the terrified boy, voice lowered to an intimidating growl. 'I know what you like, Fingal. I know what you do in the woods.'

The blue eyes closed.

Robert slapped the angelic face. Hard.

Fingal's eyelids flew open.

Robert held the boy there with his body, feeling the arousal in the groin which pressed back against his. 'You want to tell me, don't you?' He watched four red finger indentations form on the boy's pale cheek.

Fingal paled further, making the mark of Robert's hand stand out more.

'You want more of this –' Robert back-handed the beautiful face roughly and rammed his thigh against Fingal's crotch '– don't you?'

The youth's sharp intake of breath was carried off in the cries of circling herring gulls. The outline of his stiffening cock was not as easily disguised.

Robert focused on huge blue eyes, not wanting to think about the hardness in his own jeans. 'Tell me.' The words were hardly audible.

Fingal's head fell forward. 'The cottage.'

Robert seized a handful of hair, dragging the youth's head up. 'Yes, I'll take you back to the cottage, but if you don't tell me what I want to know, you'll wish I'd left you here.'

Fingal blinked. 'Behind the cottage.' The voice was hoarse with exertion.

Robert lowered his face. 'What's behind the cottage?'

Azure eyes gazed at him pleadingly. 'The stones behind Corrie Cottage, beyond the loch. At midnight.'

Robert almost whooped with satisfaction.

Twenty-Three

F ingal had been very helpful, given the right stimulation. Once the boy had started talking, it had been almost impossible to stop him.

Robert now knew that the cult would leave Castle Dunbar at exactly ten thirty, travelling on foot across the hills, to arrive at the standing-stones at eleven o'clock.

At midnight, the sacrifice would take place.

An icy hand clutched at his guts. Crouched in a tall bank of reeds, Fingal's airgun clasped in his fist and wearing a dark robe the youth had reluctantly provided, he shifted his position.

The last four hours had been hell. Robert had considered concealing himself somewhere near Castle Dunbar and accosting the procession as soon as it emerged.

But armed or not, there were far more villagers than he could hope to take on. He would be easily overpowered. And he doubted, even with Angelo's life at stake, he could actually use the air-rifle.

Overhead, the sun was low in the sky, suffusing the hills in a rosy glow. Shards of light glanced off the black-flecked standing-stones, making the rock glitter through the dusk.

Robert pulled back his sleeve and looked at his watch: quarter to eleven. His stomach flipped over with dread.

The cult would have left. The procession had began. A frisson of expectation joined the dread. His mind returned to the plan.

According to Fingal, Angelo's part in the ritual would come at the climax of the ceremony. Until then, his was more of a passive presence. The islanders would be occupied with other rites. If, as Fingal had informed him, everyone would be wearing robes, a figure lurking on the fringes of the activity would not be noticed. He would have ample opportunity to snatch Angelo from under his captors' noses.

A tiny rowing boat was moored in a rocky inlet at the foot of the steep cliffs. The craft looked barely sea-worthy, but it should be capable of getting them off the island.

And afterwards? Robert tried to slow his breathing. He didn't want to think about afterwards: his whole being was centred on the task in hand. What happened later could be dealt with later.

His leg was cramping. Robert shifted his weight to the other foot. Reeds poked the back of his neck. An unearthly silence had descended over the island, heavy with a sense of expectation. His heart pounded more loudly than ever. He craned his head left, to the mountain path which led overland from Castle Dunbar.

Something sparkled in the dusk. Then something else. Robert staggered to his feet. Beneath the folds of the robe, his legs were stiff and sore. He barely felt the discomfort as his eyes focused on the line of torches making its way along the foot of the largest mountain. His heart faltered, then thumped back on course.

In the distance, the sound of a lone piper drifted through the still air.

Robert shivered, sweating beneath the heavy cloak.

As the procession neared, the music increased in volume. From his vantage point above the standing-stones, Robert watched the long snake of torches weave towards him. The tramp of at least fifty pairs of feet on gravel beat out a rhythmic tattoo beneath the drone of bagpipes. Robert narrowed his eyes, trying to make out faces. But every member of the approaching cavalcade wore a dark hood pulled over their faces.

Except two.

Striding in front, Rhona Dunbar shimmered in a white, flowing gown, her long hair cascading over her slender shoulders.

Behind, flanked by four robed figures, Angelo's coffee-coloured skin dappled and shone under the flickering torches.

Accompanied by the hooded piper, the Lady Laird marched between two large black-flecked pillars into the centre of the circle. Angelo followed.

Robert narrowed his eyes as the accompanying figures fanned out, one flank veering right, the other veering left until they shadowed each of the upright rocks and obscured his view. Sinking to a crouch, he moved forward onto his stomach and began to wriggle across the ground towards the activity.

He paused behind a bush, squinting through a circle of smoking torches.

Rhona Dunbar stood at one end of the large, horizontal slab in the centre of the ring, the hooded piper at the other. Angelo stood between them.

Robert lifted his head higher, transfixed by the naked Argentinian. Angelo's body was completely hairless. He looked more like a god than ever, his smooth skin bathed in the red glow of the sun and the orange light of the flaming torches. Then Robert's gaze focused on the straps around the man's shaved cock and balls. He inhaled sharply, trying to reconcile the absence of chains and ropes with the unmistakable look of fear which was frozen on Angelo's face – and the glistening rod of flesh which poked almost vertically up from the man's crotch.

Angelo blinked. Deep inside, muscle stretched and rebelled. The plug in his arse was chafing. Every step should have been agony, but he had grown surprisingly used to the large object inside him. In fact, he had found a strange pleasure in the way the plug rubbed and caressed his most intimate area.

The music which had accompanied his walk faded away. The ring of hooded figures disappeared and he heard a thundering in his ears.

The thunder of hooves.

As if woken from a dream, he shook his head and gazed around.

Rhona smiled at him. 'It is time, Caballo. Make yourself ready.'

Angelo stared at the smooth altar.

One hooded figure broke ranks, moving forward. Its hands held heavy ropes, which they extended to the Lady Laird.

The smile never left her aristocratic features. Rhona took the ropes and moved towards him.

The granite was cold as he lay down, allowing her to bind and secure him once more. Words brushed his ears.

'Only for a little while, Caballo. You must be prepared for the Kelpie.' She slipped something soft and padded under his buttocks, raising the lower part of his body up off the cold stone.

Angelo smiled up at her noble face. He tried to form words, but his throat seemed to prevent any sound other than moans.

Rhona nodded, then reached behind him.

He felt her fingers move against his skin as she unbuckled the harness around his arse. Then a warm palm hefted his balls, as if weighing them.

'Good! You are heavy with power. But we need more. There is much at stake here.'

Angelo tried to thrust himself into her hand. The hardness inside him was stimulating his body beyond anything he had ever known.

Rhona released his bollocks and he felt her fingers around the base of the plug.

Then the sensation of contentment ebbed away, to be replaced by a yawning emptiness as the Lady Laird eased the plug from his arsehole. Angelo threw back his head and howled like an animal. His hole gaped, then clenched wildly. A night breeze wafted against spasming muscle. Finally, words came. 'Put it back in! Fill me! *Madre mía*!' Angelo's head thrashed from side to side. He levered his body from the cold stone, yearning for the feeling he'd only dreamt about. He needed the pressure inside him more than life itself.

Rhona moved away, and when Angelo next focused, green twinkling eyes bored into his.

Malcolm lowered his hood and loosened the cord around his waist. The dark robe fell away, revealing the rugged face and the powerful body. Malcolm's red hair spilled forward as he bowed his head. 'This is an honour, Caballo. I have been weak, and have wasted my seed within the past two days.'

Angelo bucked upwards, his gaze transfixed by the hardening member which jutted out from between the fisherman's powerful legs.

'But your presence here is filling me with strength once more, Caballo.' Malcolm ran a rough fist down the length of his own cock, pulling his foreskin back to reveal the plush head. 'You will make me hard in a way no man has ever made me hard before.'

As Angelo watched, unable to tear his eyes away, the tall redhead was handed a small stone by a faceless, hooded figure. Malcolm took the pebble and, pressing the fingers of his other hand each side of his piss-slit, dropped the object inside.

'Thus I am sealed. The sacred fluid will not be splilled until the time is right.'

Then another figure appeared, holding a bowl. Malcolm cupped one hand into the liquid, then slathered it over his stiffening length.

Angelo moaned, arching his back in anticipation as the fisherman leant over him and the thick head of Malcolm's cock slid into his aching body. He felt the first inch spread him wide. The second and third opened his arse wider still. Angelo thrashed in his bindings as the fourth, fifth and six inches of the fisherman's sealed cock continued to plough steadily up into him. The large head was burrowing into the deepest regions of his arse, opening and stretching the tight velvet tunnel the way only a flesh-and-blood prick could.

Angelo lunged upwards off the stone altar as Malcolm's turgid sack impacted with the shaved cheeks of his arse. His own cock was restrained in an iron grip – not one drop of pre-come could escape. He gazed at the fisherman's sweating face, mouth lolling open with desire. 'Fuck me – please fuck me!'

Malcolm's green eyes stared back. 'With pleasure, Caballo.'

The airgun lay forgotten beside the bush and Robert was on his feet, stumbling over the hem of the long robe as he half-crouched, half-ran towards the circle.

Angelo's howls rang in his ears.

Slipping into a space previously occupied by the bowl-bearer, he stood there trembling. Robert had been expecting ritual sacrifice, the slaughter of chickens or some other fowl – everything but this. Riveted, he watched Malcolm's hard arse-cheeks tighten and relax with every thrust into Angelo's body. At his side, a hooded figure was fondling himself through thick fabric. On the other side, a torch swayed from side to side as a faceless man pulled his prick free from beneath the robe, a heavy fist sliding up and down the engorged length.

At the head of the altar, where Angelo thrashed and moaned like a wild beast, Rhona Dunbar stood motionless, pale arms stretched high above her head, eyes gazing towards the shadowed mountains. The piper's tune had taken on a more raucous tone, sounding like the neighing of a horse.

All around him, figures were stroking themselves. Robert could see many wore the same tight cock-and-ball restraints against which Angelo's shaft was throbbing visibly.

Abruptly, Malcolm pulled out and turned.

Robert gazed at the shining length of the fisherman's prick, then up to where the rugged face was creased with pleasure. As Malcolm stepped back into his place within the circle, a second figure stepped forward and removed its hood.

Angelo braced the soles of his bare feet against sweat-slicked granite and thrust upwards into the night sky.

A vast, tattooed body stood between his legs. Douglas McVey bowed his head in supplication. 'We have waited eons for this moment, Caballo.'

Angelo gazed open-mouthed at the blacksmith's decorated torso, at the rearing hooves and flying manes. The stallions were licked by painted flames which seemed to come alive in the amber glow of the torches. The man's skin gleamed, every bulging muscle and stretched sinew glistening with power. The thick silver rings glinted in each brown nipple, catching and reflecting the light surrounding the altar.

Douglas raised his head, eyes boring into Angelo's. His brawny fist gripped the heavy organ which sprouted from between his tree-like thighs. 'My cock is honoured, Dark Rider. We both salute you.'

Angelo's eyes focused on the head of the thick member. The single circlet which had bisected the turgid flesh yesterday was now augmented by a series of others. A cluster of silver studs encrusted the tip of the blacksmith's throbbing length. On each side of the man's furry bollocks, a chrome pin gleamed. A shudder shook Angelo's sweating body.

Douglas ran a heat-seared thumb over the pierced flesh. The engorged prick bucked against his scarred palm and an expression of growing lust furrowed the iron face. 'They will increase my pleasure – and yours, Caballo.'

Angelo's balls contracted in their sack of shaved skin. The cock looked like a weapon. The aching muscles in his arse contracted abruptly, then spasmed open. He struggled against the ropes, unwilling to tear his eyes from the advancing rod of flesh and unable to ignore the arrows of desire which stabbed at his own cock.

A hooded figure moved forward and held out what looked like a small ball-bearing.

Douglas took the silver sphere between a large thumb and forefinger, then squeezed the head of his massively swollen prick until the large slit popped open.

Through a haze of lust and longing, Angelo's brain remembered the way the blacksmith had sealed his cock with thumb and finger, yesterday. He watched Douglas drop the chrome orb inside his gaping slit, straining and gasping at the way delicate cock flesh expanded to hold the bead in place.

Already encrusted with silver, the man's glans now looked more like some fearsome weapon than ever.

Douglas drenched his length in the proffered bowl of oily liquid and moved closer.

Suddenly afraid, Angelo shrank back, hauling at his bonds.

The man's studded prick loomed towards him, fat and straining.

Angelo threw back his head and stared up at a midnight-blue sky. Through his blurred vision, a huge yellow moon gazed down at him. Then something thick and unstoppable was pushing at the tender lips of his arse. Angelo gasped, feeling nubs of forged steel press against his aching flesh. The gasp was echoed below. He grunted, then hissed as the breath left his body and the swollen head pushed its way in.

The blacksmith's rough, spark-scarred hands gripped Angelo's thighs, widening them further as he sank relentlessly into him.

Angelo felt every metal-scabbed millimetre as the cockhead bored home. He clenched his fists; his teeth and the walls of his arse tightened, providing a firm sheath for the sword of throbbing meat. Tiny chrome bosses stroked inside him, a vanguard of sensation which ploughed ahead and dragged the girth of more fleshy reinforcements behind. The metal bead pushed against the rounded gland behind Angelo's bladder.

A roar escaped his lips. Then Angelo was heaving at his restraints. The muscles in his arms stretched tight. Veins stood out on his neck.

Douglas gouged on past, the other piercings dragging against Angelo's prostate and causing tidal waves to spasm up and down the inside of his arse.

It felt as if the man was forming a new tunnel, mining previously unexplored seams of sensation. The coarse rope bit deeper around Angelo's wrists as he tried desperately to free his arms. He wanted to grab the blacksmith's huge sweating shoulders and haul the man into his body. He wanted to fuck himself on the metal-embossed cock until the inside of his arse was raw and tingling.

Then the coolness of the ball-pins made contact with the shaved skin of Angelo's buttocks. He lay there, moaning, while rippling walls of muscle clenched and reclenched around the throbbing flesh inside him.

Douglas filled his entire body. Angelo could feel the man's breath and smell the blacksmith's musky odour. Vibrant tattoos danced before his eyes. Glinting nipple rings swam in front of his face. Beneath his back and shoulders, the granite altar was awash his sweat.

Coarse hands roved over his body. Angelo leant up against them, revelling in the rough touch. His balls knitted together, swelling further. The need for release was almost unbearable. Then a deep bass voice resounded in his ears.

'I taught you well, Dark Rider. And you will give the knowledge back ten-fold.'

Slowly, the vastness began to recede. Angelo thrashed, tightening his arse-muscles and trying to hold the man inside him. But Douglas's retreat was as steady and relentless as his conquering had been. A sob caught in Angelo's throat.

A calloused hand stroked his burning cheek. 'Soon, Caballo.' Douglas's voice trembled with desire.

Angelo stared up at the moon, empty and yearning. Movement between his aching thighs told him the tattooed giant had gone.

Seconds later, another movement told him it was not over yet.

His feet had taken root. His heart hammered in his chest. Robert's eyes darted between Douglas McVey's striking form, Rhona Dunbar's increasingly loud incantations and the writhing body prostrate on the altar.

Angelo's dark curls were plastered to his head and lank with sweat. His coffee-coloured arms and dark, hairless legs hung limp. Even at this distance, Robert could see the pink crinkled opening to the man's body, inches below the swollen, leather-bound member.

Beneath the fabric of the coarse robe, his own cock inched ever upwards.

Another hooded shape moved into his line of vision, and Angelo's grunt of acceptance rumbled in his ears. Then someone tapped his shoulder.

Every nerve in Robert's body jangled. He spun round, staring into Fingal's angelic face.

The youth's eyes were shining. He stretched out a hand, gripped the edge of Robert's hood and pulled.

Robert's heart leapt into his throat. But the damage was done. Face revealed for all to see, he saw others were disrobing. He recognised several fishermen, Duncan the taxi-driver, Cameron Dunbar – even Miss Nicol, whose steely features had taken on an almost benign quality.

Fingal's voice caressed his ears. 'I understand now, and I think you do too.'

Head spinning, Robert stood mesmerised by the islanders' smiling faces. Fingal talked on.

'You were right, Robert – you are one of us now, and the ritual is for everyone. The Kelpie is very close. Look!' He pointed to the one person who was still dressed.

In the centre of the circle, Rhona Dunbar twisted and turned, spine arching as she moved. Silver hair whirled around her shoulders. The gauzy fabric of her gown swirled over slender hips and down around her small bare feet. A husky voice soared like a descant above the low hum of the islanders' chant.

'*Thigeadh do rioghachd, agus an agus, agus an agus!*'

The piper, who had been waiting silently just outside the circle, now placed the chanter's mouthpiece between his lips and began to fill the instrument's bag with air. Seconds later, the Lady Laird's hoarse words had a skirling accompaniment.

Fingal's whisper cut through the growing sound. 'She calls to the Kelpie, offering her body to him for ever and ever, as Lady Flora Dunbar offered herself one thousand years ago tonight.'

An impassioned cry from Angelo made Robert's head jerk towards the altar.

Between his parted legs, Hamish Campbell's stocky body appeared from within the folds of darkness.

Angelo stared at the policeman's cock. It was as stocky as the man himself, short but very thick. Hamish wore the same silver-coloured ring around the base of his balls, while the shaft itself was naked and gleaming.

The policeman bowed. 'We are grateful, Caballo.' Slate-grey eyes pierced his.

Angelo could only grunt and strain at the tethers.

Unceremoniously, Hamish shoved a round, beige-coloured object into his slit.

Angelo watched the bearded face crease with pleasure at the act.

Then the policeman lowered his ruddy face, kissed the tip of

Angelo's prick and positioned himself against the spasming opening to the Argentinian's body.

Angelo lunged upwards. Frustration and desire were building to an unbearable peak of longing. He wanted to be stretched. He wanted to feel the policeman's shaft force its way into him. Through unfocused eyes he watched veins stand out on Hamish's face, mirroring the pencil-thick tubes on the man's stout cock.

Then Hamish was in him, pushing his way past quivering muscle and up towards Angelo's very heart. The man fucked in short, savage jabs, the head of his prick battering against the rounded gland just behind Angelo's bladder.

Heels and shoulders taking all his weight, Angelo jerked upwards, meeting and returning each of those vicious thrusts with an energy and need he never knew he had. His balls burned, his cock was on fire. He wanted to tear off the bindings and spurt into the night.

Then, following the pattern set by Malcolm and Douglas, the policeman withdrew with a shudder, and walked away.

Sweat poured from his hair, coursing into already damp eyes. Angelo was whimpering now. As each of his subsequent lovers arrived and departed, the turgid sack between his legs became more and more swollen. Within its leather bindings, the skin on his cock was stretched impossibly tight. The slender strand which bisected the large head pulled until Angelo felt it was about to snap.

Noise filled his head – the chanting, the drone of the pipes and Rhona's increasingly deep pleas. Another man withdrew from his body, and Angelo found himself eye to eye with the Lady Laird.

Silence descended abruptly.

Rhona's eyes looked different – wider, bluer. She tossed her head and her great mane of silver hair whirled around her face.

Angelo was aware of a slackening around his arms and legs. Ropes still attached to his wrists and ankles, he raised himself upright on the granite altar. His legs refused to close. He sat there, swollen balls resting on the cool surface and stretched out his arms towards the white-robed figure.

Rhona tossed her head a second time. Somewhere behind those

ice-blue eyes Angelo glimpsed a wilder stare. She exhaled noisily, slim fingers unfastening the buttons of her filmy gown. 'It is time, Caballo.'

Angelo could only nod. Rhona's voice was soft, but much lower than before. He watched smooth shoulders appear from beneath the fabric, marvelling at the smooth, almost flat curve of her chest, and the strong muscles of her stomach.

Then the rest of her robe fell away.

Angelo blinked, staring between sinewy milk-white thighs.

The figure before him had the blondest pubes he had ever seen.

And the largest cock.

Robert rubbed his smarting eyes on the back of his hand. At his side, Fingal chuckled.

'The Kelpie has been well tricked, no?'

Robert shook his head, trying to make sense of what he was seeing. Fingal attempted an explanation.

'She is Rhona – and she is Cameron's wee brother. The Dunbars have always been eccentric.' The youth chuckled again and made an obscene gesture with his fist and forearm. 'Their eccentricity has come in handy – the Kelpie usually only deals with female members of the family. This generation has none.'

Robert goggled.

Fingal shrugged. 'In legend, Kelpies deceive mortals. For once, mortals have deceived a Kelpie. Come on.'

Robert's knees trembled as Fingal led him towards the altar.

Lady Rhona turned, smiling. 'You brought the Dark Rider to us. It is only fitting you be near when he fulfils his destiny.'

Robert stared down at Angelo. His lover looked so beautiful. His dark skin glowed with life, a life which throbbed up from swollen balls into his bulging cock.

He moved around, bare feet sliding on wet grass, until he was standing directly behind Angelo.

Eclipsed by black pupils, dark eyes shone up at him.

Robert's cock pulsed against the back of Angelo's neck as he leant forward and cradled the sweat-soaked head in his arms.

'Not one drop will be spilled until the time is right, Caballo.'

Lady Rhona was straddling the altar now, unrolling what looking like a tube of chicken-skin over the full ten inches of gleaming, aristocratic cock jutting up from between her thighs. She stared at Angelo. 'Come to me, Dark Rider.'

Reclining on the black-flecked stone, Angelo lifted his hips and slid forward.

Robert glanced nervously at his watch: two minutes until midnight.

Overhead, the sky was a deep crimson colour, rays of red fanning out from the distant sun which hovered over the horizon to pierce the darkness around the moon.

The villagers had formed a tight circle surrounding the altar, fanning out to fill the area within the standing-stones. Dozens of naked, sweating bodies were stroking themselves and each other, merging into a writhing mass of arms, legs, cocks and arses. The air was filled with the rasp of fist on flesh and the stink of sexual tension.

In front of him, outlined against the two sides of the sky, Angelo and Rhona Dunbar faced each other, thighs spread. From one dark and one pale body, two very different pricks jutted up into the still air. The Lady Laird's shaft was thick and angry-looking and would have done justice to any stallion, while Angelo's bound and trussed prick reared and buckled like a caged beast.

Then, in one smooth movement, Rhona Dunbar edged forward and down. A slender fist gripped the jutting member. 'Ride me, Caballo – ride me, Dark Rider!'

Hips raised, Angelo slid into her lap, bracing his arms against the black-flecked stone of the altar.

Robert gasped and moved too, still holding the sides of his lover's head.

Thighs straddling a slim waist, pale legs thrusting out from behind his coffee-coloured back, Angelo hovered there, an inch above the head of the throbbing cock. He threw back his head and stared up.

Robert locked eyes with his lover. He saw uncertainty, fear and longing in the dark pupils.

'Ride me, Caballo!' Rhona's voice was breathless with need. 'Ride the Kelpie until the ground moves under us!'

He couldn't help himself. Robert knew this had to be. His own cock thrusting between Angelo's shoulder-blades, Robert dipped down and covered his lover's mouth with his. And pushed. He shivered, feeling the strong body tense as he lowered Angelo onto the pole of flesh. Robert continued the kiss, sealing his lover's mouth with his lips. Angelo's pants of desire trembled through Robert's body, down his throat and into the very heart of him. He slid his arms up under coffee-coloured limbs and gripped Angelo's shoulders.

Then a jolt pulled them apart, and the ride began.

Angelo twisted his fingers in thick blond hair. Eyes rolling in his head, he tried to brace himself against each thrust but the jabs came so thick and fast it was all he could do to hold on.

Rhona was gripping his waist, driving up into him with a ferocity which belied the calm features. With each jab of the thick shaft, taut pale abdominal muscles slammed against his cock, then dragged down with each withdrawal. Leather thongs dug increasingly painfully into his aching length.

Angelo planted his bare feet on the granite alter behind Rhona and raised his knees to grip her sides. She was thrusting up into him with such force his balls were about to explode. He clenched his teeth, howling in Robert's arms. At the base of his balls, the silver circlet strained, barely able to keep the pressure at bay. Crisscrossed leather thongs tightened further beneath his fingers. His shaking fingers slipped from soaking blond hair. Angelo wrapped a fist around his trussed cock, and felt another clenching deep in his guts.

Then another hand covered his, pale fingers groping past darker knuckles. In an instant the bindings slipped from his shaft and the ring behind his balls snapped open. The sensation made his whole body tremble – even the altar beneath him shook. The emphasis suddenly changed. Angelo lunged forward, pushing the blond figure onto its back and impaling himself more securely on the thick staff of flesh.

Free of all restraints, legs braced, Angelo began to ride.

He hauled himself up the length of the throbbing cock, then slammed back down on the rod, feeling the impact of the Lady Laird's balls on his arse cheeks. His own shaft was slapped between their two bodies as he rode faster. Sweat flooded over his face and dripped onto his mount.

All around him, slick flesh shimmered in the light from dozens of torches, which were now planted in a circle on the ground. Giant shadows galloped past his half-shut eyes, thrown against the granite stones. Angelo fucked himself faster. The walls of his arse tightened and relaxed along the length of the cock inside him, gripping it tightly as it rammed up into his body.

The need for release was stronger than ever. Pressure pounded within his arse, inside his balls and behind his eyes.

In his head, blood thundered like hooves. The sound galloped up the length of his cock, stretching the foreskin to breaking point as his shaft was buffeted and crushed between his stomach and the writhing torso under him.

Angelo dipped lower over the snorting Rhona, impaling himself again and again. He gripped her shoulders, pistoning with his hips until he felt the cock spear the very heart of him.

Then the world ebbed away and he was back on Caliban. Two bodies become one synchronised being. He could no longer tell where mount stopped and rider began. They were racing towards a joint goal, although what this goal was or where they would find it, Angelo still had no idea.

But it didn't seem to matter. A greater power had control of his body.

A strange odour rose up, over the stink of sweat and sex which surrounded their coupling. The air was suddenly charged. Angelo felt static prickle over his skin.

Then the altar was moving and they were both falling, the Kelpie's cock still buried in Angelo's arse.

★　★　★

Robert leapt back. Every hair on his naked body stood on end.

The earlier tremors had been enough of a shock, but this time the earth was quivering with more force than before.

He sank to a crouch in front of Angelo, who was still riding the Lady Laird as if his life depended upon it. His own cock trembled in a parallel with the waves of movement which shimmered beneath his feet. Panic was swept away by the sight of Angelo, writhing and ecstatic, his strong body pieced by the furious cock. Robert's guts clenched. A familiar heat built in his balls. He was about to come, and he couldn't stop himself.

Around him, he felt a shared second of apprehension, as dozens of others hovered on the brink. Then a joint roar from in front of him tipped his body over the edge.

An ear-splitting crack echoed around him.

Heat exploded in his arse. Angelo lunged forward, propelled by momentum and the overwhelming clenching in his balls. He grabbed his flexing cock, his other hand stretching up into the night. The moment was frozen in time, held there by the joint tremors of a double climax. He was aware of molten lust driving its way up his aching shaft, gathered from every nerve in his being. Then thick, white spunk shot from his slit, arcing up over Rhona's writhing torso and splattering on the grass behind her head. The cock inside him spasmed again. Angelo roared, hips bucking forward and up as a second volley tore itself free from his body.

Through a haze of release, he could see other cocks flexing and shuddering around him. With every jut of Rhona's hips, he shot again and again. His arse-muscles spasmed vigorously in parallel with each wave of orgasm, forcing Rhona's cock from his body. The organ flexed beneath his balls, losing the chicken-skin condom and leaking its thick milky cargo onto Angelo's shaved thighs. Angelo shot a final time. His balls lay drained and empty against a pale, quivering abdomen. His legs turned to rubber. All strength had left his body. One limp arm flailing behind him, he fell backwards on soaking grass. Wet earth resounded with the trembles from his exhausted body.

Angelo moaned, curling himself into a sticky ball. One

outstretched hand snaked across the grass. His skin was bathed in sweat, greasy with effort. Vision returning to focus as the last ripples of climax faded, he shook his fuzzy head and blinked through receding tremors.

The circle of naked figures were on their knees. Tiny stones and pebbles littered the surrounding area, shot from dozens of slits.

Angelo inhaled deeply, sucking air into his burning lungs. A new smell augmented the overwhelming stench of maleness.

A rich, dark, cloying smell.

He raised his face from the ground. A viscous film covered his skin. Angelo stared at the gooey blackness which drenched the grass, then ran a finger down his cheek.

The digit came away black-smeared. Then Rhona's husky voice soared through his confusion, her words breathless with excitement.

'The earth has disclosed its ancient treasures!'

Angelo staggered to his feet, then slipped in a pool of thick, black liquid. Flat on his back again, he found himself staring up at Robert's pink, wild-eyed face.

'Oil! You've struck oil!'

Angelo blinked. The words sank in.

Three sets of hands grabbed him, hauling him upright. Rhona Dunbar's long blond hair was matted with the sticky substance. Cameron's face was streaked with smears of the stuff. 'The legend has come true! The Dark Rider has saved Kelpie Island!'

Angelo collapsed back into Robert's arms.

Naked villagers surged forward, embracing them both. Angelo stared from his lover's delighted face to a spot just beneath the altar, from which thick, bubbling liquid continued to ooze out of a crack in the ground onto the surrounding earth. Robert's arms tight around him, Angelo smiled up at the ecstatic sea of faces, then slipped into a blackness of his own.

Twenty-Four

R obert twined his fingers with Angelo's as they stood at the edge of the cliff. He stared out at the autumn sunrise.

A lot had happened since the strange events of midsummer's eve. He smiled, glancing for the hundredth time at the letter gripped firmly between the fingers of his other hand and thought about perhaps the strangest event of all.

Angelo's lips nuzzled his neck. 'I always had faith in you.'

Robert reread the publisher's letter, still unable to take in the news. They liked his novel – written in a six-week frenzy – and were offering a five-figure sum for *Island of Dreams*. An independent film company were already interested in the movie-rights, and wanted to shoot on location.

Robert smiled. More revenue for the Dunbars, although following the surveyor's report, he doubted money would be a problem for any of the islanders – at least for the foreseeable future. He turned his head, to where the tall rig was rhythmically pumping the black gold from deep in the bowels of the earth. He sighed.

Angelo's teeth bit the skin on his neck, nipping playfully. 'What's wrong – they not offering you enough?'

Robert laughed, gripped Angelo's waist and pulled the man against him. 'I have more than enough already.' He gazed into eyes darker and more liquid than the crudest oil.

Angelo blushed, and smiled lopsidedly.

Robert's cock twitched. He pressed himself against his lover's thigh and rested his head on a broad shoulder.

What had occurred, three months ago, had brought good fortune in so many ways.

The Laird and Lady Laird had paid off the mortgage on the island, on the strength of future income.

Malcolm and the other fishermen had sold their fishing boats and pooled their resources into a ferry service, shuttling first geologists and then oil-workers from the mainland over to the island. A joint venture with Duncan of Duncan's Automobiles was presently involved in the purchase of a helicopter. Robert shivered, hoping the man's skill in the air was more reliable than his land technique.

Strong, coffee-coloured arms wrapped themselves around him, and Robert felt Angelo's thick desire hard against his hip. The shiver subsided into tiny ripples of contentment. The handsome Argentinian had obtained the contract to build temporary accommodation for the incoming workers. That, plus the upgrading of the island's infrastructure, would satisfy Angelo's need for physical work for a long time to come.

Robert raised his head, tilting his face upwards.

Full lips met his in a powerful kiss.

Robert moaned and felt his lover's response through their twining tongues. Then tentative words drifted into his ears.

'Can I be – of service?'

Angelo chuckled. Robert grinned, easing himself away. The need in Fingal's voice was echoed by a desire in them both. Hand in hand, they walked towards the figure in the doorway.

Kneeling on the newly purchased four-poster bed, Robert looked down at the golden head between his thighs, then smiled across at Angelo.

The naked Argentinian was rubbing the tip of his cock up and down the pink, newly shaven crevice of Fingal's arse, while the boy's lips nuzzled Robert's bollocks.

Robert slipped a hand under the bum-fluffed chin and tilted the boy's head upwards.

Fifteen minutes ago, it had been Angelo who had gazed into those sky-blue eyes, while Robert played with the man-boy's tender arsehole. The angelic face was creased with lust, lips and nose smeared with sweat and two men's pre-come. Fingal's irises had almost disappeared, black pupils swollen with desire.

Two sets of blue eyes met. Robert's cock flexed against the boy's chin. 'Who owns you, Fingal?'

'You do, Mr McLeod.' The man-boy's voice was husky. He was naked, except for the tiny black jockstrap he always wore for these duties. His slender wrists were bound loosely behind his back, keeping his eager fingers away from his own and other men's pricks.

Three months had transformed the sullen Fingal from petulant mischief-maker into devoted slave, a role the boy had seized with both hands. They'd had a long talk. Fingal didn't love Robert – he loved life, and wanted to experience all he could of it. Next year, if the youth continued to provide sterling service through the dark winter months, Robert and Angelo would take Fingal to London. But Robert had a feeling their young companion was now happier on Kelpie Island than he could ever be elsewhere.

Robert contined to stare, watching the boy's expression as Angelo removed his cock from Final's shaved crack and replaced it with a well-greased finger.

The boy shivered, his body hypersensitised to every change in its treatment. 'And Caballo –' His voice cracked with need. 'I am the joint property of Mr McLeod and Mr Caballo.'

Robert nodded. He sank his fingers into the boy's long, gleaming hair and repositioned the angelic face at his groin. His cock stuck up almost vertically, licked and sucked into ninety-degree erection by the most willing mouth he'd ever encountered. Robert leant forward, pressing his length against Fingal's pink cheek.

The man-boy gasped, tried to lower his face in order to service the cock, but Robert held him firmly, enjoying the feel of the boy's hot skin against the throbbing flesh of his shaft. A frisson of pleasure shimmered across his balls. Robert gasped. He moved his hand to the back of the boy's neck, gripping the blond ponytail.

Fingal grunted.

Robert knew the man-boy's slender cock was raging inside the tight black pouch of the jockstrap. Fingal needed a firm hand, all right, and there was nothing turned the boy on more than having his neck gripped and his face pressed against swollen man-meat –

At the other end of the crouching figure, Angelo was unwrapping a condom. Fingal inhaled sharply, spreading his legs further at the sound.

– unless it was another cock, pushing its way into his arsehole.

Robert looked up, watching his handsome lover carefully unroll the sheath of latex over his dark, engorged length. His own cock flexed against Fingal's face as Angelo's rod glistened and shone through the manmade membrane. The sight made his guts clench. Robert pressed down, lowering Fingal's face further until his tight balls rested against the boy's scalp.

Angelo was watching, one hand stroking his length, the other continuing to finger the boy's sweet hole.

Robert's hips jutted forward. The knowledge of Angelo's eyes on him added to the pleasure of rubbing his heavy bollocks over the back of the golden head.

In a strange way, Fingal had brought them together by keeping them apart. Now, ever since that night, three months ago, they fucked with him, through him, over him and the act brought them closer together.

Robert's jealousy had almost lost him Angelo. That would never happen again. Feeling the friction of the boy's thick hair, he dragged his balls across the back of Fingal's head one last time then dipped down and positioned the head of his cock against a pair of bruised lips.

In a parallel movement, Angelo was now resting his sheathed tip against another opening to the boy's body. Crouching behind the lithe body, Angelo reached over and stroked Robert's cheek.

Robert twisted his head, kissing his lover's fingers and tasting Fingal's manly musk on Angelo's hand.

Then they both thrust forward.

Fingal grunted, pushed onto Robert's length by the force of Angelo's cock entering him from the rear.

The man-boy's mouth had always been eager. His arse had needed a little more training to bring it to the point where it would take either Robert or Angelo's cocks at will.

Robert gripped Fingal's shoulders, supporting the boy as he sucked. Inches away, Angelo's breath brushed his face. Robert grinned: this would be special – it wasn't every day he sold a novel, and he wanted to celebrate. Abruptly, he pulled his slick cock from the boy's wet mouth. The member slapped back loudly against his stomach.

Fingal gasped in protest, then confusion as Robert deftly untied the slender wrists.

Angelo raised one perplexed eyebrow.

Robert smiled. 'Get him onto his back.'

Realisation at what Robert had in mind spread over the darkly handsome face. In seconds, they had flipped Fingal over. His hands were free, but both ankles were now firmly tied halfway up corresponding bed-posts. The boy's legs were supported, his thighs spread wide and open.

Robert stared at the dark rosette between two pink arse-cheeks. It looked so small, so tight he began to have second thoughts.

But Angelo had no such doubts. He tore open another condom and, holding Robert's cock steady in his fist, rolled the tube of latex over the throbbing length. The movement made Robert's shaft flex and buck like a wild beast, and he had to grit his teeth against the pleasure.

Then they were kneeling, side by side, between the man-boy's naked thighs, each holding their cocks.

Fingal's head and shoulders were raised off the bed as he watched apprehensively. The fingers of one hand were pulling at small, erect nipples. His pupilless eyes darted from the blond to the dark head and back again.

Robert watched as Angelo reached forward, rubbing the bulge in the boy's jockstrap. The sight made his balls spasm. It gave him so much pleasure to watch Angelo with another man. Fingal's eyes were fixed on Robert's face as the Argentinian slipped a finger inside the pouch to caress the boy's hardness. But Robert knew what Fingal really wanted – the one thing guaranteed to have the boy's tight arse-lips spasming open for their joint pleasure.

Eyes never leaving the scene before him, he stretched an arm down, over the side of the bed, and located the hazel twig.

The very sight of the switch had Fingal once more flat on his back, tearing at the bedclothes with scrabbling fists.

Robert flexed the branch in the air, heard the familiar swoosh then crack as he brought it down hard across the boy's stomach.

On cue, Fingal's back arched. He yelped, then the sound lowered into a groan of satisfaction as Angelo slid back into the now-spasming pink rosette.

As his lover edged up onto his knees, his sweating, coffee-skin flanked by pale, writhing legs, Robert delivered a second whack to Fingal's groin. The hazel twig landed across the hard bulge in the black pouch.

This time, Angelo groaned, and Robert knew his lover was feeling the tight clench and unclench of the man-boy's arse-muscles around his cock. He moved up the bed, to where Fingal was thrashing around on the mattress. He flicked the switch again, watching the boy's back arch until only his shoulders were in contact with the bed.

Inside the condom, a droplet of pre-come drooled from Robert's slit. Fingal was buffeted between each flick of the cane and each thrust of Angelo's prick. At the apex of the man-boy's passion, Robert gripped the boy's flailing arms, hauling him up and slipping under the sweat-drenched body.

His shaft lay along the top of Fingal's crack. Robert felt the force of Angelo's thrusts ripple up his length. The boy was a conduit, something which joined rather than separated. Tossing hazel twig aside, he reached down and gripped Fingal's arse-cheeks.

The boy's head lolled against his shoulder. Three feet below, Robert felt Angelo's slick prick brush past his hand. Then slow down.

Fingal was moaning.

Angelo paused, the head of his cock held vice-like by the boy's arse-lips.

Robert circled the tight ring with the fingers of one hand, tipping Fingal forward with the other until the boy sprawled in Angelo's arms. He could see his lover's shaft, lubed and gleaming between stretched, sweating arse-cheeks. Biting back a sudden wave of increased arousal, Robert licked then eased his index finger into the boy's hole.

Fingal grunted, then began to pant.

Robert kissed the top of the golden head and got a mouthful of damp hair, then edged a second finger into the boy. Angelo was thrusting again, bucking Fingal up and down in his lap. Soon Robert had three, then four fingers curved parallel to his lover's cock.

Then Angelo's husky baritone seeped through the wet sound of their bodies. 'Take him with me, Robert. Now.' Fingal's head hung over Angelo's shoulder, his sweating back gleaming in candlelight. Two broad hands were spreading the boy's pink arse-cheeks wide and welcoming.

The thought of feeling Angelo's length nestled beside his, their cocks held snug and tight inside the same arsehole almost pushed him over the edge. Robert gripped his prick, pressing his fingers hard against his lover's shaft as he edged his own alongside.

Fingal's grunts became howls of ecstasy as a second shaft pushed its way into his body. Together, Robert and Angelo made a joint girth of almost eight inches, stretching the boy's fuck-tunnel until he was sure they would split him in two.

Robert's whole body was tingling with sensation: the friction of his lover's cock as it ground against his, the tight fleshy embrace of Fingal's warm arse and the expression on Angelo's face as they sat there, legs entwined and arms around the beautiful boy impaled on both their shafts.

The fuck was brief but wild. Every movement of every limb and member had an echo in someone else. One minute Robert's tongue was in Fingal's ear, the next he was tasting Angelo's mouth over the man-boy's shoulder.

Fingal came first, screaming his release as Robert and Angelo slammed their twin cocks up into his body. Robert felt his lover's prick flex beside his, then gasped as wet warmth filled his own condom.

Angelo slumped back on the bed, taking Fingal with him. Robert followed, aware only of an intense orgasm which seemed to be multiplied by three.

An hour later, cocks cleaned by Fingal's other hole, Robert and Angelo walked around the outside of the cottage.

The entire building was at present under reconstruction, thanks to the proceeds obtained at auction in London from the sale of Bethran McLeod's exquisite volume of Edwardian erotica.

The slim tome was at present with a private collector in New York. The twenty thousand pounds the American had paid was now safe in the Caballo/McLeod joint bank account.

The smell of frying drifted into Robert's nostrils.

Angelo's hand lingered on Robert's waist, then slipped down onto his arse.

Robert grinned. Fucking with the two men always gave him an appetite. He pulled Angelo back towards the open door.

Feet away from it, they paused for a moment, gazing at the standing-stones, beyond the loch. Angelo's voice was low. 'I still cannot remember much.' He kissed the top of Robert's head. 'Apart from the size of Rhona's cock, and the pounding she gave me, it's all a bit of a blur. You were there – what actually happened?'

They had never really talked about the ceremony. Even now, it all seemed like some bizarre dream. Robert laughed. 'You were all high on Cameron's aphrodisiac home-brew! The seismologists in Edinburgh say an earthquake of that magnitude was scheduled to happen, sooner or later.' He slapped Angelo's tight rear. 'Just Mother Nature coming up trumps for once – nothing to do with kelpies or water-spirits or anything else!'

'What about the white horse? I did see it a couple of times.'

'You need to get your eyes tested.' Robert gazed into dark, bottomless pupils. 'I think you'd look very sweet with glasses.' He pinched a handful of Argentinian arse.

Angelo laughed, chasing Robert into the cottage.

And from a hill high above, a gleaming white stallion tossed its head in annoyance, before fading back into the mist.

IDOL NEW BOOKS

Also published:

THE KING'S MEN
Christian Fall

Ned Medcombe, spoilt son of an Oxfordshire landowner, has always remembered his first love: the beautiful, golden-haired Lewis. But seventeenth-century England forbids such a love and Ned is content to indulge his domineering passions with the willing members of the local community, including the submissive parish cleric. Until the Civil War changes his world, and he is forced to pursue his desires as a soldier in Cromwell's army – while his long-lost lover fights as one of the King's men.

ISBN 0 352 33207 7

THE VELVET WEB
Christopher Summerisle

The year is 1889. Daniel McGaw arrives at Calverdale, a centre of academic excellence buried deep in the English countryside. But this is like no other college. As Daniel explores, he discovers secret passages in the grounds and forbidden texts in the library. The young male students, isolated from the outside world, share a darkly bizarre brotherhood based on the most extreme forms of erotic expression. It isn't long before Daniel is initiated into the rites that bind together the youths of Calverdale in a web of desire.

ISBN 0 352 33208 5

CHAINS OF DECEIT
Paul C. Alexander

Journalist Nathan Dexter's life is turned around when he meets a young student called Scott – someone who offers him the relationship for which he's been searching. Then Nathan's best friend goes missing, and Nathan uncovers evidence that he has become the victim of a slavery ring which is rumoured to be operating out of London's leather scene. To rescue their friend and expose the perverted slave trade, Nathan and Scott must go undercover, risking detection and betrayal at every turn.

ISBN 0 352 33206 9

HALL OF MIRRORS
Robert Black

Tom Jarrett operates the Big Wheel at Gamlin's Fair. When young runaway Jason Bradley tries to rob him, events are set in motion which draw the two together in a tangled web of mutual mistrust and growing fascination. Each carries a burden of old guilt and tragic unspoken history; each is running from something. But the fair is a place of magic and mystery where normal rules don't apply, and Jason is soon on a journey of self-discovery, unbridled sexuality and growing love.

ISBN 0 352 33209 3

THE SLAVE TRADE

James Masters

Barely eighteen and innocent of the desires of men, Marc is the sole survivor of a noble British family. When his home village falls to the invading Romans, he is forced to flee for his life. He first finds sanctuary with Karl, a barbarian from far-off Germanica, whose words seem kind but whose eyes conceal a dark and brooding menace. And then they are captured by Gaius, a general in Caesar's all-conquering army, in whose camp they learn the true meaning – and pleasures – of slavery.

ISBN 0 352 33228 x

WE NEED YOUR HELP . . .

to plan the future of Idol books –

Yours are the only opinions that matter. Idol is a new and exciting venture: the first British series of books devoted to homoerotic fiction for men.

We're going to do our best to provide the sexiest, best-written books you can buy. And we'd like you to help in these early stages. Tell us what you want to read. There's a freepost address for your filled-in questionnaires, so you won't even need to buy a stamp.

THE IDOL QUESTIONNAIRE

SECTION ONE: ABOUT YOU

1.1 Sex (*we presume you are male, but just in case*)
Are you?
Male ☐
Female ☐

1.2 Age
under 21 ☐   21–30 ☐
31–40 ☐   41–50 ☐
51–60 ☐   over 60 ☐

1.3 At what age did you leave full-time education?
still in education ☐   16 or younger ☐
17–19 ☐   20 or older ☐

1.4 Occupation _____

1.5 Annual household income _____

1.6 We are perfectly happy for you to remain anonymous; but if you would like us to send you a free booklist of Idol books, please insert your name and address

_____

_____

_____

_____

SECTION TWO: ABOUT BUYING IDOL BOOKS

2.1 Where did you get this copy of *Dark Rider*?

Bought at chain book shop ☐

Bought at independent book shop ☐

Bought at supermarket ☐

Bought at book exchange or used book shop ☐

I borrowed it/found it ☐

My partner bought it ☐

2.2 How did you find out about Idol books?

I saw them in a shop ☐

I saw them advertised in a magazine ☐

I read about them in _____

Other _____

2.3 Please tick the following statements you agree with:

I would be less embarrassed about buying Idol books if the cover pictures were less explicit ☐

I think that in general the pictures on Idol books are about right ☐

I think Idol cover pictures should be as explicit as possible ☐

2.4 Would you read an Idol book in a public place – on a train for instance?

Yes ☐   No ☐

SECTION THREE: ABOUT THIS IDOL BOOK

3.1 Do you think the sex content in this book is:

Too much ☐   About right ☐

Not enough ☐

3.2 Do you think the writing style in this book is:
      Too unreal/escapist   ☐   About right   ☐
      Too down to earth   ☐

3.3 Do you think the story in this book is:
      Too complicated   ☐   About right   ☐
      Too boring/simple   ☐

3.4 Do you think the cover of this book is:
      Too explicit   ☐   About right   ☐
      Not explicit enough   ☐
Here's a space for any other comments:

SECTION FOUR: ABOUT OTHER IDOL BOOKS

4.1 How many Idol books have you read?

4.2 If more than one, which one did you prefer?

4.3 Why?

SECTION FIVE: ABOUT YOUR IDEAL EROTIC NOVEL

We want to publish the books you want to read – so this is your chance to tell us exactly what your ideal erotic novel would be like.

5.1 Using a scale of 1 to 5 (1 = no interest at all, 5 = your ideal), please rate the following possible settings for an erotic novel:
      Roman / Ancient World   ☐
      Medieval / barbarian / sword 'n' sorcery   ☐
      Renaissance / Elizabethan / Restoration   ☐
      Victorian / Edwardian   ☐
      1920s & 1930s   ☐
      Present day   ☐
      Future / Science Fiction   ☐

5.2 Using the same scale of 1 to 5, please rate the following themes you may find in an erotic novel:

Bondage / fetishism	☐
Romantic love	☐
SM / corporal punishment	☐
Bisexuality	☐
Group sex	☐
Watersports	☐
Rent / sex for money	☐

5.3 Using the same scale of 1 to 5, please rate the following styles in which an erotic novel could be written:

Gritty realism, down to earth	☐
Set in real life but ignoring its more unpleasant aspects	☐
Escapist fantasy, but just about believable	☐
Complete escapism, totally unrealistic	☐

5.4 In a book that features power differentials or sexual initiation, would you prefer the writing to be from the viewpoint of the dominant / experienced or submissive / inexperienced characters:

Dominant / Experienced	☐
Submissive / Inexperienced	☐
Both	☐

5.5 We'd like to include characters close to your ideal lover. What characteristics would your ideal lover have? Tick as many as you want:

Dominant	☐	Caring	☐
Slim	☐	Rugged	☐
Extroverted	☐	Romantic	☐
Bisexual	☐	Old	☐
Working Class	☐	Intellectual	☐
Introverted	☐	Professional	☐
Submissive	☐	Pervy	☐
Cruel	☐	Ordinary	☐
Young	☐	Muscular	☐
Naïve	☐		

Anything else? _____

5.6 Is there one particular setting or subject matter that your ideal erotic novel would contain:

_____

5.7 As you'll have seen, we include safe-sex guidelines in every book. However, while our policy is always to show safe sex in stories with contemporary settings, we don't insist on safe-sex practices in stories with historical settings because it would be anachronistic. What, if anything, would you change about this policy?

_____

_____

SECTION SIX: LAST WORDS

6.1 What do you like best about Idol books?

_____

6.2 What do you most dislike about Idol books?

_____

6.3 In what way, if any, would you like to change Idol covers?

_____

6.4 Here's a space for any other comments:

_____

_____

_____

_____

Thanks for completing this questionnaire. Now either tear it out, or photocopy it, then put it in an envelope and send it to:

Idol
FREEPOST
London
W10 5BR

You don't need a stamp if you're in the UK, but you'll need one if you're posting from overseas.